Urgent needs . . . extreme measures!

"Tell me, who's that with Wentworth Lister? That woman—talking to him?"

Unwin frowned his cleft frown: "Demelza Poldark, it looks like."

"How the devil has she got in here? Who could have introduced her? And now she's talking to Longshanks Lister—just as she intended! God's my life, she'll hang her husband if she's not careful —and go to prison for contempt of court herself. She's playing with fire! . . ."

Unwin said: "I told you the first time I set eyes on her that she was a dangerous woman."

JEREMY POLDARK

A Novel of Cornwall
1790-1791

Winston Graham

BALLANTINE BOOKS • NEW YORK

With the exception of actual historical personages identified as such, the characters are entirely the product of the author's imagination and have no relation to any person in real life.

Copyright 1950 by Winston Graham

All rights reserved. Published in the United States by Ballantine Books, a division of Random House, Inc., New York. Originally published under the title *Venture Once More.*

ISBN 0-345-26002-3

This edition published by arrangement with Doubleday & Company, Inc.

Manufactured in the United States of America

First Ballantine Books Edition: July 1977

Back cover photograph copyright BBC-TV

BOOK ONE

Chapter One

In August 1790 three men rode along the mule track past Grambler Mine and made towards the straggling cottages at the end of the village. It was evening and the sun had just set; clouds had been driven up the sky by a westerly breeze and were beginning to flush with the afterglow. Even the mine chimneys, from which no smoke had issued for best part of two years, took on a matured mellow colour in the evening light. In a hole in the taller of the two, pigeons were nesting, and their flapping wings beat against the wider silence as the men passed. A half dozen ragged children were playing with a homemade swing suspended between two of the sheds, and some women standing at the doors of cottages, hands on elbows, watched the horsemen ride by.

They were soberly dressed, respectable riders in a clerkish black, and they sat their horses with an air of importance; not many such were seen nowadays in this half-derelict, half-deserted village which had come into being and had existed solely to serve the mine and which, now that the mine was dead, was itself perishing of a slower decay. It seemed that the men were going to pass right through—as might have been expected—but at the last one nodded his head and they reined in their horses at a more dejected-looking shack than anything they had yet seen. It was a one-story cob hut with an old iron pipe for a chimney and a roof patched and re-patched with sacking and driftwood; and at its open door on an upturned box sat a bowlegged man sharpening a piece of wood. He was under the average height, strongly built, but getting up in years. He wore old riding boots bound with string, yellow pigskin breeches, a dirty grey flannel shirt which had lost one sleeve at the elbow, and a stiff black leather waistcoat, whose pockets bulged with worthless odds and

5

ends. He was whistling almost soundlessly, but when the men got down from their horses he unpursed his lips and looked at them with wary bloodshot eyes; his knife hung over the stick while he sized them up.

The leader, a tall emaciated man with eyes so close together as to suggest a cast, said:

"Good day. Is your name Paynter?"

The knife slowly lowered itself. The bowlegged man put up a dirty thumbnail and scratched the shiniest spot on his bald head.

"Mebbe."

The other made a gesture of impatience. "Come, man. You're either Paynter or you're not. It's not a subject on which there can be two opinions."

"Well, I aren't so sure 'bout that. Folk is too free with other folk's names. Mebbe there can be two opinions. Mebbe there can be three. It all depend what you d'want me for."

"It *is* Paynter," said one of the men behind. "Where's your wife, Paynter?"

"Gone Marasanvose. Now if you be wanting she . . ."

"My name is Tankard," said the first man sharply. "I'm an attorney acting for the Crown in the coming case of Rex versus Poldark. We want to ask you a few questions, Paynter. This is Blencowe, my clerk, and Garth, an interested party. Will you lead the way inside?"

Jud Paynter's wrinkled teak-coloured face took on a look of injured innocence, but under this conventional defence there was a glint of genuine alarm.

"What are ee coming troubling me for? I said all I had to say afore magistrates, an' that were nothing. 'Ere I am, living a Christian life like St. Peter himself, sitting before his own front door interfering with no one. Leave me be."

"The law must take its course," said Tankard, and waited for Jud to get up.

After a minute, glancing suspiciously from one face to the other, Jud led the way inside. They seated themselves in the shadowy hut, Tankard staring distastefully about and lifting his coattails to avoid the litter as he sat down. None of the

6

visitors had delicate noses, but Blencowe, a pasty, stooping little man, looked back wistfully at the sweet evening outside.

Jud said: "I don't know nothing about'n. You're barking up the wrong door."

"We have reason to believe," said Tankard, "that your deposition before the examining justice was false in every particular. If——"

"You'll pardon me," said Garth in an undertone. "Perhaps you'd be letting me speak to Paynter for a minute or two, Mr. Tankard. You remember I said, afore we came in, that there's more ways . . ."

Tankard folded his thin arms. "Oh, very well."

Jud turned his bulldog eyes upon his new adversary. He thought he had seen Garth before, riding through the village or some such. Snooping perhaps.

Garth said in a conversational, friendly tone: "I understand you were Captain Poldark's servant at one time, you and your wife, for a great many years and for his father afore him?"

"Mebbe."

"And after working faithful for him all those years you were suddenly put off, turned from the house without a word of warning."

"Ais. Tweren't right or proper, I'll say that."

"It is said, mind you, this is but hearsay, y'understand, that he treated you shameful afore you left—for some fancied misdeed—used his horsewhip and near drowned you under the pump. Would that be so?"

Jud spat on the floor and showed his two great teeth.

"That's against the law," interposed Tankard, squinting down his long thin nose. "Offences against the person: common assault and battery. You could have proceeded, Paynter."

"And it can't have been the first time, I'll wager," said Garth.

"No, nor it wasn't either," Jud said after a minute, sucking at his teeth.

7

"People who ill-treat faithful servants don't deserve them these days," said Garth. "There's a new spirit abroad. Every man is as good as his neighbour. Look what be happening in France."

"Ais, I d'know all about that," said Jud, and then stopped. It wouldn't do to let these prying busybodies into the secret of his visits to Roscoff. All the time this Poldark stuff might be a blind to trap him into other admissions.

"Blencowe," said Tankard. "Have you the brandy? We could all do with a tot, and no doubt Paynter will join us."

. . . The afterglow faded, and the shadows in the littered hut grew darker.

"Take it from me," said Garth, "the aristocracy is finished. Their day is over. Common men will be coming into their rights. And one of their rights is not to be treated worse than dogs, not to be used like slaves. D'you understand the law, Mr. Paynter?"

"The Englishman's house is his castle," said Jud. "And habeas corpse, and thou shalt not move thy neighbour's landmark."

"When there's trouble at law," said Garth, "like what there was here in January, it's often hard for the law to act like it should. So it acts as best it may. And when there's riot and wrecking and robbery and suchlike, it says nothing about those who follow if so be as it can lay hold on those who lead. Now in this case the ringleader is plain to be seen."

"Mebbe."

"No mebbe about it. But reliable evidence is hard to come by. Evidence of responsible men like yourself. . . . And, mind you, if the law sees it cannot prove a case against the ringleader, then it will look further and smoke out the lesser men. That's the truth of it, Mr. Paynter, as sure as I'm sitting here; so it's best for all that the right man should stand in the assizes."

Jud picked up his glass and set it down again, it being empty; Blencowe hastily proffered the brandy bottle. There was a comfortable bobbling sound as Jud upended it.

8

"I don't see why for you d'come to me, when I wasn't there at all," he said, caution still uppermost. "A man can't see farther'n he can blaw."

"Listen, Paynter," said Tankard, ignoring Garth's warning sign. "We know a great deal more than you think. These inquiries have been in train for near on seven months. It would be better for you if you made a clean breast of it all."

"Clean breast indeed——"

"We know that you actively co-operated with Poldark on the morning of the wreck. We know you were on the beach all through the rioting of that day and the following night. We know you played a leading part in resisting the officers of the Crown when one was seriously injured, and in many ways you are as culpable as your master——"

"I never 'eard sich loitch in all me life! Me? I was never nearer the wreck nor what I am now——"

"But as Garth explained, we're willing to overlook this if you will turn King's evidence. We've a weight of testimony against this man Poldark, but wish to make it stronger. It's plain you owe him no loyalty. Why, on your own showing he's treated you shamefully! Come, man, it's common sense to tell us the truth, as well as your common duty."

With some dignity Jud got to his feet.

"Also," said Garth, "we'd make it worth your while."

Jud pivoted thoughtfully on his heel and slowly sat down again. "Eh?"

"Not official, of course. It wouldn't do to come official. But there's other ways."

Jud stretched his head to peer out through the door. There was no sign of Prudie. It was always the same when she went to see her cousin. He looked sidelong at each of the men in the hut, as if he might weigh up their intentions unnoticed.

"What other ways?"

Garth took out his pouch and rattled it. "The Crown's out for a conviction The Crown's willing to pay for the right information, like. Strictly on the quiet, of course. Strictly between friends. Like offering a reward for an arrest, as you might say. Isn't it, Mr. Tankard? Nothing different from that."

Tankard did not speak. Jud got his glass and sucked up the rest of the brandy.

Almost under his breath he said: "First threatenings an' now bribery. Bribery as I'm alive! Money for Judas, I reckon they'm thinking. Stand up in a court o' law agin an old friend. Worse'n Judas, for he did it on the quiet like. An' for what? Thirty bits o' silver. An' I'm reckoning they wouldn't offer me that much. They'd want for me to do un for twenty or ten. Tedn reasonable, tedn proper, tedn Christian, tedn *right*."

There was a short pause.

"Ten guineas down and ten guineas after the trial," said Garth.

"Ha!" said Jud. "Just what I thought."

"It's possible it could be raised to fifteen."

Jud got up, but slowly this time, sucked his teeth and tried to whistle, but his lips were dry. He hitched up his breeches and two fingers went into a waistcoat pocket for a pinch of snuff.

"Tesn't fair to come on a man like this," he grumbled. "Me head's goin' round like a trool. Come again in a month."

"The assizes are fixed for early September."

Tankard also got up. "We shouldn't require a long deposition," he said. "Just a few sentences covering the main facts as you know them—and an undertaking to repeat them at the appropriate time."

"An' what would I say?" asked Jud.

"The truth, of course, as you can swear to it."

Garth interrupted hastily: "The truth, of course, but maybe we could guide you as to what we most want, like. It is the assault upon the soldiers that we're wishing to have witness of. That was on the night of the seventh-eighth of January. You were on the beach at the time, weren't you, Mr. Paynter? No doubt you saw the whole incident."

Jud looked old and wary. "Naw. . . . Don't remember nothing 'bout that, now."

"It might be worth twenty guineas if so be as your memory came round to it."

"Twenty now and twenty after?"

". . . Yes."

"Tes worth all o' that for such a stramming big story."

"It's the truth we want, man," said Tankard impatiently. "Were you or were you not a witness of the assault?"

Garth put his pouch upon a rickety old three-legged table which had once belonged to Joshua Poldark. He began to count out twenty gold coins.

"What," said Jud, staring at the money, "when that there soldier got his head cleaved open, an' all the rest of 'em was pushed off of Hendrawna Beach fasterer than what they came on. I laffed at that. Didn' I laff! Was that what you was meaning?"

"Of course. And Captain Poldark's part in it."

Shadows were filling the hut with the approach of night. The clink of coins had a liquid sound, and it seemed for a moment as if all the light that was left lingered over the dull gold island of the guineas.

"Why," said Jud, swallowing, "I reckon I mind that well enough. Though I took no part in it myself, see. I was—thereabouts all the time." He hesitated and spat. "Why didn't you tell me you was meaning that all along?"

The following day a young woman on a horse went through Grambler in the other direction, passed Sawle Church, skirted Trenwith and presently began to go down the steep track into Trevaunance Cove. She was a dark young woman, a little above average in height, dressed in a close-fitting blue riding habit, a pale blue bodice and a small tricorn hat. Connoisseurs would have disagreed as to whether she was beautiful, but few men would have passed her without a second glance.

Leaving the smelting works, whose ochreous fumes had blighted the vegetation of the cove, she rode up the other side to where Place House, squat and solid against wind and storm, brooded over the sea. As she got down it was plain that the young woman was nervous. Her gloved fingers fumbled with the bridle of her horse, and when a groom came out to hold him she stumbled over what she had to say.

"Sir John Trevaunance, ma'am? I'll ask if he be in. What name shall I say?"

"Mistress Poldark."

"Mistress Poldark. Er—yes, ma'am." Did she imagine the slight glance of added interest? "Will you come this way, please."

She was shown into a warm little morning room from which a conservatory led off, and after sitting pulling at the fingers of her gloves for a few minutes she heard footsteps returning, and a manservant came to say Sir John was in and would see her.

He was in a long room like a study, overlooking the sea. She was relieved to find him alone except for a great boar hound that crouched at his feet. She found him, too, less imposing than she'd feared, being of a figure not much taller than herself, and ruddy-complexioned and rather jovial about the eyes and jowl.

He said: "Your servant, ma'am. Will you take a seat."

He waited until she had chosen the edge of a chair and then sat at his desk again. For a minute she kept her eyes down, knowing he was looking her over and accepting the scrutiny as part of the necessary ordeal.

He said warily: "I haven't had the pleasure before."

"No. . . . You know my husband well. . . ."

"Of course. We've been associated in business until . . . recently."

"Ross was very grieved to give up the association. He was always that proud of it."

"Hrrrm! Circumstances were too much for us, ma'am. Nobody's fault. We all lost money in the transaction."

She looked up, and saw that his scrutiny had gratified him. It was one of the few comforting factors in Demelza's excursions into society, this faculty she had of pleasing men. She did not see it yet as power, only as a buttress to faltering courage. She knew that her visit here was irregular by any standards of etiquette—and he must know it as well.

From where they were sitting they could both see the smoke drifting across the bay from the smelting works, and after a moment he said rather stiffly:

"As you—hrrm—no doubt know, the company has been re-formed—under new management. It was a blow for us all when the concern failed, but y'understand how I was placed. The buildings were on my land—indeed under my very nose—I'd sunk more capital than anyone in the concern, and it would've been crazy to let 'em rot away in idleness. The opportunity came to obtain fresh capital and it was only common sense to take it. I trust Captain Poldark understands how it was."

"I'm sure he does," said Demelza. "I'm sure he'd only wish you well with any new venture—even if he wasn't able to partake in it himself."

Sir John's eyes flickered. "Kind of you to say so. As yet we barely meet expenses, but I think that will improve. Can I offer you some refreshment? A glass of canary, perhaps?"

"No, thank you . . ." She hesitated. "But p'raps I should like a glass of port if twouldn't be putting you out."

With an ironical eyebrow Sir John rose, and pulled the bell. Wine was brought and polite conversation made while it was drunk. They talked of mines and cows and carriages and the broken summer. Demelza grew easier in manner and Sir John less wary.

"To tell the truth," said Demelza, "I think it is the caudly weather that's making trouble with all the animals. We have a fine cow called Emma; two weeks ago she was yielding rich, but now the milk's gone into her horn. Same with another, though that was not so surprising——"

"I've a fine Hereford, worth a mint of money," Sir John said. "Calved only for the second time two days ago and now sick and ill with a paraplegia. Had the cow doctor, Phillips, over five times. It will break my heart if I have to lose her."

"Is the calf safe?"

" Oh yes, but it was a bad time. And afterwards Minta not able to stand. Something is amiss with her teeth too—loose in the jaw—and a sort of separation to the joints of her tail. Phillips is completely defeated, and my own man no better."

" I mind when I lived at Illuggan," said Demelza, " there was a case like that there. The parson's cow was taken ill with just that sort of complaint. And after calving too."

" Did he find the cure?"

" Yes, sir, he found the cure."

" What was it?"

" Well, it wouldn't be for me to say whether the parson did right, would it? He wasn't above calling in an old woman, called Meggy Dawes—she lived just over the stream, I remember. A rare hand at curing warts and the King's Evil. Once, a boy went to her with a kenning on the eye. It was a bad one, but no sooner did she——"

" But about the cow, ma'am."

" Oh yes. Is she to be seen, Sir John? I'd dearly like to see her to be sure if it is just the same complaint as in the parson's cow."

" I'll take you to her myself, if you'll be so good. Another glass of port to sustain you?"

A few minutes later they made their way across the cobbled yard at the back of the house and into the shippon where the cow lay. Demelza noticed the massive stonework of the outhouses and wished they were hers. The cow lay upon her side, her soft brown eyes mournful but uncomplaining. A man rose from a wooden seat and stood respectfully by the door.

Demelza bent to examine the cow—with a professionalism of manner that came from her seven years at Nampara, not at all from her Illuggan childhood. The animal's legs were paralysed—and her tail had a curious disjointed appearance about halfway along its length.

Demelza said: " Yes. It is exactly the same. Meggy Dawes called it Tail-Shot."

" And the cure?"

" It is her cure, mind you, not mine."

"Yes, yes, I follow that."

Demelza passed the tip of her tongue over her lips. "She said to slit open the tail here, about a foot from the end, where the joint has slipped, and put in a well-salted onion— then bind it in place with some coarse tape—keep it there about a week, then leave off the tape. Only a little food once a day, and a cordial made of equal parts of rosemary, juniper berries and cardamon seeds without their hulks. I remember well. That's what she said."

Demelza glanced experimentally at the baronet. Sir John was chewing his bottom lip.

"Well," he said, "I've never heard of the cure, but then the disease is rare too. You are the first person who seems to have encountered it before. Damme, I've a mind to try it. What do you say, Lyson?"

"'Tis better'n seeing the animal suffer, sir."

"Exactly what I feel. I have heard that these old women are wonders when it comes to the lesser-known distempers. Could you repeat the instructions to my man, Mrs. Poldark?"

"With pleasure." After a minute or two they walked back across the yard and into the house.

Sir John said: "I trust Captain Poldark is keeping in good heart over his coming trial."

As soon as he spoke he regretted having been so incautious. One felt that she had deliberately avoided this subject, so putting on him the onus of mentioning it. But she did not take up the case as passionately as he had feared.

"Well, of course we're very unhappy about it. I think I worry more than he does."

"It will soon be here and over now, and a good chance of acquittal, I think."

"D'you really think so, Sir John? That comforts me greatly. You'll be in Bodmin yourself during the assizes?"

"Um? Um? Well, that I don't know. Why do you ask?"

"I have heard tell there is to be an election during September, and with the assizes on the sixth I thought you might by chance be there."

"You mean to help my brother? Oh, he's well able to

look after his seat." The baronet glanced without trust at her composed face as they re-entered the big room he used as an office. It wasn't easy to guess what she was thinking. " Even if I was in the town I should have too much in hand to attend the court. Besides, with respect, ma'am, I shouldn't wish to see an old friend in distress. Shall wish him well, of course —but no one wants to seek entertainment in the spectacle."

" We've heard tell there are to be two judges," she said.

" Oh, not two to the case. Two will share the assize between 'em, I expect. Wentworth Lister is not an ill fellow, though it's years since we met. You'll have a fair trial, be sure of that. British justice will see to it." The boar hound had come across, and he took a sweet biscuit from a drawer and gave it to the dog.

" It is fair puzzling to me," said Demelza, " how a man—a judge—can come down all the way from upcountry and listen to a case and get the hang of the rights and ways of it all in a few hours. It don't seem possible to me. Does he not ever ask for the truth in private before the case begins?"

Sir John smiled. " You'll be surprised how quickly a trained brain can sum up the true facts. And remember, it will not depend upon the judge but upon the jury, and they are Cornish folk like ourselves, so there's good cause to look on the bright side. Another sip of port?"

Demelza refused. " It's a little heady, I suspicion. But very taking in flavour. When all this is over we'd like for you to come and see us one day, sir. Ross asked me to say that."

Sir John said he'd be charmed, and the dog dropped crumbs from his biscuit all over the floor. Demelza rose to go.

He added: " I shall pray for good results from your treatment for Minta."

So did Demelza, but she didn't show her doubts. " Perhaps I might have news of her?"

" Of course. I'll send word over. And in the meantime . . . should you be passing this way again—only too pleased."

" Thank you, Sir John. I sometimes ride the coast for my health. It is uneven for a good horse, but I like the views and the bracing air."

16

Sir John went with her to the door and helped her to mount, admiring her slim figure and straight back. As she rode out of the gates a man on a grey horse came in.

"Who was that?" said Unwin Trevaunance, dropping his grey riding gloves on top of a pile of tin cheques. Sir John's younger brother did everything deliberately, giving consequence to actions which hadn't any. Thirty-six or -seven, tall, lion-faced and masterful, he was a much more impressive personality than the baronet. Yet Sir John made money and Unwin did not.

"Ross Poldark's wife. Attractive young woman. Hadn't met her before."

"What did she want?"

"That I don't yet know," said Sir John. "She did not appear to want anything."

Unwin had a cleft between his eyes, which deepened when he frowned. "Wasn't she his scullery maid or some such?"

"Others have risen before her, and with fewer talents, I'd swear. She has a certain elegance already. In a few years it will be hard to tell her from a woman of breeding."

"And she came for nothing? I doubt it. To me she looks a dangerous woman."

"Dangerous?"

"We exchanged a glance as she left. I'm not unskilled in summing people up, John."

"Well, neither am I, Unwin, and I think I'll take the risk." Sir John gave another biscuit to the hound. "She has a ready cure to offer for Minta, though rot me if I think it'll work. . . . Did you find Ray?"

"Yes. Oh yes. I told him Caroline wanted to break the journey down here to be in Bodmin during the election; but Caroline has written him also, so it was no news. Like her to ask me to ask her uncle and then to write herself!"

"She's only a girl. Be patient with her, Unwin. You'll *need* patience. She's temperamental and wayward. And there are others will think her a good catch beside yourself."

Unwin bit at the top of his riding crop. "The old man's an

ingrained miser. There he was this morning, turning over the accounts with his scabby hands, and the house—no mansion at the best of times—nearly falling down for want of repair. It's really no fit place for Caroline to spend half her life."

" You'll be able to alter all that."

" Aye. Someday. But Ray's no more than fifty-three or -four. He might live ten year yet." Unwin went to the window and stared out across the sea, which was quiet this morning. The low cloud over the craggy cliffs had darkened the colour of the water to a deep veined green. Some sea gulls had perched on the wall of the house and were throatily crying. To the tall man, accustomed now to London life, the scene was melancholy. " Penvenen's got some uncommon views altogether. He was giving it as his opinion this morning that Cornwall is over-represented in Parliament. Says the seats should be redistributed among the new towns in the midlands. Stuff and nonsense."

" Take no notice of his little foibles. He often says these things to annoy. It is a way he has."

Unwin turned. " Well, I hope we have no more elections for another seven years. It will cost me upwards of two thousand pounds just for the pleasure of being returned—and you know that doesn't end it—or begin it for that matter."

Sir John's eyes took on a cautious bloodless look, as they always did when money was mentioned. " Your profession's of your own choosing, my boy. And there's others worse off. Carter of Grampound was telling me he would have to pay as much as three hundred guineas a vote when the time came." He got up and pulled the bell. " Mistress Poldark was asking me if I should be in Bodmin for the hustings. I wonder what her purpose was in that?"

Chapter Two

The morning was well gone when Demelza turned Caerhays towards dinner and home. As she skirted the grounds of Trenwith House she wished she could have dropped in for a few minutes' friendly chat with Verity. It was something she greatly missed and could never get used to. But Verity was in Falmouth, if not further afloat—happily married, it seemed, in spite of all foreboding; and she, Demelza, had been the active conniver in the change, so she could not complain. Indeed it was Verity's elopement which had caused a sharper breach between the families, and, in spite of Demelza's self-sacrifice of last Christmas, the breach was not properly closed. The responsibility was not now Francis's. Since the illnesses of last Christmas and little Julia's death he seemed most anxious to show his gratitude for what Demelza had done. But Ross would have none of it. The failure of the Carnmore Copper Company lay insuperably between them. And if what Ross suspected about that failure was right, then Demelza could not blame him. But she would have been much happier with it otherwise. Her nature always preferred the straightforward settlement to the lingering bitter suspicion.

Just before she lost sight of the house she saw Dwight Enys coming along the track in her wake, so reined in her horse to wait for him. The young surgeon took off his hat as he came up.

"A fine morning, ma'am. I'm glad to see you enjoying the air."

"With a purpose," she said, smiling. "Everything I d'do these days is with some purpose or another. Very moral, I suppose, if you look at it that way."

He answered her smile—it was difficult not to—and allowed his horse to walk along beside hers. The track was just wide enough for them to go abreast. He noticed professionally how slight she had stayed since her illness of January.

"I suppose it depends whether the purpose was moral or not."

She pushed in a curl that the wind had dislodged. "Ah, that I don't know. We should have to ask the preacher. I have been to Place House doctoring Sir John's cattle."

Dwight looked surprised. "I didn't know you were expert in that."

"Nor am I. I only pray to God his Hereford cow takes a turn for the better. If it dies I shall have advanced nothing."

"And if it lives?"

She glanced at him. "Where are you bound, Dwight?"

"To see some of the folk of Sawle. I am increasingly popular with the patients who can afford to pay nothing. Choake gets ever lazier."

"And more unfriendly, like. What is at back of all this— this trying to get Ross convicted?"

The doctor looked uncomfortable. He flicked the loose loop of the reins against the sleeve of his black velvet coat. "The law, I suppose . . ."

"Oh yes, the law. But something else. Since when has the law been so fussy about strippin' a wreck or rough-handling a few excise men—even suppose Ross had any part in that, and we know he did not. It is only what's been going on since I was born and for hundreds of years before that."

"I'm not sure that that's true—not altogether. I'd do anything to help Ross—and will do, you know that . . ."

"Yes, I know that."

"But I don't think it's any good blinking that you can ignore the law ten times, but the eleventh—if it gets you—it will hold on like a leech, and no letting go till the thing's thrashed out. That's the truth. Of course, in this case one wonders if, now the law *has* moved, there may not be other influences at work also——"

"There's men been round asking questions even of the Gimletts, our own servants. There can scarcely be a cottage in the district that hasn't had its caller, all trying to pin the blame on Ross! It's the law, no doubt, but the law wi' plenty of money to spend and time to waste—for there's none of his own folk will give him away, and they might know it. Ross has his enemies but they're not among the miners who helped him at the wreck!"

Sawle Church, its tower leaning like Pisa, was reached, and Dwight halted at the head of Sawle Combe. On the hill some women were cutting a sloping field of corn; it was stacked round the edge but as yet uncut in the middle, and looked like an embroidered handkerchief.

"You will not come down this way?"

"No, Ross will be expecting me back."

"In so far," said Dwight, "in so far as there is any influence at work beyond the law, I should not put it down to pompous nobodies like Surgeon Choake who have neither the money nor the venom to do serious harm."

"Nor do I, Dwight. Nor do we."

"No . . ."

He said: "For your information, I have not visited the Warleggans for twelve months."

She said: "I have only met George properly. What are the others like?"

"I know them very little. Nicholas, George's father, is a big hard domineering man, but he has a reputation for honesty that is not lightly to be had. George's uncle, Cary, is the one who keeps in the background, and if there is anything shady to be done I should guess he does it. But I confess they have always been gracious enough to me."

Demelza stared across at the silver-blue triangle of sea blocking up the end of the valley. "Sanson, who lost his life in the wreck, was a cousin of theirs. And there are other things between Ross and George—even before the smelting company. It is a good time to pay off old scores."

"I should not worry overmuch about that. The law will only take account of the truth."

"I'm not so sure," she said.

On Hendrawna Beach the scene was quite different from Trevaunance Cove. Although there was little ebb and flow about the rocks, on the flat sandy beach the sea roared, and a low mist hung over it in the still mild air. Coming back from his usual morning walk as far as the Dark Cliffs, Ross glanced across at the cliffs where the shacks of Wheal Leisure were built, and could hardly see them through the haze. It was like walking in a vapour bath.

Since the loss of Julia and the opening of the prosecution against him, he had forced himself to make this walk daily. Or if the mood took him and the weather was favourable he would go out in the new dinghy and sail as far as St. Ann's. Such activity didn't lift the cloud from his mind, but it helped to set it in proportion for the rest of the day's tasks. His daughter was dead, his cousin had betrayed him, his much-laboured-over smelting scheme was in ashes, he faced charges in the criminal court for which he might well be sentenced to death or life transportation; and if by some chance he survived that, it would be only a matter of months before bankruptcy and imprisonment for debt followed. But in the meantime fields had to be sown and reaped, copper had to be raised and marketed, Demelza had to be clothed and fed and cherished—so far as it was in his scope to cherish anyone at this stage.

It was Julia's death which still hit him hardest. Demelza had grieved no less than he, but hers was a more pliant nature, responding involuntarily to stimuli that meant little to him. A celandine flowering out of season, a litter of kittens found unexpectedly in a loft, warm sunshine after a cold spell, the smell of the first swathe of hay: these were always temporary reliefs for her, and so sorrow had less power to injure her. Although he didn't realise it, much of the cherishing this year had been on her side.

After the storms of Christmas it had been a quiet winter; but there was no ease in the district, Ross thought, any more than there was ease in himself. Copper prices had risen only enough to bring a slight increase of profit in the mines now open, nothing to justify the starting of new ventures or the reopening of old. Life was very close to survival level.

As he left the beach and climbed over the broken wall he

22

saw Demelza coming down the valley, and she saw him at the same time and waved, and he waved back. They reached the house almost at the same time, and he helped her down and gave the horse to Gimlett, who had come hurrying round.

" You've dressed up for your morning ride to-day," he said.

" I thought twas bad to get slovenly and be seen about as if I didn't care for being Mrs. Poldark."

" There are some who might feel that way just at present."

She linked his arm and put pressure on it to get him to walk round the garden with her.

" My hollyhocks are not so well this year," she said. " Too much rain. All the crops are late too. We need a rare hot September."

" It would make it stuffy in the court."

" We shall not be in court all the month. Only one day. Then you'll be free."

" Who says so? Have you been consulting your witches?"

She paused to pick a snail from under an old primrose leaf. She held it distastefully between gloved finger and thumb. " I never know what's best to do with 'em."

" Drop it on that stone."

She did so and turned away while he crushed it. " Poor little bull-horn. But they're so greedy; I shouldn't mind if they were content with a leaf or two. . . . Talking of witches, Ross, have you ever heard of a cow illness called Tail-Shot?"

" No."

" The back legs are paralysed and the cow's teeth come loose."

" A cow's teeth are always loose," Ross said.

" And the tail has a queer unjointed look—as if it were broken. That gives it its name. D'you think twould cure the disease to open up the tail and put in a boiled onion?"

Ross said: " No."

" But it would do no harm if the cow was going to get better anyhow, would it?"

" What have you been up to this morning?"

She looked into his distinguished bony face.

"I met Dwight on the way home. He is going to be at assize."

"I don't see what need there'll be of him. Half Sawle and Grambler will be there, it appears to me. It will make quite a Roman holiday."

They walked round in silence. The garden was motionless under the lowering clouds, leaf and flower taking on the warmer, firmer substance of permanent things. Ross thought, there are no permanent things, only fleeting moments of warmth and companionship, precious stationary seconds in a flicker of troubled days.

The clouds broke in a shower and drove them in, and they stood a minute in the window of the parlour watching the big drops pattering on the leaves of the lilac tree, staining them dark. When rain came suddenly Demelza still had the instinct to go and see if Julia were sleeping outside. She thought of saying this to Ross but checked herself. The child's name was hardly ever mentioned. Sometimes she suspected that Julia was a bar between them, that though he tried his utmost not to, the memory of her courting infection to help at Trenwith still rankled.

She said: "Is it not time you went to see Mr. Notary Pearce again?"

He grunted. "The man frets me. The less I see of him the better."

She said quietly: "It is my life, you know, as well as yours that's at hazard."

He put his arm round her. "Tut, tut. If anything happens to me you will have much still to live for. This house and land will be yours. You will become principal shareholder in Wheal Leisure Mine. You will have a duty—to people and to the countryside . . ."

She stopped him. "Nay, Ross, I shall have nothing. I shall be a beggar again. I shall be an unfledged miner's wench——"

"You'll be a handsome young woman in your first twenties with a small estate and a load of debts. The best of your life will be ahead of you——"

24

"I live only through you. You made me what I am. You *think* me into being handsome, you *think* me into being a squire's wife——"

"Stuff. You'd surely marry again. If I were gone there'd be men humming round here from all over the county. It isn't flattery but the sober truth. You could take your pick of a dozen——"

"I should *never* marry again. Never!"

His hand tightened on her. "How thin you are still."

"I'm not. You ought to know I'm not."

"Well, slim then. Your waist used to have a more comfortable feel."

"Only after Julia was born. That was . . . different then." There, the name was out now.

"Yes," he said.

There was silence for a minute or two. His eyes were lidded and she could not read his expression.

She said: "Ross."

"Yes?"

"Perhaps in time it will seem different. Perhaps we shall have other children."

He moved away from her. "I do not think any child would be grateful for having a gallows bird for a father. . . . I wonder if dinner is ready."

When Dwight parted from Demelza he rode down the steep narrow track to Sawle village, into the bubble of the stream and the clatter of the tin stamps. It was a short enough time since he had come to this district, a callow young physician with radical ideas about medicine; but it seemed a decade in his life. In that time he had earned the confidence and affection of the people he worked among, had inexcusably broken his Hippocratic oath, and since then had painfully re-established himself—entirely in the eyes of the countryside, who laid the blame on the girl, very partially in his own, which at all times were self-critical and self-exacting.

He had learned a great deal: that humanity was infinitely variable and infinitely contradictory, so that all treatment

25

consisted of patient experiment and trial and error; that the surgeon and the physician were often mere onlookers at battles fought under their eyes; that no outward aid was one quarter as powerful as the ordinary recuperative power of the body, and that drugs and potions were sometimes as likely to hinder as to help.

If he had been a self-satisfied man he might have found some comfort in having come this far, for many of the surgeons and apothecaries he met had learned nothing like this in a lifetime and were never likely to. He avoided members of his own profession, for he found himself constantly at loggerheads with them. His only comfort was that they were often as much at variance among themselves, having only one element in common, an absolute and unquestioning confidence that their own method was infallible—a confidence that seemed in no way shaken when one of their patients died. If a sick man collapsed under treatment that was the fault of the sick man, not of the method.

What Dr. Thomas Choake believed Dwight was not sure. Since their early quarrel they had seen little of each other; but as they practised over much the same territory they were bound to have occasional contacts. Choake always had an instant remedy to hand—sometimes he seemed even to have decided on a remedy before he saw the patient. But whether these remedies sprang from a fixed theory of medicine or merely from the impulses of his own brain Dwight was never able to tell.

This noon Dwight had several patients to visit, the first a call on Charlie Kempthorne. Two years ago Kempthorne had had a consumption of both lungs, the top only of each affected, but enough to spell a death sentence. Now he was apparently well, and had been all this year, was free of cough, had put on weight and was working again, not as a miner but as a sailmaker. He was at home, as Dwight had expected, and sitting at the door of his cottage busy with a coarse needle and thread. He grinned all over his lean over-brown face when he saw the physician, and got up to greet him.

26

"Come inside, sur. Tis a pleasure to see you. I bin saving some eggs till you passed by."

"I'm not here to stay," said Enys pleasantly. "Just a visit to see you're following instructions. Thank you all the same."

"Tis no 'ardship to go on with the treatment. Here I sit in the dryth, day in day out, stitching away—and makin' more money than I did as a sumpman!"

"And Lottie and May?" Kempthorne had two scrawny little daughters, of five and seven. He had lost his wife in a drowning accident three years ago.

"They'm down to Mrs. Coad's. Though what they d'learn I'm vexed to think." Kempthorne wet the thread in his mouth and paused with it between finger and thumb to look at the other man slyly. "I suppose you d'know there's more fever abroad. Aunt Sarah Tregeagle asked for me to tell you."

Dwight did not comment, having a distaste for discussing diseases in general terms with his patients.

"The Curnows have it, and Betty Coad and the Ishbels, she asked for me to tell you. Of course, tis no more'n you've reason to expect in August month."

"A fine big sail, that."

Charlie grinned. "Aye, sur. For the *One and All* of St. Ann's. She need all her canvas."

"Would you make sails for the revenue boats as well?"

"Only if so be as I could stitch in a flaw so that they ripped when giving chase."

From here to the open square at the foot of the hill it was not safe to ride a horse, and Dwight walked thoughtfully down the steep rutted track of Stippy-Stappy Lane. These cottages, the better ones of the village, occupied one side of the lane; on the other, beyond the overgrown Cornish wall, the valley fell steeply into a gully where a part of the Mellingey River ran away to the sea and worked the tin stamps. Each house was about six feet below its neighbour, and at the last of them Dwight tethered his horse. As he knocked at the door a shaft of brassy sunlight fell through the clouds on the

27

clustered cottages below, giving their roofs a wet gleam, anticipating the rain.

Here lived Jacka Hoblyn, who had his own tin stamp, Polly his wife, their daughter Rosina, a semi-cripple, and their younger daughter Parthesia, a lively little creature of eleven, who opened the door. There were two small rooms downstairs, with lime-ash floors, in one of which Rosina carried on her work as a sempstress and patten maker. Parthesia said her mother was in bed and hopped ahead of him up the outside stone staircase to the raftered loft where they all slept. Having seen him in, she skipped off again in search of Father, who she said was sick too.

Polly Hoblyn, who was forty and looked fifty-eight, greeted him brightly; and Dwight smiled back, taking in all the usual symptoms of an attack of the tertian ague: the muscle tremors, the pinched pale face, the dead white fingers. It was an unusually bad attack. The encouraging circumstance was that he had been called in—however tentatively and apologetically—to deal with it. Two years ago people with the ordinary complaints bought stuff, if they could afford it, from Irby, the druggist at St. Ann's, or from one of the old women of the neighbourhood; certainly they never dared call in Dr. Choake unless they had broken a limb or were *in extremis*. That Dr. Enys did not mind administering to folk who could pay only in kind, or not even that way, they were slowly coming to appreciate. Of course there were those who said he experimented on the poor people; but there are always uncharitable tongues.

He mixed the woman a dose of Peruvian bark; then, having watched it go down between the clenching teeth, he put out two fever powders to be taken later and a dose of sal polychrest and rhubarb for to-night. At this point the light in the doorway darkened as Jacka Hoblyn appeared in the doorway.

"Good day to ee, Surgeon. Thesia, bring us a nackan from down b'low. I'm sweaten like a bull. Well, what's amiss with Polly?"

"The intermittent fever. She should stay in bed two days

at least. And you? I think you have the same. Come over here to the light, will you."

As he got near, Dwight caught the strong whiff of gin. So it was one of Jacka's times. Parthesia came dancing up with a square of red cloth, and the man mopped his heavy brow with it. His pulse was small, hard and quick. The fever was at a later stage, and would cause an overmastering thirst.

"I got a touch. But moving around is best for it, not loustering tween the blankets. Fasterer you move, fasterer he go."

"Now look, Hoblyn, I'd like you to take this now, and this powder in water before you go to bed to-night. Understand?"

Jacka ran a hand through his upstanding hair and glowered at him. "I don't 'old with doctor's traade."

"Nevertheless, you should take this. You'll be far better for it."

They stared at each other, but Dwight's prestige was just too much for the streamer, and with some satisfaction he watched the strong dose of soluble tartar disappear. The night powder, if Hoblyn was sufficiently alert to drink it, contained ten grains of jalap, but that didn't so much matter. Dwight felt a greater concern for the health of the three women than for the man.

As he was leaving he saw Rosina limping up the hill with a jug of milk. She was seventeen, and her fine eyes had not yet been spoiled by endless hours of close sewing in a bad light. She smiled and curtsied as they met.

"Your family should be improved to-morrow. See your mother takes her powder."

"I will surely. Thank you, sur."

"Your father gets—troublesome when he is in liquor?"

She blushed. "It make him ill-tempered, sur; hard to get along with, as you might say."

"And—violent?"

"Oh, no, sur—or but seldom. And then he d'make it up to we afterwards."

Dwight slid past the little bow window of Aunt Mary

29

Rogers's shop and reached the huddle of broken-down cottages at the foot of the hill known as the Guernseys. Here the worst squalor began. Windows stuffed with board and rags, doors propped beside the openings they had been designed to fill, open cesspools, with rat runs from one to another, broken roofs and lean-to shacks where half-naked children crawled and played. Coming here, Dwight always felt conscious of his own decent clothes: they were phenomena from another world. He knocked at the first cottage, surprised to see both halves of the door closed, for the room within depended for its light on what came through the door. A week ago he had delivered Betty Carkeek of her first-born son when two fishwife-midwives had done their worst and failed.

He heard the baby crying inside and after another minute Betty came to the door, opening the top half a suspicious inch.

" Oh, tis you, sur. Do you come in." Betty Carkeek, née Coad, was not the sort who faded away, given half a chance, but he had been relieved when the fourth and fifth days were past without any sign of childbed fever. She should do well enough now. He followed her into the stone hut—it was hardly more—stooping his head on the threshold, and saw Ted Carkeek sitting over a small fire stirring some sort of an herb brew. Ted and Betty had only been married a month, but staying home when there was work to do, and work so hard to get, seemed a poor way of showing your devotion.

He nodded to the young man and went to look at the baby. Ted got up and moved to go out, but Betty stopped him, and he grunted and went back to watching his brew. The child was snuffly with a cold and its breathing rapid; Dwight wondered what the inexperienced girl had done; one was always struggling against ignorance and neglect.

" Your mother not here, Betty?"

" No, sur. Mother's some slight."

Of course. Kempthorne had mentioned the Coads. " The ague?"

" Yes, I reckon."

The stuff on the stove began to bubble and the fire spat as beads of moisture fell on it. Smoke curled away from the open chimney and wove itself about the blackened rafters.

" And yourself?"

" Proper, you. But Ted's not so smart——"

" Hold your clack," said Ted from the fireplace.

Dwight took no notice. " You're up too soon," he said to the girl. " If Ted is home he can look after you."

" Tis I been tending on he, more like."

Ted made another impatient movement, but she went on: " Let Surgeon see ee, Ted. There's nought to be gained by sceedling there by the fire. He's no telltale, we did ought to know that."

Ted grumpily rose and came into the light of the door. " I sprit open my shoulder, that's all. Physic won't do him no good."

Dwight pulled back the sack the boy had over his shoulder. A musket ball had glanced off the bone and come out, leaving in the first place a clean enough wound. But there was a good deal of inflammation now, not improved by the poultice of boiled yarrow leaves.

" Have you clean water here? What's that you're brewing on the fire?" Dwight went about dressing the wound, making no comment on the circumstances.

And because he didn't ask, the explanation came, though not until the dressing was done and he had bled the man and was ready to leave. Ted Carkeek was partner with four others in a cockleshell of a boat with which in quiet weather they would venture the long and hazardous voyage to France to pick up spirits and bring them back for sale. Theirs was no large-scale business like Mr. Trencrom's; but by means of four or five runs a year they were able to make enough to help things along. They had left last Saturday and returned Wednesday, putting in to Vaughan's Cove, a strip of beach connecting at times with Sawle Cove, to find Vercoe and two other excisemen waiting ready to lay hands on them. There had been a scuffle, their boat had sunk, drifting on the rocks

31

in the confusion, and Ted Carkeek had been shot in the shoulder. A disagreeable affair, and one which might have repercussions.

"Twasn't as if we was doin' wrong," Ted said indignantly. "Tis only turning a penny like other folk—and now we've to start again from naught, if so be as we're left be. Like as not we'll have soldiers in searching the houses, like what they did in St. Ann's!"

Betty said: "What we all d'want to know is, how the gaugers knowed where they was going to land. Tisn't natural. Someone's been talking."

Dwight fastened the clasps of his leather bag, giving a last uneasy glance in the direction of the child. There was little he could do for so young a baby; in any case Mrs. Coad would certainly make her daughter disobey him and give it some witch's brew of her own. The child would survive or not according to its constitution. He said: "The excise men have long ears. You'll need to rest that shoulder, Ted."

"It edn the first time that's happened," said Ted. "Old man Pendarves and Foster Pendarves was caught in April. Red-handed. It's not natural, I'll lay."

"Did many in the village know of your trip?"

"Oh . . . yes, I s'pose. Tis hard for 'em not to guess when you're gone half the week. But not where we was going to bring the stuff in. That were knowed by only six or seven. If I could lay me hands on the one that couldn't make to hold his tongue—or, still more, give us away on purpose . . ."

It was dark and stuffy in the room, and Dwight had a sudden urge to put his hands up to the slanting beams and push them away. These people might as well live in a cave, shut off from light and sun.

"Are others of your family ill, Betty?"

"Well, not ill as you'd say. Joan and Nancy has fever too, but they're sweating nicely and on the mend."

"Have they been nursing your baby?"

Betty stared at him, more anxious to say the right thing than the truthful. "No, sur," she got out at last.

Dwight picked up his bag. "Well, I should not let them."

32

He turned to leave. "Don't be too free with your suspicions, Ted. I know it is easy to advise, but once you get suspecting people it's hard to know where to stop."

As he left the cottage and crossed the square towards the fish cellars where several families eked out an existence, he was frowning at the problems the outbreak of fever had brought him. All this summer he had been troubled by a new virulence in this seasonal complaint—not merely by the virulence of taking it bad the way Mrs. Hoblyn had done, but by the emergence of new symptoms when people should have been on the mend. Discolorations of the skin developed, and swellings and then a new loss of strength. Two children had recently died—apparently from this—and several adults were much more ill than they ought to have been. Even the children who got better were feeble and yellow, with tumid bellies and weak legs. If measles came they would go off like flies. He had tried all his favourite weapons but none of them seemed to do any good. Dwight sometimes wondered if he ought to invent a new complaint called privation disease to cover the ills he found.

Chapter Three

Ross rode in to Truro on the following Monday. Demelza would have gone with him had she not sensed that he preferred the journey alone. He was like that at present.

When he got in he called at once on Mr. Nathaniel Pearce.

Last February, when the law had so suddenly and unexpectedly moved in the matter, Ross had still been feeling the worst effects of his bereavement and his several failures, and he had endured the justice's examination in an angry and resentful mood. It had early been clear that he must employ some lawyer to act for him—and who more natural than his own and his father's, Mr. Notary Pearce, who also was his co-partner in Wheal Leisure and his creditor to the sum of fourteen hundred pounds?

But several times during the months of waiting Ross had wished himself sufficiently of one mind to make a change before it was too late. Pearce was a good negotiator, adept in conveyances, a sharp and adroit enough man where money was concerned; but there were younger and keener men to prepare briefs for the assizes. Also in this bitter cleavage which had broken out between two factions in the county during the last few years, Pearce was one of the few men with a foot still in each camp. He was a friend of Ross's and a friend of the Warleggans. A shareholder in Wheal Leisure, he nevertheless banked with the Warleggans—although he sometimes did legal business for Pascoe's. He was a personal friend of Dr. Choake's, but had loaned money to Dwight Enys. In principle it was all very good; detachment and impartiality were to be admired. But lately, with ruin and broken homes following in the wake of the struggle, it just wasn't wholesome any more.

Ross found him in better spirits than usual. The chronic gout that was settling on him had eased, and he was using his new mobility in a furious attack on boxfuls of ancient legal papers that filled the room. A clerk and an apprentice were helping in the orgy, carrying boxes to his desk and then bearing away the crackling yellow parchments which Mr. Pearce weeded out and flung upon the floor.

When he saw Ross he said: " There now, Captain Poldark; what a pleasant surprise; do take a chair, if there is one— Noakes, clear a chair for Captain Poldark—I am just sorting a little of the older stuff; nothing modern, you follow, selecting a little of the older stuff for disposal. You're keeping well, I hope; this uncertain weather suits some people." He scattered a dozen mothy letters on the floor and set his bob wig straight. " My daughter was saying only yesterday— Noakes, take these boxes with you: all this Basset and Tresize stuff has to remain *intacta*. . . . A little joke there, Captain Poldark, if one knows the subject of the 1705 files. . . . The older families naturally expect their lawyers to preserve all correspondence relating; but space is the obstacle; one needs cellars. My daughter was saying wet summers are healthy summers, do you agree?"

"I'll not keep you long," said Ross.

Pearce glanced at him and set down the bundle of papers he had grasped. "No. Quite so. But I have a free morning. There are one or two things. Noakes—and you, Biddle—you can leave us. Never mind the boxes. Dear, dear, not in front of the desk. That's right. . . . Now, Captain Poldark. We're quite cosy. One minute, just to poke the fire. . . ."

So they settled to be cosy in the hot, paper-littered room, and Mr. Pearce scratched himself and informed Ross what arrangements had so far been made for his downfall. The assizes would be formally opened on Saturday the fourth, prox., though no business would be transacted until the Monday. Ross would be required to present himself to the Governor of the Prison not later than Thursday the second. The Hon. Mr. Wentworth Lister and the Hon. Mr. H. C. Thornton, two of His Majesty's Judges out of the Court of Common Pleas, were to hold the commission. Probably H. C. Thornton would deal with the *nisi prius* side, and Wentworth Lister would handle the Crown cases. The lists were very crowded because when the winter assizes had been due to take place there had been so much fever in Launceton that the lawyers had refused to come down, and nearly all the cases had been postponed until the summer. It was likely, however, that Ross's trial, being considered an important one, would be put forward to the Tuesday or the Wednesday.

"Who is leading for the Crown?"

"Henry Bull, I believe. I could have wished for someone different—though, mind you, I've never seen him, don't know him, except by repute; and by repute he's a trifle hard-hitting, shall we say. No great lawyer, one understands, but keen to get his verdict. Still, that's as may be. You've a great deal of good will, Captain Poldark; it all helps; dear me, it's of high importance where a jury is concerned." Pearce reached forward with his curtain rod and jabbed at the fire again.

"Good will and ill will," said Ross, watching the other's face.

35

"Indeed, one doesn't hear of it. Naturally, there may be some; we all have enemies; it's hard to come through life without them. But not many, I'm thinking, being committed in a magistrate's court as you were, can have had their bail money paid in by two of the magistrates on the bench. And after the things you said it was, I declare, a considerable tribute. You were a thought—hrr—hrr—reckless, to say the least, as I've suggested before."

"I only said what I thought."

"Oh, I've not doubt of that; indeed not. But if one may venture the suggestion—it doesn't always do, Captain Poldark, to say exactly what one thinks without regard to one's circumstances—that's if one wishes to—er—— In this case, with Lord Devoran and Mr. Boscoigne sympathetic towards you, some—some formula might have been found if you had not committed yourself so willingly. I hope, when the opportunity comes for you to speak in court, you will have greater regard for your safety. In my view—humble as it is—a lot will hang on your attitude then."

"Hang is the word." Ross got up and made his way among the papers to the window.

"Let us hope not. Dear me, no. But, remember, you will have a jury to consider—always very susceptible to good and bad impressions. You can do a great deal for yourself, believe me. Of course, counsel will advise you when you see him— and I do trust you'll accept his advice."

Ross watched a spider crawling up into its web in a corner of the windowpane. "Look, Pearce, there is one thing I have not done and must do—that is, make a will. Can you have it done—drawn up now so that it may be signed before I leave?"

"Why, yes, it's not impossible so long as the testamentary conditions are not involved. Noakes can be got in when you please."

"It should not be involved at all. A simple straightforward statement that I leave all my debts to my wife."

Pearce picked up a book and allowed a fat finger to travel experimentally along its edge for dust. "Not so bad as that,

36

surely, ha, ha! Things are somewhat tight for the moment, but no doubt they'll ease."

"They'll ease if they're allowed to ease. If things go wrong at Bodmin, you'll barely see your money back. So it's self-interest as well as common justice to get me my freedom." There was a faint ironical spark in Ross's eyes.

"Just so. Just so. We shall all work for it, believe me. A great deal depends on the jury. I confess I should feel a small matter more settled if there had not been so much trouble in France. We have to face it. That disturbance in Redruth in the autumn; ten years ago it would have been a case for the petty sessions—now one hanged and two transported . . ." Mr. Pearce scratched under his wig. "Shall I call in Noakes again now?"

"Please do."

The lawyer levered himself out of his chair and pulled the bell. "We still have the defence statement to complete. It's *essential* if you're to plead not guilty that . . ."

Ross turned from the window. "Leave it to-day. I don't think I'm in the mood. When the jail is waiting I may bring my mind to a better grip of the affair. . . ."

He had a standing invitation to dinner with the Pascoes, and when he left Mr. Pearce's office, as it was by then two o'clock, he walked at a leisurely pace towards the bank, which was in Pydar Street. Another bad day; August was refusing to relent. A cold northwest wind was bringing heavy showers, and the hot sun that broke between had no time to dry the streets before the clouds blew up again for the next storm. In this town where little rivulets ran down the side of the streets even in the dryest of summers, and half-hidden streams bubbled in every side alley, a town that one could not leave except by bridge or ford, one got a sense of saturation. In low-lying places the muddy pools were slowly submerging the cobbles and joining to become lakes.

To avoid one stretching half across Powder Street, Ross turned up the slit of Church Lane, and the wind, suddenly finding new venom, blew at his coattails and tried to snatch his hat. Another man behind him was not so lucky, and a black felt with a wide brim came hobbling along the wet cobbles to finish up at Ross's feet. He picked it up. As its owner came along he saw that it was Francis. So much had happened in their relationship since the angry scene of last August that they met like strangers, remembering the old emotions but no longer feeling them.

"God's my life," said Francis. "What a pesky wind. One is blown down this alley like a pea down a pipe." He accepted the hat but did not put it back on his head. His hair continued to blow about. "Thank you, Cousin."

Ross nodded briefly and moved to pass on.

"Ross . . ."

He turned. Francis was thinner, he noticed. The threat of stoutness had gone; but he looked no better for it. "Well?"

"We meet irregularly, and that no doubt's too often for you. It's not a view I'd criticise; but there's a thing or two I want to say in case another year passes before the opportunity occurs again."

"Well?" Ross's unquiet eyes stared past the other man.

Francis hunched up the high velvet collar of his coat. "Talking in this funnel's trying on the temper. I'll walk with you a few paces."

They fell into step. Francis did not speak until they reached St. Mary's Church and turned along beside the railings of the churchyard.

"Two things, I think, in the main. You cannot want my good wishes or be in a mood to appreciate them, but when you go to Bodmin next month you may know that you have them just the same."

"Thanks."

"The second is that should my help be of any use you may have that also."

"I don't think it can be."

"Nor I, in the main concern, or I'd proffer it with greater eagerness. But in one eventuality . . ."

He hesitated and stopped, both in speech and in motion.

38

Ross waited. Francis was rapping at the railings with his stick.

"Gravestones are a good place for confidences, no doubt. Supposing things should go wrong with you next month, how is Demelza fixed?"

Ross raised his head as if conscious of some challenge—not from Francis, but from this circumstance which was rearing itself in other people's minds as well as his own. "She'll survive. What is it to you?"

"Only that help may be offered in a variety of ways. I'm no doubt as nearly bankrupt as you, or nearer; but if after next month you are in prison and I out, she can turn to me if she needs help or advice. I have a name still in the county and happen to have a little hard money put by. She may have that if she needs it, or anything else I own."

It was Ross's impulse to say, What, turn to a traitor and a sneak thief like you, who betrayed and ruined a dozen good men and a fine project for the sake of petty spite; but he had no proof, and anyway it was over and gone. Resentment and bitterness and old grudges were dead things which rotted the hands that grasped them. Something Demelza said last winter just after Julia's death: "All our quarrels seem small and petty. Oughtn't we to find all the friendship we can—while there's still time?"

He said: "Is that Elizabeth's view too?"

"I haven't consulted her. But I'm sure it would be."

The sun had gone in for the next shower. The light was hard and metallic, the street still and colourless as in a steel engraving.

"Thank you. I hope the offer will not be necessary."

"That's my hope too, of course."

The thought welled up suddenly in Ross that but for this man *none* of the rest might have happened. The copper company on its feet, his child alive. No stopping it this time. Yet here he was, soberly talking as if nothing had happened. A blow in the face.

He said in a changed voice: "I have just made my will.

Pearce has it. No doubt he'll be capable of discharging his duties if the worst comes to the worst." He raised his crop in a half salute, not meeting his cousin's eyes, and turned on his heel to continue to the Pascoes'.

Harris Pascoe was behind the counter when he went in; but the banker at once beckoned him to come to the side, and they entered the private room together. Over a glass of brandy Pascoe said:

"We have young Enys to dinner—the first time for several months. Joan is pleased, but I am a little doubtful of the attachment. It has run on so long that I don't think it will come to anything. Especially after Dwight's affair with that w-woman last year."

"The girl threw herself at him," Ross said. ". . . I hope I shall not be the skeleton at the feast to-day."

"No indeed. Your visits are as rare as Enys's. Come along in. I can join you in a minute."

"There was business in my visit as well," said Ross. "To do with my approaching assize call."

He found a certain detached interest in watching the responses of various people when he mentioned his coming trial. In some people's eyes a morbid speculative gleam would betray itself behind the show of sympathy; others would shy away as if they had been told you were going to have your leg off. Harris Pascoe wrinkled his mouth in distaste and made a show of fixing his spectacles more firmly behind his ears.

"We hope for a happy outcome of that."

"But in the meantime a prudent man puts his affairs in order."

"There's very little more to do at present, I think."

"Except become solvent."

"Ye-es. Q-quite so. Quite so. Would you like to look at your account while you are here?"

They went into the bank, and Pascoe opened one of the great black books, dusted a little stale snuff off a page and coughed.

"The position in a nutshell is this. You have a credit balance of a little over a hundred and eighty pounds. You have a permanent mortgage on your property with the bank of two thousand three hundred pounds, bearing seven per cent interest. You have a further indebtedness outside, I understand, of—of one thousand pounds, is it?—b-bearing interest at forty p-per cent—repayable when?"

"This December or next."

"This December or next. And your income—in round figures, as it were?"

"Not more than three hundred a year net."

Harris winced again. "Er—yes. That's after living expenses are paid, I suppose?"

"Ordinary expenses of food, yes."

"Well, it just won't go, will it? You'll remember when you c-contemplated taking out that second bill I advised you instead to sell the mine shares. However, I'm not here to say I told you so. Any other substantial debts?"

"No."

A bluebottle had entered through an open window and was exploring the room with great vigour. The banker pushed the ledger along the desk, and Ross signed his name against the last entry in his account.

"I am concerned," he said, "to see some sort of security for my wife. I try not to take a pessimistic view of this trial, but no good comes of being an ostrich." He raised his deceptively sleepy eyes, and there was a touch of irony in them again. "There are various ways in which the law can deprive her of my support—so if she comes to widowhood or grass widowhood before her time I should take some comfort in knowing she would not be without a home."

"I think you can be assured of that," the banker said quietly. "Your liquid assets will meet the second mortgage. If they do not quite I will make up the difference."

They walked back into the private room. "You have the disadvantage of being my friend," Ross said.

"Not all d-disadvantage."

"I've a long memory—if the law will allow me to keep it."

41

" I'm sure it will." In some embarrassment, since the conversation seemed to be becoming emotionally charged, he went on in a different tone. " There is one thing I should t-tell you, Poldark, though it's not yet public property. I am enlarging the scope of my business and taking partners into it."

Ross had his glass filled. It was not good news to him, who at the moment felt himself dependent on the personal good will of the banker, but he could not show that.

" A considerable step, but naturally you wouldn't take it without good reason."

" No. I think I have good reason. Of course, when my father began his tin discounting it was a d-different matter. Business was simple and straightforward thirty years ago, and we did not issue bank notes until I was married. We have always held a high r-reputation, and so long as such a trust existed there was no need for complicated systems of finance. But things have changed and we must move with the times. Nowadays a bank is subject to all k-kinds of new responsibilities and stresses—and they are more, I think, than one man—or one family—should shoulder."

" Who are to be your new partners?"

" St. Aubyn Tresize, whom you know. He has money and prestige and wide interests. The second is Annery, the solicitor. A warm man. The third is Spry."

" I don't know him."

" From Come-to-Good. A quaker. I shall be managing partner and we shall be known as P-pascoe, Tresize, Annery & Spry. I think the meal will be ready now. A drop more brandy just to top up your glass?"

" Thank you."

As they moved towards the stairs which led up to the living rooms of the house, Pascoe added:

" In fact it was our experience of last autumn which finally decided me to take this action."

" You mean the failure of the Carnmore Copper Company?"

" Yes. . . . No doubt, fighting it out as you fought it out—

in the arena all the time—you could feel the pressure of the hostile interests, the other copper companies and the banks concerned, plainly enough. But sitting here—you know I hardly ever go out—sitting here in this quiet bank one was aware of s-subtle stresses too."

" Also hostile."

" Also hostile. I was not, as you know, directly interested in the copper venture. It is not my business as a custodian of other people's money to take speculative risks. But I was aware that if I had been so concerned I should not have been strong enough to stand the strains that could have been put on me. Credit is an unpredictable thing—as unstable as quicksilver. One cannot box it up. One can only give it away —and once given it is elastic up to the very point of breakage. Last autumn I realised that the days of the one-man bank are over. It—disturbed me—shook me out of a comfortable rut in wh-which I had been for many years. All this year I have been feeling my way towards some broader organisation."

They went up the stairs to dinner.

Chapter Four

When Francis got home it was just after six. He had had to ride into the teeth of the wind all the way, and there had been a half dozen torrential showers, some of them with more than a suggestion of hail, to stream off his horse's head and his cape and to strike at his face under the insecure hat, to trickle down his neck and soak his riding breeches above the leather leggings. Twice too he had nearly come off when his horse slipped in mud-filled ruts more than a foot deep. So he was not in a good temper.

Tabb, last of the two remaining house servants, came to take his horse and began to say something; but a gust of wind and another flurry of rain bore it away and Francis went into the house.

It was a silent house these days; and already it showed

43

signs of poverty and neglect: wild weather and salt air is hard on man's work, and there were damp stains on the ceiling of this fine hall and a smell of mildew. Portraits of the Poldarks and the Trenwiths stared coldly across the unfrequented room.

Francis tramped to the stairs, intending to go up and change, but the door of the winter parlour flew open and Geoffrey Charles came galloping down the hall.

"Daddy! Daddy! Uncle George is here and has brought me a toy horse! A *lovely* one! With brown eyes and brown hair and stirrups I can put my feet in!"

Francis saw Elizabeth had come to the door of the winter parlour; so now there was no escape from greeting an unexpected visitor.

As Francis went in George Warleggan was standing by the fireplace. He was wearing a snuff-coloured coat, silk waistcoat and black cravat, with fawn breeches and new brown riding boots. Elizabeth looked a little flushed, as if the surprise call had pleased her. George came seldom these days, being not too sure of his welcome here. Francis had queer moods and resented his indebtedness.

Elizabeth said: "George has been here an hour. We were hoping you would be back before he had to leave."

"Quite an honour these days." Francis bent to satisfy Geoffrey Charles with admiration for his new toy. "Now I am here you'd best stay till this shower is over. I've been anointed many times on the way home."

George said evenly: "You've lost weight, Francis. So have I. We shall all look like sans-culottes before the century is out."

Francis's eyes travelled over George's broad frame. "I notice no change for the better."

The cream curtains in this room were inches farther across the windows than Francis liked them; they diffused the light, giving it a tactful and opaque quality which irritated him. He went across and pulled them sharply back. When he turned he saw that Elizabeth had flushed at his last remark as if it were her responsibility.

"We ordinary people," George said, "are affected by the

vagaries of fortune. Our faces, our figures are marked and warped by all the storms that blow. But your wife, my dear Francis, has a beauty which is untouched by ill luck or indifferent health and only grows more radiant when the tide turns."

Francis threw off his coat. " I think we all need drink. We can still afford drink, George. Some of the old instincts remain."

" l have been pressing him to sup with us," Elizabeth said. " But he will not."

" Cannot," said George. " I must be back at Cardew before dark. I had been as far as St. Ann's this afternoon on mining business and could not resist calling on you when so near. You come so little to town these days."

George was right, Francis thought cynically as his wife took a wineglass from him, Elizabeth's beauty was too pure to be affected by everyday circumstance. George still envied him one thing.

" And how's mining?" he asked. " One advantage of being out of it is that one can take a purely academic interest in its vagaries. Are you thinking of closing Wheal Plenty?"

" Far from it." George poked the carpet with his long malacca stick and then stopped because just there the pattern of the carpet was wearing thin. " Tin and copper are both rising. If it goes on we may be able to restart Grambler one day."

" If that was possible!" said Elizabeth.

" Which it is not." Francis drained his glass at a draught. " George is romancing for your benefit. Copper would have to double its price to justify a new outlay on Grambler now it is closed and derelict. Had it been saved from closing there might have been another story. It will not reopen in our lifetime. I am fully resigned to spending the rest of my days as an impoverished farmer."

George humped his shoulders. " I'm sure you are making a mistake. You're both making a mistake of remaining shut up here. There is plenty to be had of life even in these depressed days. Poldark is still a good name, Francis, and if you

45

moved in society more opportunity would come of bettering yourself. There are patronages to be had, if nothing better, paid offices which carry no obligation and no loss of prestige: indeed, the reverse. I could become a burgess any day if it pleased me, but at present it pleases me to keep out of the political field. As for you . . ."

"As for me," said Francis, "I am a gentleman and want no patronage—either from gentlemen or others."

He said it without emphasis, but the sting was there. George smiled, but it was not the sort of observation he would be likely to forget. Few people had the courage to make such remarks to him nowadays.

Elizabeth made an impatient movement. "It's surely not reasonable to quarrel when there is friendship—when there are friendships to be had. Pride can go too far."

"Talking of the Poldarks," Francis went on, taking no notice of her. "I saw that other representative of the name in Truro to-day. He didn't seem unduly depressed by his forthcoming trial, though he was not anxious to discuss it with me. One can hardly blame him."

Francis bent again to speak to his son and the others were silent.

George eventually said: "I wish him an acquittal at his trial, of course. But I don't think the outcome will affect your good name, Francis. Am I my brother's keeper? Still less so, then, of a cousin."

Elizabeth said: "What chance is there of an acquittal, do you think?"

"A lovely horse," said Francis gently to Geoffrey Charles. "A lovely horse."

"I don't see how there can be a *clear* acquittal," George said, dabbing his lips with a lace handkerchief and watching Elizabeth's expression. "Ross was a free agent at the time of the wrecks. No one coerced him into doing what he did."

"If one believes he did it!"

"Naturally. That will be for the court to find. But the fact that he has treated the law with contempt on a number

46

of previous occasions will be inclined to weigh to his detriment."

"What previous occasions? I know of no others."

"Nor is the court supposed to," Francis said, straightening up. "But it will not be left in ignorance. I came on this pretty little sheet in Truro to-day. There are sure to be others in Bodmin before next week."

He took a crumpled paper out of his pocket, straightened it, and, avoiding Geoffrey Charles's outstretched fingers, passed it to Elizabeth.

"I thought of showing it to Ross," Francis added, "but decided it was discreeter to leave him in ignorance."

Elizabeth stared at the paper. It was a typical broadsheet, run off a cheap press, the ink blurred and unevenly spread.

True and Sensational Facts in the life of Captain R-s-P—d—k, bold adventurer, seducer and suspected murderer, shortly to stand his trial on Criminal Charges at B—m-n Assizes next. Price One Penny. Written by an Intimate Friend.

After a minute she put the paper down, and looked at Francis. Francis looked steadily, interestedly, back at her. The thing was written in the form of a biography, and none of the salacious rumours of the last two years was missing—all set out as if the facts were beyond dispute.

Francis offered it to George, but he waved it away. "I have seen them about. One of our coachmen was caught reading a similar thing yesterday. They are not important."

"Not important," said Francis gently, "except to Ross."

"Come here, boy," George said to his godson, "you have the reins entangled with the saddle. Look, this is the way it goes."

Elizabeth said: "But if all this is believed it will prejudice the jury, will prejudice everyone! They talk of a fair trial . . ."

"Don't distress yourself, my dear Elizabeth," George said.

47

" These scurrilous broadsheets are always going about regarding someone or other. No one takes account of 'em. Why, only last month there was some sheet issued purporting to show in the most lurid and circumstantial detail that feeble-mindedness and insanity runs all through the Royal Family and that the King's father, Frederick, was a pervert and a degenerate beyond recall."

" And isn't it so?" Francis asked.

George shrugged. " I suppose there is some sludge of truth in the basest slander."

His meaning was obvious.

" It states," said Elizabeth, " that Ross served in the American war only to escape charges of this sort being brought against him before. But he was only a boy at the time—there was some boyish escapade, I know, but nothing serious. And this—about Demelza. . . . And this——"

Francis read: " ' *Furthermore, there are numerous brats scattered throughout the countryside whose parentage might be in doubt did there not exist the strange Circumstance of the scar wherewith the Devil hath cursed all the Captain's offspring—this scar being so like unto his own that the same branding iron might have been Employed. Here in good earnest we find——* ' "

" What does that mean?" Elizabeth asked.

" Jinny Carter's child has a scar," said Francis. " Jinny Scoble, as she now is. The pamphleteer has been to some trouble to scrape up all the—er—what did you call it?—all the sludge. ' By an Intimate Friend.' I wonder who it could be. Not you, George, I suppose?"

George smiled. " I earn my bread in a more orthodox manner. Only a bankrupt would sell his services that way."

" Money is not always the strongest inducement," said Francis, his gibe turned against him.

George bent his head to rest his chin on the knob of his stick. " No, perhaps spite could play its part. . . . Anyway, the matter is unimportant, isn't it? If the stories are all untrue they can be refuted."

But he had touched Francis on a raw spot and his characteristic turning of the point when he had made it did not quite come off. It had long been George's practice to swallow insults and to pay them back at leisure. Francis had been brought up to no such self-control. It was fortunate that just then Geoffrey Charles fell off his horse and pulled the animal over on top of him, for when the clamour had subsided the worst moment was past. For two reasons Elizabeth exerted herself to prevent a recurrence of it. First, George almost owned the things they stood in. Second, on personal grounds, she did not want to lose his friendship. Admiration such as he brought was rare enough in the life she led. She knew it was her due, and the knowledge made it all the harder to be without.

Chapter Five

Bodmin at the time of the summer assizes of 1790 was a town with three thousand inhabitants and twenty-nine public houses.

A historian passing through two centuries before had noted the unhealthiness of the situation, the houses in the mile-long main street being, he pointed out, so shut off from sun by the hill behind that no light could have entrance to their stairs nor open air in their rooms. When it rained, he added, all the filth of the outbuildings and stables was washed down through these houses into the street; and, further, the main water supply ran openly through the churchyard, which was the ordinary place of burial for town and parish.

The intervening years had not changed the situation, but there was nothing so far as Ross could see in the hard-bitten look of the inhabitants to suggest they suffered any unusual apprehensions from sickness or pestilence. Indeed in the previous summer, while cholera raged in the districts around, the town had escaped.

He presented himself at the gaol on Thursday the second of September, and Demelza followed on the Saturday. He

49

had been opposed to her being at the trial at all, but she had insisted so vehemently that for once he gave way. He reserved a room for her at the George and Crown, and a place for her on the midday coach, but unknown to him she had been making extra arrangements of her own. Bailey's Flyer began its long run from the west country at Falmouth, and when she met it at Truro at eleven forty-five Verity was travelling in it.

They greeted each other like old lovers, kissing with a depth of affection that trouble brought to the surface, each aware of the other's love for Ross and of a uniting purpose.

"Verity! Oh, I'm that glad to see you; it's been an age—and no one to talk to as I talk to you." Demelza wanted to board the stage at once, but Verity knew they had a quarter of an hour's wait, so steered her cousin-in-law into the inn. They sat in a corner by the door and talked in earnest confidential tones. Verity thought Demelza looked years older than at their last meeting, and thinner and paler, but somehow it all suited her dark hair and brows and wayward eyes.

"I *wish* I could write like you," Demelza said. "Letters that tell something. *I* can't write, no more'n Prudie Paynter, and never shall. It is there, there in my mind, but when I pick up the quill it all puffs away like steam out of the spout of a kettle."

Verity said: "But tell me now, who is to be for Ross's defence, and what witnesses will be called in his favour? I am so *ignorant* of these things. How is the jury chosen? Is it of freemen and will they look on such a crime indulgently? And the judge . . ."

Demelza tried to satisfy her from the information she had. She was surprised to find Verity as unlearned in the law as herself. They struggled with its complexities together.

Verity said: "Andrew would have come, but he is at sea. I should have been happier with him to lean on. But perhaps it's for the best. . . . You don't know, I suppose, if Francis will be at the assizes?"

"No. . . . No, I don't think so. But there will be a great many there. We're lucky, so they say, to have accommoda-

50

tion, because there's an election this coming week—between Unwin Trevaunance and Michael Chenhalls on the Basset side, and Sir Henry Corrant and Hugh Dagge on the Boscoigne. There'll be a big fuss about that."

"You're well informed. Is that Unwin Trevaunance, Sir John's brother?"

"Yes. We—I—have got to know Sir John a slight bit. Of course Ross have known him for years—but I . . . He happened to have a sick cow—and I cured her—or she got better of her own—and so I've been over there once or twice and have details of the election."

"A sick cow?"

Demelza coloured a little. "It was nothing important. Verity, I don't want for you to mind if I act strange this week end. It is only a track of my own I'm following, like, and maybe it will lead somewhere and maybe it will lead to a dead end. But it is just the way I feel about things, and I hope you'll understand. Are you really happy with Andrew?"

"I'm very happy, thank you—thanks to you, my dear. But what is it you intend to do this week end?"

"Maybe nothing at all. It is only just a warning. And have you met your stepchildren yet?"

Verity opened her new velvet bag, took out a handkerchief, then drew the strings of the bag together again. She frowned at the handkerchief.

"No . . . not yet. I haven't met them yet because—James is away still and—but I'll tell you about it later . . . I think we should take our seats now."

They went out to the waiting coach, with its fresh horses stirring restlessly in the traces and the postboys to hand them up. They were the first in the vehicle, but a moment later three more entered, and several climbed on top. It was to be a crowded journey.

The clash of election and assize had given the soberer citizens of Bodmin some anxious thought: the coincidence was maladroit, to say the least; inns would be packed to suffocating one week and empty the next; the solemn process of the law might be disconcerted by the no less important but noisier processes of an election contest in which some bad blood was already being shown. Everyone knew that there were two mayors in the town, each representing a rival patron; but no one yet knew which would prevail during this all-important week.

The election of the members of Parliament, in more cordial circumstances, might have been put through in a couple of hours and no one the worse, since there were only thirty-six electors, members of a Common Council under the mayor. Unfortunately the dispute as to the mayoral office raised questions about the validity of the Council, each mayor having his own version of the electoral roll. Mr. Lawson, one mayor, had among his common councillors his brother, his wife's brother, a cousin, a nephew, and four sons, and this was a situation which Mr. Michell, the other mayor, passionately challenged.

As to the law, the lists were crowded with cases from the deferred spring assizes, the gaol crowded with felons, and the inns crowded with litigants and witnesses. On the Friday Ross had his first interview with his counsel, Mr. Jeffery Clymer, K.C., a burly man of forty with a possessive nose and one of those chins which no razor's edge will whiten. All considered, Ross thought it a good thing the barrister came in his robes or the turnkey might have been reluctant to let him out again.

Mr. Clymer thought the case of the Crown v. R. V. Poldark would not come on before Wednesday morning. In the meantime he thumbed through Mr. Pearce's brief, shot questions at his client, tutted over the answers and sniffed at a handkerchief soaked in vinegar. When he left he said he would be round on Monday with a list of witnesses who had been subpoenaed to appear and a draft of the line of defence he would advise his client to pursue. The one tentatively sketched out by Mr. Pearce was quite useless—it admitted altogether too much. When Ross said that was the defence Mr. Pearce had prepared on his instructions, Clymer said fiddle-

52

sticks, it wasn't for a client to issue instructions of that sort; a client must be guided by his legal advisers or what was the good of having them. You couldn't plead not guilty and say in the next breath, I did it after all. It was an infernal pity Captain Poldark had made such admissions and offered such expressions of opinion to the examining justice. Asking for trouble, that's what you'd call it. Whole purpose of the defence now must be to remove that impression, not emphasise it. Ignoring Ross's look, he said it would profit them both if Captain Poldark would spend the week end thinking this over, and also in casting back in his memory for any new recollection that would help. After all, he said, rubbing his blue chin, no one but the prisoner could know *all* the facts.

One condition of Ross's consent to Demelza's presence in the town was that she should make no attempt whatever to see him in gaol. In fact she was not altogether loth, for she would not then have to account for her movements. Only to Verity need she make excuses, and at the worst Verity had no control over her.

As soon as they got to the inn there was trouble, for the landlord had put up another double bed in their room and claimed the right to let two other women share it. Only a long and painful argument and some extra money from Verity won them their privacy. They had a meal together and listened to the slamming of doors, the cries of ostlers, the hurrying feet of the maids and the singsong of drunken wayfarers under the window.

"I think we shall have to plug our ears to sleep," said Verity, taking the pins out of her hair. "If it's like this at seven what will it be in another three hours?"

"Never worry," said Demelza, "they'll all be drunk insensible." She stretched herself, arching her back like a cat. "Oh, that old coach: joggle, joggle, bump. Three times I thought we were going to upset or spend the night in the mud."

"It has given me a sick headache," Verity said. "I shall take a draught and lie down early."

"In another hour I believe I should have felt the same. What were you going to tell me about your stepchildren, Verity?"

Verity shook out her hair and it fell in a cloud about her shoulders. The action was like some new and secret blossoming of her personality. She did not look eleven years older than Demelza now. Happiness had brought the keen intelligence and vitality back into her eyes, and an extra roundness to her cheeks and made the wide generous mouth less unproportionate.

"It's nothing," she said. "Nothing beside what is happening to Ross."

"I want to hear," said Demelza. "Have you not even seen them once yet?"

". . . It is the only flaw at present. Andrew is very fond of his children, and I hate to feel they will not come because I am there."

"Why should you feel that? It is naught to do with you."

"It should not be. But . . ." She split one side of her hair into three parts and began to plait them. "It is a very peculiar position, with Andrew's first wife dying as she did and the children being left so young—with that scar; their mother dead, their father in prison; brought up by relatives. Their father has always been at a disadvantage with them. They have come to see him occasionally, but never since we married. Of course James could not, for he is with the fleet and depends on the movements of his ship; but he has never once written. And Esther is only at Plymouth. . . . Andrew hardly mentions them now, but I know he thinks about them. I know he would be very happy if we could come together. I have wondered sometimes whether to go to Saltash to meet Esther—not telling Andrew, while he is away."

"No," said Demelza, "I wouldn't do that. She should come to you."

Verity stared at her reflection in the mirror, then at Demelza, who was changing her stockings. "But suppose she never comes."

"Get Andrew to invite her."

54

" He has already done that, but she has made excuses."

" You must use a bait, then."

" A bait?"

Demelza wriggled her toes, and her eyes considered expressively the three pairs of shoes she had to choose from.

" Is she fond of her brother?"

" I believe so."

" Then get him to Falmouth first. Perhaps it is only shyness with them both, and he might be easier to entice in the first place."

" I should like to think you're right, for he must be home soon. He was expected back at Easter, but his ship was diverted to Gibraltar . . . What is that?"

Above the noises of the inn and street a man was shouting. He had a loud voice and a bell.

" The town crier," said Verity.

Demelza had just taken off her riding habit, but she went to the window, which was at floor level, and knelt and peered through the lace curtains.

" I can't hear what he's saying."

" No . . . it is to do with the election."

Through the mirror Verity looked at Demelza's crouched figure which had some of the alertness of a young animal— the cream satin underskirt, the little décolleté bodice of Ghent lace. Three years ago she had lent Demelza her first dainty underclothes. Demelza was a quick learner. Verity's lips moved in an affectionate smile.

The crier was not coming their way, but in a temporary lull in the local noises they caught some disconnected words. " Oyez! Oyez! Hear ye, hear ye . . . by the sheriff's precept . . . Notice of election . . . The mayor and aldermen of the borough of Bodmin . . . Speaker of the House of Commons, does command, issue and proclaim on Tuesday, the seventh day of September, in the year of our Lord . . ."

" Does that mean the election is to be Tuesday? I thought it was Thursday," Demelza said.

" The notices will be posted now. We can see them tomorrow."

55

" Verity . . ."

" Yes?"

" You are tired to-night?"

" I shall be well enough in the morning."

" You will not mind if I go out by myself for a little?"

" To-night? Oh no, my dear! It would be the height of
folly! You'd never get along the pavements. You'd be in
grave danger."

Demelza went across to the things she had unpacked, considered them in the failing light. " I should keep to the main
streets."

" You don't realise what it is like! In Falmouth, even on
a normal Saturday night, it's impossible to venture without
escort. *Here*, when there is free drinking, and the town's
crowded with sightseers . . ."

" I am no lent-lily to snap off at the first touch."

" No, my dear, but it would be madness, I assure you.
You don't realise . . ." Verity watched the other girl's face.
" If you're resolved, then I must come with you."

" That you cannot. . . . You've helped me so often, Verity,
but in this you cannot help me. It is—just something . . .
between Ross and me. . . ."

" Between . . . Did Ross ask you to do this?"

Demelza wrestled with her conscience. She knew the mischief which had come from her white lies before. But also
the good!

" Yes," she said.

" In that case . . . But are you sure he meant you to go
out alone? I can scarcely believe that he could ever have
agreed to . . ."

" I am a miner's daughter," Demelza said. " I was not
brought up gentle. Gentleness—is that the right word?—
came upon me when I was half grown. I have Ross to thank
for that. And you. But it don't alter me underneath. I still
have two marks on my back where Father used the belt.
There's naught a few drunks could do but what I couldn't give
them back. Tis all a matter of being in the mood."

Verity watched her cousin's face a minute longer. There

was a strength of line belying the soft feminine expression of mouth and eye.

"Very well, my dear." Verity made a gesture of resignation. "I am not happy about it, but you are your own mistress now."

Chapter Six

There was no moon to light the town that night, but every shop, tavern and house contributed its share to the yellow flicker of the streets. In accordance with custom both parties in the election were offering free drinks to their supporters, and there were already numbers of people stumbling as they walked, or sitting in a lazy stupor in alcoves or against a handy wall.

When Demelza came out she turned down the hill and in a few minutes was in the main thoroughfare, which this afternoon she had thought the narrowest and most crowded in the world. The shops and inns and houses, tight squeezed, had along their frontages a succession of slated porticoes reaching into the roadway on stone posts and forming an unbroken way down both sides of the street. The space left for traffic was little more than wide enough for one coach, and, since in the case of shops the porticoes were often used for the display of goods, pedestrians found themselves out in the road much of the time. Such an arrangement might have served for the normal life of the town; it was inadequate now.

The street was crammed with people, milling about, pushing up one side and down the other, rough but good-tempered so far. A few yards from the Queen's Head she came to a stop, unable to go farther because of the press. Something was going on at the hotel, but at first she could only see the scarlet and orange banners which hung from the upper windows. People were shouting and laughing. Near the portico against which she was standing a blind man was whining and trying to find his way through; a woman quarrelled with a

57

brass worker over the price of a bell; a man, half drunk, was sitting on a stone step used for mounting horses, stroking the cheek of a vacant-faced full-bosomed young country girl on the step below. Two ragged urchins in cut-down coats came suddenly to blows and rolled over, scratching and biting, in the dried mud. A half dozen people laughed and formed a ring, hiding them from view.

There was a sudden shout and a rush towards the Queen's Head, and the press here was eased. A window of the upper room of the inn had been opened and people were cheering and shouting at the figures in the window. Others were rolling and fighting in the road just below. Another great cheer and a rush. The people above were throwing things down, scattering them in the road. An urchin came doubling and ducking through the crowd, holding his hands under his armpits, his face contorted but triumphant. Three men were fighting, and Demelza had to duck under the portico to avoid them. One crashed into the stall of the brass worker, who came out with a flood of shouts and curses to drive them off.

" What's to do?" Demelza asked him. " What are they about?"

The man eyed her up and down.

" Scattering red-hot coins, they be. From a frying pan. Tis the custom."

" Red-hot coins?"

" 'S. Tis the custom, I tell ee." He went in.

She worked her way nearer and could see the cook at the window in his tall hat, and two men with huge red and gold favours in their buttonholes. There was a great scream and a rush as more money was flung down. The human beings milling together in the flame and shadow had lost some part of their individuality and moved with a mass impulse not quite their own, not quite the sum of all the separate souls. She felt if she was not careful she might become a part of the mob in the yellow dark, be caught up in it, and lose her individual purpose and volition, being sucked towards the window with each wave that broke. She found herself beside the blind man.

58

"You'll not get through by yourself, old man," she said. "Where do you want to go?"

"Guildhall, Mrs.," he said, showing broken teeth. "Tes up along, no more'n a short way."

"Take my arm. I'll help you." She waited for the next rush, and then thrust her way forward, finding comfort in being able to join with somebody, be of use to somebody, against the rest.

The blind man breathed gin over her. "Tes rare an' kind of ee t'elp a poor old man. I'll do the same for ee one day." He cackled as they got through the worst of the press. "Tis a rare dring to-night, you; an' worse to follow, I misdoubt."

"Where is the Basset headquarters?" she asked, peering up the street. "I thought this afternoon it was up here?"

The blind man squeezed her arm. "Well, tes no more'n a few paces now. But 'ow would it be if ye came along of me —up Arnold's Passage. I can give ee a nice little drop o' dripshan. Warm ee up, twould."

She tried to get her arm free, but his fingers were tight and playing a little tune on her arm.

"Leave me go," she said.

"No offence, Mrs. No 'arm meant. I thought you was a docy little maid. I can see naught, ye follow—so tes all a question of feel wi' me, and ye feel young and friendly. Young and friendly."

Two riders came down the street, picking a slow way among the people, trying to quiet their horses, often unable to go forward at all. She steered the blind man past them and then wrenched her arm free. He tried to catch her fingers but failed, and she pushed her way ahead.

As she got opposite the Guildhall another great press of people came down the street from the west, shouting and singing and carrying someone precariously on a chair. She was just able to slip into the arched entrance of the Crown. They seemed about to go right past, but some stopped, and a man stood on another's shoulders to try to reach the blue and gold flag just above them. He had caught at a corner, when a dozen or more men rushed past Demelza out of the hotel, sent the climber flying off the other man's shoulders and in a minute a fight was in progress. Someone threw a brick, and Demelza retreated farther into the yard and tried to tidy herself. Then she went in.

How to dress for her purpose had been a difficult decision and unsatisfying when made. She wanted to look her best, but could not have faced the streets in evening things. So the result was a compromise which sapped some of her dearly needed confidence.

"Yes'm?" An impudent page boy was standing before her. She saw by his eyes that he had not quite placed her in the social scale.

"Is Sir John Trevaunance staying here?"

"Not's I know, mum."

"I think he's here now. He told me he'd be here this evening." A rash claim.

"I can't say, mum. They're dining. There's guests."

"Still dining?"

"Should be over soon'm. They started in at five."

"I'll wait," she said. "Do you leave me know so soon as they're finished."

She sat down in the lobby of the hotel, trying to appear unconcerned and at ease. Outside the noise was worse, and she wondered how she would get back. She tried not to be nervous. Waiters were scurrying backwards and forwards from a room on her left. She did not want to be found sitting here like a beggar waiting for alms. She beckoned one of the waiters.

". . . Is there a withdrawing room where I may wait for Sir John Trevaunance in greater comfort than here?"

"Er—yes, madam. Top o' the stairs. Can I get you a refreshment while you wait?"

A brilliant idea. "Thank you," she said. "Would you bring me some port."

This was not the election dinner, which would be on Monday, but a preliminary gallop, as Sir Hugh Bodrugan called it. And, since there were a few women present, the evening was on a discreeter level than Monday's would be. A few of the weaker brethren were tipsy; but most carried it off in good style.

At the head of the table were Sir John Trevaunance and his brother Unwin. Between them was Caroline Penvenen, and on Sir John's left was Mrs. Gilbert Daniell, with whom the other three were staying. Beyond her was Michael Chenhalls, the other candidate, and next came Miss Treffry, the mayor—*their* mayor—Humphrey Michell, and Sir Hugh Bodrugan. Among the other guests were notables of the town and district, wool merchants and civic officials.

When the ladies left them the men sat over their port for half an hour before pulling in their sprawling legs and standing about in yawning, chatting groups amid the débris of the meal. The noise at the front of the hotel was not noticeable in the long dining room, but when they got upstairs the shouts and the cheers and the scuffling and the laughter were plain enough. As Unwin mounted the stairs beside his elder brother, Caroline Penvenen came towards him carrying her tiny dog. Her face was a study in charming petulance.

"Horace is upset by the noise," she said, drawing her long fingers over the silky head and ears. "He is of a nervous disposition and inclined to fret when frightened."

"Horace is a very lucky dog to have so much affection centred on him," said Unwin.

"I shouldn't have brought him, only felt he would be lonely with old Mr. Daniell for company. I feel sure he would have found it quite desolate to sit in that dismal drawing room all the evening, with a draught whistling under the door and an old man *snoring* probably in the best chair. . . ."

"I would point out, my dear," said Sir John in a lowered voice, "that we are Mr. Daniell's guests—and that Mrs. Daniell is just behind you."

Caroline smiled brilliantly at the younger man. "Sir John does not approve of me, Unwin. Did you know that? Sir John is convinced I shall disgrace him yet. Sir John thinks that woman's place is in the home, and not being obtrusive and a responsibility at election times. Sir John does not look with favour on any woman until she is at least thirty and past mischief; and even then . . ."

It was while the two men were politely trying to convince her otherwise that Demelza came out of a side room and saw her quarry close at hand. She came towards them with less hesitancy than she would have done half an hour ago, wondering all the same who the tall striking girl was with the red hair and the fiery grey-green eyes.

When Sir John saw her he looked surprised.

"Why, Mrs. Poldark; this is a pleasure. Are you staying here?"

"For the time, yes," said Demelza. "There is a big commotion outside. I wonder if it is to do with this election?"

Sir John laughed. "It's my belief so. . . . May I introduce . . . I don't think you will have met Miss Caroline Penvenen—although she is a neighbour of yours for part of each year, at Killewarren. Mrs. Demelza Poldark, from Nampara."

The ladies expressed themselves charmed at the acquaintance, though Caroline was summing up Demelza's dress and Demelza knew it. "I stay with my uncle," said Caroline, "Mr. Ray Penvenen, whom you may know. I have no parents and he reluctantly takes the responsibility of an orphan niece, as monks take a hair shirt. So at times I remove the penance by removing myself; and others wear the shirt for him. I was but then condoling with Sir John in the matter."

"Believe me," said Unwin, who did not look very pleased at Demelza's arrival, "you do yourself less than justice. If responsibility you are, which I doubt, there are many who would have it. You have but to say the word for half the men in the county to be at your side. And if——"

"Men?" said Caroline. "Must it only be men? What's wrong with women? Don't you agree, Mrs. Poldark, that men put a false estimate on their own importance?"

"I'm not sure as to that," said Demelza. "For, you see, I'm married and am on the wrong side of the fence, like."

"And is your husband all that important? I shouldn't

admit it if it were the truth! But, Unwin, were you not telling me there was a Poldark to be tried at the assizes this year? Is it any relation to this lady?"

"That's my husband, ma'am," said Demelza, "so perhaps twill be understood why I hold him in some extra worth just now."

For a second or two Caroline looked confused. She patted her dog's snub nose. "And did he do wrong? What is he charged with?"

Gruffly Sir John told her, and she said: "Oh, la; if I were the judge, then I'd sentence him forthwith to be returned to his wife. I thought excise men were not classed as human beings these days."

"I wish you were judge, then," said Demelza.

"I'd like to be, ma'am, but since I'm not I wish your husband well, and hope he'll come home again to domestic bliss."

The conversation was broken by Michael Chenhalls, who said:

"They're shouting for us, Unwin. I suggest we go out on the balcony before they try to break into the hotel."

"As you please."

"I'll come with you," said Caroline. "I like to hear a mob when it is baying."

"Baying for me?" said Unwin.

"No . . . just baying."

"You as well may get a brick thrown as a bouquet."

"That's as it should be. Spice in the pudding."

They moved off towards the room with the balcony, and Demelza was alone with her quarry at last. She didn't think she would be left so for long.

"A taking young lady, Sir John."

Sir John dryly agreed. "She's but eighteen, you'll understand, and a thought high-mettled. She'll settle down."

"I am not many years older."

He looked at her with a quizzing interest. This was the fourth time they had met, and there were few women he had so quickly come to friendly terms with.

63

"Marriage has a maturing effect. . . ." He chuckled. "Though, drat it, take the ring off and you'd *look* little older."

Demelza met his gaze very frankly. "I don't want to take it off, Sir John."

He shrugged uncomfortably. "No, no. Naturally not. No one'd wish it. Naturally not. Have no fear, ma'am, your husband'll get a fair trial. Perhaps more than fair. And Wentworth Lister's a very able man. No prejudices. I can vouch for that."

Demelza glanced around. Well, she must plunge in now.

"That," she said, "was what I wanted to see you about. . . ."

On the balcony the candidates had been greeted with an immense roar, as if a lion had opened its mouth.

When she could make herself heard Caroline said: "They look like a field of turnips—only not so neatly set. What a rabble, dear Unwin. What is to be gained from pandering to them like this?"

"A custom," said Unwin, bowing his fine head towards the mob. "It's only for five or six days, and then they can be forgotten for as many years. I hope you're looking gracious, for it all helps."

"Could I ever look anything else? You know, I should make you a very fine wife . . ." Unwin turned. ". . . *If* I decided to marry you. What could be more tactful than my behaviour to-night: criticising Mrs. Daniell's house within Mrs. Daniell's hearing; mentioning the Poldark case before Poldark's wife. What a triumph I should be among your parliamentary friends!"

Unwin didn't reply, but bowed and waved to the people below. Down the street towards the Queen's Head the maelstrom was beginning to move.

Caroline pulled her beautiful embroidered shawl about her shoulders. "I hope Horace isn't biting the footman. His teeth are sharp, and he has a knack for choosing the painful places. What a pretty woman that Mrs. Poldark is. It's her eyes and skin that make it all. Pity she doesn't know how to dress."

"We can go in now," said Unwin, the cleft deepening between his brows. "The novelty of seeing us is wearing off and if we stay longer they'll start expecting something else."

"D'you know," said Caroline, "I should like to go to the assize for a day. I've never seen the way it all works, and I believe it would be very diverting."

They turned to go in. "Diverting if you got fever."

"Oh, then I should be in bed for a few days and you should visit me. Does that appeal? Come, you promised me. What is the use of having influence if you don't use it?"

. . . In the lobby behind them Sir John pushed his wig back to mop his forehead.

"My dear madam, I have no influence of that sort! You don't know what you're asking! I tell you, it would prejudice your husband's case, not help it!"

"Not if it was put in the right way, surely."

"Yes, if it was put any way. His Majesty's judges are not to be suborned by this sort of approach when a case is sub judice!"

Demelza felt her heart growing cold with disappointment and despair. She allowed her eyes to travel interestedly over Sir John's face. "It is only that if you was to tell him all the truth about it before the case began he would know what to expect. What's amiss with that? Isn't it the truth they want? Is it real justice they want to give—or is it some other sort: law justice, made up on what lies the witnesses tell in the box?"

Sir John gave her a look more of sorrow than of anger. It was rather plain where her friendship and charm had all this time been leading.

"My dear ma'am, it's a little late to explain, but I can only assure you I'm advising you right. For one thing, Wentworth Lister wouldn't listen to me. It would be more than my friendship was worth. Ecod, I should be out of favour with every legal man in the country!"

Sir Hugh Bodrugan had seen her now. In a minute he would be over.

She said: " It was not as if it was money you was offering him—but only truth. Is that so much to be despised?"

" That may be how you look at it. But how would he know it was the truth?"

" Just now—when I was sitting here before you came up— I heard a man say your brother had paid two thousand pounds for this seat in Parliament. Is that so, Sir John?"

" What's that to do with you?"

At his cold tone she gave in. " I'm sorry. I meant no 'arm —no harm coming here to-night. I—don't understand, that's all. I don't see why it is right to pay electors for voting one way and so mortal hard to *ask* a favour of a judge. Perhaps twould be better if we did offer to pay him."

" Then you *would* be sent to gaol. No, ma'am; be assured it's best to leave it all alone." At her change of tone his had grown more sympathetic. " Don't think I do not sympathise! I hope and believe Poldark will be a free man by the end of the week. The surest way of attaining the opposite—the *opposite*, ma'am—would be to try to influence his lordship in any way. It is one of the peculiarities of life in England. I cannot explain why it should be so, but the law has always been above corruption. . . ."

He was looking towards the door where Caroline and Unwin and the Chenhalls were re-entering. So he did not catch the expression that flickered in Demelza's eyes. It was only there for a second, like a flag of defiance over a part-surrendered fort.

Chapter Seven

On Sunday morning there was a procession to church, headed by the legal fraternity in the town. It came down St. Nicholas Street right past their inn, and Demelza and Verity knelt and watched it go. Demelza's knees came over weak at the sight of the two judges in the full regalia of their office— scarlet robes and heavy wigs: one of them tall and rawboned, the other of middle size and stout. She hoped that Wentworth Lister was the stout one. The enormity of her proposition to Sir John was brought home to her at sight of the material he had to work on. In the afternoon, rallying, she called at the hotel again and took tea with Sir Hugh Bodrugan, as invited. It was a respectable genteel occasion, and for once, with him, she was successful in keeping the conversation decent. But he wouldn't be an easy man to hold at arm's length for long.

On Monday morning Mr. Jeffery Clymer had his final interview with Ross. He read rapidly through the new notes Ross had made, drawing his black eyebrows together until they were a continuous irregular portico above his eyes, like the porticoes of Fore Street.

Then he said: " It won't do, Captain Poldark. Just won't do."

" What's wrong with it?"

" What I told you on Friday. Got to realise, my dear man, criminal court is not a pitched battle, it's a field of manoeuvre. You may speak the truth, the whole truth and nothing but the truth; but it all depends *how* you speak it! Got to be tactful, persuasive, throw yourself on the mercy and indulgence of the law. Be humble and innocent, not stiff-backed and defiant. Say what you like after the verdict; before that have a care. Weigh every word. Look: this is the sort of case you must put forward."

Ross took the parchment from the plump hairy hands of the barrister and tried to concentrate above the clatter of the cells. After a minute or two he put it down.

" There are limits even if one's neck is at stake."

Clymer looked his client over, summing him up professionally, the long strong frame, the bony well-bred face, high-strung under its reticence, the scar and the hair and the blue-grey eyes. He shrugged. " If I could speak for you, that's what I'd say."

" If you could speak for me, I might let you say it."

" Well, then, what's the difference? Of course, it's your own life to do with as you please, your own freedom—if

67

that's what you call it. Got a wife? Got a family? Don't you think it's worth making this concession for them? Mind, I make no promises *with* this line. But with yours you would as well do without me and save your guineas."

In another cell some men were brawling, and at the back of this one two thieves were dicing for a neckerchief another had left behind. Got a wife? Got a family? Don't you think it's worth making concessions? Would it really be for Demelza's sake or for his own? The thought of captivity was stifling to one of his restless nature. In these few days he had seen enough. Was he justified in changing his defence at the last moment in an attempt to save his own skin?

He said shortly: "Have you the list of witnesses for the Crown?"

Clymer handed him another sheet and wafted a handkerchief before his nose while Ross read it.

Vigus, Clemmow, Anderson, Oliver, Fiddick . . . "No one can say the law has been slipshod in making up its case."

"It never is, once it's *got* a case. Persevering—that's what you'd call it. Where a couple of hundred people are involved in a crime it usually fastens on one or two men—the most likely, perhaps the most culpable, though not always—it fastens on one or two and tries to force the others to turn King's evidence. Makes one or two the scapegoats, as it were. You're the scapegoat, Captain. Unfortunate. These men ʼr friends?"

"Some of them."

"Doesn't follow, of course. Friend will turn nastier than an enemy to save his own skin. Bad thing about human nature —got a yellow streak. Came from Cain. Never know when it's going to show. We've all got it somewhere and fear brings it out."

"I suppose," Ross said, hardly listening, "these men have no choice but to appear if the law subpoenas them . . . Paynter! I didn't expect him."

"Who's that? Something fresh?"

"A man who was my servant for years."

"Was he in this?"

68

" Oh yes. I woke him first and sent him to rouse Sawle."

" Sawle a man?"

" No, a village."

Mr. Clymer wafted vigorously. " Terrible smell in here, terrible smell. Was this Paynter on the beach when the excise men turned up?"

" On the beach but too drunk to know anything."

" Trouble with some people—when they don't remember, they invent. That's often the defence's opportunity. Sharp-witted man?"

" I wouldn't say so."

" Ah. No doubt you could shake him. Though some of these dullards are wickedly obstinate in the box. Bullheaded, that's what you'd call 'em."

Ross handed the list back. " Wednesday morning, do you think?"

" Wednesday morning." Clymer stood up and folded his gown about him. " Don't know why I'm troubling. If you want to hang it's your own affair." The gaoler had come forward but he waved him away. " Remember seeing a man strung up at Tyburn once. They cut him down for dead but he grimaced and twitched for quite five minutes after."

" I've seen that happen when a man's head was shot off by a cannon ball," Ross said. " It's a still more peculiar sight when the head and the body are some paces apart."

Clymer stared. " Yes? . . ."

" Yes."

" Ha, well . . . I'll leave this draft defence with you. Think it over. But don't regret you didn't use it *after* the verdict. There's nothing to be done then. The prosecution will have plenty of harsh things to say about you without your helping 'em in any way out of a mistaken sense of pride. Pride's all right in its place. Got plenty myself. Couldn't get along without it. But a court of law's not the place for a display of it."

Dwight Enys put up at a little inn in Honey Street. A sudden illness in Mellin Cottages had delayed him so that he did not reach Bodmin until Monday afternoon. At the assize court he saw that Ross's name was not on the list for Tuesday; then he called at the George and Crown, but found only Verity there.

He left soon and dined quietly at the inn. Having hurried, he now found himself with one day to kill. In the morning he thought he would visit the lazar house he had passed a mile or so out of the town. He had never seen a leper and it might add to his knowledge to observe them.

The tiny dining room of this inn was separated from the tap room only by half-height swing doors, and as he was finishing the cold pigeon pie there was some little commotion and he heard the word "surgeon" mentioned. It was not, however, his business and he helped himself to the apricot jellies and the cream. After a minute the owner of the inn pushed through the door and, seeing Dwight, came perspiring over to him.

"Begging your pardon, sur, but be you a surgeon or an apothecary or some such like?"

"I am."

"Well, sur, a footman has this minute run over from the Priory House to say there's someone taken tedious sick, and was there a physician to be had? Tis urgent, so I'm told. Twould be obliging to the Daniells and a keenly act as you might say. . . ."

In the taproom was a liveried footman looking breathless and a shade anxious. A Miss Penvenen was the lady who was took ill, a Miss Caroline Penvenen; a guest staying in the house. No, he hadn't seen her himself and didn't know what was amiss except that it was urgent and their own apothecary lived at the far end of the town.

"Very well. I'll be with you in a minute." Dwight ran up the stairs and picked up the small bag of medicines and surgical instruments he seldom travelled without.

It was a fine night and only a few yards to the Church Square and up the hill at the other side. They turned in at a gate and came to a big, square, gentleman's residence overlooking a small park. Water glimmered through the ornamental trees.

The footman led the way into a square hall lit by massive candles which flickered and bobbed like servant girls as they went by. Through a half-opened door Dwight saw a table set for supper, gleaming knives, polished fruit, flowers. A man's voice talking in a measured even tone; used to being listened to. Up the stairs. Good wrought-iron work and plenty of white paint. Two Opies and a Zoffany.

Along a red-carpeted passage and a turn. The footman knocked at a door.

" Come in."

Dwight was ushered in and the footman withdrew. Sitting on a low couch was a tall, slender, strikingly handsome girl in a richly patterned dressing gown of white lawn.

" Oh, are you an apothecary?" she demanded.

" A physician, ma'am. Can I be of help to you?"

" Yes. That's if you know the use of drugs the way an apothecary does."

" Of course. What is the matter?"

" You attend on the Daniells regular?"

" No. I'm a stranger to the town. Your footman came to the inn where I was staying and said you were urgently ill."

" Yes, I see. I only wanted to be sure." She got up. " *I* am not ill, though. It's my little dog, Horace. Look. He has had two fits and now's half awake only, as if faint. I'm greatly concerned about him. Will you attend to him at once, please."

Dwight saw that beside her on the sofa was a small black pug curled on a silk cushion. He looked at the pug and then he looked at the girl.

" Your *dog*, ma'am?"

" Yes," she said impatiently. " I've been worried out of my life for half an hour. He'll not drink and scarcely knows me. It's all this commotion and excitement there's been, I'll swear. I shouldn't have brought him; I have only myself to blame."

It was a beautiful room, decorated in scarlet and gold. Candles on the dressing table reflected in endless multiples through double mirrors. No doubt the chief guest room. A lady of consequence. He said gently: " Your footman made a mistake. It would be a farrier you really sent him for."

He caught the flicker in her eyes before she bent her head. " It's not my custom to employ a horse doctor for Horace."

" Oh, some of them are skilful enough."

" That may be. I don't choose to employ them."

He didn't move.

She said sharply: " I want the best advice. I'll pay for it. I'll pay your ordinary fee. Come, what is it? You can have it in advance."

" That can wait until I have the honour of attending you."

Their glances clashed. Something in her attitude had irritated him even more than the nature of the call.

" Well," she said, " are you going to treat the dog, or do you not know your trade well enough? If you're a beginner, perhaps you had better go and we'll call someone else."

" It was what I was about to suggest," he said.

As he reached the door she said: " Wait."

He turned. He noticed that there were faint freckles across the bridge of her nose.

She said: " Have you never had a dog of your own?" The tone of her voice was different.

" . . . Yes, I had once."

" Would you have let him die on a point of—formality?"

" No . . ."

" Then will you let mine?"

" I imagine it's not as serious as that."

" I hope not myself."

There was a moment's hesitation. He came back into the room. " How old is he?"

" Twelve months."

" Fits are not uncommon at that age. An aunt of mine had a spaniel . . ."

He bent to examine Horace. There didn't seem much wrong with the animal except that its breathing was stertorous.

Pulse was fairly steady and there was no sign of fever. At the best of times, he thought, it would be a miserable little beast. For one thing it was much too fat and pampered. Dwight was aware that its graceful arrogant young mistress was closely watching him.

He looked up. "I see no cause for anxiety. There's an excess of some of the vital humours, and I'd advise you to follow a lowering system of treatment. Keep him very short of sweetmeats and pastries. And let one of the servants give him regular exercise each day. Real exercise. Running and jumping. He's got to get rid of the poisons causing these convulsions. In the meantime I'll write you a prescription that you can get a druggist to make up."

"Thank you."

He took out his notebook; she meekly fetched him a pen and ink and he wrote out a prescription for a paregoric of black cherry water and Theban opium.

"Thank you," she said, taking the slip. "You were saying?"

"What?"

"About your aunt."

His mind had moved on beyond that. He suddenly smiled, the last anger going. "Oh, my aunt had a spaniel, but that was many years ago. He used to have fits when she played the spinet. One hesitates to say whether he was musical or the opposite."

Caroline's smooth young face, which had been so taut a few minutes ago, flashed its own answering smile, though there was still a glint of disappearing hostility at its edge.

"What is your name?" she said.

Tuesday dawned with heavy showers which made the dry mud into wet mud but didn't affect the spirits of those who were determined to make the most of election day. Dwight went first to the assize building, but there was no notice yet of the following day's list so he felt entitled to introduce himself to Mr. Jeffery Clymer to find out.

Mr. Clymer was at breakfast, his mauve chin paler for the

73

morning's shave, and in a great confusion and hurry; but he allowed Dwight a seat at the table and a glimpse of Wednesday's cause list. The cases which were to come before the Hon. Mr. Justice Lister were briefly stated.

R. v. *Smith for misdemeanour*

R. v. *Boynton for larceny*

R. v. *Polkinghorne and Norton for vagrancy*

R. v. *Poldark for riot and assault*

R. v. *Inhabitants of the township of Liskeard for non-repair of highway*

R. v. *Corydon for receiving stolen goods*

R. v. *Inhabitants of the Parish of St. Erth for obstruction of estuary*

Dwight put the paper back on the table. "How can all those be possibly got through to-morrow?"

"Have to be, my dear man," said Clymer, chewing. "Crowded list. Don't want to be here all month. Due in Exeter the sixteenth. But don't worry; they'll be run through all right. A lot of 'em are simple cases."

"Including that of Rex. v. Poldark?"

"Oh no, hum . . ." Mr. Clymer paused to pick his teeth with his little finger. "Far from it. But we shall get through. Could only wish for a different attitude on the part of my client. Stiff-necked, that's what you'd call it. Doesn't understand the law. And still unrelenting. Perhaps the look of the judge will make him change his tune. Wentworth Lister's no milksop. Well, well, I must be off. Got a case at eleven. Old woman accused of poisoning her grandson with ground glass. She's seventy-two and not a penny piece. Better all round if she was hanged to make an easy passing, but we must see what the judge says."

As Dwight got up to go a servant tapped at the door.

"If you please, sir, a Mr. Francis Poldark to see you."

Mr. Clymer gulped at his coffee. "Another Poldark? What does this mean? Do you know him, sir?" When Dwight had briefly answered, "Another witness, d'ye think?

74

This fellow Pearce doesn't know his business if he allows people to come in with their stories five minutes before the trial. No mention of him in the brief at all!"

"He was ill at the time of the wrecks. But he may have called to make general inquiries about his cousin."

Mr. Clymer irritably unbuttoned his morning gown. "Not Captain Poldark's wet nurse, y'know. Have other business to attend to. Foster!"

"Sir?" The clerk put his head round the door.

"Bring me R. v. Penrose and R. v. Tredinnick."

"Yes, sir."

"All this election farce. Most untimely and unsettling. Place overcrowded with drunken rogues and pickpockets. No service in the hotels. Bedbugs. Disgraceful: that's what you'd call it." The barrister turned to the gaping servant. "Well, show him up if you must. Show Mr. Poldark up!"

"I'll take my leave before he comes," Dwight said. "That will be one less in your way. We shall meet to-morrow."

"Be there by ten. The early cases may be run through very quick."

On the way down the stairs Dwight met Francis coming up. Francis said:

"I came in great haste, but hear the case isn't until to-morrow." He was dusty and unkempt.

"That's true."

"Do you know where I can get a room for to-night? The town is fermenting with people."

"I think you may have to go some distance out."

"Which inn is Ross's wife staying at?"

"The George and Dragon. But your sister was saying they were crowded too."

Francis looked up quickly. "My sister?"

"They're staying together." Dwight's professional eye could not help registering that Francis looked pallid and out of condition. The stamina had gone with the flesh he had lost. "Your wife isn't with you?"

". . . The court is no place for a woman. What are all these damned flags and banners waving in the breeze?"

75

Dwight explained. "Oh, of course, I had forgot. Cornwall abounds in rotten boroughs and suitable people to fill 'em. Think you this man upstairs has any forensic ability? So many of them are braggarty, pot-bellied old roués, caring only for their fees and a handy wench when it's over."

Dwight smiled. "I found him irritable but alert. I shall judge better to-morrow." They passed on, and then Dwight turned again. "If you should be out of a place to sleep to-night and nothing at all in view, you may share my room, though there's only one bed in it. The London Inn, near the church."

"You may be held to that. If there's floor space I can use a rug and lie easy enough. Thank you."

Dwight left the hotel and turned up the street. It was fine now and a walk would do him good. Just out of the town a carriage drawn by four grey horses, with a driver and a postilion in green and white livery, passed him on the way in. As it lurched along, going slowly because of the appalling state of the road, Dwight saw George Warleggan alone inside.

When Dwight got back from his visit to the lazar house—where he had found only seven resident lepers, most of them drunk, and the building nearly falling down for want of elementary repair—he was only just in time to squeeze into the Guildhall to watch the election.

The platform at the end was filled with the town's notables, and Dwight was surprised to see the tall red-haired girl as the only woman among them. Outside was a good deal of noise, for the hundreds of people who could not get in were jammed in the street shouting rival slogans. Proceedings began with the usual sheriff's precept; then a fat man called Fox, who was a county magistrate, got up to administer the oath to the returning officer. Here was the crux of the matter. The two mayors, Michell from one end of the platform, and Lawson from the other, jumped forward and claimed their right to be that man. A long legal argument followed. Both sides had brought barristers to put their claim, but neither

76

convinced the other, and tempers grew frayed. People in the hall began to shout and stamp their feet, and the floor shook.

Dwight stared over the bobbing heads and wondered how Horace was faring. He glanced at the people crushed around him, some in wigs, some with their own hair tied in bows at the back, others, labourers and workingmen, with lank uncut hair falling to their shoulders. Two near him had got skin diseases and a third was far gone in consumption and spat blood into the straw underfoot. In the corner was a woman who had lost her nose with the French disease.

Suddenly a compromise—of sorts—was struck on the platform, though it was come to more because of the noise of the mob outside than from any will to make concessions. The mayors were to be joint returning officers and would be jointly sworn in as such. Anyone could see that this would lead to further trouble when the election proper began, but at least it allowed progress of a sort.

Growing tired of it all, Dwight edged a step or two nearer the door, though he did not see much prospect of getting out until it was all over. Silence fell on the people around him and he saw that the first voter had stepped up. This was Alderman Harris, a man with a stomach equal to his great reputation, and he recorded his vote—for Trevaunance and Chenhalls—amid a burst of cheering and only a few catcalls. Then came Roberts, a Whig Quaker, who was also allowed to pass unchallenged. Another Whig followed and, acting as warily as his rival, Michell passed him without comment. A third Whig, however, was too much to swallow. The barrister acting for the Basset interests objected on the grounds that Joseph Lander had long been invalidated from membership of the corporation on the grounds of insanity and that he had been three times put in the stocks for indecent behaviour.

This caused an uproar, and two men near Dwight started fighting. One of them shoved Dwight against the woman who had lost her nose, and she opened a mouth like a door and screamed as if she were being murdered. When she was at last quieted, Dwight saw that a doctor was standing up giving evidence that Joseph Lander's mother and father were

77

incestuously related and both had died insane—but before he could follow the argument the two men were fighting again; and when one of them was hauled insensible from under the other's feet Joseph Lander had passed from the scene.

The young physician began to wish he hadn't come. Every other man who came up to vote was challenged, and the argument lasted interminably. One man, obviously at death's door, was carried up on a stretcher and put on the floor while they quarrelled over him like seagulls over a strip of offal. Sir Hugh Bodrugan, stocky and hairy and authoritative, was allowed to pass unchallenged, just because, Dwight thought, no one dared face him out. What he was doing on the corporation was a mystery; but there were several like him, men who lived miles away and had no connection whatever with the town.

The girl was looking hot and bored; and suddenly she leaned towards Unwin Trevaunance and began to whisper in his ear. Trevaunance in some obvious irritation argued with her, but she rose and slipped out of a side door. Dwight began to fight his own way out.

It was a long struggle, much resented and resisted, but he got there in the end and found himself hot and bruised and breathless in the passage. This passage was choked with people, and the stairs leading to the street were worse. He turned towards the back, knowing that Caroline Penvenen could not have gone out by the front door.

At the end of the passage the crowd thinned a bit, and two special constables were guarding the door which led to the platform. They stared at him with suspicion as he came up.

"Which way did Miss Penvenen go?"

One of them nodded. "Down thur, sur."

Dwight saw a door in the opposite wall, and pushed his way through to it. It led into the back room of the shop next door and thence to the main street. When he came out he thought she had gone, for the crowds were shouting and dancing about the ale-houses opposite, and the porticoes made it hard to get a view down the street. Then he turned and saw her standing against the wall beside the shop door, watching him.

She was hatless, evidently caring nothing for convention; her rich auburn hair, rather coarse in texture, curled to her shoulders. The pearls about her neck were worth any footpad's risk.

"Dr. Enys," she said as he bowed. "Why are you following me?"

Again he felt that prick of irritation. "I saw you leave and thought you might need my help."

"Should I be likely to?"

"Election day is not the quietest of times."

"I found it all very dull."

"Naturally. But there are those who do not."

The shop door burst open and a servant came out. He stopped at sight of them and touched his forelock.

"Oh, Mistress Penvenen, ma'am, the master asked me to see ee home safe. He couldn't leave his self, not just now. Tis——"

"I need no foster mother to escort me home," she said impatiently. "Go back to Mr. Unwin and look after him. He'll need it maybe. Go on! Go on!" she added as the man hesitated. "I don't want you."

A section of the crowd was chanting the marching song again, but others were booing derisively. Someone aimed a brick at the Guildhall window, but it missed and broke to pieces on the wall, scattering a shower of smaller stones on the people underneath.

"Rabble," said Caroline. "Like the shirtless beggars and thieves who pretend to hold France. England would be happier for a few thousand less of them."

The shopkeeper behind them was busy putting up his shutters. There was a clatter of heels as someone clambered across his portico, and he pushed his way out into the street and began swearing and shouting at him to come down.

"In a mass," said Dwight, "a rabble, yes. And a drunken rabble's a dangerous thing; I wouldn't trust its behaviour a yard. But take each man to himself and he's likeable enough. A weak creature, as we all are, liable to jealousies and petty spites, as we all are, selfish and afraid, as we all are. But often generous and kind and peaceable and hard-working and good to his family. At least as much all those things as the average gentleman."

Caroline looked at him. "Are you a Jacobin, like your friend Ross Poldark?"

So she had been making inquiries about him. "It's clear you don't know Ross Poldark."

"No. I expect to see him to-morrow—and hope for better entertainment than I've had to-day."

Dwight said sharply: "No doubt you're the sort of woman who takes a window at Tyburn—for the pleasure of seeing someone choked to death."

"Is it any business of yours if I am?"

"No. I'm thankful not."

"I find you a little impertinent for one of your station, Dr. Enys."

"I don't suppose my station to be that of a lackey, ma'am."

"You might establish your claim with some show of gentility then."

His flush didn't fade. "This is a rough county, Miss Penvenen. As you'll see if you look around you. . . . Not that I've noticed any strict attention to the conventions on your part."

She lifted her head. "There are limits, don't you think? And it seems only necessary for me to mention Poldark's name for you to fly into a rage and overstep them. Is he your hero, Dr. Enys? Shall you be able to make a rabid speech to-morrow in his defence? Be careful that you don't forget your manners then, or the judge will not give you a hearing."

"The judge is not a woman, ma'am."

"And what do you mean by that?"

"I mean he's not likely to be swayed by prejudice."

"Not even by an odious conceit such as some men suffer from?"

"Oh, conceit. I shouldn't put that as the special property of one sex. . . ."

As he spoke his attention was taken by an extra commotion across the road. Two men were fighting or struggling, it seemed for the possession of some papers.

"It's very gracious of you to instruct me," Caroline said. "I wonder you're so solicitous for one you so greatly despise."

"You quite misunderstand what I . . ." He broke off.

"Naturally."

There were cries and shouts and laughter from across the street, and some papers flew high in the air and scattered over the crowd. Other men had joined in the struggle now. Dwight muttered his excuses to Caroline and ran across the road. He tried to force his way through the ring of spectators.

It was hard going, for no one would move an inch for another, but at last he got through and found Francis struggling with three men who were apparently trying to restrain his violence towards a fourth who cringed among a heap of papers in the gutter.

"Mangy moulting carrion crow," Francis was saying, in quite a quiet voice considering his struggles. "Let me pluck a few more feathers. You wanted to distribute 'em, did you not, and I'll do it for you. This way . . ." He half broke free, but they grabbed him again.

"Hold hard, sur," said one. "Ye've plucked 'im near to the bone, I bla'."

There was a laugh. Francis had had a good deal to drink. The man in the gutter, a tattered black-coated fellow, was holding his head and groaning, but with an eye on the sympathy of the crowd. Scattered about in the mud were dozens of broadsheets, and Dwight picked up one which lay at his feet. The leaflet was entitled *True and Sensational Facts in the life of Captain R—s— P—d—k.*

"Things that grow in dunghills breed pestilence," said Francis. "They should be trod back before they move from their middens. Let me go, fellow. Take your scabby hands off me."

"Mr. Poldark . . . are these men annoying you? What has gone wrong?"

Francis raised an eyebrow. "Dr. Enys. Well, it would be

81

a mistake to imagine that by clinging to me like blowflies they're amusing me at all." He wrenched himself free, the men having slightly relaxed their grasp at the sight of Dwight's sober bearing. "God damn it, there's no respect for quality in this town! One cannot squash—ah, there he goes!"

Seeing his attacker free again, the tattered man in the gutter had turned, like one of the worms Francis had compared him to, and wriggled his way between the legs of the spectators. France threw his stick after him, but it only caught a fat man on the shins.

"And now he goes free, to lay his eggs elsewhere. Well, I fancy these he has left are well addled." Francis ground the papers in the mud. Then he pulled his cravat round to the front and tried to adjust it. "Go on, go on!" he said to the gaping crowd. "There's no more entertainment for you. Back to your spawning."

Dwight said: "These scurrilous sheets. But it won't help to take the law into one's own hands."

"What are they doing but taking the law into their own hands trying to poison the public's mind before the trial? It's a monstrous encroachment on individual rights. I'll wreck every one of 'em I come across."

Dwight made a noncommittal reply and turned to go.

"As for you," said Francis to the man who had held him, "when the constables of this flea-ridden town want your help no doubt they'll enlist it. Until then restrain your interfering humours or they may lead you into trouble." He ran a hand through his hair. "Come and drink with me, Enys."

"I'm sorry . . . I was engaged when I heard the commotion and—broke off a conversation." Dwight peered back over the crowding people but could see no sign of Caroline.

"Conversation," said Francis, "is what I require. Intelligent conversation. I have spent the day in the company of rogues and thieves and bawds, beginning with the biggest blackguard of them all. Now I crave an hour's respectability. Suitably primed, I think you could dispense it."

Dwight smiled. "Another time I'd be honoured. But at the moment, if you'll excuse me . . ."

He pushed his way back to the Guildhall and looked every way. But she was not to be seen. Evidently she had no fear at all and had gone off on her own.

Unnoticed by him, a sudden silence had fallen on the crowds. Now he heard someone speaking, and knew it was the announcement of the election result. But he was too late to catch what was being said. All he heard was the roar of the crowd at the end—and that was a roar of frustration and annoyance.

Whatever the result, rivalry hadn't been appeased by it.

Chapter Eight

Verity sat on the low window seat watching the forty or fifty horses being driven by the hotel grooms down from the grazing fields above the town. Every evening about this time they came clattering and snorting past, forcing a dangerous way along the narrow street. Every morning they were driven up.

She had spent much of her time at this window since she came, peering down on the heads of passers-by, just as in Falmouth when Andrew was away she would sit in the window above the porch working at her embroidery and gazing out over the harbour. There was no such view here, just a narrow hilly street and an endless movement of people to and fro.

She had heard the result of the election an hour ago, a fiasco which would inevitably lead to more petitions and counter-petitions before Parliament and endless quarrels within the town. The two returning officers had shown different results. Mr. Lawson had returned a Whig and a Tory, Mr. Michell two Tories. The town was in a ferment.

By now Andrew would be in Lisbon. To-morrow, while Ross was standing his trial, he would be setting sail for home. His son James, at Gibraltar, was no great distance from him, but could as well be in another hemisphere. Sometimes she

83

doubted whether she would ever meet his two children; in her heart, in spite of what she had told Demelza, she had grown to fear it more than desire it. James and Esther were the standing evidence of Andrew's first tragic marriage. Perhaps they felt that themselves and so would not come. Perhaps they merely felt that the new wife had pushed them out. In any event Andrew Blamey's second marriage so far was an unqualified success, and Verity was terrified that his children might endanger it.

There was a knock at the door, and Joanna, the untidy serving maid, stood there, hair awry under a mobcap, and a streak of dirt across her cheek.

" If ee plaise, ma'am, a gent to see ee. Name of Mr. Francis Poldark."

Verity's heart lurched. " Mr.—*Francis* Poldark? . . ."

" Iss, I bla. He say you d'know he. Perhaps tis the other leddy——"

" It is this lady," said Francis, entering. " I am her brother, wench, so there's no bawdy tattle for you when you go below. Get down to your taps and leave us be. And wipe your snotty nose."

Joanna, gaping, slid out, and brother and sister faced each other for the first time for fourteen months, since the day when, abetted by Demelza and in the face of his bitterest opposition, Verity had run away and married Andrew Blamey.

Her heart sinking, she saw at once that he was drunk. And she knew how much that meant. Six or seven years ago their father had been known to complain that Francis would never have a head on him and slid under the table after the first bottle like any common clerk. But time and patience had cured all that. It needed real perseverance these days.

" You alone?" he said.

" Yes . . . I—didn't know you were in the town, Francis."

" Everyone's in the town. Apothecary, ploughboy, poor man, thief . . . I thought you were staying with Demelza."

" She's gone out this evening. We've been together all day."

He frowned at her as if trying to see her with the unprejudiced eyes of a stranger. His shirt was torn at the neck and his coat stained with mud. Only she knew how passionately he had resented her marriage. Since they grew up his love for her had been selfish, possessive—a little more than brotherly. His distrust of Blamey's bad record had been the centripetal force round which the other little resentments clung.

"Mrs. *Blamey*," he said contemptuously. "How does it feel to be called Mrs. Blamey?"

"When you came . . . I hoped . . ."

"What? That I was come for a reconcil—conciliation?" He looked round for a seat and moved across the room to find one, sat carefully in it, putting his hat on the floor beside the chair and stretching out one muddy riding boot. His movements were too deliberately steady. "Who knows? But not with Mrs. Blamey. My sister—that's different. A treacherous slut." But he said it without conviction or venom.

She said: "I've so wished to come back and see you all— I've been asking Demelza. All your sickness over Christmas —and Demelza's loss. In Falmouth we've had our share, but . . . How is Elizabeth? Not with you, I suppose?"

"And how is Blamey?" said Francis. "Not with you, I suppose? Tell me, Verity, d'you find married life less of a snare than the rest of us? We plunge into it, poor deluded devils, convinced there is something within that we're missing and must not miss. But it is a gin, is it not, with iron teeth—and once it fastens on us . . . How is Blamey; lashing his sailors, I conceit, in Biscay or the Baltic. You've got stouter, you was always such a thin kipes of a girl. Have you brandy or rum in the room?"

"No . . . only port."

"Of course, Demelza's drink. How she loves it. She should take care or she'll become a tippler. I saw Ross in Truro, two weeks gone; he seemed very little put about by all the legal fuss and the lying scabby rumours. Like Ross, that. He's a hard nut and they'll not crack him with a mere assize, however much they count on it." He stared at her with a pursed, angry face, but looking through rather than at her. "I

85

wish I were Ross and going to stand before my judges to-morrow; I'd tell them a thing or two, I'd shock them. Francis Poldark, of Trenwith, Esquire."

One more effort. "I'm glad you've come, Francis. I should be so relieved to feel all the heartburning was over. It has been my one unhappiness since I left."

He ripped a bit of torn lace off the edge of his cuff, idly rolled it between finger and thumb, and flipped it across the room in the direction of the fireplace. "Happiness—un-happiness: tags to tie upon the same mood! Pretty ribbons that mean no more than the flags of this cursed election. *Aarf!* as Father used to say. This morning I quarrelled violently with George Warleggan."

She got up. "I'll order you some refreshment, my dear." When she had pulled the bell: "We're all praying for an acquittal to-morrow. They say it's by no means hopeless. Demelza has been about some business of her own all week. It is something to do with the trial, but I don't know what. She can't rest."

"Acquittal! Nor would I in her shoes. This morning I went round to the counsel who's defending Ross and said to him: ' Tell me the truth now, I want no cuckoo-spit, but the truth: what are his chances for to-morrow?' And he said: ' As for the third charge, there's a very fair chance; but I see no getting out of the first two—on his own admission and on his pig-headed attitude now. There is still time to change and make a fight of it, but he will not do so, so it is a lost cause to begin.' "

The serving maid came to the door again, but for a moment they were both too preoccupied to heed her. At length Francis sent her scurrying off for gin.

He said: "I met George at the Garland Ox just after. He looked so damned opulent and self-satisfied that I couldn't stomach him. My gorge rose and I vomited a good deal of spleen. It did me a world of good."

They were silent for a long time. She had never seen him like this before. She didn't know if the change had come in twelve months or only in to-night. Two things struggled in her mind, concern for him and concern for what he had said about Ross.

"Was it wise to quarrel with George? Don't you still owe him money?"

"I greeted him by saying: 'What, are the carrion gathering before the buck's killed?' When he showed signs of swallowing that outwardly but resenting it inwardly I thought it time to place my opinion of him beyond a doubt. His damned suaveness didn't avail him. With a politeness to match his own, I dwelt on his looks, his clothes, his morals, his parentage and his earlier ancestry. We quarrelled with a becoming vigour. The position between us had needed clearing up for some time."

"Clearing up," said Verity restlessly. "It will be a very happy clearing up if he forecloses on you. He has been an old friend, I know, but I wouldn't consider it beyond him to pay you out for an insult in whatever way he can."

Joanna came back with the gin. Francis tipped her and watched her go. He slopped some of the spirit into a glass and drank it. "Oh, no doubt he thinks he'll take it out of me to-morrow. But he may be defrauded." Francis stared with a peculiar expression at his empty glass. He might have been staring at the bitter procession of his life, ever dwindling in thought and achievement down a vista of days till it came to this desolate moment, when the dregs were all that remained. It was a moment when lunacy and unreason became part of the wider comity.

"To-morrow is still remote," he said. "It may never happen."

"The whole procedure was cursed irregular," said Sir John Trevaunance, dusting snuff off his sleeve. "Ecod, if I'd been there it would never have been allowed to happen."

"Easy to talk," said Unwin, like a sulky giant. "Neither would give way, and the crowd was howling outside. We had to give 'em some result or they would have wrecked the place. As it was, when Michell and Lawson went to the window together I thought they would be stoned."

"Michell's returns were sent straight off?"

"Yes, by post rider. But so were Lawson's."

"It's important which the sheriff has in his hands first. There's no reason in it, but a greater regard is usually taken of the first in."

They were at the reception following the election dinner. It had been decided after hurried consultation to go ahead as if there had been a full-scale Tory victory. The Boscoigne faction was doing the same and at the Guildhall reception which followed the dinners there was an intermingling of the rival parties. Both judges were present and several people of rank in the county who had not been concerned in the election.

"There'll be pressure on me to stand aside," said Unwin viciously. "There's a smell of it already. Without me Chenhalls and Corrant can occupy the seats comfortably. If I have to go, Basset will hear of it."

"There's no question of your stepping aside." Sir John chewed his bottom lip. "In fact, since you're second in both polls, you're really the only one who's fully elected."

A set dance was in progress, and Unwin watched Caroline's tall graceful movements as she danced in a square with Chenhalls and some cousins of the Robartes. "Well, we are three members for two seats. That will not pass."

"It's only a question of time," said Sir John, staring at a dark young woman talking to one of His Majesty's judges. "When the plea is heard before the Chancery Court Lawson's mayoralty will be declared illegal, there's no doubt. That will automatically make his election figures invalid. Anyway, they smack of fraud. Whoever heard of a Whig mayor returning one candidate of the other colour when there are two of his own?"

"It suggests impartiality."

"Nonsense, it suggests fraud. But in any case, if this should not be thrashed out before Parliament reassembles, don't hesitate to claim your seat. There have been similar occurrences in recent years at Helston and Saltash. Daniell reminds me that at Saltash two rival electoral bodies have existed for a very long time, and different committees of appeal have held first one body to be legal and then the other. More than that, Unwin. In an election to fill a single seat four or five years ago, the rival electoral bodies each elected a member—and *both* have taken their places in the Commons."

" Yes, I heard something of it in the House."

" Well, that was in '85 or '86. And Daniell assures me that in spite of petitions and counter-petitions both elected members continue to sit. If that can happen, there's no reason to be despondent about the present result. I believe it to be most important that you regard yourself as re-elected and act accordingly."

The dance came to an end and was politely applauded. Without looking towards the Trevaunances, Caroline drifted off with Chenhalls in the direction of the supper room. Relations between the lovers had not been of the sweetest to-day. She had insisted on attending the hustings—much against all his advice. Then, suddenly bored, she had slipped out in the most obvious way when Unwin couldn't possibly leave to accompany her, and had sent his servant scuttling back when he told him to follow. After all that she'd arrived back in the hall just as the results were given, and had snapped his head off when he asked the cause. When I am your husband, he thought, looking towards her as she stood in the doorway . . . Her shoulders gleamed whitely even in this subdued light. *If* I am your husband; and that was a disturbing thought. This election had been more expensive than ever. Doubts as to the results made his position much more unstable—whatever John said. And there were mounting debts in London. He started towards her, but Sir John clutched his arm.

He looked at his brother impatiently, expecting more sage but unwelcome advice. But Sir John was staring the other way.

" Tell me . . . who's that with Wentworth Lister? That woman—talking to him."

Unwin frowned his cleft frown. " Demelza Poldark, it looks like."

89

"Cod, well . . ." Sir John swallowed. "I thought so. So she wouldn't take no for an answer."

"What d'you mean?"

The other said expressively: "How the devil has she got in here? Who could have introduced her? And now she's talking to Longshanks Lister—just as she intended! God's my life, she'll hang her husband if she's not careful—and go to prison for contempt of court herself! She's playing with fire!"

"I've seen her about with Hugh Bodrugan."

Sir John took out a handkerchief and mopped his face. "Well, I had no hand in it, that's one thing! Hugh always was a lecherous fool; she'll have had to pay her forfeits there. Well, I wish her luck of the encounter. She'll need it."

Unwin said: "I told you the first time I set eyes on her that she was a dangerous woman."

Demelza was well aware that she was playing with fire. As soon as she saw the tall cadaverous judge at close quarters she knew this was going to be the hardest meeting of her career.

She had put on her pale mauve silk with the half-length sleeves and the flowered apple-green bodice and underskirt. It was the one Verity had chosen for her three years ago.

Sir Hugh Bodrugan did not know Lister, but had got Mr. Coldrennick, the M.P. for Launceston, to introduce them. Then, grunting and hairy, he had gone off with Coldrennick and left Demelza with her quarry, as promised.

The Hon. Mr. Justice Lister was about sixty years of age, six feet tall, with long tapering legs, slightly bowed, and an austere lined face stamped by forty years of courtrooms. He was not enjoying himself in this reception because he was a shy man when away from his work, and had no interest in the powder and patch of fashionable assemblies. He had come because the accommodation in the judges' lodgings was so cheerless that he had dined out every night—and now could not refuse the organisers, who had been his hosts.

When he met this young woman he fully expected her to ask him a few inane questions and simper at him and move on, as other young women had done. He had no interest in women, except that they appeared as the motive power behind a good many of the felonies which came under his scrutinising eye. He was a bachelor and a pessimist.

But this young woman had lingered longer than most. At the moment she had asked him a question and he had not caught it. He lowered his head.

"What did you say?"

"Does your lordship dance?"

He shook his head. "But don't let me deter you. No doubt you have partners enough waiting to claim the privilege."

"Oh no, my lord. I should better prefer to watch. I believe it is the onlooker who most enjoys the dance."

He put out his bottom lip. "I am of an age, madam, when the spectacles of others in effort is more rewarding than the effort itself. I should not have imagined you were."

"But what has age to do with it?" Demelza asked. "Isn't it wise to—to keep out of the crush sometimes so as we may see what we look like when we're in it?"

He glanced at her a little more keenly. "If you observe that rule in matters of more serious import you will make a good deal of your life."

"In matters of more serious import," Demelza said, "life don't always give you the choosing."

"Every subject's soul is his own," said Lister. "How he uses it is no one else's responsibility."

"Oh yes, my lord, I believe you truly. But sometimes tis like a bird in a cage. It can sing never so sweet but being dropped down a well will not put an end to it."

He smiled dryly. "You argue with a ready wit, ma'am."

"Your lordship's too kind. Of course it is a pre-presumption on my part. I am really so ignorant about all these things. You know so much."

"We know what we are allowed to know," said Lister. "Conscience is nearer judgment than knowledge."

"I wonder," she said, "if that ever worries you?"

"What?"

"Judgment, I mean," she went on hastily at his look, "isn't

91

it hard to judge to perfection unless you d'*know* to perfection? Forgive me if I don't understand."

"My dear madam, there is room for improvement wherever we look. Infallibility exists in divine creation, not elsewhere."

. . . In the refreshment room Unwin said: "In what way have I offended?"

"In no way, my dear," said Caroline, her fingers travelling over her hair. "Why should you have?"

"That I don't know. I lay myself out to please you all ends, incurring the disapproval of my party to get you to the hustings—but to-night you ignore me for Chenhalls or any other middle-aged beau who comes along. I'm surprised you've not danced with Bodrugan yet."

"Thank you, dear, I prefer bearbaiting out of doors." Caroline's sweet voice had a touch of ice. "But why should I not dance with the middle-aged beaux if they give me pleasure? I'm not yet tied to your apron strings—and thankful too, for they would be gloomy tiresome sulky depressing apron strings to-night, and hardly to be borne."

Unwin took a grip on himself and smiled. "I'm sorry, Caroline. It is this accursed election—pray forgive me. As soon as the situation is cleared up I shall be better company, I promise. I should be now, given half a chance."

"Always it was 'when the election is over.' Now apparently it is not over. Oh, John! John!"

"Yes?" said the elder Trevaunance acidly. He disliked being called by his Christian name by this wand of a girl. He bore it only for his brother's sake.

"Do you know a physician who lives in or around Sawle by the name of Enys? Dwight Enys, I believe."

"M'yes. Lives on Poldark land or just on the Treneglos estate. Young feller. Know nothing about him much. Why?"

"He is in the town, I believe to give evidence at to-morrow's assize. Has he private money, I wonder?"

"Why? Have you met him?" Unwin asked suspiciously.

"By chance he was the man we called in to see Horace. I told you about him. And very stiff-necked at being summoned to attend a pet dog."

92

"Infernal impudence. Had I been there I should have told him so."

"Oh, *I* told him so. But impudence is not so grave a sin, Unwin. Do you think? It shows a certain resilience and spirit. . . ."

. . . In the ballroom conversation had shifted a little away from the dangerous subject. Wentworth Lister was staring at the dark girl with narrowed eyes. "Modesty, a Greek philosopher once said, is the citadel of beauty and of virtue; the first of virtues is guilelessness, the second the sense of shame. It is a precept which has helped me in my estimate of women over many years."

"And your estimate of men?" said Demelza.

"Yes, and in that too." The dance came to an end and the judge glanced slowly round the room. It was warm in here, and he was sorry he had put on his third pair of stockings.

"Pray do not let me detain you longer," he said rather resentfully. "I'm sure you must have other and more pleasant claims upon your time."

Demelza moistened her lips. "Judas; I was thinking I was trespassing on yours."

To this he had to give a polite denial, and she in turn glanced quickly about. Though there were plenty of people moving around them, none just at that moment seemed bent on disturbing the tête-à-tête. The judge was not an attractive figure.

"I wish they would play something softer next time," she said. "It is hard to be heard. They make too much use of the flute and the pipes."

He said: "You play yourself, perhaps?"

"Only a very little." She smiled at him with sudden brilliance. "And sing—when I'm alone, like."

"I agree with you in a preference for the violins and the viols. As for singing, there is none worth hearing to-day."

Something in his tone caught her animal-sharp ears. It was a single breath of feeling among the dry rushes of his character.

"The Cornish do a rare lot of singing."

His lips smiled. "They put their voices together. No doubt that is what you mean. The church choir on Sunday."

"Of course—it is not maybe like what you get in London."

"There is little in London either. Little that is uncontaminated by modern tendencies. Frivolous and insipid glees. Italianate pasticcios and simpering artificiality. To catch the pure stream one must go back two hundred years—or more."

Lister closed his mouth sharply and took a pinch of snuff. Having dusted away the powder with a lace handkerchief, he clasped his hands behind his back and stared across the room as if determined not to be lured into further expressions of opinion.

Demelza said desperately: "What's wrong with the church music, my lord? I don't rightly follow you."

"Ha!" said Lister.

The Trevaunances had reappeared out of the supper room. Caroline's flame-coloured head just topped Sir John's, and was little below Unwin's.

Demelza said: "It is the first church I have heard with one of those organ pieces. There is one in Truro, but I never heard it. It is a grand sound, but I rather prefer the older way when it is well done."

The judge sniffed and dabbed. "You are fortunate that your ear is not entirely ruined by modern tendencies. No doubt you have never heard of singing in organum?"

"No, my lord. It is not singing with the organ?"

"It is certainly *not* with the organ. . . ."

. . . Sir Hugh Bodrugan had talked out the implications of the electoral position with Mr. Coldrennick and wanted something more to drink. He was sick and tired of Bodmin and would be glad to get home to-morrow to his dogs and his horses and Connie with her curses, and room in his great ramshackle house to stretch and sprawl and belch. This was all too confined for him. Only bright thing in his visit was meeting Demelza Poldark, who was always sharp-witted enough to keep him awake and freshen things up. He stared across at her where she was still talking to the tall spindly judge. She was damned elusive, that was the trouble. A bit of angling

94

was all part of the fun, he knew that; he didn't want his fish landed too easy; but so far he'd only kissed her twice—but once on the mouth—and squeezed her a couple of times in interesting places. A damned tantalising long-legged minx. It was time he was getting back to her.

He said just the last part to Mr. Coldrennick, breaking in on some dull observations about burgage tenures.

" Yes," said Mr. Coldrennick, " I suppose so. Must confess I've seldom known the learned judge so conversational. Young Mrs. Poldark has a way with her."

" Oh, she's a way with her," said Bodrugan grimly. " Damme, yes. It's the will that's lacking."

As they got near they could hear the judge's voice. " My dear young lady, no harmony, even of the most primitive kind, existed in the church until the tenth or eleventh centuries. Plainsong was begun then by higher and lower voices singing at a distance of a fourth or a fifth instead of in unison. It was no doubt years before it was found that thirds and sixths, instead of being more were less discordant and infinitely more melodious and variable in effect. There is a Scottish hymn—ah—to St. Magnus . . ."

" Hrrm-hm!" said Sir Hugh Bodrugan.

The Hon. Mr. Justice Lister raised his head and gave the interrupter a look he usually reserved for malefactors. At sight of it Coldrennick would have sheered away, but Bodrugan was not to be intimidated by anything.

" Ha, there, it's time for a bite of something more to eat, m'dear. There's such a shindy of people that I need you to steer me across in the right direction. Your lordship'll pardon us, no doubt."

" I'm not at all hungry, Sir Hugh," Demelza protested. " Perhaps twould be possible to wait awhile. His lordship was talking about church music, an' it is a rare instruction I should like to go on with."

" Nay, it will wait until another occasion, won't it, my lord. Church music, ecod! That's a subject for election night."

" A subject for any night," said Lister, " if you have the

disposition to grasp it. There are those, plainly, who have not." He was going to add something more from between his tight-held lips, but two ladies came up from the direction of the supper room, and there were others approaching. He said to Demelza: "There is also certain Elizabethan music, madam. Byrd and Tallis are names to remember. And—in a lighter and different fashion—Thomas Morley."

"I'll remember them," she said, and thanked him in her most careful style. Bodrugan was waiting to move away, and the other women now spoke to the judge. But after a moment he turned again to Demelza. There was a faint glimmer of approval in his deep-set eyes as he looked her up and down.

"I don't recall your name, madam, or whom I've had the pleasure of addressing."

"Poldark," she said, and swallowed. "Mrs. Ross Poldark."

"I am obliged to you," he said, and inclined his head. The name clearly meant nothing to him—yet.

Chapter Nine

After dark the streets reached their peak of noise and drunkenness, and Dwight's first intention was not to go out again. Caroline would be at the ball, but he had no invitation, and in any case no evening clothes. After supper he sat for a while in his bedroom reading a medical book, but the wilful Miss Penvenen and her doings kept intervening. She existed at the corner of his eye, in the depths of his ear, in the back of his mind. He remembered the rustle of her silk dress like something new and heard for the first time, he saw the tip of her tongue once when she licked her lips, he heard her voice, cool and irritating but as unforgettable as a line of music. Eventually he threw the book on the bed and went down to the taproom for a couple of drinks, but it was noisy and overcrowded, so, for lack of something better to do, he decided to stroll up the hill to the tiny hospital, which was under the charge of a Dr. Halliwell. Bodmin was one of the few towns progressive enough to have such an accommodation—mostly, if you were injured, you died in the street or in your own bed—and he thought it might be interesting to compare this tiny provincial establishment with the great institutions which flourished in London.

So he just missed Francis, who turned into the inn after he had left.

Francis asked for him and, on being told he was out, said that he had been promised a share of his room for the night. The innkeeper eyed him doubtfully, trying to size him up, impressed by his gentlemanly speech and bearing which weighed against his muddy tattered clothes, suspecting he was drunk yet not quite reconciling that with his fine-drawn expression and resolute speech.

"I'm sorry, sur, but twouldn't be for the likes of me to let one gent into another gent's chamber wi'out a by-your-leave. Twouldn't be playing fair, like."

"Nonsense. Dr. Enys invited me. What time will he be back?"

"I dunno, sur. He didn't say."

Francis put down his saddlebag. "It is a common custom in times of need to ask two gentlemen to share the same chamber. And you know it. And we are not strangers but friends. Come, tell me what Dr. Enys is paying and I'll give you the same."

"That and gladly when Dr. Enys comes in."

"I am not prepared to wait all the night for it." Francis took out a purse and from it some gold coins. "I'll pay you my rent now, so that you can't be the loser."

The landlord's eyes boggled. "It's but a small chamber, your honour, and but a single bed."

"I have no care for the size of the bed."

The landlord stared again and then turned to the potboy. "Here, Charlie, take this gent up to number six."

Francis paid his dues and followed the boy up the creaking stairs. Once in the room and rid of the boy he shut the door and turned the key. A low narrow chamber with a plain deal table before the empty fireplace, a single bed by the half-shuttered window, two candles flickering, lifting the shadows beside the bed. He leaned against the door for a minute, taking in the room, then picked up one of the candles and carried it to the table. Then he undid his bag, took out a clean shirt, washed himself, put on the shirt and a clean neck-cloth. He sat down at the table, took some sheets of paper from his bag, and after some thought began to write. All this was undertaken with deliberation but it was not quite the deliberation of drunkenness. He had passed through drunkenness to a deadly sobriety beyond.

For five minutes the room was possessed by a new quiet made explicit by the single scratching whisper of the pen. Occasionally there were noises outside, or a burst of laughter would drift up through the squat walls from the taproom like echoes of a remote world. Just now and then one of the candle flames would tremble and a flicker of smoke come into being and detach itself and drift away. He wrote with a concentration which came from both outward and inner urgency: he was not only writing against the clock but against some imperative mechanism within himself which told him that the thing he had to do could wait no longer.

At length he signed his name, got up, went to his bag again, took out a pistol. It was a single-barrel duelling weapon of the flintlock type employing a heavy bullet and a light charge of powder. He primed it and set it on the table beside him. Then he looked round. All was ready. The silence of the room had become oppressive, it beat in his ears; it echoed the terror of the final initiative, the last compulsion of mind and muscle to which all this had been proceeding as a river hurries to the annihilation of the sea.

He raised the pistol to his head.

The hospital, Dwight found, consisted of a few rooms on the first floor of a squat building near the assize court. Beneath it was the Reading Society; you visited the ground floor to gain a book, the first floor to lose a leg. He was not fortunate enough to find Dr. Halliwell, who had not yet returned from a day's shooting, but a stout dropsical woman, after a brief suspicious argument at the door, showed him round the two wards.

The beds were arranged much on the London principle, built into the walls, with wooden sides, rather like great drawers pulled out of a cabinet, each ward being lit by a single lantern in which a squat candle steadily burned. The crowds and events of the week had brought their crop of accidents and illnesses, so the hospital was fairly full. There was the usual close and horrid smell. The patients were four in a bed, lying head to feet; and there did not seem to have been much attempt to sort them out according to their various infirmities. Under the lantern a woman who had had her hand amputated shared a bed with another in the first stages of labour, and the third in their company, to any trained eye, was plainly dying. She had a flushed, feverish face, and pale violet blotches on her hands, and her breathing was halting and strained.

"A doxy found in the streets," said the stout woman, hitching up her stomach. "Give birth to twin boys a week past. She'll be gone afore morning, if you ask me. . . . This other one's been in labour no more than an hour yet. Tis her father's child, they say, though *she'll* say naught. We put 'em in together for company like. . . . This here be the men's ward."

Dwight did not stay long. He did not know Dr. Halliwell, and one could never be sure that his visit might not be unwelcome. When he got out into the street again he took some grateful breaths of the night air. It had been raining heavily while he was inside, and more was blowing up from the west; but it had not at all damped the spirits of the revellers, and there were dozens still roistering in the streets. He saw two of the more respectable merchants being pushed home in wheelbarrows.

The innkeeper met him with the news of the unexpected visitor. Dwight had forgotten all about his morning invitation to Francis, and their encounter this afternoon made him wish he'd never issued it. He went up the stairs expecting to find his guest sprawling asleep on the bed, and his irritation was increased when he found the door locked. He thumped on it impatiently, hoping his guest was not too drunk to hear. There was no reply. It was too bad, for there might be no means of waking the man before morning. The landlord probably would not have another key, even supposing this one was not blocking the keyhole on the other side.

Dwight thumped again with all his strength. The dark narrow passage was cobwebbed in every corner, and there were cracks along the walls where they bulged as if some superior weight was leaning on them from the other side. A claustrophobe would have shrunk and hurried through before they collapsed together and trapped him. From one of the wider cracks near the door a black beetle showed up for a moment as if disturbed and resenting the noise. Suddenly Dwight heard a movement inside the room and the key turn.

With relief he lifted the latch and went in and was surprised to see the bed empty and unused and Francis walking slowly back to the table on which the two candles burned.

His irritation going, Dwight laughed a little awkwardly.

"You'll excuse the noise. I thought you might be asleep."

Francis did not reply but sat down at the table and stared at two sheets of paper in front of him. He didn't look as drunk as when they last met. With mounting surprise Dwight noticed the clean shirt, the neat neckcloth—and the completely bloodless face.

He said: "The landlord told me you'd come. I thought you might have difficulty. The town is fairly seething."

"Yes," said Francis.

Aware of some deeper tension within the room than he had yet penetrated to, Dwight slowly unbuttoned his coat and threw it off, stood for a moment in his shirt sleeves, uncomfortable, hesitating. The other man's silence forced him to go on.

"I was sorry for leaving so sharply this afternoon, but, as I explained, I had to rejoin a friend. You've supped, I suppose?"

"What? Oh, yes."

"If you're writing a letter go on with it."

"No."

Silence fell. Dwight stared at the other more closely. "What's wrong?"

"Are you a fatalist, Enys?" Francis brought his brows together in a sudden grimace of nervous resentment. It broke over his frozen face like a storm. "D'you believe we are masters of ourselves or merely dance like puppets on strings, having the illusion of independence? I don't know."

"I'm afraid I'm a little tired for a philosophical discussion. Have you some personal problem before you that puts the question more conveniently?"

"Only this." Francis swept the papers impatiently aside and picked up the pistol they had covered. "Five minutes ago I tried to shoot myself. The thing misfired. Since then I have been debating whether I should try again."

A glance showed Dwight that the other man was not joking. He stared at Francis, trying to find something to say.

"You're a little shocked," Francis said, and pointed the pistol at his face and squinted down the barrel, his finger on the trigger. "Of course it wouldn't have been in the best of taste—to have made use of the hospitality of your chamber for such a purpose—but none of my own was to be had, and to do it in some dark corner of a street is faintly vulgar. I'm sorry. Anyway, the thing's not done yet, so you have a talkative companion for a few moments instead of a silent one."

Dwight stared at him, resisting the impulse to say or do the obvious things. A wrong move might be fatal. After a long minute he forced himself to relax, to move across to the ewer and basin by the window so that his back was towards the other. He began to wash his hands, and found they were not quite steady. He felt that Francis was closely watching him.

"I don't understand you," he said at length. "I don't understand why you could possibly wish to destroy yourself —and, if you did, why you should ride twenty-five miles to a strange town to do it."

There was a rustle of papers as if Francis were putting them together.

"The deceased behaved irrationally before he died. Is that it? But who behaves rationally even when wanting to stay alive? If we were thinking brains suspended in fluid . . . But we're not. We have viscera, my dear Enys, as you should know; and nerves and blood and things called emotions. One can develop a quite unreasoning prejudice against spilling one's blood on one's own doorstep. Impulses are hard to put under a slide rule."

"If this was an impulse, then I hope it's past."

"No, it is not. But now you are here give me your opinion. What happens to a resolve when you put the barrel to your head and pull the trigger and the hammer clicks and nothing takes place? Do you accept the jibe, not having had the foresight to buy fresh powder or the intelligence to realise that powder kept long in this damned Cornish atmosphere gets damp? Or is it the last humiliation to shirk another try?"

Dwight began to dry his hands. "It's the only sensible course. But you didn't quite answer my question. Why suicide? If I may say so, you're young, propertied, respected, have a wife and son, safely got through serious illness, are under no cloud——"

"Stop," said Francis, "or I shall weep for joy."

Dwight half turned, and out of the corner of his eye saw that the pistol now lay on the table again, a hand resting lightly on it. "Well, if you were your cousin, I might see a greater reason for all this. He has lost his only child, is likely to have some sentence to-morrow, failed last year in an enterprise he put all his heart to . . ."

Francis got up, pushing the table aside with a squeak, stalked across the room. "God damn you, be quiet. . . ."

Dwight set down the towel. "No doubt Ross still has his self-respect. Which you perhaps have lost. . . ."

Francis turned. At close quarters his face was streaky with dried sweat. "What makes you say that?"

The pistol was a long way away. Dwight felt a little more confident of being able to deal with this situation.

"I think there must be a loss of self-respect before suicide can be even thought of."

"You do, eh?"

"Yes, I do."

Francis made the facial movements of a laughter which was more bitter for its silence. "There are times when it may be the only means of restoring one's self-respect. Can you conceive that, or is it outside your scope?"

"It's not outside my scope to imagine such a situation. But I'm not able to imagine why you should feel yourself in it."

"Let's see, what were those gracious words you used: young, propertied, respected? But young by what standards? And propertied, did you say? The question is, who owns property in these bankrupt days? Usually some upstart sneering moneylender with a smooth voice and the ethical code of a cuttlefish. . . . And respect?" Francis said the word savagely. "Respected by whom? We are back at the same old gate, respect of oneself, which is the impasse. Drink loosens the disillusion but sharpens the paradox. A pistol ball has no morning after."

Dwight went across and lit another couple of candles on the mantelpiece. The shadows at the end of the room lifted, showing the faded flock paper, the dusty antlers of the stag. The light was like a creeping sanity, moving over the dark places of the mind. "A pistol ball is very—dramatic," he said slowly.

"Sudden solutions usually are. You ought to know that—in your profession. But you can't rule them out because they offend your sense of propriety."

"Oh, I don't. All the same, I prefer things on a more homely level. Let's have a drink and talk it over. What's the hurry? We've all night before us."

"Dear God . . ." Francis let out a slow breath and turned away. "My tongue's like burnt paper. . . ."

In the street outside someone was laughing inanely. Dwight went to the cupboard.

"I've brandy here. We can sample that." He heard Francis folding the papers and stuffing them into a pocket. When he turned Francis had picked up the pistol again, but was taking out the bullet. Half done, he hesitated and the glitter came back into his eyes.

"Drink this," said Dwight quickly. "Cheap gin will poison you and bring up all sorts of unhealthy thoughts."

"The thoughts were there without the gin."

"Well, you can tell me about them if it pleases you. I don't mind."

"Thank you, but I'll keep my sorrows to myself." He accepted the glass and looked at it. "Well, here's to the devil. I don't know whose side he has been on to-night."

Dwight drank without comment. The emotional storm was blowing itself out. Chance had prevented Francis from making his gesture. In exhaustion he would now wish to talk of anything but to-night's motives. But that was just why it was important that he should do so. Only by getting him to talk it out of himself could one make reasonably sure that the crisis should not happen again.

Chapter Ten

Before the Reformation the Franciscans had been a power in the town, owning much of the property at its heart; and although the monks no longer walked the streets in their grey habits or cared for the sick and poor, the property remained as their monument, turned to secular use but unmistakably ecclesiastical in design. Of such was the Refectory of the Grey Friars, where the assizes were held.

Its Great Hall, a hundred and fifty-odd feet long and sixty in height, with its east window of stained glass, was an impressive chamber; but it bore its age—a matter of five hundred years—with increasing uncertainty, and there were other drawbacks to its use as a court of justice.

The weather turned from warm to sultry overnight, and when dawn broke a thick mist had fallen over the town. It did not clear much as the sun gained power, and when the judges walked across from their lodgings in their wigs and ermine the fog drifted about them like wet smoke.

Demelza had had a terrible night, dozing to find nightmares round every corner and starting into a wakeful reality which was no escape. She felt that she had failed utterly last evening, that the outcome of all her efforts had been a futile conversation without issue and without point, that she had failed Ross in every way.

It was not until last night that she had realised how much she had been privately and foolishly building on her own efforts; all these weeks of waiting she had fed on the hope of being able to give crucial help. Yet it was some native good sense which had prevented her from pressing her overtures with the judge when they at last met. She bitterly blamed herself now for not casting herself and her story on his mercy; but if she had been confronted with the opportunity again she would have done just the same. Ill judgment might have conceived the meeting, but good judgment had saved it from the worst disaster.

Verity had been nearly as upset as she when she returned. Francis had called, in a strange drunken mood, and had departed in a stranger, which left her in a state of increasing anxiety. Worried almost equally for both the Poldarks, she too had hardly slept, and when she saw Francis ahead of her going into the assize courts she felt sudden relief, as if she had not expected to see him safe and well to-day. But the other care remained, and when she got inside, the anxiety was doubled by what she saw of the earlier cases that came on.

Places had been saved for them near the front of the hall, which was already crowded when they took their seats. Guards and turnkeys, jurors and witnesses, barristers and notaries filled the front of the hall, and behind were the public places. The few front rows here had been saved for people of note, and many who were in town for the elections had come to see the fun. Verity saw Unwin Trevaunance with a red-haired girl, and Sir Hugh Bodrugan and several ladies and gentlemen of quality with fans and snuffboxes. In a corner by himself, holding a long malacca stick, was George Warleggan. Behind these rows were the rabble.

The hall, though high, was ill ventilated and stuffy, and one could tell that it would soon grow hot with the press. There were men at the door and inside selling hot pasties and chestnuts and lemonade, but they were driven out just before ten o'clock. Then the clerk of the court rapped with his hammer and everyone stood up, and the Hon. Mr. Justice Lister, connoisseur of church music, came in, bowed solemnly to the court, and sat down with the sheriffs and aldermen. He pulled the great bunch of aromatic herbs nearer to him and put a vinegar-soaked handkerchief on the top of his papers. Another heavy day was begun.

The first case was soon disposed of. Demelza could not follow the matter at all. The counsel speaking had such a plummy voice that she only caught one word in three, but she gathered it was something to do with what were called the prisoner's recognisances. These being discharged, the man was marched out of the dock again. Then there was a hum of interest as three men and two women were ushered in together. One of the men was Ross Poldark. His dark coppery hair was well combed, the scar, as always at times of stress, noticeable on his cheek. He looked paler from his week's imprisonment. She remembered Jim Carter's fate.

They were swearing in a jury, but she heard nothing of it. She was thinking of Ross as she had seen him for the first time, that day years ago at Redruth Fair. To her it seemed a century—yet though she had grown older, changed beyond recognition or imagining, he had become curiously younger to her while remaining in essence the same. He was a man of moods, yet he was her constant, something unchanging, infinitely reliable, the pivot of her life. There could never be anyone else. Without him she would not be more than half alive.

Mr. Justice Lister looked hollow-eyed and inhuman this morning, capable of any enormity. The jury were sworn in and there were no objections. Now, to Demelza's surprise, all but one of the prisoners were led out again, Ross among them.

The trial of the Crown versus Boynton, F.R., for larceny had begun.

She didn't listen to it. It passed over her head in a sickly haze which would be remembered more vividly than it was experienced. Only some time later she heard the jury find the prisoner guilty of stealing a pair of knit-thread lady's stockings, value two shillings and sixpence, and a packet containing half a thousand pins, value sixpence, from a haberdasher's shop. She heard Mr. Justice Lister take into account that this was a first offence and sentence him to be burnt in the hand and discharged. Hardly had he been led away than the two women came in and the next case was on. She realised with a dreadful sinking apprehension that Ross was next.

The two women were vagrants. They had been caught flagrantly begging. They had no visible means of support. It was a plain case and the jury speedily found them guilty. But this was a crime on which the Hon. Mr. Justice Lister felt rather strongly and he delivered a long and damning homily on the evils of such a life. Looking at him, Demelza realised there was no mercy here. His diction was beautiful, his phrases as elegantly rounded as if they had been written out the night before. But the substance was to condemn. Abruptly, without any raising of the voice or change of expression, he sentenced the two women to be whipped and the case was over.

At this there was a good deal of stirring in the court, for some of the men wanted to push their way out to see the women stripped and flogged in the church square, and others were as anxious to take the vacant places; so it was in the midst of this confusion that Ross was led in. This time as he passed to the dock he glanced a moment aside and his eyes caught Demelza. A faint encouraging smile flickered across his face and was gone.

"Quiet," said Verity. "Quiet, my dear. We must try to keep calm." She put her arm round Demelza and held her tight.

It was clear now that this was the important case of the

day. More barristers-at-law came in, and the bench on which they sat was full. Demelza tried to see some change in the judge's expression, some flicker of interest, but there was none. He might never have met Mrs. Ross Poldark the night before. Mr. Jeffery Clymer sat just below the dock, where he could maintain contact with his client. Henry Bull, K.C., leading counsel for the Crown, had left the preceding cases to his junior, but this one he was handling himself. A dark man and handsome in a coarse way, with skin so olive and eyes so amber as to suggest a touch of the tar brush. It had been to his disadvantage all his life; he had had to struggle hard against the whispering voices of his colleagues and rivals—and the struggle had left its mark.

The clerk of arraigns began proceedings by saying:

"Ross Vennor Poldark, hold up thy hand. Gentlemen of the jury, look upon the prisoner. He stands indicted by the name of Ross Vennor Poldark, of Nampara, of the County of Cornwall, Esquire, who, on the seventh of January in the year of our Lord seventeen hundred and ninety, not having the fear of God before his eyes but being moved and seduced by the instigation of the devil, did incite divers peaceable citizens to riot, and furthermore did commit riot contrary to the laws of the land. And furthermore that the said Ross Vennor Poldark feloniously, wilfully and with malice aforethought, with force and arms, did plunder, steal, destroy and take away divers goods belonging to two ships in distress. And furthermore . . ."

The voice went on, it seemed to Demelza for hours, saying the same things over and over again in different words. She felt really faint now, but tried to hide it. Eventually the voice stopped. Then Ross said: "Not guilty," and the clerk said: "Culprit, how will thou be tried?" and Ross said: "By God and my country." Then the dark foreign man got up and began to say it all over again.

But here was a difference. The clerk had droned his words —legal phrases dry and brittle as seed husks which didn't seem to have any life in them. Mr. Henry Bull, K.C., breathed on them and brought them to life with a vengeance. He was

telling a simple story to the jury—no official stuff in this—
just a simple story which anyone could follow.

It seemed that in the great gale of January last, which they
would all no doubt remember, a ship—a Cornish-owned ship,
mark you—got into distress and was driven ashore on Hendrawna Beach, just below the house of the prisoner, a man
comfortably circumstanced, a mine owner and a landowner
with an ancient name. The jury might have expected that such
a man's first thought—he being the first to see the ship—
would have been for the safety of those on board. Instead, as
evidence would be brought to prove, his only concern had
been to rouse the lawless spirits of the neighbourhood in
great numbers, so that when the wreck came in it should be
plundered with the utmost dispatch. And that it was plundered, in a matter of a few hours, and without a thought for
the safety of the crew or any attempt to help them ashore,
witnesses would be called to show. The man who stood in
the dock had personally swum out to the wreck before anyone
else and personally directed operations for the dismember-
ment of the ship. At this time there had been one passenger
still left on board. No one knew whether prompt help could
have saved him. It was only known that no such help was
given and that the man lost his life.

Counsel further suggested that the prisoner had had
watchers posted all along the cliffs keeping a lookout for
further prey, for when yet another ship, the *Pride of Madras*,
was driven ashore a few hours later, all the dissident and
lawless sweepings from five parishes were waiting to welcome her in—and it was doubtful if, even supposing the
crew could have got her off again with the flood tide, she
could not have been held ashore by sheer weight of numbers.
All this at the instigation of the prisoner, who must bear the
perfidy of the acts of his followers. Some of the crew of this
ship had been severely beaten as they struggled ashore and
robbed even of their clothes. They had been left insensible
and naked in the freezing cold, and it was virtually certain
that among those who lost their lives there were several who
should be alive to-day had they received the Christian treat-

ment any distressed sailor was entitled to expect. Their ship had been torn to pieces in a single tide. The ship's master, Captain A. V. Clark, would be called to testify that he had not been so barbarously used when cast ashore among the savages of Patagonia two years earlier.

Even this was not all—by no means the worst of it—and Henry Bull wagged a long brown forefinger. When His Majesty's excise men, supported by a small contingent of dismounted dragoons, had come upon the scene the prisoner had come before them and warned them not to interfere, at peril of their lives—had threatened them in the most direct and offensive manner. When they disregarded this and went down upon the beach they were set on by the prisoner and others, and a serious fight had developed and one of the excise men, John Coppard, had received very serious injuries. There were, in fact, two deaths on the beach that night among the rioters, and many injured. Reliable witnesses put the numbers of the wreckers at two thousand.

The voice went on, welling sometimes in Demelza's ears, at others growing faint and far away. Indiscriminately it piled up the calumny, the truth, the lies and the half-truths, until she felt she must scream. It was very hot in the hall; the windows were steaming up and the walls running with moisture. She wished now she had never come—anything better than listening to this. She tried to stop her ears, but that was no use. If the worst was to be heard she had to listen.

At last Bull came to the close of his speech. It was not within his present scope to call the jury's attention, he said, to the previous acts of lawlessness which had disfigured the prisoner's character. But . . .

Here Mr. Jeffery Clymer, who had been drawing circles and squares with his pen, leapt to his feet and vehemently protested—a protest which was upheld by the judge, and Mr. Bull was forced to withdraw. This he did willingly, having planted what he wanted in the jury's mind. It was not permissible to say *anything* about the prisoner's previous character, he went on; *but*—and here was the big but—it was admissible and very relevant to draw deductions from certain statements prisoner had made to the examining justice—statements which attempted to *justify* his actions, statements which branded him as an obvious Jacobin and an admirer of the bloodshed and tyranny across the water. Such men, Bull went on to imply, were doubly dangerous at times like these. Each member of the jury must be possessed of some property. If he wished to keep that property intact, men like the prisoner must be made an example of. The flame of sedition and unrest must be stamped on at its very outset. A sometime soldier and gentleman had a special responsibility. For him to side with the rogues and riffraff of the towns, encouraging them and instructing them in acts of violence they would not by themselves have the wit or intelligence to conceive, was an outrage on society. Such a man deserved to be put away. Hanging was barely good enough. Justice must be done, and he demanded no less than justice.

When he sat down there was a visible stirring in the court; and then after a minute junior counsel for the Crown got up and added a further speech of his own, it being the custom in serious cases to allow two speeches for the prosecution and none for the defence. At last it was over and the first witness was called. This was Nicholas Vigus.

He came into the courtroom blinking, hesitating, a cherub surprised in some nefarious practice. In an age when wigs were so much worn, the smooth fresh tight skin of his head seemed in indecent contrast with the pockmarks in his face. In his thin sly voice, growing more confident as he went on, he testified that on the morning in question he had been wakened soon after dawn by the prisoner thunderously knocking on the next-door cottage and calling "Zacky! Zacky! Good pickings for all! There's a wreck coming ashore and we'll strip her to the last plank!" Later he deposed to seeing the prisoner on the shore leading operations and generally directing the crowds, also that the accused had been the first to swim to the ship and board her. Also he had directed operations against the second ship and been generally active all through the day. Witness had seen accused go up to excise officers when they arrived and have high words with them but had not been near enough to hear what passed. Later he had gone away and not been present at the fight. That concluded his evidence. Everyone looked at Ross.

Ross cleared his throat. The beginning for him. Till now he had been unable to disrelate himself from a spectator's part, critical, unstirred, noting the colour of Mr. Henry Bull's fingernails more than his invective, judging the ages and occupations of the jury without much thought to the fact that they were judging him. Now he must stir himself to fight, must feel this thing personally and passionately if he were to survive. The conflict between Clymer's advice and his own inclinations was still unresolved. But sight of Demelza had made him feel that he must fight.

"Was there a very strong gale blowing that morning, Nick?"

Vigus blinked slyly at Ross, the confidence ebbing again. "'S, I reckon."

"It's true, isn't it, that the Martin cottage is not next door to yours but next but one."

"'S, I reckon. Daniel's is between."

"You must have had good hearing to have been sure of what I said so far away."

"Oh, 'tisn't so far away. I 'eard what you said sure 'nough."

"Have you always resented it that I didn't wake *you*?"

There was a little cackle of laughter at the back of the court.

"Made no diff'rence to me," said Vigus sullenly. "I wasn't consarned with a wreck."

"But you were on the beach all through the day?"

"Off and on, like. I went down to see what was to do."

"Did you not play any part in salvaging things that were being washed ashore?"

"No. I aren't one of those sort."

"Not ever?"

"No."

"D'you mean you live near the beach and yet never pick up things that are washed ashore from wrecks?"

"Oh . . . sometimes. But not this time. Not when tis a proper wreck with men drowning, and the like."

"Did you help the men who were drowning?"

"No-o."

"Why not?"

"I didn't happen to see any."

"Did you see me swim out to the first wreck?"

". . . Yes."

"Didn't I carry a line with me?"

"Mebbe. I don't recall."

"What does that suggest?"

"Don't know. It don't suggest nothing to me."

Ross glanced at Mr. Clymer, who instantly shook his wigged head. Nick Vigus was allowed to go. Three more witnesses were brought in to testify to certain aspects of the story and to confirm what Nick Vigus said. Then the usher spoke again.

"Call Jud Paynter."

Demelza stared at their onetime servant as he sidled slowly to the witness box, walking rather as if he hoped he wouldn't be noticed getting there. It was quite unbelievable to her that he should be in this company—prepared to testify against Ross, barefaced in a court of law. Verity put a restraining hand on her arm again as she seemed about to stand up. Jud mumbled through the oath, then looked round for somewhere to spit, but thought better of it and glanced at Mr. Henry Bull who was waiting for him.

"Your name is Jud Paynter and you live with your wife in Grambler village?"

"Ais."

"Tell us what happened on the morning of the seventh January last."

"Well . . ." Jud cleared his throat. "Me and the old woman was asleep—that's Prudie, see . . ."

"You mean your wife?"

"Well . . . yes, sur, in a manner o' speaking . . ." Jud smiled apologetically. "Prudie and me was asleep when along come Cap'n Ross makin' a rare to-do, and afore I can

113

spring up and unclitch the door 'e bursts it off its hapses and rushes in and says there's a ship ashore down to Hendrawna Beach. 'Do ee bestir yourself good an' fine,' he says. We was always the best of friends, Cap'n Ross and me. Many's the time when 'e was a little tacker no biggerer'n pot high——"

"Yes, yes. Keep to the point. What then?"

Jud's bloodshot eyes roamed round the court, carefully avoiding contact with all comers.

"Yes, what then?"

"Then he says to me he says, 'Do ee go run and roust all the men ye can—for like as not thur's women and childer on the ship,' he says, 'and they must be saved from a watery grave. . . .'"

There was a moment's irritable consultation between the law officers.

"Come, my man, recollect yourself," said Henry Bull. "Think again."

Jud stared up at the Gothic roof for inspiration. Then he licked his gums.

"Well?"

"Well, that's what 'e said, sur. Sure 'nough."

"And I tell you to think again. What you say is not in accordance with your sworn statement."

"What?"

"You did not say this when giving testimony before the Crown's attorney and his clerk."

"Eh?"

"Tell us what you originally said."

"That's what I said: no more'n no less."

"Nonsense, man. Have I your lordship's permission? What you said was—let me read it to you—'When Captain Poldark came to my hut he told me to hurry down and rouse my friends because there was a wreck, and the sooner it was stripped the better, before the preventive men turned up.' That was what you said."

Jud squeezed up his face for a second, and then let it set into a look of hurt reproach.

"Nay, *nay*, sur, I never heard such words out of me mouth! Yer worship, I never thought upon no such thing. Tedn fair, tedn just, tedn *right*."

"This statement, I would remind you, Paynter, was made before witnesses and signed with your mark. It was read over to you before you signed."

"Well, I'm 'ard of hearing," said Jud, staring barefaced at the counsel. "Tes more'n likely they mistook what I did say an' I mistook what they did say. Tes more'n likely, that's for certain."

Mr. Bull angrily swung his gown behind him and bent over his brief. He proceeded to lead Jud through the story of the day, but very soon there was another disagreement and another angry argument. Upon it came Mr. Justice Lister's cold quiet voice.

"Do you know, witness, what the punishment is for perjury?"

"Perjury?" said Jud. "I ain't never done nothing like it, yer worship. I can't even write me own name, leave alone other folk's. And I was never near the wrecks but once and then twas to lend a 'elping 'and wi' the folk struggling in the waves. Nobody'd do less'n lend a 'elping 'and."

The judge gazed at Paynter for a long steady moment, then said: "I don't think this witness is going to assist your case, Mr. Bull."

Mr. Clymer got up in a very fatigued manner. "May I draw your lordship's attention to the fact that in the first instance, when called before an examining justice, Paynter gave no such evidence as he is alleged to have done at a later date. He seems to have denied knowledge of the events we are dealing with."

There was some angry argument and rustling of papers. But Henry Bull was not giving up. "There is some very important evidence at a later stage, your lordship. If I might put that to the witness . . ."

"Very well."

"Now, Paynter," said Bull, fixing him with an eye, "turn your mind to the events on the night of the seventh. You were present when the excise men and the soldiers came upon the beach. In your statement you say that the prisoner, Captain Poldark, was the leader of the men who attacked the excise officers and that you saw him strike John Coppard, who fell to the ground seriously injured. That is a true statement, is it not? Remember his lordship's warning: you are on oath. You can be sent to prison yourself!"

Jud sucked his two teeth and hesitated. "Nay!" he said suddenly, almost under his breath. "I don't know nothin' 'bout'n."

"What? What's that?" said the judge.

"Tes all a new story to me, your worship. I never heard such words out o' me mouth. Tedn true. Tedn nothin'!"

Henry Bull took a deep breath. He turned sharply to the judge. "My lord, I ask your permission to call Mr. Tankard and Mr. Blencowe."

Mr. Justice Lister moved the aromatic herbs before his nose.

"I would remind you, Mr. Bull, of the case of Nairn and Ogilvie—which cannot be unfamiliar to you—when the court remained in session without a break for forty-three hours. I do not intend that to happen here—and you have a lot of witnesses yet to call."

Bull flapped his gown irritably. "M'lord, this is a matter of the gravest importance. This man has just made a very serious charge against two junior officers of the Crown. It seems to me vital——"

"I should have thought, Mr. Bull," said his lordship wearily, "that the situation was plain to the meanest intelligence. This witness has clearly committed perjury at some period of the proceedings. Whether he committed it at an earlier stage or is committing it now is not surely of great importance to your case, since the evidence of a perjured witness can hardly bear much weight. Whether the Crown wishes to charge him on that account is a matter for the appropriate officers to decide. I should certainly not oppose it. But it must also be perfectly clear that this man is of such low intelligence and limited mental capacity that it would in any case be difficult to draw a distinction between wilful and natural stupidity. If you will accept my advice you will turn him out of the box and get on with your case."

"Of course it is as your lordship pleases," said Bull sulkily, and Jud was ushered unceremoniously from the court.

Chapter Eleven

While the next witnesses were making their procession to and from the box Verity watched the jury. They were decently dressed, sober-looking men, mostly of middle age: small gentry and tradesmen. In Cornwall as a whole there would be a certain lack of condemnation for the things Ross had done or was accused of doing. Wrecks were looked on as legitimate spoil. Excise men were the most hated and despised of people. But Henry Bull had been cunning in his final appeal. Among propertied people there was now an almost universal dread of a miners' insurrection. Jacobin clubs which had opened in England to lend the French revolutionaries support, the wild scenes in Redruth last autumn, the recurring bread riots, and the seething discontent of which they were a symptom, all tended to a feeling of horrid insecurity. One saved one's twenty pounds a year, one built a new linhay or bought a new farm cart with a sense of uncertainty about the future. It was very unsettling, and if a riot such as this they were hearing about was allowed to pass without heavy punishment for the ringleader . . .

Captain Clark was in the box, and described the scenes on the beach that night as a Dante's Inferno, with great bonfires blazing, hundreds of drunken men and women capering and fighting, mules laden to breaking point with spoils from his ship, assaults upon his poor shipwrecked crew, how he and two other men stood guard over the passengers with knives and a drawn sword to save them from being torn to pieces.

When it was done there was an unaccustomed silence in the court. The sailor had brought the scene vividly to life, and it seemed that the people in the court were picturing it, some of them shocked that their countryfolk should have gone so far. Eventually Ross said: "Captain Clark, do you recall my coming to you on the beach and offering you and your crew shelter for the night in my house?"

Clark said: "I do indeed, sir. It was the first act of common charity shown us on that dreadful night."

"Did you avail yourself of it?"

"Yes, most certainly. Nineteen of us in all spent the night in your home."

"You were well treated there?"

"Most kindly treated."

"Did you, while you were on the beach, hear me or see me encouraging anyone to wreck your ship?"

"No, sir. . . . I may say it was dark except for the bonfires. But I hadn't set eyes on you until you came forward and offered us shelter."

"Thank you." Ross leaned over and had a whispered consultation with Mr. Clymer. "Captain Clark, did you see the meeting between myself and the sergeant of dragoons?"

"Yes."

"Was there any quarrel between us?"

"As far as I remember, you warned him not to go down to the beach and he accepted your warning."

"Would you consider it a friendly warning that I offered, meant to avoid bloodshed?"

"It could have been. Yes, I think it's fair to say so."

"There was no fight between us?"

"Not when I was there, certainly not."

"Did I accompany you into the house?"

"You did."

"Thank you."

"One moment, Captain," said Henry Bull, whisking up as the sailor was about to leave the box. "How long did the accused stay with you when you entered the house?"

"Oh, about ten minutes."

"And when did you see him next?"

"About an hour later."

"Were there any excise men in the party when you met the troopers?"

"Not that I saw or noticed."

"There was nothing, so far as you know, to prevent the accused leaving the house again as soon as you were settled, and having a further argument with the soldiers?"

"No, sir."

"Thank you. Call Captain Ephraim Trevail."

A short thin man came to the stand, and stated that he had witnessed the fight between the excise men and the soldiers, and verified that he had seen Ross as the ringleader and identified him as the man who had struck John Coppard down. So far as Ross knew he had never seen him before, but he could not shake his evidence. Mr. Jeffery Clymer passed up a note telling him not to press a hostile witness. Then Eli Clemmow was called and told exactly the same story. It was more than three years since Ross had seen this man. He felt his anger rise.

When it was his turn to speak he said: "Where do you live, Clemmow?"

The man's lips slipped back to expose his prominent teeth. They were like a special malice which had been kept hidden until now. "Truro."

"How was it that you were at Hendrawna, nine miles away, when the wreck came in?"

"I wasn't. I 'eard tell about the first wreck and walked over to see the fun."

"At one time you lived on my land, didn't you?"

"'Sright."

"But I turned you off, d'you remember, because you were a constant worry and disturbance to the neighbourhood."

"You mean you turned *brother* out of house and home—for doin' nothing 't all!"

"You hate me for it, don't you?"

Eli checked. "Nay . . . nay. I care naught for ee."

Mr. Clymer passed Ross a note which read: "Can you shake him as to detail?"

Ross said slowly: "Tell me, Clemmow, which of the two wrecks came in closest to my house?"

The lips sucked but there was no reply. After a time Ross said: "Did you hear my question?"

"Twas dark when I got there."

"Which was the bigger of the two ships?"

After a long pause: "*Pride o' Madras.*"

"How many masts had she?"

". . . two or three."

"How did you know which she was?"

"I—'eard tell."

"Was the bigger one nearest my house or farthest away?"

Another pause.

Ross said: "I suppose you saw the bonfire on Damsel Point?"

". . . Yes."

"There was *no* bonfire on Damsel Point or near it. You were never on Hendrawna Beach that night, were you? You never left Truro."

"Yes, I were! You're only tryin' to trick me!" Eli Clemmow's face was white and tight. He went on to explain; but Mr. Henry Bull, rising again, cut him short.

"Have you ever been to sea, Mr. Clemmow?"

"Well—er—no, not so's you could say 'to sea.' But——"

"So that if there were two shipwrecks on a beach in the dark, some distance from each other, you might find it hard, having no expert knowledge, to say which was the larger?"

"Yes, that's true 'nough!"

"Much harder, no doubt, than if you had helped actively to wreck the ships and assault the crews?"

Eli nodded gratefully.

"Did you notice where the bonfires were particularly?"

"No. They was about—just 'ere and thur."

"How far were you from the struggle which developed between the prisoner and the excise men?"

"Which it is *alleged* developed," said Mr. Jeffery Clymer, getting up and sitting down again all in one movement.

"Which it is alleged developed?"

"Oh . . . close as you are to me."

"And the story you have told on oath—that is a true eye-witness account of what took place?"

"Yes, true as I'm standing here!"

Demelza's faintness kept coming in waves. It would lean over her and then at the last moment move away again, leaving her shaken and sick. The excise man, Coppard, had been called, had confirmed the general story, but, to give him credit, had been vague as to whether he had been attacked by the accused or even whether the accused man had been there at all. The sergeant of dragoons had come and gone. The afternoon was half spent, and so far there had been no break for refreshments. Two street sellers had got in through the half-closed doors and were doing brisk if illicit business in the back rows. The heat and the smell were stifling.

The last witness for the prosecution was Hick, the justice who had taken all the depositions, including Ross's own. Some difficulty had arisen on the Truro bench when it became known that the law expected them to proceed with this case. Some of the magistrates were so favourably disposed towards the accused man that it would have been plainly unfair for them to have taken charge. Others, such as the Rev. Dr. Halse, were equally prejudiced against him. In the end the nonentity, Ephraim Hick, had been chosen to preside. Hick's main interest was the brandy bottle—but the depositions had come through with a fair enough degree of impartiality.

Hick now had to put in this testimony and this testimony was dangerous in the extreme.

From the answers the prisoner had made at his interrogation it appeared that he fully admitted the charge of having roused the neighbourhood when the first wreck came in. To the question, "What purpose had you in mind?" he had answered, "There were families in the district who were starving." Question, "Did you lead these people to the wreck?" Answer, "They needed no leading. They knew the district as well as I did." Question, "Did you incite them to attack the crew of the *Queen Charlotte*?" Answer, "None of the crew of the *Queen Charlotte* was attacked." "Were you the first to board her, and, if so, what was your purpose in so doing?" "My purpose was to see what cargo she carried." "Was any of the crew left on board when you reached her?" "No, only one passenger, and he was dead." "Was he dead when you reached the ship?" "Of course. Are you accusing me of murdering him?" "Did you help your friends to board the ship by means of a line?" "Yes." "Did you make any effort to get the body of the dead man ashore?" "None whatever." "Did you help to wreck the ship and carry away its cargo?" "No." "Were you present while this was being done?" "Yes." "Did you make any attempt to stop it?" "None at all. I am not a magistrate." "But you were the only gentleman present, the only person with sufficient authority to stop this plundering in its early stages?" "You exaggerate my influence."

Later on the interrogation went on: "Were you among the first persons to see the second shipwreck?" "I believe so." "Did you encourage your friends to attack the crew of the *Pride of Madras*?" "Certainly not." "Did you stand by and let them be assaulted without protest?" "They were not assaulted by any men known to me. By this time great numbers of miners were on the beach from farther afield." "That doesn't answer my question." "It is all the answer I can give you. I was not able to be in every place at the same time." "But you went aboard the *Pride of Madras*?" "I did." "Long before offering the shipwrecked sailors any help?" "Some time before." "Did you approve of this riot which had started?" "I did not consider it a riot." "Do you approve of it now?" "Do you approve of whole families being without enough food to keep them alive?"

At the end the accused had denied all knowledge of the attack upon the soldiers and excise men.

This concluded the Crown's case.

There were only five witnesses for the defence. First were

John and Jane Gimlett, who were called to testify that the prisoner had not left the house again after entering it with the shipwrecked crew. The first hour, while they were serving hot drinks to the castaways, he had spent by the bedside of his sleeping wife, who was seriously ill. Henry Bull did much to intimidate them but nothing at all to shake them. If the prisoner had left the house again it could not have been until very much later—until well after the time of the assault. Then came Zacky Martin and "Whitehead" Scoble, who testified to Ross's seemly behaviour at an earlier stage. Last witness was Dwight Enys.

He did not know how the case had gone up to this time. The sun was out now, and beat down through the tall windows. Among the spectators he caught sight of a vivid auburn head. So she was here as she had said.

It was a strange position to be confronted by Ross and asked to give his testimony. After speaking for a moment or two he turned more directly to the judge.

"My lord, I am the physician who attended on Captain Poldark's wife and child during their attack of malignant sore throat (*morbus strangulatorius*). During this attack I was very constantly in the house, and I know that Captain Poldark had had no sleep for almost a week. His only child died, and she was buried the day before the wreck. His wife was still dangerously ill. I attended him professionally the night before the wreck, and formed the opinion that he was on the verge of a mental breakdown. That breakdown, I consider, did take place—and any strangeness in his actions during the next two days is almost wholly to be attributed to that condition."

There was silence. Everyone was listening intently now. Henry Bull glanced at Ross, whisked his gown and got up. This witness's testimony was dangerous to the prosecution's case.

"You are an apothecary, Dr. Enys?"

"No. A physician."

"I understand that is a distinction without a difference—at least in the provinces."

"I don't know all the provinces. In fact there's a very great difference."

"Cannot almost any man set himself up as a physician if he wants to?"

"He has no right to."

"What right have you?"

"I am a licentiate of the London College of Physicians."

Mr. Bull stared out of the window. He had not expected that reply.

"You have travelled a long way to practise, Dr. Enys."

"I am a Cornishman by birth."

"How old are you, may I ask?"

"Twenty-six."

"And have you been qualified long?"

"Nearly three years."

"Three years. . . . And under whom did you study in London?"

"I studied the theory and practice of physic under Dr. Fordyce in Essex Street, midwifery under Dr. Leake in Craven Street—and some surgery with Mr. Percival Pott at St. Bartholomew's Hospital."

"Oh, surgery too! Very interesting. And under whom did you study mental afflictions?"

"Under no one in particular. . . ."

"Then your views on the subject can hardly be expected to carry much weight, can they?"

Dwight stared at the King's attorney. "You must know, sir, that no practical medical instruction is available on this subject. It is one of which knowledge can only be gained by clinical experience——"

"Which no doubt you must have had in great measure."

". . . I have had some experience. I couldn't say in great measure."

"You'll have visited and studied at Bedlam, of course."

"No, I have not."

"Not? You haven't even been there?"

"No."

"Indeed, then——"

"I'm not suggesting that Captain Poldark was *insane*. I am saying, that in my view he was temporarily—not himself, through grief and lack of sleep."

"Would you excuse him on those grounds?"

"Certainly. Yes."

"Do you think that everyone who loses a child in infancy is justified in creating a riot throughout three parishes with great loss of property and considerable loss of life?"

"I do not believe that Captain Poldark created the riot. But if he acted strangely in certain ways I believe he did so because of a temporary unsettlement of his reason. He's not a man normally given to lawless acts."

"That is a matter which will come out after the verdict," said Bull silkily. "At present I suggest you do not bring his character into it."

"I can only give you my opinion as his physician."

"We have already heard that. Thank you, Dr. Enys."

Dwight hesitated. "It is an opinion I would stake my reputation on."

"We do not know what your reputation is, Dr. Enys. But thank you just the same."

"One moment." It was the Hon. Mr. Justice Lister. Dwight stopped. "You say you formed this opinion of the prisoner the night before. On what did you base your opinion?"

"On . . . on his general behaviour, my lord. He was not entirely coherent in his remarks. When his daughter died a great many people came for the funeral. All classes came, from the highest to the lowest. He's held in very great respect, you see. But because his wife was ill, it was impossible to give them any sort of refreshment—as is customary, my lord, at funerals in Cornwall. The fact weighed heavy on Captain Poldark's mind. He went on and on repeating his regret that he hadn't been able to feed them. He wasn't drunk—he drank very little at that time. It was, in my view, solely a mental condition."

"Thank you," said the judge, and Dwight left the stand.

There was another stirring in the court. People got up and

stretched their legs and spat and rustled papers. But no one moved to go out, and those pressing to enter were unable to. It was the prisoner's last chance now, to sway the court and the jury if he might by his eloquence—or, if that were lacking, as it usually was, to read the defence he had prepared with the help of his counsel and trust that that would serve.

Chapter Twelve

It was now or never. His own defence, stating what he had felt and done, briefly and bluntly. . . . Or Clymer's mock humility, denying everything, even putting new interpretations on what he'd said in the magistrate's court. . . . Or a compromise, using the more temperate part of his own and the less disingenuous of Clymer's. If he attempted that he would stumble and falter.

They were waiting. . . .

"My lord," Ross said, "this case has taken much of your time already. I'll try to take as little more as may be necessary to ask your clemency—and the jury's understanding. The worst that can be said of me has been said by the counsel for the Crown. Witnesses have been called in support of his case, and I have called witnesses to disprove it—or certain parts of it. The best that can be said of me has been said by them. You have heard both sides and can form your own conclusions.

"It's true that on January the seventh last there were two wrecks on Hendrawna Beach, just below my house, that my servant informed me of the first one when it was just coming light, and that I took a horse and told several people of the neighbourhood. If you ask me my motive, I cannot remember. At least, I did it, and in due course a great number of people came upon the beach and the ships were stripped bare. I was there most of the day—but although my house was afterwards searched, no goods from the ships were found there. In fact I took none. Rather strange, don't you think, for the ringleader of a lawless mob to take none of the spoils for himself?

"Now as to this lawless mob. In his speech the counsel spoke of there being more than two thousand people on the beach. That is true. But later he spoke of these people as being the—if I remember rightly—the dissident and lawless sweepings of five parishes. I wondered if he knows how sparsely the countryside is populated in this district. The whole population of five parishes would not be above six thousand, including women and children. Does he suggest that every able-bodied man in those parishes is a dissident and lawless scoundrel? I don't feel that, as reasonable people, you will agree with such an estimate."

Ross turned back to the judge, warming a little to his theme because for the moment it was not so directly concerning himself.

"No, my lord, of the two thousand on the beach not fifty came with any intent to break the law, not ten but would be loyal and faithful subjects of the King when given chance to be so. All the rest came—as people will come whatever their class—to witness a sensational happening, whether it is a fire, or a wreck—or an assize—or an execution. They needed no invitation from me. They would have quickly been there without it. Perhaps half a hundred were there more quickly because of my summons. That was all. There is a mine on the cliffs almost overlooking the beach. When someone at the workings caught sight of the wreck—as they must have done soon—do you not think his action would have been the same as mine: to rouse his friends—without searching into his heart for this or that motive, but just to rouse his friends?"

As Ross paused to collect his thoughts, someone sniggered loudly at the back of the court. He knew at once who it was. Eli Clemmow had done just the same thing three years ago at the petty sessions when Ross had been speaking on Jim Carter's behalf. Then it had had the effect of breaking the continuity of his reasoning and diverting the attention of the justices. It must not happen that way again.

"Gentlemen of the jury," he said, "as to what happened

when those people got on the beach and saw the ships wrecked, I must ask you to think for a moment of the traditions of our county. That attempts are made or have ever been made to lure ships on the rocks by means of false lights is a calumny which has been spread only by the prejudiced or the ignorant. But that people search the beaches for flotsam and look on the leavings of the tides as their own especial property is too commonly known to need emphasis. The law says such flotsam belongs to the Crown—or perhaps to this or that lord of the manor—but in fact when the stuff is of little value no attempt is made to reclaim it from the people who found it. In times of dire want these little pickings have often been the means of keeping people—honest decent people—alive. So a habit—a tradition is formed. What happens, then, when a whole ship comes in? People flood to the beach to see the wreck, and to help in the rescue work— there are two widows in my parish who would not be widows if their husbands had not tried to save shipwrecked sailors. But when the rescue work is done, are they to stand idly by and wait for the arrival of the excise men? The law says yes. The law, of course, is right. But when men have seen their children without a crust for their bellies or a rag for their backs, it's hard for them to reason as they should."

He had got the attention of the court again.

"The counsel has suggested that these people are revolutionaries—that I am a revolutionary—branded with the desire to overthrow authority. I answer, quite simply, that nothing could be further from the truth. We are not. As for the assaults upon the crew of the second ship—this was a disgraceful episode which I will not attempt to excuse. But it was done by men in drink and by men from far afield who had come—certainly not at my invitation—when news of the first wreck had travelled to them.

"Finally, as to the attack on the excise men. No defence or excuse is needed because I was not there. I never saw the excise men. They never saw me. I warned the sergeant of dragoons not to go on the beach at that juncture because everyone was by then very excited, and I wished to avoid bloodshed. By the time these men arrived there was very little they could do."

Ross looked through Clymer's notes again, but found nothing more he could, even in this new mood, bring himself to add.

"So that is all I have to say. I pray I am equal to whatever fortune is in store for me, and put myself upon the candour, the justice and the humanity of your lordship, and upon yours, my countrymen, gentlemen of the jury."

He bowed and sat down in the back of the dock, and as he did so there was a little grumble of approval at the rear of the court.

Verity whispered: "I don't think we could get out now if we wanted to. The doorway and benches are so crammed."

"No. We must stay. I shall be all right."

"Here, try these smelling salts again."

"No, no. Listen."

"There are three charges," said the Hon. Mr. Justice Lister coldly, "on which this man stands before you. He is charged with riot, with wrecking and with assault upon an officer of the Crown. You have heard the evidence, and it is your duty to bring in a verdict in accordance with that evidence. You may find him guilty on all three charges—or on any one of them.

"Now as to the third charge—namely assaulting and injuring an excise officer—there is some conflict of evidence. Two witnesses have sworn to his being the man, two have given testimony that he could not possibly have been there. The excise officer himself is doubtful on the point of identity, and none of his colleagues has been called to assist the prosecution. It was a dark and wind-swept night and it is possible that there has been a confusion of identity. It is a matter for you to decide whether you prefer to accept the testimony of his two servants who swear that he never left the house again or the testimony of Trevail and Clemmow, who declare that they saw him strike the officer down. But where there is a reasonable element of doubt, let me remind you, it is an axiom of English law that an accused man should receive the benefit of it."

To Demelza's fevered imagination it seemed that he glanced towards her as he spoke.

"As to the first two charges, these are very differently based. The prisoner admits that he summoned people to the wreck, but claims—appears to claim, that his aim was as much to succour the shipwrecked as to pillage the vessel, and that the riot inadvertently developed without his encouragement or desire. That, if I interpret him correctly, is his defence now—and it is the crux of the matter; yet certain of his statements and certain of his actions at the time lay themselves open to a different interpretation. If, for instance, he was *really* concerned to save the passengers and crews, why was he not more active in doing so? How was it that, between swimming out to the first ship and a belated offer of shelter to the people of the second ship—many hours later—he apparently made no efforts on their behalf? They did not see him. He says he did not see them. But he admits to being on the beach. What was he doing there all those hours?"

Mr. Justice Lister was speaking without notes. In fact he had taken none during the trial.

"The prisoner's physician has been called to testify to Captain Poldark's distressed condition at the time of the wrecks—suggesting virtually that he was not responsible for his actions at the time. Whether you consider such testimony sufficiently weighty to be of vital importance is for you to decide. I would only point out that such a condition, if it ever did exist, can hardly have prevailed at the time of the justice's examination—which took place *six weeks later*. You have heard the statements made by the accused at that examination carefully read to you, and I have no doubt they are present in your minds. You will remember he was asked: 'What purpose had you in leading your friends to the wreck?' To which his reply was: 'There were people in the district who were starving.' Later he was asked: 'Did you approve of this riot which had started?' And he answered: 'I did not consider it a riot.' What then, you may wonder, did he consider it? Did he look on it as a justifiable act of robbery and pillage?

"Now you may say, 'But if the third charge is unproven, it is difficult to prove an illegal act against the prisoner in person on the other counts. Where is the testimony providing concrete evidence of his guilt? For instance, did anyone see him carry off one stick or stone from either of the ships?' The answer is, no. But in law, if you are satisfied that a riot took place, it is only necessary to be further satisfied that the prisoner was sufficiently involved in the affair as to be guilty as a principal. A common intent to commit a felony makes the act of one the act of all—and it is not necessary even to be present at the actual commission of the felony for a man to be held guilty. For instance a man could be out of sight of a murder, but if he were keeping watch for the murderers and cognisant of their intent he would be held guilty."

The court was very silent now. Demelza's heart was going colder and colder.

"Further, in law, where several people join together to commit an act which is itself unlawful, and a worse crime comes from anything done in the prosecution of that unlawful design—then one and all are guilty of the worse crime, however abhorrent it may personally be to some of them, and however little they may have had intent to commit it. It remains therefore for you only to decide on the evidence you have heard: first, whether in fact the prisoner was on the beach at the time of the wreck; second, whether he was there with others with the intent to strip the wreck; third, whether such a pillaging and riot and assault took place."

His extraordinary memory had absorbed it all like a sponge: now at a squeeze it all came out again—sometimes seeming to be a little in the prisoner's favour, but mainly against him. One could not suspect Mr. Justice Lister of any prejudice: he was not loading the scales but merely assessing their respective weights and finding one side heavier than the other. He was performing the duty for which he had received his commission from the King, and by reason of which he held his elevated position in society.

"The prisoner," he ended, "has attempted to find mitigating circumstances for the crimes of riot and wrecking in the distress generally prevailing among poor people at this time. This is an irrelevance which you are in duty bound to ignore. He has devoted a part of his final plea to a defence of his own countryfolk, who are, in any case, not on trial at this assize at all. You may consider this a not unadmirable sentiment on his part, but you would be failing in your obligations to society if you allowed sympathy or a narrow emotional patriotism to influence you in any decision you deemed to be right. I will ask you now to discharge the duty which you have undertaken by your oaths, regardless of the consequences and regardless of everything except your desire to do justice between the Crown and the accused. Will you now consider your verdict."

In the general buzz that broke out Verity saw the judge glance at the clock. It was almost four and there were several cases yet to come. The jury put their heads together, whispering self-consciously, aware of everyone's eyes on them. Several times Verity had thought Demelza was going to faint, but thankfully she had seen her gain a greater control of herself this last ten minutes. It was as if the worst had already happened and now she was reacting against the blow.

"You may retire if you wish," said the judge to the foreman.

The foreman nervously thanked him and again consulted with his fellows. Then he leaned over to the usher and the usher went to the judge. The clerk of the court rapped with the hammer and the judge stood up, bowed and went out. The jury had decided to retire.

It's all over, thought Ross, and so much better if I'd stuck to my guns and made the speech I wanted. Hedging at the last moment. Cowardice and compromising. Pretending to myself that it was for Demelza. My own weakness and cowardice and Clymer's damned overbearing manner. And it will avail absolutely nothing at all. Even if I had gone the whole hog and crawled on my belly the way he wanted. As it is, two stools. Not even the satisfaction of feeling that I told them exactly what I thought—about the trial, about the distress, about the wreck. Dirt in my mouth.

The judge with his thin sour face. A human machine for administering the law. If I go to prison I really shall come out a revolutionary—climb up and slit his throat one night as he snores in bed. Far safer to hang me.

And Demelza? Difficult to see her without turning one's head. Just see the colour of her skirt out of the corner of my eye, and her hands on her lap. They can't keep still, can they, darling? Perhaps I should have crawled, really crawled, for her sake. Mercy, mercy. The quality of mercy is not strained, it droppeth as the gentle rain from heaven upon the place beneath. What the devil are the jury arguing about? It must be perfectly plain to them, just as plain as to the judge, who practically directed them.

Surprise to see Verity here. Must write to her and ask her to look after Demelza. Should have thought of that before. Demelza will take advice from her. Perhaps it was as well Julia died: wouldn't have been nice to grow up knowing . . . But perhaps if she hadn't died none of this would have happened. Perhaps Dwight wasn't too far off the truth. Nonsense, I was in my right mind, sane as could be. Must write and thank him nevertheless. Sober young fellow. Pity he got in that mess.

Suppose I shall get a few minutes with Demelza when it's over. But what to say . . . Meetings like that are robbed of their sense by being so limited. What *were* the jury doing? Tis mightiest in the mightiest, it becomes the thronèd monarch better than his crown. His sceptre shows the force of temporal power. . . . Temporal power. The Hon. Mr. Justice Lister. Temporal power . . . The jury were coming back.

It had only been ten minutes, but, as Zacky said at the back of the court, it seemed like a month. They filed slowly in,

133

the twelve good men and true, looking as self-conscious as when they went out, and the foreman had a guilty look, as if he thought himself liable to be charged with a lesser felony and brought before the court for judgment. Everyone stood while Mr. Justice Lister came back, and silence settled suddenly on the court as he sat down.

The clerk rose and said: " Gentlemen of the jury, have you agreed upon a verdict?"

" We have," said the foreman, swallowing nervously.

" Do you find the prisoner guilty or not guilty?"

" We find him . . ." The foreman stopped and started again. " We find him not guilty upon all three charges."

For a last moment the silence hung like a wave, and then broke. Someone at the back of the court started to cheer, and others took it up. It was answered almost at once by boos and cries of " Shame!" Then it stopped, and a backwash in tiny rivulets of conversation lapped about the court. The clerk's gavel hammered them out of existence.

" If there is any further disturbance," said his lordship, " the courtroom will be cleared and proceedings taken against offenders."

Ross remained where he was, not quite knowing whether to believe the verdict or whether there was some further male-volence the law might be capable of. After a moment his own self-contained blue eyes met the judge's.

" Prisoner at the bar," said Mr. Justice Lister. " You have been tried on three charges by a jury of your fellow country-men and found not guilty. It only remains for me, therefore, to order your discharge. But before you go I wish to offer you a word or two of advice. It would not be proper for me to comment on the verdict brought in by this jury—except that you should feel in your heart a gratitude towards God for a deliverance which owes much to mercy and little to logic. In a few moments you will be leaving this court a free man— free to rejoin your deserving wife, and to begin a new life with her. Your able defence—and your reputation in other fields— marks you as a man of talent and capacity. I urge you in your own interests to subdue those instincts to lawlessness which may from time to time come upon you. Take warning from to-day. May it bear fruit in your heart and in your life."

Tears were beginning to fall on Demelza's hands.

Chapter Thirteen

They went home that same evening. He had a morbid distaste for the interest his presence aroused in the town, and his whole concern was to get away from staring eyes. There was no coach, so they hired horses and left at half past six.

Demelza had wanted Verity to go with them and to stay for a few days at Nampara before returning to Falmouth, but she obdurately refused; instinct told her that at this stage they should be by themselves. Dwight, too, was to have ridden with them, but he was involved at the last moment in helping some injured man. The rest of them—Jud Paynter and Zacky Martin and Whitehead Scoble and the Gimletts—were coming on by stage wagon to-morrow and walking from St. Michael.

So they left Bodmin quite alone; left the buzzing town, from which the crowds drawn by the election were already beginning to dribble away. By next week, when the judges and the counsel were posting on to Exeter, Bodmin would be back to normal.

It was dusk before they passed Lanivet and dark by the time they were half across the moors. Mist had blown up again and once or twice they thought they had missed the way. They talked scarcely at all, and discussion as to the right road was a welcome topic when other words would not come. At Fraddon they rested for a while, but soon were in the saddle again. They reached Treneglos land about nine-thirty and later made a detour to avoid Mellin Cottages. This was another inducement to return early, to be home before the news spread so that there were no cheering cottagers to welcome them. The uncomplex Demelza would not have minded in the least—a triumphal procession was what the occasion deserved—but she knew how Ross would hate it.

So they came upon their own property at last: the stone posts where the gate had once hung, the descending valley among the wild nut trees. As always fog made the land secretive and strange; it was not the familiar friendly country-side they knew and owned, it reverted to an earlier and less personal allegiance. Ross was reminded of that night seven years ago when he had come home from Winchester and America to find his house derelict and the Paynters drunk in bed. It had been raining then, but otherwise just such a night. There had only been the dogs and the chickens and the dripping of moisture from the trees. He had been numb with the blow of Elizabeth's engagement to Francis, angry and resentful of a hurt only half realised, desperately alone.

To-night he was coming back to a house yet more empty because Julia was not there, but riding beside him was the woman whose love and companionship meant more than all the rest; and he was returning free of the cloud which had shadowed his life for six months. He should feel happy and free. During his time in prison he had thought of all the things he should have said to Demelza and would never have the opportunity of saying. Now with unexpected reprieve came the old cursed constriction on his tongue, blocking up emotional expression.

The mist was less thick in the valley, and presently they saw the black shape of their house and crossed the stream and reined in at the front door beside the big lilac tree.

Ross said: " I'll take the horses round if you'll get down here."

Demelza said: " It seem funny without even Garrick to give a friendly bark. I wonder how he is, over to Mrs. Zacky's."

" Likely to scent your return at any moment, I should think. A half mile is nothing to him."

She slipped down and stood a moment listening to the clatter and clop as the horses were led round to the stable.

Then she opened the front door with its familiar friendly squeak and went in. The smell of home.

She groped into the kitchen, found the tinderbox and scraped it. By the time Ross came in she had a fire flickering and a kettle perched precariously on the sticks. She had lit the candles in the parlour and was reaching up to draw the curtains.

As he saw the stretch of her young body, the dark hair lank with the clammy night, the olive colour in her cheeks, an impulse of warmth and gratitude towards her came to him. She had never for a moment expected him to rejoice at his deliverance. She might not understand the causes, but some instinct told her that spiritually he was still—at the most—a convalescent. It would take time, perhaps a long time.

She looked round, met his gaze and smiled. " There was some water left in the pitcher. I thought we could brew a dish of tea."

He took off his hat, flung it in a corner and ran a hand through his hair. " You must be tired," he said.

" No. . . . Glad to be home."

He stretched and wandered slowly round the room, glancing at things he had virtually said good-bye to a week ago— now renewing their acquaintance as if after many years. The house was isolated and empty in a dark, still world. The pulse of living had died while they were away.

" Shall I light up a fire in here?" she asked.

" No. . . . It must be late. My watch has stopped—and I see the clock has stopped. Did you forget to wind it?"

" Could you expect me to remember that?"

" I suppose not." He smiled rather absently, went across to the clock Verity and Demelza had bought three years before. " What do you think the time is?"

" About eleven."

He set the hands and began to wind up the weights. " I should have thought later than that."

" We'll ask Jack Cobbledick in the morning."

" How will he know?"

" By the cows."

Ross said: " Couldn't we ask them to-night?"

She laughed, but with a slight break in her voice. " I'll go'n see if the kettle's singing."

While she was gone he sat in a chair and tried to arrange his thoughts, to sort them out so that he knew what his own feelings were. But relief and relaxation were still so entangled with the old tensions that nothing clear would come. When she returned with cups and a steaming teapot he was wandering round the room again, as if after his week's captivity even these confining walls were irksome.

She said nothing but poured out the tea. " P'raps Jack half suspicioned someone would be back to-night, for he left a jug of milk. Come and sit down, Ross."

He sat in the chair opposite her, accepted a cup, sipped it, his lean introspective face showing the strain more now than at any time. This side she could not see the scar. The tea was warm and grateful, soothed one's stretched nerves, hinted at the old companionship.

" So we're to start life afresh," he said at length.

" Yes . . ."

" Clymer said I was amazing lucky—that a Cornish jury was the most pigheaded in the world. He charged me thirty guineas; I thought it not unreasonable."

" I thought he did nothing at all."

" Oh yes. . . . Again and again it was his guidance. And the speech I made—was partly his." Ross's face twitched. " God, how I disliked that!"

" Why? It was a handsome speech, I thought. I was so proud of you."

" Proud . . . Heaven forbid!"

" And others thought the same. Dwight told me he'd heard that was what got you off."

" Which is worse. To have to go crawling for one's freedom."

" Oh no, Ross! There was no crawling in that. Why should you not defend yourself—explain what you did?"

" But it was not true! At least . . . if it was not false it was an evasion of the truth. I had no thought of saving life when

138

I roused the neighbourhood. It was the Warleggans' ship. That was all I cared about. When I found Sanson dead in the cabin I was glad! That was what I should have told the jury this afternoon—and would have but for Clymer and his counsels of expedience!"

"And now to-night you would not be free, but perhaps sentenced to transportation. Do you think, Ross, that that would have been a good exchange—just for stretching a story so's to put it in the best light? And if you'd said what you wanted, would it have been more than half the truth, *more* the truth than what you did say? Dwight was right, an' you know it! You were crazed with grief—and the jury's verdict was the only fair one."

Ross got up. "Whitewashing my neighbours too. We knew they were all on the beach for what they could get, and with little thought to the shipwrecked sailors. Who would blame them?"

"Right enough. Who would blame them—or you?"

Ross made an angry, disquieted movement. "Let's talk of other things."

But instead they talked of nothing, and silence fell. The house seemed to hold itself together about them. She tried to bring up the election, but it didn't make sense. Eventually he sat down again and she refilled his cup.

"I'd dearly love to go on doing this forever," she said.

"Drinking tea? You'd find it incommoding after a while. . . . But why?"

"It is the *homely* thing," she said.

One of the candles began to sputter, and she got up and snuffed it. The smoke it had made drifted upwards in a dark spreading curl.

"It's you and me," she said, " in our own house; nothing between us—no interruption. Maybe it's because I'm just of common stock, but I want the home about me: candles burning, curtains drawn, warmth, tea, friendship, love. Those are what d'matter to me. This morning—even a few hours ago—I thought it was all gone for ever."

"Common stock? Don't believe it." After a minute he

added: "Nor was Julia of common stock, and she was like you."

"That is the other thing I want," she said, taking the opening.

"What?"

"A fire—and perhaps a cat by the hearth . . . but mostly a child in the cot."

His jaw muscles tightened, but he didn't speak.

"What is it?" she asked.

"Nothing. It's time for bed. To-morrow I am to become a farmer again—eh?"

"No, tell me, Ross."

He stared at her. "Was not the last experience enough for you? I want no more fodder for the epidemics."

She stared back at him, horrified. "Not ever?"

He shrugged, uncomfortable and a little surprised at her expression. He had thought she felt the same as himself.

"Oh, it may be they will come in due course. We cannot help that. But not yet, pray heaven. And they can never take Julia's place. I should not want them to. I should not want them at all yet."

She was about to say something more but checked herself. She had known in court to-day that she was with child again, and since the moment of his acquittal had been keeping the knowledge to herself like some secret to be betrayed in due time, when it would perhaps help him in the struggle back to normal life again, give a new interest, a renewed purpose. Now the gold had suddenly peeled off and revealed something tawdry and inferior—and unwanted. She went round snuffing the other candles, getting the smoke in her eyes, thankful that he was staring into the fire. The triumph of the day gone. She was as desolate as he.

Just then there came a tentative knock on the front door. At first they thought they had mistaken it, but it came again. In surprise Ross went out and across the hall and flung it open. The flickering light of a horn lantern showed up half a dozen people standing in the mist. There was Paul Daniel and Jack Cobbledick, and Mrs. Zacky Martin and Beth Daniel and Jinny Scoble and Prudie Paynter.

"We seen the light," said Mrs. Zacky. "We thought to come'n see if twas you back, my son."

"Praise the Lord," said Beth Daniel.

"Es it all right?" asked Paul Daniel. "Are ee free and it all over?"

"You're early for carols," said Ross, "but come in and take a glass of wine."

"Aw, no, we'd no thought t'intrude, my dear. Twas only wanting to know, and seeing the window alight . . ."

"Of course you must come in," said Ross. "Aren't you all my good friends?"

Chapter Fourteen

Later that night a coach drew up outside the largest of the town houses in Princes Street, Truro, and a chilled and yawning postilion got down to open the carriage door for George Warleggan. George got out, ignoring his servants, and walked slowly up the steps. Finding the door bolted, he pulled irritably at the bell. Another sleepy footman let him in, took his hat and cloak and stared after him as he mounted the handsome staircase. There was no look of sleep in George's eyes.

At the top of the first flight he hesitated, saw a light under his uncle's door, and went across. Cary was in a shabby old dressing gown and a nightcap but was working over his accounts by the light of two candles. When he saw who had come in he took off his steel spectacles and put down his pen. Then he blew out one of the candles, since less light would be needed for talking.

"We expected you yesterday. Did you have to lie there the night?"

"The trial did not come on until to-day—and was not over until four. Then one had to eat."

141

Cary breathed through his nose and eyed George. "I should have stayed another night. A wonder you did not break your axles in the dark or flounder in a bog."

"We did once, but came out with some effort. I was not prepared to spend another night in a dirty noisy inn, with indifferent service and no curtains to the bed." George went over to a decanter on the table and poured himself a drink. He sipped it, aware that Cary was still watching him.

"Well," said Cary, "I assume you are not here at this time of night for the pleasure of my company?"

"He got off," George said; "the accursed ignorant jury disregarded all the evidence and found him not guilty—because they liked the colour of his eyes."

"On all counts?"

"On all counts. So the judge gave him a lecture, telling him to be a good boy in future, and then he was discharged."

Cary sat perfectly still. His little brown bright eyes were fixed on the single unwavering candle flame. "Was it not even suggested that he had murdered Matthew? I tell you, *that* should have been the charge!"

"And I tell you, my dear uncle, it would not have held for a moment. Matthew was found drowned. There was not an atom of proof and we could not have manufactured it. As it was, the evidence we tried to strengthen in our own way was of little value. Some of it, even, was of advantage to the other side. That man Paynter. I must see Garth in the morning. . . ."

"And what of the other things?" said Cary. "His misdeeds in the past. It is little more than twelve months since he broke in Launceston gaol and took out a prisoner—and nothing done about it. And then soon after he was helping that murderer Daniel to escape. Does all that count for nothing?"

George took his glass over to a chair and sat down. He studied the colour of the wine. "The law, as you should know, deals in one thing at a time. It also deals only in past convictions, not past suspicions. The judge had the facts before him, but he had no chance of using them. We are thwarted, dear Cary, and must accept our defeat." It was as if George was salving his own frustration by taunting the other man.

There was a rap at the door and Nicholas Warleggan came in. He was more properly ready for the night, in a flowing gown and a black skullcap.

"Well, Father," said George in ironical surprise, "I thought you were at Cardew."

"Your mother went alone. I heard the carriage stop. Well, what was the result?"

"He was acquitted of all charges and now no doubt is back at Nampara sleeping the sleep of a free man."

"The man responsible for Matthew's disgrace," Cary said, "and later for his death."

Nicholas Warleggan glanced sharply at his brother. "There is always the danger of a suspicion becoming an obsession." To George he said: "So your efforts have been useless. I have been most uncomfortable about it all through."

George still twirled his glass round by its stem. "Your conscience gets ever more restive on our account. My dear uncle, why do you buy cheap wine? I call that economy very unsuitable."

"It is perfectly palatable to me," said Cary. "If you do not like it you need not drink it."

George glanced at his father. "What have we done but exert pressure which would assist the law? Of course we shall drop it, for there is nothing more to do. Is there, Cary?"

"I shall not relax my efforts in any way," said Cary, scarcely opening his mouth. "Poldark is in deep water financially. We can yet see him in prison or drive him out of the county."

"In other words," said George, "there are more ways than one of killing a cat. You cannot blame us, Father, if we take an interest in his mine."

"I have no objection whatever to any proper business move," said Nicholas, padding across the room. "I have no love for any of the Poldarks—arrogant, overbred, indolent squireens. If you can purchase the outside shares in his mine, by all means do so: it is one of the most profitable for its

143

size in the county. But retain a sense of proportion. In a few years, George, with my prestige and your ability we shall be in a position where the Poldarks will not be worth our notice—they are not in fact even now. It's not becoming to our position or dignity—this feud——"

"You have no thought for Matthew," said Cary sharply.

"No, in that respect I have not. He was morally at fault and brought his troubles on himself."

"Did you see Pearce yesterday?" asked George.

Cary sniffed. "Yes. He says Mrs. Jacqueline Trenwith is not prepared at present to dispose of the shares. I don't like Pearce. He quibbles. He thinks he can run with the hare and hunt with the hounds."

"We can cure him of that. His convictions wear away very easily. Sit down, Father; you walk about as if the house were on fire."

"No, I'll go to bed," said Nicholas. "I must rise early in the morning."

"While I was in Bodmin," George said, "I also had a brush with Francis Poldark. We chanced to meet, and he being then sober but anxious to amend the condition, I invited him to an inn where we drank together. But once in the inn he grew offensive and tried to pick a quarrel with me."

"What did he say?"

"He accused me quite openly of being behind this charge against his cousin, of trying to ruin his family in any underhand way I could, of behaving in the ill-bred manner he would expect of the grandson of a blacksmith—who still lived in a hovel near St. Day because the family of Warleggan was ashamed to own him."

There was silence in the room except for Cary's breathing. Nicholas Warleggan's neck had gone a dull red.

Cary said: "And you sat there and allowed *that* to pass?"

George looked at his hands. "With these I could have broken his back. But I've had better things to do with my life than learning to be a pistol shot, and I had no intention of allowing a weakling like Francis to dictate my behaviour."

"Quite right," muttered Nicholas. "It was the only way

to act. But I'm perplexed that he should have done this. Only last year he was at bitter loggerheads with his cousin . . ."

"That, I think, is what troubles him," George said pleasantly. "It doesn't lie easy on his conscience."

"And how did you leave him?" said Cary.

"In polite enmity."

Cary made an angry gesture, shutting one of his account books with a snap. "All his finances are in our hands. We can break him to-morrow—financially, which is the better way. . . ."

George hunched his shoulders. "No. . . . We can't do that. At least not so obviously. For the moment I intend to make no move at all."

"Why not? You care nothing now for his good will."

"Not *his* good will," said George, getting up. "But there is another person to consider."

BOOK TWO

Chapter One

As the autumn lengthened and winter came in Ross made a determined effort to set aside the troubles and anxieties that were past and accept in earnest the life of a small farmer squire with a mining interest—the life he had abandoned with regret only two years ago. But although he had left the happy routine with reluctance, he couldn't recapture the pleasure by simple means of a return to it.

Also some chill had come upon his relations with Demelza. Her thoughts were not as open to him. Dating strangely from his acquittal, the laughter had gone, and the instant understanding. He tried more than once to break down this new reserve but failed, and the failure left its mark on his own responses.

Although he was thankful enough to be free of the menace of the assizes, the lesser but still serious danger of his own approaching bankruptcy kept him company most days. Even a sale of all his shares in Wheal Leisure would not balance his debt. A proud man, he hated indebtedness of any sort. He still hated the memory of the trial. Although he had probably gone free as a result of his change of front at the last moment, he constantly despised himself for having made it.

A few weeks after the trial Verity wrote:

My dear Cousin Ross,

I am writing you this time instead of Demelza because what I have to say is perhaps a little more to you than to her, though of course you may let her read this if you wish.

First may I say again, thank God for your deliverance—and in that prayer Andrew truly and sincerely joins. I know how wicked it was that the charge was ever brought against you, and in that respect acquittal was no more than your right. Yet there is the deepest cause for thankfulness in each one of your friends that there was no miscarriage of Justice —and the true hope that any embitterment which the arrest caused in you has been salved by this happy Outcome.

While I was in Bodmin I saw Francis twice. The first time he called at the inn and, although he was somewhat the worse for drink, I felt that he had come to see me in the intention of making up the Quarrel between us; but when it came to the Point he had not the words and so went away unsatisfied. Therefore after the trial I sought him out and spoke to him again.

This second meeting confirmed the other opinion formed at the first: that something is gravely wrong with him. He is frighteningly bitter—in the way you are sometimes, Ross. Yet not like you, because I think he is more likely to do a mischief to himself than to others.

I know you and Francis have quarrelled, but have very strongly the Feeling that he wishes to be reconsiled. I don't know what was the full cause of the quarrel except that of course it began as a result of my elopement with Andrew— so I feel doubly concerned for the outcome. If he makes some further approach to you I beg you to be accommodating if not for his sake then for mine, who still love him in spite of all his faults. It may be that you could help him back to a proper balance.

I don't like developments in France. It is unwholesome for a King to be led into Paris as if he were a prisoner, and there is much Feeling here about it. Try not to speak too openly in favour of liberty and freedom, Ross, for one can be so misunderstood. One is snapped up at the first mention of such things—by people who only twelve months ago were all in favour of reform. You will think this letter is quite a Lecture.

We went to Gwennap yesterday at the invitation of one of Andrew's friends. A dreadful place and bleak as a desert with hillocks of cinders and large engines creaking and groaning. All the whims are worked by mules, and poor impish, half-starved children hang over them flogging them round without respite. Steam and vapour hung over the scene like a pall. One wonders how Wesley dared to go there. Being even half-way home gave me a decided twinge.

I hear my stepson may be back in England *this* summer —a mere twelve months after his ship was due. I hope to meet him then.

My dearest love to you both,
Verity

In December Demelza was making rushlights with Mrs. Gimlett, an employment that needed some practice and skill. The rushes had been cut in October and put in water so as to prevent drying or shrinkage. After they were stripped they had been laid out on the grass to whiten and " take the dew " for a week, and then dried in the sun. The last treat-ment was to dip the rushes in scalding fat so that when with-drawn it congealed about the stem. Last year she had bought six pounds of grease from Aunt Mary Rogers for two shillings, but this year, in the desperate need for the smallest economy, she had saved her own fat, even the scummings of her bacon pot, and was hoping it would do as well.

These small economies were the only way she could make some contribution to the general need. Sometimes, too, in this quiet December she had got Ross's dinghy out and rowed twenty or thirty yards offshore where she had been able to catch mackerel and skate enough for the whole household. Ross did not know of this, and Gimlett was impressed to help her and sworn to secrecy. To-day the kitchen was full of the sputterings of the grease, and some of the smoke and steam of the process, when there came a ran-tan on the front door which she knew to be the knock of a stranger.

Jane Gimlett went to the door and reappeared after a minute hastily wiping her greasy hands.

" If you please, mistress, it is Sir Hugh Bodrugan. I asked him into the parlour. I hope twas the right thing to do."

Sir Hugh had been calling irregularly for the last eighteen

months but she had not seen him since the trial. The thought came to her that if she went in to him like this with spots of grease on her face it might cure him of his interest. But vanity and a sense of her own low beginnings were too strong. She flew upstairs and made quick repairs.

When she went in he was sprawling in Ross's best chair examining the silver duelling pistols which he had taken down from the wall; he was wearing a red hunting coat and brown corduroy breeches and, since she had last seen him, a new wig. He got up and bowed over her hand.

"Y'r servant, ma'am. Thought I'd call and refresh our friendship. Pleasant time we had in Bodmin, but a shade inconclusive." The bawdy twinkling black eyes met her own as he straightened up. They were almost on a level, she slightly the taller.

"Maybe you looked on it different from me, Sir Hugh. I found it exhausting."

He laughed. "Well, ye've got a husband no one expected you to have. I trust he appreciates the escape. And I trust he appreciates you."

"Oh, we appreciate each other, Sir Hugh. We are very happy, I assure you."

A shadow of discontent passed across his face. "But not above helping a neighbour in distress, eh?"

"In distress," she said, looking away from his bold glance. "I didn't know baronets was ever in distress.''

"Oh yes," he said with a thick chuckle. "They are mortal like other men. Liable to all the ills and disappointments—and all the temptations, as you must know."

She went to the table at the side. "Can I offer you port, sir, or is brandy more to your fancy?"

"Brandy, please. It lies easier on the stomach."

As she poured out the drink she knew he was watching her and was sorry that her frock was a cheap one, though she knew well enough that he was not really interested in her frock.

He came over for the glass and took it with his left hand, putting his arm round her waist as he did so. After a moment they were seated again, he gulping at his glass, she on the edge of a chair at a discreet distance and gently sipping.

" Tis not that sort of distress, I trust?" she said gravely.

" It well could be, ma'am, it well could be."

" Then I fear I have no cure for you."

" You have it, miss, but withhold it, being hard of heart. However at this instant that's not the distress I seek your aid for. It's my mare Sheba."

She stared at him over the rim of her glass, the dark wine making some added glimmer in the dark of her eyes. " Sheba? What is wrong and what can I do for you?"

" She's sick, with some infernal fever that she can't throw off. Her eyelids are swollen and she has a racking cough. She can barely walk, and her knee joints crack at every movement as if they were dry sticks."

" I'm sorry to hear it," she said, putting out one slipper and then, as he glanced down, withdrawing it. " But why do you come to me?"

Sir Hugh blew through his lips. " Why do I come to you? Because I was consulting Trevaunance on the problem this morning, and he says you cured a pedigree cow of his when all the farriers had failed! That's why. Is that not a good reason?"

Demelza blushed and finished her port. As she did so she heard a horse outside and Ross dismounted at the door. Gimlett ran past the window to lead Darkie to the stables.

" It was mostly a matter of good fortune, Sir Hugh. It so happened——"

" All cures are good fortune one way or another, but everyone hasn't the honesty to acknowledge it. Trevaunance was telling me that you're learned on herbs and gypsy lore. If you——"

" Oh no," Demelza began. At that juncture Ross came in.

He looked surprised and not too pleased to see the thickset hairy baronet sprawling in his chair and talking to Demelza in such a familiar manner. He had never quarrelled with Sir Hugh, but had never liked him. Also, as a result of his visit to Truro, he had his own affairs very much on his mind, and he had only half his attention to spare for an unexpected visitor.

"Sir Hugh has called———" Demelza began.

"My mare Sheba is ill, Poldark, and I've called to solicit your wife's good offices. She's been ailing for more than two weeks—Sheba, I mean—and Connie's in the greatest of a passion over it; she swears it is the groom's fault. Anyway, it ain't natural for the mare to be ill so long and she but six years old. Treneglos was saying one of his had it and died of it! We can't *afford* to lose her. It ain't natural at all."

Ross dropped his riding gloves on a chair and poured himself some brandy. "How can Demelza help you?"

"Well, I hear she's a rare hand with herbs and spells and suchlike. Trevaunance only told me this morning, or I should have been over before. Damn it, the farriers have no more idea than the man in the moon!"

"The farriers———" Ross began.

"I was just saying to Sir Hugh," Demelza said hastily, "that Sir John was putting too much store on a little advice I gave him back in August month. It was no more'n a word I dropped about his sick cow, and she grew better by accident."

"Well, come over and drop a word about my sick mare, and see if *she* gets better by accident. Cod, it will do no harm surely."

Demelza hesitated, opened her mouth to speak.

"After all," said Sir Hugh, "it is no more than repaying one good turn with another. We're neighbours and should do what we can to be neighbourly: that's what I thought at Bodmin. Come yourself, Poldark, if you've the mind. Connie'll victual you well enough, I'll say that for her. We dine at three. I shall expect you to-morrow, what?"

"I'm sorry," Ross said. "I have business which will keep me at the mine all day. Perhaps we can arrange one day next week."

Demelza got up to refill Sir Hugh's glass. "Maybe I could go, Ross?" she said gently. "Not to dine, but just for half an hour to see the mare. I can do naught, of course, but if Sir Hugh really wants it and nothing less will satisfy him . . ."

Bodrugan took the drink. " That suits me fine. I'll expect you any time after eleven. And anything you want—medicines, plasters, clysters, herbs—just say the word. I'll have a groom ready to ride to Truro."

After a few more sentences Ross went upstairs, but Sir Hugh was not hurrying. He finished his brandy and took a third, while Demelza wondered how Jane was managing the rushlights. At length he left, stocky, authoritative and vigorous—squeezed Demelza's hand lengthily, climbed on his big horse and cantered across the bridge and up the valley.

She went into the kitchen and found Jane had finished the job and was cleaning up the mess. After about ten minutes she heard Ross come down again, and she followed him back into the parlour.

" Did you eat in Truro? We've some pie left."

" I ate in Truro."

She glanced at him, took in his bleak expression, thought it a criticism of her attitude towards Sir Hugh.

" We're neighbours, Ross. You couldn't expect for me not to receive him."

" Who? Oh, Bodrugan." Ross lifted an eyebrow. " I suppose you will not go to-morrow."

" Of course I'll go," she said, a faint edge on her voice. " I promised, didn't I?"

He said with irony: " D'you really suppose he wants you to cure his mare? I had a greater regard for your intelligence than that."

" You mean you've no regard for my intelligence at all."

" I've a great respect for it—sometimes. But you must realise what Bodrugan is after. He makes it very plain."

Because it was three-quarters true she resented it the more. " I think I ought to be able to judge that for myself."

" No doubt you think so. But be careful that his title doesn't dazzle your eyes. It has that effect with some people."

" Especially," she said, " a common miner's daughter who doesn't know any better."

He looked at her a moment. "That's for you to demonstrate."

He turned to go, but she was at the door first.

"You're detestable—saying things like that!"

"I'm sure I didn't start this argument."

"No, you never do start arguments, do you, with your cold looks an' your bitter tongue! You just freeze everyone up an'—an' despise everything that isn't up to your standard. It's—it's unfair and horrible! Perhaps that's what you want me always to feel. Perhaps you're sorry you ever bothered to marry me!"

She turned and was out of the door, slamming it behind her, and he heard her running up the stairs.

. . . Supper was late that evening.

Mrs. Gimlett said her mistress had a headache and would not be down, so Ross ate the meal alone. It was a dish of boiled rabbits with savoury garnishings, but he imagined that it had not quite the flavour as when Demelza cooked it. Afterwards there was apple tart and cream and hot scones. When he had finished he put some tart and cream in a dish and a couple of the scones and took it upstairs.

He found her in their room lying on the bed. It was her favourite retreat in her rare moments of despair. She had her face in the pillow, and she didn't move when he came in or when he sat on the bed.

"Demelza."

She might have been dead for all the response this produced.

"Demelza. I've brought you some tart."

"I don't want nothing to eat," she said in a muffled voice.

"All the same, a mouthful or two can be put away somewhere. I want to talk to you."

"Not now, Ross," she said.

"Yes, now."

"Not now."

He stared at her tangle of hair, at her figure's tantalising twisted grace.

153

"You've got a hole in your stocking," he said.

She wriggled and after a moment sat up. Her face was streaked and she wiped it with a corner of lace, hating him but not wanting to be unsightly in his eyes.

"Eat this, my dear."

She shook her head.

He put the dish down. "Look, Demelza, if there have to be quarrels I like them to have a good substantial basis with a nice groundwork of grievance on both sides to work on. But I don't see a basis for this in a fat hairy old man who comes here pestering you for favours. In your heart I think you know Bodrugan just as well as I do. So perhaps there is some other irritant at work. Do you know what it is?"

She made a little gesture which did not convey much.

"You speak of my cold looks and bitter tongue," he said. "But after living in this house six or seven years and being married to me for over three, my peculiarities can't be any surprise to you. I admit them, but they've not grown on me overnight like Billy Thomson's beard. You've suffered under them and thrived under them for long enough. So I can't help but feel there is an underlying cause which makes them no longer bearable. I've noticed a falling off in the hours we spend together and in the sort of satisfaction they bring. Haven't you?"

She said indistinctly: "It is not of my seeking."

"Perhaps," he said, "we expect too much if we expect the early glow to last. We had fifteen or eighteen months that were as near perfect as any man or woman could wish for; but now at the beginning of this second stage we're disappointed that absolute happiness has gone and each is inclined to blame the other. So minor irritations magnify and we come to a quarrel. That's the plain truth, is it not?"

"If that's how you see it," she said, keeping her head away.

"Isn't that how you see it? Well, not yet, but perhaps you will come to see it that way."

Not only does he not want our child but he no longer wants me, she thought.

"In the meantime," he went on gently enough, "let's strive for tolerance in our irritations. I'll do my most to avoid condescension towards you—which is the last thing I feel. And if you find my company cold as well as dull, try to excuse it, because I've subjects enough to engage me, and a passing sourness of expression is much more likely to be concerned with a passing thought than being a sign of dissatisfaction with you."

After saying that, he leaned forward and kissed her on the cheek and left her again, having only succeeded in considerably deepening the misunderstanding between them.

A good deal later that night she came downstairs and found him at the table in the parlour with all his books around him. In the old days she would have sat on the arm of his chair and tried to make out how he came by the balance; but that would not do now. A half-full brandy bottle was at his elbow, and she wondered if it had been new to begin the evening. He glanced up with a brief smile when she came in, but soon was working again.

She went across and poked the fire, threw on another couple of billets of wood and sat quiet watching the blue tentative flames.

She could hear the stream hissing, and an owl screeched sometimes in the dark. A quiet night. All December so far had been the same, a time of early dews and wet leaves underfoot and darkness lingering in the day as if it were the earth's natural element. It was gentle weather—but gentle with the atmosphere of decay. There seemed nothing new or young in the world.

Suddenly she looked up from biting her finger and saw that Ross was watching her. To cover her thoughts she said:

"Do you still not get paid for being head purser of the mine, Ross?"

"It saves money and I draw a greater profit."

"And so does everyone else. Where Father used to work they paid the head purser forty shillings a month. We are so poor now that it would help."

"But not enough." He began to fill his long pipe. "These are not all cost books. Some are for my own accountings. I shall not be able to meet my obligations in three weeks' time."

"Did you see your moneylender to-day then?" She tried to say it casually, though she knew all it meant to them both.

"Pearce would be flattered by your name. Yes, I saw him. He has agreed to extend the loan for another year."

"Then . . ."

"Pascoe has also agreed to add interest to mortgage with his bank, while cautioning me that, now he has partners to consider, he may not be able to do it for a further year. But he's unlikely to have the need, for I can't find the four hundred pounds' interest for Pearce, nor near it, without selling out of the mine; and without that we shall not drag on a very long time."

She felt suddenly ashamed of herself for having picked this day to quarrel with him.

"How much are you lacking?"

"A little over two hundred pounds."

"Could you not . . ."

"Oh yes, I could perhaps borrow the money—that much—from some friend, but what's the use? I should only get in even deeper. It would have been better, as Pascoe advised, to sell a year ago to the Warleggans and have done with them and started free of the worst debt."

"It's not like you to be down in the mouth, Ross. But even borrowing from a friend wasn't quite what I meant. We have—some things, a few things, which did ought to bring us in money."

"Such as?"

"Well . . . there's my ruby brooch. You said that was worth a hundred pounds."

"The brooch is yours."

"You gave it me. I can give it back if I want to. And there's Caerhays. I can manage well without a horse. I scarcely ever go beyond what I can comfortably walk. I

156

always *did* walk. An' the frock would fetch something—and this clock, and the new carpet in our room."

"I couldn't consider it. If I went to prison you would have to live on those things and what they brought. I'm not just going to empty them into the bottomless pit."

"Then there's some of the farm stock," said Demelza, more happy now she had something definite to consider. "All rare good stock but more than we properly need. It seems simple enough to me. If you pay off this interest debt you can make more money somehow. But if we sell the mine shares these other things'll be no manner of use to anyone. *They* won't bring us in money to live on. Wheal Leisure does. Besides . . . it wouldn't be like you to give in to the Warleggans."

She had touched the raw spot. He got up, thrusting back his chair, and stood while he lit his pipe from a piece of twisted paper.

"You always did argue like a lawyer."

That pleased her. The light flickered about her face.

"You'll do that, won't you, Ross?"

"I don't know."

"We could raise two hundred pounds," she said. "I'm sure we could."

Chapter Two

The following day Demelza rode a little defiantly off to meet the Bodrugans at Werry House. She was in a reckless mood, and for the moment it didn't seem so much to matter that she knew nothing whatever about horses. When she saw the sick mare she had a rush of misgivings, but it was plain that Sir Hugh expected her to prescribe some vile-smelling nostrum and that he put down as false modesty her expressed wish not to interfere. She'd cured Sir John's Minta and could at least make an attempt to do the same here.

She stared at the mare for some time and then glanced up to meet a look of curiosity and challenge on Constance Bodrugan's face. Well, if that was the way they felt . . . If the mare died they could well afford the loss, and it might ease Sir Hugh's attentions once and for all. . . . If she had to commit a crime she might as well do it with a flourish. . .

She ordered all the blisters, clysters, ointments, salves, pills and poultices of the professional horse doctors to be thrown away. That cleared the air quite a bit. Then she told them to go out and gather nine leaves of heart-fever grass and nine flowers of the scarlet pimpernel and tie them in a silk bag round the mare's neck. When these were eventually brought she recited a poem over the animal.

> " Herb Pimpernel, I have thee found
> Growing upon Christ Jesu's ground.
> The same gift the Lord Jesus bare thee
> When His blood He shed to spare thee;
> Herb and grass this evil pass
> And God bless all who wear thee—Amen."

It was a doggerel she had heard old Meggy Dawes of Illugan recite: she rather thought Meggy used it as a cure for warts, but anyhow it couldn't do any hurt.

Then she prescribed the same cordial of rosemary, juniper and cardamon which she had recommended for the pedigree Hereford. After that they all went back to the house and she took two glasses of port and a biscuit and watched a litter of puppies chewing the rug at her feet. The port just in time helped to kill off the growth of self-criticism. She refused an invitation to dinner and left before one, her virtue unimpaired, followed by the blustering good wishes of Sir Hugh and the speculative glances of Constance Lady Bodrugan. She could guess what Constance would say if the mare died.

Ross didn't mention the visit over dinner, but at supper he said:

" What was the matter with Bodrugan's blood mare? Influenza, d'you think?"

So he had taken it for granted that she had gone in spite of his disapproval. " I don't know at all, Ross. It might well be. She's awful bad, with a quivery feel to the muscles like Ramoth before he died."

" What did you do for her?"

Uneasily she told him.

He laughed. " You'll have every veterinarian in the county up in arms. You're stealing their fire."

" I don't care for that. But she's a rare lovely animal. I hope she comes round. I expect twould be quite a loss if she died."

" She must be worth upwards of three hundred guineas."

Demelza dropped her knife and went pale. " You're joking, Ross!"

" I may be wrong, of course. But King David was her sire. And he——"

" Judas!" Demelza got up. " Why didn't you tell me before?"

" I thought you knew. Anyway, I'm sure you'll have done her no harm."

Demelza went to the side table. " It was *mean* of you not to tell me, Ross."

" I thought you knew! Bodrugan is always boasting of it, and you have had his acquaintance for more than a year. But perhaps when you meet you don't talk of horses."

She did not take him up on that quip, but moved the dishes restlessly about. After a minute she came back to the table and sat down again.

" By the way," he said, " what did happen in Bodmin? How was it you came to meet Sir Hugh while you were there? And why does he seem to think you're under some obligation to him?"

She said: " I don't know how they dared send for me."

At much the same time that Demelza was rashly making her second essay in animal medicine, Dwight Enys, applying all his conscience and skill to the less valuable human animals of Sawle, was making discoveries about his own shortcomings.

Doctoring, he found, was not only a constant fight against other people's ignorance but also against one's own.

It was Parthesia Hoblyn's gums which gave him the clue to the disease which had been spreading through the village all autumn. If any excuse could be found for his own incompetence it lay in the paludal fever which had so constantly masked the more serious complaint. In this case, as in most of the others, the girl had taken the fever, had recovered, had taken it again, and after the second attack all the life had gone out of her and she had been breathless and exhausted with the least effort. Discoloration of her arms like bruises had made him suspect, first, her father and then, when he proved blameless, the disease known as purpura. He had given her an occasional fever powder to clear the blood, and had ordered her to sit out on mild days and drink cold water —a course that Jacka Hoblyn strongly disapproved of. (Busy about the house, he said: that was what she should be; it would work off the bad humours far better than sitting at the door breathing in all the moisture and the steams.)

And then Dwight met Ted Carkeek (whose shoulder wound was long since healed and almost forgotten) and Ted by chance mentioned that his father had died at sea; and going from him Dwight came straight into Vercoe, the bearded excise officer from St. Ann's—an ex-naval man—who stopped to ask him about his wife with an abscess under her tooth and went on talking about life aboard ship; and straight afterwards Dwight called on the Hoblyns and saw Parthesia's gums—and everything then was suddenly plain and he was abusing himself for having been so criminally blind. These listless blotchy ailing people of Sawle, with their nose bleedings and their sallow skins, were the victims of an outbreak of scorbutus. Choake, presuming he now came into the village at all, had not spotted it; and *he* had not spotted it, so people went on suffering and being wrongly treated.

"Parthesia, I'm going to change your medicine. I think you need a change, do you not? I haven't the ingredients here," he said to Rosina, who was standing by the chair, " but think a sulphur medicine might help. In the meantime, have you any source of fresh vegetables in or around the village?"

"Vegetables? No, sur. We don't belong to have vegetables—not above a few potatoes—before April or May."

"Or fruit—lemons in particular, or lemonades . . . no, of course you haven't. I have green things sometimes myself. Can you not get them in Truro?"

"They're too dear for the likes of we. Those things d'run away with the money in no time."

He looked thoughtfully into Rosina's beautiful eyes. "Ye-es. . . . Still I must urge you to afford them. It's vital. They'll do Thesia far more good than all my draughts or all your mother's home doctoring."

Rosina said: "I'll ask Father. Maybe we could perhaps send in for some when the next mule train go in."

He went away thinking it over. Counsels of perfection which the Hoblyns, being people just above the privation level, might possibly be able to follow. But what of the rest? They could no more get fresh vegetables or fruit than if they were becalmed in the Pacific Ocean. Yet what good would his sulphur potions or diaphuretic salts be to them without it? At the best palliatives. Probably not that. It was infuriating. Amid all the doubts and disappointments of medicine there existed for this disease a certain cure—and the cure was unobtainable.

Nor could he himself afford to feed a village, or some chosen families, on green stuffs of his own buying.

Trenwith House was still the province of Thomas Choake; but Dwight, by roundabout and unsought ways, had come to have an interest below stairs in Mrs. Tabb who, having fallen and badly cut her arm a few days before, would have no one but Dr. Enys to dress it. She had walked to his house but had gone queer when she got there, so he had said he would call next time and save her the seven-mile walk. He found the wound not suppurating much, and applied a blister of Spanish fly to help it. Having left an ointment for later use, he walked down the stairs escorted by Tabb—and saw Elizabeth Poldark in the hall.

"Dr. Enys. We don't often see you in our house."

"No, ma'am." He smiled. "I try not to poach on a colleague."

She said slowly: "The game is only preserved on professional visits."

"Thank you. I'll remember that. I've not seen your husband since we met in Bodmin."

"Francis told me of your kindness. We were all most relieved at the outcome of the trial. . . . Will you take a glass of wine?"

They turned towards the winter parlour. "If refinement of taste is enough, then our married life has been an idyll," Francis had said on that long night in Bodmin. Refinement of taste? Was that all this woman had to offer? Her young withdrawn loveliness always caught at Dwight's heart. Oh, he knew he was impressionable, but . . .

In the parlour Aunt Agatha crouched over a smoky fire. The old lady's hands trembled and fumbled unceasingly about in her lap, like wrinkled grey moles searching for something they could never find; but her spirit was as determined as ever, and the sharp old eyes looked Dwight over as he was reintroduced. Of course she remembered him at Ross's baby's christening party, she said, it being her habit nowadays never to admit she could forget anything. She could always tell an attorney's face. They seldom—what? what? Yes, that's what she'd said. And what was doctoring like in Truro these days? In her young days there'd been a Dr. Seabright with a big following. Used to prescribe fresh horse dung as a cure for the pleurisy. Lived over what was now Pearce's Hotel. Very popular, but he caught farcy cutting up a horse and was dead within the month.

"Aunt Agatha will not hear us; she's very deaf," Elizabeth said, and turned the conversation to commonplaces of the countryside. Dwight expanded as he always did in sympathetic female company, and only now and then did the memories of that night come to disturb him. They blew across his brain like phantasms of a not quite real experience. The unwinking candles; Francis's disembodied face, bitter and drawn; the harsh confidences, originally sought, but when given half turned away from; through it all ran Elizabeth, Elizabeth, the loved but the unloving, the Galatea who never woke.

Perhaps some shadow crossed Dwight's face, for Elizabeth broke off what she had been talking about.

"Dr. Enys, may I ask you a question? . . . From something he said I've come to suspect that my husband—that Francis tried to commit suicide when he was in Bodmin. Do you know if it is true?"

That was a poser. In embarrassment Dwight glanced at the old lady, who was still watching him as if she could hear every word.

"Your husband and I shared a room in Bodmin, as you know. The atmosphere of the town was very excitable at that time and Mr. Poldark was—susceptible to the general feeling of recklessness and hard drinking. We—talked a long time together, well into the night, and I think his having someone to talk to helped him over a difficult period. I don't think you need worry about it."

Aunt Agatha said: "Shingles I had, I recollect, and he gave me blood from a cat mixed with cow milk to put on the sore place mornings and evenings. And treacle water at nights. He was a skirt little fellow, I mind, but as bright as a bee."

"You haven't answered my question, Dr. Enys," Elizabeth said.

"That's the only answer I can give. . . . I've known nowhere worse than this district for wild rumours, and I should advise you to ignore them."

There was a glint in Elizabeth's eyes as she turned. "Perhaps you don't realise how cut off we are here from the general social world, Dr. Enys."

"No . . . I hadn't realised it."

"Our cousins from Nampara don't come, we can no longer afford to entertain, and Francis is seldom in a mood for polite visiting. So perhaps it will explain to you why I am put to this strait in begging information from a—stranger."

Dwight said: "I should be sorry if you looked on me as

163

that. I shall be only too happy if I can be of help or value to you—and I hope you'll call on me in any way you think fit."

"In those days," said Aunt Agatha, chewing at her gums, "no gentleman never went out without his sword. Didn't *dare*. I mind seeing a highwayman hanged at Bargus. Pretty-looking man, he was, in a crimson suit o' clothes and a gold-laced hat. Went off very well, too, bold as brass to the last kick. You wouldn't have dared rode from Truro like that, young man, dressed as if you was going to a burying."

"I live between Nampara and Mingoose," said Dwight in a raised voice.

"Yes, I know tis easy enough now. Here to Truro they say's as safe as your own backlet. All the spirit's gone out of the world."

Elizabeth said: "Francis will have told you of the estrangement between ourselves and our cousins?"

"I know of it, yes."

"Do you think Ross is settled down after all his trouble?"

"I always feel," Dwight said, "that Ross is like a volcano. He may be quiet forever—or erupt to-morrow."

He caught a look in her eyes which seemed to show agreement. He went on: "Demelza I've seen less of than before." (Which was true enough. Sometimes indeed it might have been that Demelza was trying to avoid him, though he could think of no reason.)

"Where's Geoffrey Charles?" said Aunt Agatha. "Where's the boy . . .?"

"Would you think," Elizabeth said, "that they were happy together?"

". . . He's going to be a tartar," said the old lady. "Not seven yet and up to all manner o' saucy tricks. I'd give him a good nooling. No cheeil's right without a stick to his back once in a while."

Dwight said: "Perhaps I should answer that if I knew the answer."

"She was good to us last year," Elizabeth said. "Without her one or more of us might have died. Would you take her a message from me? Tell her—would you say that we once spent a happy Christmas together at Trenwith and say that we should like them to come again this year. Impress it on her, would you, that we really want them, need them? D'you mind doing this for me?"

"Of course I will."

"Perhaps you'd join us yourself. We shall have no special attraction to offer you, but——"

He thanked her, said he would be delighted, and took his leave. On his way out he saw Francis coming in, walking up the drive from the direction of the main gate. They didn't directly pass each other, but Francis raised an ironical finger to his forehead. He was roughly dressed and his boots were caked in mud, but he looked better than when last Dwight had seen him.

The short day was closing, and it would be dusk before he reached Grambler. The sullen sea was already blurred where it could be glimpsed between the declivities of the land. The damp mild pall of clouds drifted across from the coast in infinite deepening layers of brown like forerunners of the long night.

As he came out on the main track above Grambler he saw a squat bowlegged figure tramping ahead. It was Jud Paynter, and in a hurry. He glanced behind nervously at the sound of a horseman, but his aggrieved face cleared when he saw who it was.

"Evening, Paynter." Dwight was riding past when Jud raised his hand.

"Handsome weather we're 'aving, Mester Enys. Proper job for the time o' year. Twill pass the winter away."

Dwight replied conventionally, then he slackened his reins to move on again.

"Mester Enys."

"Yes."

"I s'pose tes axing more'n you could do to keep aside of me till we get to Grambler."

"Not if there's some good reason. It's only half a mile."

"'Alf a mile can be a cant of a way. Aye, an' thur's reason, sure 'nough. Thur's a couple o' great men inching up behind me, and I aren't taking to the notion at all. No, not me. Not Jud Paynter. I aren't aiming to be churched just yet. See any sign of 'em, did ee?"

"What d'you mean?"

"What I d'say, that's what. Just in St. Ann's I am, about me ordinary, proper, reasonable, human, respectable, decent, fair an' honest business when first I seen the two of 'em eyeing me as if I was a green goose ready for the Christmas pot. Ullo, I says. Footpaths, I says. Or some such, I says. I'd best be off home, else they'll likely slit me throat when I aren't looking. Tes a crying shame," Jud went on, "what the country's coming to. Can't stir outside your own front door wi'out blackguards lying in wait. Tedn right. Tedn proper. Tedn *fair*."

"Do they suspect you to be carrying money?"

"Me?" said Jud, startled. "I aren't carrying money. Not more'n a few pence to buy an honest glass o' rum."

"Why should anyone try to rob you, then? Why not me? My horse alone would be the better prize."

Jud shrugged. "There you are. Tes the way of things. Maybe they think there'd be more of a dido if you was ditched. Nay. Tes the widows an' orphans, that's what the bad men d'go for."

"Which are you?" Dwight asked.

"Who, me?" said Jud. "Why, I been an orphan ever since me mother and father died."

They made slow progress, Dwight having difficulty in keeping his horse in check, Jud panting along grumbling behind. Dwight had a pot of ointment to deliver in the village, so he left that and was just overtaking Jud again when he reached his shack. Prudie was at the door.

"So there ye are, you splatty old pig," she said, and then she recognised the horseman. "Avnoon, Dr. Dwight," she added sheepishly.

"Good day to you, Prudie. You must be glad to see your husband safely home."

"Home, an? I ain't 'ad sight or sound of him these pretty

many days. Reckon he b'long to think he can go off an' come back just when he d'take the fancy. Dirty old gale."

"You know where I been," said Jud. "Know it fine an' well. Earning money, I been, to keep ee in lazy idleness. And Doctor d'know just so well as you, though he may pretend elsewise."

Dwight said: "A good run?"

"'Twas none so poor."

"Was that why the men were following you?"

"What men?" demanded Prudie, wiping her swollen red nose on her sleeve.

Jud looked uneasy while Dwight explained.

"Tes naught to do wi' the trade," he said. "Tes just as I told ee. Footpaths looking for some poor 'elpless old man to rob. I tell ee tes a bad business when law and order d'go for naught. I——"

"Well," said Prudie, "I can't suppose what's amiss with 'im. Ever since he come 'ome from that trial he's been like this—scared to go abroad after dark, 'e is. Scared of 'is own shadow oft times, I reckon. Say 'bo' to him an' he'll run like a meader."

"Tedn true! Tedn right! I aren't afraid of nothing except what tis natural to be afraid of. An' I aren't no meader, see, so there!"

"Be as it will, tis somethin' to do wi' that trial," said Prudie. "Dear knows what tis, but you was there, Dr. Dwight, my son, an' mebbe *you* can guess. Like as not Jud was tiddly when he went in the stand, an' tis a mystery to me how he wasn't locked away there and then!"

"But what has that to do with his being afraid now?"

"That's what I been saying till I'm swelled out wi' saying it," Jud stated violently. "What you got t'eat, wife? I'm leary enough without all this slack-jaw. Ef ye paid more heed to yer cooking and less to yer talkin' the world'd be a sight betterer place. There's no peace, not in the home nor out of it!"

Dwight took the hint and began to move on. Prudie's voice followed him like an organ with all the stops pulled out.

"Law or no, tis on account o' something to do wi' that there trial. You can't fox me, ole man. All the time, soon as it go dark, you're hoppin' and dodging like a flea on a hot plate. Thur's somethin' behind it, an' I'll get to the root of un yet!"

Dwight's last view was of Jud going grumpily into the cottage, and Prudie's threats and warnings blew after him through the wide dusk.

Chapter Three

The brooch fetched seventy pounds. The pawnbroker said prices had come down since they bought it; also there was not the sale for expensive jewellery in Cornwall. Ross said it was as much as they could reasonably expect. Demelza's horse, Caerhays, fetched thirty-five guineas, and the carpet ten. Ross said the frock was *not* to be sold. Very well, he should go to prison and she would never wear it again and the moths would get at it and it would go out of fashion, and it was too big already about the waist because she had lost weight and he should go to prison; but the frock was not to be sold. Demelza took a warmth and comfort from that.

Then they started on the farm stock. They sold their two-year-old colt, Sikh, for ten guineas, and their two best cows for fourteen guineas apiece. It was not a good time of year for disposing of farm stock. Ross sold with the bitter consciousness that the people who bought his animals would be able to dispose of them in three months' time at a profit. They got two pounds, twelve shillings and sixpence each for two month-old heifer calves. Without oxen, ploughing would be almost impossible, so there could be no economy there. They sold their pigs and almost all their poultry. Jane Gimlett was in tears, and Jack Cobbledick only just avoided them. With some twenty-five pounds still to be got Ross went round his farm. Of all his livestock, built up carefully over seven years, he now had one cow, due to calf in

April, one horse, his team of oxen, a half dozen chickens and a few ducks. It was while they were on this tour that Dwight arrived with Elizabeth's invitation.

"Tell them . . ." said Ross, and stopped, the anger swelling, "that we are so busy savouring the sweets of——"

"Tell them," said Demelza hastily. "But it isn't for Dwight to be our messenger, is it? Shall you accept for yourself, Dwight?"

"I think so. Christmas isn't a great deal of pleasure spent alone."

"There are worse alternatives," said Ross.

After a minute Dwight added: "Of course I should enjoy it better at Trenwith if you were there. . . ."

"Complimentary but inaccurate."

"I'll take the chance."

"There's no chance to take."

The awkward silence was broken by Garrick, who suddenly appeared and came bounding across the yard like a monstrous French poodle, wagging his stump and showing a lolling red tongue. As usual he had no respect for the decencies; Dwight had to duck out of the way, and Ross came off with a couple of muddy paw marks on the front of his shirt.

"The trouble with Demelza," Ross said, brushing himself, "is that she adopts strange animals and then doesn't sufficiently tame them. We had Sir Hugh Bodrugan over the other day."

Dwight laughed. "Sir Hugh has never shown any special ambition to lick my face."

"Not yours perhaps."

"Oh, Ross," Demelza said, "why could we not go to Trenwith?"

Ross looked at his empty yard. "D'you seriously ask that?"

"I know I should not; but . . . it is a pity to think too much in the past."

How fail when it so much influenced the present? "Tell them that we will come when Verity and Blamey are invited and not before."

"I don't think it will be very long before that happens," said Demelza. "Verity and Francis were reconciled at Bodmin."

"We can all be reconciled together, then."

After a minute Demelza said: "That's what I should like too. But if we were to make the first move . . ."

Ross thought, Oh, God, what if my bankruptcy *is* Francis's fault (and the chances are it would have happened in any case), perhaps Demelza is right. She often is. Reconciliation is what Verity wants. And Demelza wants it. And Elizabeth. The last thought wakened in him a desire, almost a need, to see Elizabeth again. He'd never got over his attachment, it was something fundamental, a weakness if you liked, overlooked but still there.

"Well," he said, "we'll think it over. At this present moment twenty or thirty pounds is more important than all the Christmas reunions. Perhaps you'd like to take out a mortgage on my property, Dwight. It would have to be a third mortgage and bear interest at a hundred per cent. There's nothing like moneylending for bringing in a fair return."

"You may have ten pounds, which is all I own. It could go to no better cause."

"Nor is it yet a lost cause, though we have moments of doubt. D'you remember Tregeagle, who had to drain out Dozmare Pool with a sea shell? Mine's the opposite task."

They moved on. Dwight began to talk about his discovery of scurvy in Sawle, and this occupied them until they returned to the house, where John Gimlett was working on a library window, repairing the rusty hinge of a shutter.

"If you're short of turf we can let you have some," Ross said. "There's enough stacked for two winters almost."

Garrick, having shown his overflowing affection, had galloped off again, but at this stage he was seen returning carrying something in his mouth. It proved to be the hindquarters of a rabbit which he laid at Demelza's feet.

"Go away!" said Demelza in disgust. "Horrid dog! Take it away!"

Ross picked up the corpse and heaved it across the stream, the dog bounding in hot pursuit.

"I wonder what Garrick would be worth in the open market," he said. "One overgrown mongrel. Carnivorous. Fights bulls and guards babies. Trained to sit on seedlings and scratch up flowers. Good crockery breaker. Suffers sometimes from bad breath. Results guaranteed."

Dwight laughed. As they went into the house he said: "Shall you be able to keep the Gimletts?"

"They won't leave. We can feed them, and that's all they want for the time. And I can't work the farm without Cobbledick."

"Seriously," Dwight said, "my ten pounds is yours if it's any use."

"Seriously," said Ross, "it will have to be the clock, Demelza, and a few bits of furniture. Then there's my father's pistols and the old telescope."

So it has all come round like in a circle, thought Demelza. Three years since we spent Christmas at Trenwith. And just such another day, cloudy and quiet. Then I was that frightened I hardly knew what I was saying. Scullerymaid going to visit the gentry. Now it's all changed. Nervous in a way, but not that way. *They're* poor. Just as poor as we—and Francis is working on his own land, and Elizabeth . . . Elizabeth has lost her terrors, and is full of gratitude to me for what took place last Christmas. Dear Verity isn't there. But I've no fear of doing the wrong thing or making a fool of myself. Yet I'm not near so happy as then. And the queer thing is I'm expecting another child, and again hiding it from Ross, though for a different reason—and it's just about four months forward, the same as last time.

"D'you remember," she said, "when we were walking this way before? Garrick kept following on and laying down when we spoke to him, just as if for once he was going to do as he was told."

"Yes," said Ross.

"And you remember we met Mark Daniel and he took Garrick by the ear and marched him home. . . . D'you ever hear anything of Mark now, Ross?"

"I don't know how he's faring with all this upset, but Paul saw him last in Roscoff."

"Don't you think it would be safe enough for him to come home?"

"No. If things get too bad in France he should go to Ireland or America; but there'd be no peace of mind for him here, even under an assumed name."

Last time there had been Verity at the door to greet them. To-day Demelza noticed the weeds growing in the drive, the grass rank under the trees, the patched-up window and the unpainted gate leading to the orchard. Tabb let them in, and the old faded Trenwiths, in their dresses and cloaks of crimson and amber, stared coldly over the ringing empty hall. As they took off their cloaks Elizabeth came out of the winter parlour.

Demelza was surprised to see her wearing the frock of startling crimson velvet with the cascades of fine lace which she had worn at Julia's christening. There had been no suggestion that this was to be a party, and Demelza, feeling that any display in the present circumstances would be looked on as bad form by these well-bred people, had come in her afternoon dress.

So she's still interested in Ross, thought Demelza, with a sharp twinge, and any gratefulness to me won't make the least difference. I might have *known*. Nevertheless she went forward with a smile on her face and was graciously welcomed. Too graciously, she at once thought. It didn't ring true, like the sick Elizabeth of twelve months ago. What a fool I've been.

Francis was not there to welcome them, but when they had taken off their cloaks he came out of the big parlour. He was a little hesitant at this first proper meeting, and the two men eyed each other for a second.

Francis said: "Well, Ross . . . so you came."

"I came."

"It's—a good thing, I think. *I'm* glad, anyway."

He put out his hand rather tentatively. Ross took it, but the clasp was not a long one.

Francis said: "We were always good friends in the past."

"The best way," Ross said, "is to forget the past."

"I'm very willing. It's a bitter subject."

That said, the reconciliation formally made, there seemed nothing to add to it, and so the constraint grew up again.

"Did you walk here?"

"Yes." A sore point, with Caerhays sold. "I see Odgers is getting some repairs done to Sawle Church at last."

"To the roof only. It has rained in so persistently these last few months that often the choir have had to sing with water dripping down their necks. I wish the damned steeple would fall down. It always persuades me I'm drunk when I get to the northwest of it."

"Someday perhaps, when a Poldark is rich again, we shall be able to do something about it."

"I think the church will have fallen down naturally before then."

"My dear," said Elizabeth, linking Demelza's arm, "I was afraid you would never bring him. If he makes up his mind there's seldom much prospect of changing it. But perhaps you are clever enough to know how to set about it."

"I'm not clever," said Demelza. Indeed I'm not, she thought. Can I hold my own this week end, like I did three years ago? This time I haven't the heart. I'm too miserable and sick in mind to want to fight for him if he doesn't want me.

"My father and mother will be here for dinner," said Elizabeth. "Also Dwight Enys. I'm afraid we shall have no visitors after. You remember last time, George Warleggan and the Treneglosses turned up and you sang those enchanting songs."

"I haven't seen the Treneglosses for ages," said Demelza, as they went into the big parlour.

"Ruth is expecting her first child next month. There'll be great excitement if it is a boy. They say old Mr. Horace

173

Treneglos is already planning for his first grandson. There's not a lot of money about these days but when a family has been in existence more than six hundred years . . . Of course, ours is older."

"What, the Poldarks?"

Elizabeth smiled. "No. I'm sorry. I meant my own family. We have records back to 971. Ross, it's like old times to see you in this room."

"It's like old times to be here," said Ross enigmatically.

"And old times," said Francis, bringing a wineglass across, "is precisely what we are doing our best to forget. Here's to new times, I say. If there are any, then they can be no worse than what's gone, and good riddance." He smiled into Demelza's eyes.

Demelza slowly shook her head, smiling back. "Old times were good to me," she said.

It wasn't the sort of meal they'd had before, either, though it was the best put on for two years. They had ham and fowls and a leg of mutton, boiled, with caper sauce, and afterwards batter pudding and currant jelly and damson tarts, and black caps in custard, and blancmange.

Demelza had never met Elizabeth's father and mother, and she was astonished at them. If keeping records since 971 made you look like that, then she'd rather have an ancestry that was decently forgot. Mr. Chynoweth was thin and wiry, with little pompous mannerisms that surprised because they claimed too much. Mrs. Chynoweth was a dreadful sight, corpulent, with one eye discoloured and a swollen neck. Not having seen her before her illness, Demelza couldn't imagine where Elizabeth had got her ravishing looks. It didn't take long either to discover that they were people with a grievance. Something had gone wrong with their lives and they resented it as a personal affront. Demelza preferred old Aunt Agatha any day, for all her whiskers and her dribbling chin. You couldn't answer her back, but her conversation had vitality and point. It was a pity someone didn't write down her flow of memories before she died and they were all gone, lost forever in yesterday's dust.

After dinner, to Demelza's horror, though she should have remembered this was the routine, the women went off on their own, leaving the men over the port; and in any nightmare Demelza could not have chosen three more fearful companions than Elizabeth—in her present mood—Aunt Agatha and Mrs. Chynoweth. They all walked upstairs and into Elizabeth's bedroom and chattered round the mirror and tidied their hair and in turn visited the noisome apartment down the passage which Demelza thought so much worse than the outdoor arrangements of Nampara; and Elizabeth adjusted Aunt Agatha's lace cap, and Mrs. Chynoweth said she'd heard the new fashions at London and Bath were verging on the indecent; and Aunt Agatha said she still had some recipes somewhere for the face: pomatums and suchlike, and lip salves, white pots and water of talk: she'd find 'em for Demelza before she left. And Elizabeth said Demelza was very quiet, was she quite well? And Demelza said, Oh *yes*, fine and well; and Mrs. Chynoweth gave her a casual glance up and down that seemed to strip her secret bare, and said the new fashion was for the waist to be right up under the arms and for the whole dress to fall quite like a candle sconce to the floor and the less worn under, the better. Demelza sat on the rosewood bed with its pink quilted satin hangings, and adjusted her garters and thought, Ross was right, we should never have come back here till Verity came; *she* makes all the difference, she's my mascot, my luck; I'm dull to-night and even port won't help; so Elizabeth'll score all round with her lovely sheeny hair and sapling waist and big grey eyes and her educated voice and her grace and poise. How is the rest of this evening and to-morrow to be got through?

Downstairs the port had circulated twice, and Jonathan Chynoweth, who had a humiliatingly weak head, was looking drowsy and talked with a slurred speech. Dwight, who had never had the money to drink regularly, was aware of his own deficiencies and kept sipping a drop and adding a drop when the bottle came round. The cousins, of course, were hardly aware that they had yet begun.

Francis said to Ross: " These are the last three bottles of the '83 port. Did you lay in much of it at the time?"

" I hadn't the money then—just back from America and the place in a ruin. I've nothing earlier than last year's. When that's done we shall have to resort to cheap gin."

Francis grunted. " Money. The lack of it is poisoning both our lives. Sometimes I could rob a bank—would, if it were Warleggan's and I could escape the gallows."

Ross glanced idly at him. " What made you quarrel with 'em?"

It was the first question which touched on the fundamentals between them. Francis instantly realised its importance and the impossibility of giving a full answer here. Yet he must not seem to evade it. " A realisation that your estimate of them was the right one."

There was a pause while the clock struck. The metallic vibrations trembled round the room long after it had finished, seeming to seek a way out.

Francis drew three straight lines down the tablecloth with a fork's prongs. " These things—soak in slowly. They're hardly noticed, until suddenly you wake up one day *knowing* that the man who has been your friend for years is a— blackguard and . . ." he waved his hand, ". . . that's all!"

" Have you moved your affairs?"

" No. I'll say that for them. I was offensive enough to George to blow his hat off, but he's done nothing about it."

" I should move them."

" Impossible. No one else would take the debt."

" Look," said Dwight uncomfortably, " I've had what drink I want, and if you'd like to discuss private money matters . . ."

" Ecod, there's nothing private in debts," said Francis. " They're everybody's property. It's the one consolation. . . . Anyway—I've nothing private from *you*."

The bottle was passed round.

" By the way," said Francis, " what has Demelza been doing with Bodrugan's mare?"

"Doing with it?" Ross said cautiously.

"Yes. I met him this morning, and he was all cock-a-hoop because his beloved Sheba was on the mend. I didn't even know the beast had been ill. He said it was Demelza's doing. The recovery, I mean, not the sickness."

The bottle came to Ross. "Demelza has some skill with animals," he said hardily. "Bodrugan came over and seemed anxious for her advice."

"Well, she's in his good graces now. He was fairly slapping his boots about it."

"What was wrong with the animal?" Dwight inquired.

"You must ask Demelza," Ross said. "No doubt she will explain."

"Quarrelling with the War-Warleggans," said Mr. Chynoweth. "A bad business. Very influ-influential. Tentacles."

"How eloquently you express yourself these days, Father-in-law," said Francis.

"Eh?"

"Let me fill your glass just this once more and then you can go to sleep comfortable."

"For twelve months," Ross said, "they've been trying to buy a share in Wheal Leisure."

"I don't doubt it. They'd be interested in any paying concern, and any belonging to you in particular."

"Wheal Leisure doesn't belong to me. I wish it did."

"Well, you're the largest shareholder. Have you had any success in linking up with the old Trevorgie workings?"

"No. We abandoned it for some of the wet months and then took it up again. I don't think the others will sanction the expense much longer."

"There's good work there somewhere."

"I know. But the men's wages mount up when you see them in the cost book."

"You remember when we went down the old workings together, Ross. It doesn't seem so long ago. There's money in Trevorgie and Wheal Grace. I could smell it that day."

"You need to put money in before you can take money out. It's one of the imperatives of mining."

"Both copper and tin have gone up again," said Dwight. He accepted the bottle and let it cool his fingers. "D'you think there's any chance of restarting Grambler?"

"Not a dog's chance," said Francis. "Here, drain up your glass, you're not keeping pace at all." He stared at Ross, whose lean restless face as yet showed no flush. "You know old Fred Pendarves. For a month now I've had him prospecting over my land. And Ellery helping him. I don't think if he lived to be eighty you'd make a farmer out of Ellery or get him to tell the front of a cow from the tail; but he's been bred to mining like a terrier's bred to ratting, and between 'em I'm hoping for some sort of a workable venture. At heart I'm just the same as Ellery: there's copper in my blood, and if I have to go on living then I've got to start mining again, not rooting up stroil or driving pigs to market."

A snore came from Jonathan Chynoweth, whose head was resting back against his chair.

"Driving pigs to market indeed," said Francis.

Ever since he came back from America, Ross thought, he and Francis had had something or other to quarrel about; but almost always when he met Francis he wondered if the quarrel was worth while. Francis had a way with him, always had had: a wry humour that carried one along, made one forget the bitterness and the possible betrayals. Perhaps the attraction was still mutual, for Francis had brightened up a lot since he came.

"Don't let me damp you," he said, "but even a hole in the ground costs money. Unless one can pick copper out of the subsoil as they did in Anglesea. . . ."

"I—have *some* ready money," said Francis. "A few hundred. It might see me through. Anyway, that's how it shall be spent."

When Francis had offered to help Demelza with money if things went wrong at Bodmin, Ross had dismissed it as a rhetorical flourish. But here it was again. Ready money in a near-bankrupt.

"Well, and have they found anything yet?"

"Oh, traces enough. There's mineral everywhere, as you

178

know. But I can't afford to take chances. I want a reasonable venture. What d'you think of this *Virgula Divinitoria*? It's supposed to be a sure test of where there is metal underground."

" The name's impressive. Do you know the English for it, Dwight?"

Mr. Chynoweth twitched and woke up. " Where am I?"

" In bed with your wife, old man," said Francis, " so have a care lest we take advantage of you."

Mr. Chynoweth blinked at him, but was too stupefied to be insulted. He reached for his glass, but before he grasped it his head was nodding again.

" I gather it's only a sort of divining rod," said Dwight. " Even supposing it worked, I think it would be disappointing to sink a shaft expecting copper and find only lead."

Ross said: " Or even a tin kettle left by one of the old men."

Francis said: " Of course you're lucky with both Wheal Grace and Wheal Maiden on your land. We never did nothing here except for Grambler. It took all our attention and all our money."

" Two derelict mines," said Ross, and remembered what Mark Daniel had said about Grace: *There's money in that mine. Copper. . . . I've never seen a more keenly lode.* " More expensive to restart than to begin a new working," he added.

Francis sighed. " Well, I suppose all your interest is in Wheal Leisure now."

" All my money is."

" And that's the same thing, eh? And I shall have to recourse to *Virgula Divinitoria* or the wisdom of old Fred Pendarves. Pass the port, Enys; you're making no good use of it."

There was a tap on the door and Tabb came in.

" If you please, sur, there's a man asking for Dr. Enys."

" What man?"

" He's from Killewarren, sur. I think he wants for Dr. Enys to go to someone who's ill."

"Oh, tell 'em to be ill on a more convenient night."

Dwight pushed back his chair. "If you'll excuse me . . ."

"Nonsense," said Francis, pouring his port so quickly that the froth circled to the centre. "If you must see the fellow ask him in here; see what he wants."

Tabb glanced at Dwight and then went out, to bring back a small clerkly man in black. They hadn't heard it begin to rain, but his cloak dripped water on the rug.

"Oh, it's Myners," said Francis. "What's amiss at Killewarren?"

The little man looked at Dwight. "Are you Dr. Enys, sir? I went to your house but was told you was here. Beg pardon for disturbing you. It is Miss Penvenen wanted to see you, and she sent me over to fetch you."

"Miss *Caroline* Penvenen?"

"Yes, sir."

So she was still in Cornwall—and no doubt her dog was having fits again.

"Has she not her own doctor?"

"Yes, sir, but she said for to fetch you. She's been ill for near on three days. It's her throat, sir, that is giving her grave trouble."

A silence fell on the table. The casual good-fellowship of Francis, Dwight's first impatience, were not proof against this. The malignant sore throat, which had struck both families last year, had hardly been heard of this. If it came in the district again . . .

"What symptoms?" Dwight said.

"I don't rightly know, sir. I'm only the bailiff. But Mr. Ray Penvenen said she was mortal sick and I must fetch you."

Dwight got up. "I'll come at once. Wait and show me the way."

Chapter Four

Penvenen land stretched up almost to the back of Grambler village, but the house, Killewarren, had its main entrance near Goon Prince and was about three miles from the gates of Trenwith.

They had not heard the rain indoors because it was coming in a fine silent slag from the southwest, moving with a tired wind. But it was more wetting than straight rain, and the night was dark with a close inner blackness more proper to a confined space than out of doors; even Myners had some difficulty in keeping to the grass-grown track that led home.

They did not talk much, because the way was often too narrow to ride abreast and the going so uneven that an incautious step might throw you. Dwight, too, had mixed feelings at the prospect of meeting the tall girl again; anxiety and a slight apprehension that was not entirely to do with her illness. More than ever he was glad he had not been free with the port.

He had never been to her home—or her uncle's home—and when they turned in at the gates he rather expected to see such another gracious Tudor residence as Trenwith, or a small but solid Palladian house like Sir John Trevaunance's; so it was a surprise to find an ill-lit, shabby, rambling building which seemed to be little more than an extensive farmhouse. They went in through a porch and hall, up some stairs and along a narrow passage to a big untidy living room at the end of it, where a man with spectacles was turning the pages of a book. He took off his spectacles when Dwight was shown in—a sandy, stocky man in a coat sizes too big for him. As he came nearer Dwight saw that his red eyelids were almost lashless and that his hands were covered with warts. Ray Penvenen, bachelor, a onetime " catch " of the county who had never been caught.

He said in a thin, rather musical voice: "Are you Dr. Enys?"

"Yes."

"My niece is ill. Dr. Choake has been attending her for two days, but she is worse and she insisted on sending for you."

As Penvenen fumbled to put his spectacles away Dwight wondered how he managed to keep his hands clean.

"Does Dr. Choake know I am being called?"

"No. We've not seen him since this morning."

Dwight said: "Of course, you know, it makes it very difficult——"

"I'm well aware of the usual etiquette, Dr. Enys, and I'm not responsible for the breach of it. It is my niece who has sent for you. But in fact I am not satisfied. She's in great pain to-night—and the throat can be so dangerous."

"Did Dr. Choake diagnose the complaint?"

"Yes. A quinzy."

"Is there any fever?"

"That we don't know. But she can hardly swallow at all."

They set off again, back down the passage and up a half dozen steps, and turned towards the south end of the house. Penvenen came to a door and stopped and knocked.

It was a big timbered room with an open fireplace in which a turf fire was flickering; wind down the chimney was fanning the smoke, and the blue damask untasselled curtains at the windows stirred furtively as the air was sucked through the door. A serving girl got up as they came in and Dwight went over to the bed.

Her tawny hair was loose and over her shoulders, and her fiery grey-green eyes a little dulled with pain, but she smiled at him with a faint sardonic twist to her lips. Then with an accompanying gesture she lifted the sheet and disclosed Horace asleep on a blue cushion beside her.

Dwight smiled back at her and took the seat the servant girl had left. He felt Caroline's pulse. It was quick but not sufficiently so to indicate a serious fever. He asked her one or two questions, which she answered by shakes or nods of her head. He saw her throat muscles quivering and then the effort she made to swallow.

" Will you open your mouth, Miss Penvenen."

She did so and he peered at her throat.

" Would you get me a spoon, please," he said to the maid. " A tablespoon." When she had gone he said to Penvenen: " What treatment has Dr. Choake prescribed?"

" . . . Two bleedings; that's so, isn't it, Caroline? A strong purge; and some sort of a draught, here. That's the lot, isn't it?"

Caroline pointed to the back of her neck.

" Oh, and a large blister. That's it. He said it was simply a question of getting the poisons to disperse."

Dwight smelled the mixture. It was probably syrup of gill and Gascoigne's powder with a few other things in cinnamon water. The maid came back and Dwight took the spoon and sat on the bed.

The left side of the throat was much inflamed and there was no sign of suppuration yet. The uvula, the soft palate and the pharynx were all involved. At least there was nothing to suggest the disease they all feared. It seemed in fact a fairly clear case of quinzy and there was not a great deal he could do to improve on Choake's treatment. Her hands and forehead were quite cool, that was the only unusual sign. She was in a lot of pain.

" Mr. Penvenen," he said, " would you kindly bring that candle over and hold it *quite* still. Just here. Here. That's it. Thank you." He pressed the tongue down with the spoon again.

Penvenen's breathing was heavy and rather stale, his nodular hand only just steady enough. Little blisters of grease followed each other down the side of the candle and congealed on the silver stick.

After a time Dwight released her and stood up. He had seen something, and a twist of excitement went through him. Penvenen also straightened, glad of the change of position, hitching the shoulders of his coat. They were all watching Dwight, but he was only aware of the green-eyed girl in the bed.

He turned his back on them and walked slowly to the fire. On the mantelshelf were things of hers. A velvet purse, embroidered and shutting with a spring; a gold repeating watch, probably French; a lace handkerchief with her initial in the corner; a pair of oiled dogskin gloves. He felt in his pocket and took out the etui that he always had with him. In it were the few small instruments that he found it useful to carry. A tooth forcer, a pair of tweezers, a fleam, tiny incision shears. He slid out the tweezers. Too short. Yet it would take an hour and a half to get the thing he really wanted. *Might* do. He had long fingers. And in another hour or so the swelling might have got so bad that what he wanted to do would not be possible at all.

He went back to the bed. " Would you hold the candle for me again, Mr. Penvenen? Miss Penvenen, sit up a little more, your head against the wood of the bed instead of against the pillow. Thank you." For a minute his eyes met hers steadily. He seemed to see into the depths of them as into the far reaches of a pool, where the spring began. " I can help you if you'll keep quite still. You mustn't jerk or jump. It may hurt a little, but I'll be as quick as I can."

" What is it?" asked Penvenen. " What are you going to do?"

" He's—going to lance my throat," she said in a whisper.

" No, I'm not. I want you to keep still. Will you do that?" She nodded. " Of course."

Penvenen could not hold the candle steady now. It flickered and bobbed; and the bed curtains got in the way; Dwight had the impulse to tear them all down. Eventually he got the light where he wanted and pressed her tongue down with the spoon. He inserted the tweezers. He could tell she had complete confidence in him; she opened her mouth wide and didn't flinch away.

It really wasn't too difficult after all. The tweezers reached quite well, and at the third attempt he got them firmly fixed

184

on the bit of foreign matter. He tried not to tear the swollen tonsil, and after a minute the thing came out, followed by a little spurt of blood.

He stood up, nearly knocking Penvenen's candle over. "Rinse your mouth now." He drew back and motioned to the maid to come forward, then went over to the fire to examine his prize. Warm and comforting to feel the triumph. Supreme satisfaction. But it would be unworthy to show it.

He turned back. Some blood had come from the throat and the usual suppurative matter. She met his eyes again.

"Is that better?" he said, a little flushed in spite of himself.

She nodded.

"It will get easier now. I have nothing here, but if your man cares to come with me I can make him up something to wash the throat. Or any apothecary will give you a melrose mixture to-morrow."

"What," said Penvenen, and cleared his voice, "what did you take away?"

Dwight said: "When did you last eat fish, Miss Penvenen?"

"I . . ." She wrinkled her nose. "On Wednesday."

"You must be more careful." He showed her the tiny piece of sharp fishbone he had taken from her throat. "It has caused you inconvenience and might have been serious if it had been left longer."

At Trenwith they spent a quiet evening, cosy but a little isolated. The rain had kept even the usual carol singers away. They played quadrille for a time to the sound of Mr. Chynoweth's snores, and when Dwight got back he changed into a pair of Francis's breeches and joined in the games and won all the money. He was quiet about his visit to Killewarren, but Demelza could see he was inwardly excited or pleased. When waiting for his cards his fingers would be drumming the chair, and there was an unusual flush on his face.

All through the evening Francis went out of his way to be

nice to Demelza; and when he chose to exert himself, which was not often these days, there were few men who could be more agreeable company. It was as if he were trying to efface in her memory the day when he had turned her out of the house. Demelza met him, as she would have met most people, with forgiveness and good will. Nevertheless she was a little uneasy for Ross, who naturally had more time with Elizabeth.

If Dwight had had leisure from his own thoughts to observe them he might have felt this regrouping strangely apt. Demelza's impish wit had an echo in Francis's wry sense of humour; socially they were well suited. And Ross and Elizabeth had much in common; all those interests and tastes which had helped to make them boy and girl sweethearts.

Just before eleven Mrs. Chynoweth helped her yawning husband to bed, and Aunt Agatha went soon after, but the others stayed till midnight had struck. Then they counted up their sixpences and drank a glass of hot punch before going off desultorily up the broad stairs. Demelza was feeling tired and overfed and got undressed and between the sheets quickly, trying not to think too sentimentally of the last time they had slept in this house. Ross sat on the bed for a minute or two talking over the evening, and then remembered his pipe which he had left in the winter parlour where they had dined. He took a candle and went back through the darkened house, his light flirting with the ancient shadows. There was a gleam under the door of the winter parlour; and when he went in he found Elizabeth clearing away the remains of the evening meal.

He explained what he had come for. " I thought everyone was upstairs," he said.

" Emily Tabb has a bad arm, and Tabb has been unwell. We can't expect them to do everything."

" Then you should press your guests. They have good will but no knowledge of how the house is run." He began to move some of the plates.

" No," she said, " I don't want you to bother. It will only take me half an hour."

"A quarter, then, if you're helped. Don't worry; I know the way to the kitchen."

She smiled, but obliquely, privately, as she turned away. Her looks had been troubling him all evening. Rich crimson flared about the unsubdued whiteness of her arms and throat, her eyes had new lights in them. She had made no provocative move at all, but in her cool cultured way her manner was not without challenge.

He followed her into the large kitchen.

"What did the Bartles do when they left you?"

"Mary is in service in Truro. Bartle was trying for work in the brewery, but I haven't heard if he got it."

"The Poldarks have fallen low," he said. "You must be sorry you married into the family."

She picked up an empty tray. "Do you think I should answer that?"

"Perhaps you think I shouldn't have said it."

"Oh. . . . You're free to say what you like, Ross. If anyone has the right, you have. I don't take offence so easily these days."

They went back into the dining room and began to fill the tray together.

He said: "I'm surprised to hear Francis has a little money put by. I wonder it hasn't been spent on ekeing out your ordinary life."

"He doesn't want to spend it that way. It's a special sum—six hundred pounds."

"Do the Warleggans know of it?"

"They gave it him."

"What?"

"It was a token payment for all the money he'd lost at the gaming tables to Sanson. They felt Sanson's disgrace was a reflection on their family and offered him this. But he won't spend it at present. He hasn't spent a penny."

Ross put a hand through his hair. "That's very strange."

They went on with the clearing.

When the last dishes were in the kitchen Elizabeth said:

"Thank you for your help, Ross. You're very kind—and forgiving, perhaps. Somehow I hadn't thought . . ."

"Forgiving?"

She avoided what she had meant to say. "But of course there has long since been nothing to forgive, has there? Your marriage with Demelza has been so happy."

He realised she had turned the conversation. He leaned back on the table behind him and watched as she stacked the plates. "I like that dress."

Her lips moved in a half-smile.

"You've grown up a little since we first met," he said.

"A little? I feel old . . . old."

"I doubt the truth of that remark."

"Why?"

"You have your mirror. My reassurance can't add anything to it."

"Oh," she said, "your reassurance isn't unwelcome." And she turned to carry a dish into the kitchen beyond.

He waited until she came back. "Demelza would have helped you willingly if you had asked her."

"Demelza . . . Of course. Yes, she would, wouldn't she?"

Elizabeth began to put some unused cutlery away in a drawer. Then she reached up to the cupboard above and tried to open it, but the door had stuck.

"Let me," Ross said, and came up behind her. He put his hand on the knob and jerked the cupboard open, and she stepped back against him. Just for a moment they were together and her hair brushed his face. He put his arm round her, his hand closing against the velvet of her other arm. Time briefly ceased to have progression and became an intimate perception of a single emotion breathed by them both—then he stepped away.

"Thank you," she said, and picked up the jar and put it in the cupboard. "It's all the rain and damp weather—makes the wood swell."

"Have you finished now? It must be nearly one o'clock."

"Almost. You go on, Ross. I don't need you any more."

"Not any more?"

She laughed slightly, but with a catch in her voice. "Well, not that way." She had still not turned to face him.

When he got upstairs Demelza was sitting up in bed darning a torn ruffle on one of his shirts. He was faintly and unreasonably irritated because she was not asleep or trying to get off, for then she would not have noticed how long he had been.

In fact she noticed more than that, some change in his face, on which she instantly put the right interpretation and a wrong emphasis.

He went across and put his pipe on the table, began to unbutton his coat.

She said: "This weather'll hold up the start of ploughing. The land'll get so soggy and sad."

"Oh, we may have some fine days next month." Because she had not asked, he forced himself to say: "Elizabeth was in the dining room clearing the remains of the feast. I helped her with a few things."

"She should've told me. I didn't like to offer."

"That's what I said."

Did you, Ross? Did you? And what else? "When I saw Elizabeth I was sorry not to have my better frock. I didn't know we were to dress up."

"You looked very nice as you were."

But she looked nicer. "Well . . . I'm glad there's peace in the family again. But I'll not be satisfied really till Verity and Andrew come as well."

"Nor I." He undressed quickly and got into bed beside her. She went on stitching.

I suppose, she thought, this had got to come someday. Elizabeth had Ross fast even though she married Francis. Then I came along and took him from her. But always there were some ties, some ropes left that wouldn't break; and when his interest in me began to slacken it was as sure as life he'd turn again to her. And now she's no longer in love with Francis. She's heart-free, though still bound in marriage. What will happen? He's hers again for the beckoning. He doesn't want me or my child. I think I want to die.

"Would you like me to blow out the light?" she asked.

"No . . . I don't mind. When you're ready."

"There's just this end to do. You must have caught it somewhere."

"All my shirts are wearing out."

He thought: Were beauty under twenty locks kept fast . . . If she went to London or Bath she'd have half the aristocracy at her feet. Instead she's immured here, in an ancient house and with a bankrupt husband, doing half her own work. It must be galling to her to feel her life's slipping away. She was twenty-six last birthday. Perhaps that's the reason for the change. But it's a change towards *me*.

"What are you thinking of, Ross?"

"Um? Oh, about the rain. The Mellingey will be in flood very soon."

What would have happened, he thought, if she'd married me? Would events have been very different? Would the results have been different? We're the slaves of our characters: would I have been happier, or she? Perhaps there are elements in her nature and mine which would have made our life together difficult.

Demelza said: "I was thankful to know it was not the morbid sore throat at Killewarren. Always now I shall be frightened out of my life of it."

"So shall we all."

"I met Miss Penvenen at Bodmin. She's a handsome girl."

"Did you, now? Where did you see her?"

"She was—we were just introduced one day. . . . Dwight was a small matter unsettled when he came back. I think he may feel a taking for her."

"Isn't she promised to Unwin Trevaunance?"

"I don't know. Twould be a pity if Dwight got into something again—I mean, made a second bad choice."

"Yes. . . ."

And what of this young woman beside him, whom he had loved devotedly for four years—and still did love? She had given him more than perhaps Elizabeth ever could: months of unflawed relationship, unquestioning trust (which he was now betraying in thought). Oh, nonsense. What man did not at some time or another glance elsewhere; and who could complain if it remained as a glance? (Chance was a fine thing.) And if there had been a cooling between him and Demelza, hers had been the first move, not his.

He said: "What *did* you do with your time while you were in Bodmin? You've never told me."

Demelza hesitated, but felt this the worst moment for confessions. "I was so worried I can't hardly remember. . . . I don't know what I should've done if it hadn't been for Verity, that I don't."

"No," said Ross dryly. So she was hiding something. Queer if she too had met someone. But who? In that seething jumble almost anyone in Cornwall. One of the Trevaunances? She had been visiting there before the trial on some strange business of her own. It would explain her interest now in Caroline Penvenen, her shying away from where they had met. Oh, it was impossible. The Trevaunances were not her sort, nor they hers. . . . He stirred restlessly.

"I've just finished," said Demelza, and put the shirt on the table and blew out the light.

They lay quiet, listening now to the purr of the rain on the glass. Demelza put her hands behind her head, but the movement was uncomfortable and she lowered them. How much longer shall I be able to hide it? she thought. There's no sign yet—I think, but Mrs. Chynoweth's one good eye seemed to see everything. Ross is not observant that way; but if Mrs. C. suspects, she'll tell Elizabeth, who'll tell Francis, who may say something to Ross. Anyway, he will have to know sometime. Put it off, put it off.

Count your blessings. He's safe from the worst things, from the debtor prison for another year, from the hangman or transportation—if he behaves—forever. He can't hardly go off with Elizabeth. Even if he's unfaithful—should that matter? In a few months or years he may tire of her. She may get old and withered, or fat and ugly. But that's much more likely to happen to me.

"Are you asleep?" he said.

"No."

He leaned over and kissed her forehead. " Good night, my love."

" Good night, Ross," she said.

After that the silence fell again and was not broken. She thought, trying to forget the heartache, if my child's a boy, perhaps it will make a difference, alter his feelings. We'll call him Jan, or Humphrey—or even Ross.

But if it's a girl . . . then we shall have no ready name.

Chapter Five

On the last day of the old year Myners brought a message to the Gatehouse where Dwight was experimenting with certain poisons to see if in small doses they had any medicinal values.

The letter, on green note paper, had been sealed with a heraldic ring and read as follows:

Dear Dr. Enys,

Having saved my life on Christmas Eve, you appear to have no further interest in my recovery. Perhaps you will be interested to know that it is now complete. My uncle and I would nevertheless esteem it a favour if you would call on us in the near future to assure yourself of this and to receive Payment and our thanks for your skill of a week ago.

I am, sir,

Yours, etc.,

Caroline Penvenen

Dwight stared at the letter and then, after a struggle with himself, went to his escritoire and wrote his reply while the bailiff waited.

My dear Miss Penvenen,

I am happy to hear of, and offer my felicitations on, your recovery. I did not, in fact, anticipate any other outcome once the fishbone had been removed. Nevertheless I should certainly have called, and ask your Pardon if my not doing so has seemed lacking in courtesy; but, as you will understand, you are my colleague Dr. Choake's patient, and it would be a breach of etiquette on my part if I continued to attend you without his knowledge or consent. In these circumstances I have regretfully had no alternative but to assume an indifference to your health which I did not feel.

As to Payment, I am amply recompensed for the small service I performed by the knowledge of your gratitude.

> I am, madam,
> > Your obedient servant,
> > > Dwight Enys

When Myners had gone back with this message Dwight turned again to his mixtures, but the experiments had lost their savour. In any case he had only his own stomach to experiment on, and he was already feeling very unwell from the last draught he had taken, so he went for a walk round the garden to see if the air would help the attack to pass off.

After an hour, when he was feeling better, Myners arrived back with another message. It ran:

Dear Dr. Enys,

To you, no doubt, the saving of my life may seem a very small Service indeed. To me, as I am sure you will understand, the matter assumes a slightly greater importance. Naturally I should not expect you to change your opinion on this point; but I should inform you that when Dr. Choake called on the following day my uncle sent him about his Business, and I have therefore been without medical attention since.

I should be obliged if you would call to-day; and enclose a guinea, which is the smallest value, little as I esteem myself, that I can put upon your visit of Christmas Eve.

> I am, sir,
> > Yours, etc.,
> > > Caroline Penvenen

Dwight went to the escritoire and sat tapping his pen in agitation. Why not admit the truth? He was in love with the girl—desperately so. And the train of incident, although the women were so vastly different, was disturbingly close to events in his love for Keren. One of Choake's patients—himself called in suddenly in an emergency—some sudden attraction—Choake turned away the following day and Dr. Enys chosen as a permanent medical man. This far the same. Of course Keren was married; but everyone knew that Caroline was promised to the younger Trevaunance. In a sense this situation was more explosive, for although he had eventually fallen in love with Keren, the infatuation had been mainly hers. Not so this time. Indeed he might be going much too fast: the infatuation might be wholly his. But the potential danger was obvious. He did not deceive himself. Despite his good breeding, Caroline was as much above him as Keren had been below him. Ray Penvenen weighed money and rank in the same scale. What was lacking in one must be made up by the other, and rumour was about that Unwin Trevaunance, despite his being a member of Parliament and brother of a childless baronet, might only just make the grade. Hence the delay in marriage.

Was he to intrude into this situation, already aware of his own feelings and half afraid, half hoping that it involved hers?

Yet how to get out of it without seeming an obvious boor? A voice within him said, Well, perhaps it would mean only this one visit; she looked a healthy young woman not given to physical ill humours. It would be pleasant to see her again, to receive her thanks. And, finding as he did so many of the big houses closed against him by this doctor or that—and not having the reputation or experience to be called in as a consultant—wouldn't it be the plainest common sense to set his feelings aside and take this opportunity of establishing himself with the richest family in the district? What other physician in his place would hesitate?

Nor would even he have hesitated if it had not been for the memory of the tragedy of Keren. That had brought home to him his own weaknesses, and it would be reckless to disregard them.

He picked up the pen again.

My dear Miss Penvenen [he wrote],

I am obliged to you for your further letter. In the first place I would assure you that it is far from likely that I saved your life. Medically one would have expected the Swelling eventually to burst and expel the foreign matter, though this not without considerable further pain and inconvenience to Yourself. In the second place I would assure you that I meant not to put any estimate upon the importance of the complaint in its relation to yourself but only to the trifling inconvenience I was put to in attending upon you.

Further, the value of your life or health is so plainly beyond computation that to express it in terms of money would seem an Impertinence, and I am therefore taking the liberty of returning the guinea you so kindly enclosed.

I will wait upon you to-morrow, Saturday, in the forenoon.

I am, madam,
Your obedient servant,
Dwight Enys

Seventeen ninety-one came in without change of weather or other outward sign to mark the beginning of a new year. Saturday was indistinguishable from Friday, grey and fine but with rain always heavy on the wind. For Dwight, however, Friday was the day he had given way to a reckless impulse; Saturday the day he must implement it. He rode over to Killewarren with the conflict still rife in his mind.

The house was no less shabby in the light of day. However much better circumstanced Ray Penvenen might be than his neighbours, he had no intention of outshining them in renewal and repair.

Caroline was waiting in the big upstairs living room with its heavy crimson plush velvet curtains and its warm turkey rugs. She looked as tall as a sunflower in a low-cut frock drawn tight at the waist and a wide green skirt. Horace came yapping at him, but she silenced him, and Dwight went across to the window where she was standing. He touched her hand.

"Dr. Enys," she said, "how kind of you to come at last. I haven't been waiting above two hours, and the time has passed quickly looking over the garden. A happy New Year!"

"Thank you. . . . And to you, Miss Penvenen." As usual he had flushed. "I'm—sorry if you've been waiting. One or two other calls took me longer than I expected. And I said the forenoon. It's only just after eleven o'clock."

"The other calls, of course, were more important than mine," she said sweetly.

"Only in that the people were more gravely ill."

"Were you so certain I was not?"

"Your letter said not."

"I might have been bravely hiding a serious disease. Did that never occur to you? Oh, faith, you can't be as good a doctor as I thought."

"I am not a good doctor. There are few such if any about. . . ."

"You think I should have kept Dr. Choake?"

"I'd prefer not to discuss it."

"Very well then, discuss me. Perhaps you would like to examine my throat again?"

"Yes . . ."

He moved nearer to her and she opened her mouth. Their faces were on a level; she was at least five feet nine, he thought. He turned her face a little more to the light. He noticed again the slight freckles on her nose. Her skin was warm and firm under his fingers.

"Say 'Ah!'"

"Ah . . ." said Caroline.

"Yes, very satisfactory. You'll have no more trouble there." He withdrew his hands, still embarrassed, and she closed her mouth.

She laughed.

"What is it?" he said.

"Nothing." She shrugged her bare shoulders, half turn-

196

ing away. "How different you are sometimes from others. To-day I might be a sword's edge, you flinch away at a touch. The other night it was not so. It was: 'Turn this way,' and 'turn that.' 'Keep your head still! Open your mouth and keep it open! Bring me a spoon! Hold the candle steady! Now!'"

He half smiled through his flush. "You were ill then."

"So one needs to be ill to call forth the physician, eh? Shall I swoon now or have a fit of the vapours?"

Something was shuffling and stamping in the room underneath.

"D'you so much prefer the doctor to the ordinary man?"

She looked out of doors, her eyes narrowed. "I have to confess a liking for a man who knows his own mind."

Dwight's heart began to thump.

"A man may know his own mind—and at the same time his own place."

Her eyes did not flicker. "That's a complaint I shouldn't have thought you *ever* suffered from."

"Well, now that you've discovered that I do, what would you suggest to remedy it?"

Caroline turned from the window. "Why, refreshment, of course. Refreshment is the remedy for all manner of embarrassments. And pray don't be frightened by the noises below. This room is over the stables and our horses are restive for lack of exercise."

He watched her while she poured two glasses of wine. He was grateful for this opportunity to collect his thoughts.

When she came back she said: "I should think your hero, Mr. Ross Poldark, must be a man who very clearly knows his own mind every instant of the day. *And*, having come to his decisions, I imagine he puts them through with the utmost ruthlessness and determination. Canary?"

"You're quite right." He took the glass. "Thank you. At least you're quite right as to the determination. But I shouldn't put his wife behind him at all in that respect."

"I've met her." Caroline sighed. "A handsome enough creature in a sort of way. But not with the 'stick at nothing' look of her husband. You must bring him over sometime. I think he would divert me."

"I'm afraid that would be difficult."

"He's not on call like a lackey—or a doctor? Is that what you were going to say? Well, I did not suppose he would be. But perhaps we can arrange it. A biscuit?"

"No, thank you."

The horses were shuffling again. She bent her head. "That's Firefly. I know his stamp. Are you fond of riding, Dr. Enys? For pleasure, I mean."

"I'm in the saddle so much about my business that I get little time——"

"We must ride together one of these days." She put a hand up to her hair. "I'll let you know. I may even venture to summon you here from a sick bedside—from some really important case, not merely a fishbone or a triviality of that nature."

"I'm sure you'll appreciate," he said impatiently, "that there are in fact serious cases about that make demands on one's time—and one's compassion. Scrofula among the undernourished children, phthisis among their fathers; the tertian fever has been everywhere this year, and scorbutus is spreading in Sawle. Thomas Choake is more interested in his hunting and those of his fashionable patients who can pay him. I deal with what I can and the rest go to ignorant rascally druggists or old women who brew rats' tails and sell them as elixirs. It's hard sometimes to maintain a sense of proportion that everyone can appreciate."

"Yes," she said after a minute, quizzically, "I think I do like you after all."

"It's very gratifying: I'm sensible of the honour. Now, I'm afraid I must be going as there are several more in this district I must see. Will you give my kind respects to your uncle . . ."

"Wait. Don't be so stiff. I should prefer five minutes more of your attention. What are all these diseases with their Latin names? They interest me. What are you doing for them?

Can you cure them? I think I should like to have been a physician or a barber surgeon—I have never had the least aversion for blood."

"I can do next to nothing for the scrofulus conditions. Once the poisonous humour betrays itself the sufferer is likely to face a lingering death. For phthisis there are two cures for every forty failures. Few people die of the tertian ague but many fall a prey to other things from its weakening effects. For scorbutus I can do everything and nothing. A doctor's drugs are useless, but certain foods can bring about an almost immediate cure. However, those foods are unprocurable by the people of Sawle, so they must bleed and die."

"What foods? Breadfruit from the South Seas?"

"No, the ordinary staples of life. Green vegetables, fruit, fresh meat. Any one of those three in sufficient quantity."

"Why do they not buy them then? I suppose they're too poor. But scorbutus is only scurvy, isn't it? Thousands of our sailors suffer from it and are no worse when they get home."

"It depends on the length of the voyage. Many die."

"But *they* cannot get the foods anyhow. Why don't the people of Sawle spend less on gin? Drunkenness is no less for all their poverty. Or why don't they run oranges instead of brandy when they sail to France?"

He said: "Oranges, when they can be had at all, are selling at twopence-halfpenny or threepence each. Meat is prohibitive. Gin costs them sixpence a quart or less. They're only human after all. And, even so, many of them are as sober as you or I."

She inclined her head. "Thank you. I'm very much complimented by the association. . . . But there, Dr. Enys, shall you do any good by attempting to preserve all these people? They will multiply and multiply and so there'll be ever more mouths to feed. Admitted it is sad to see them die, but it keeps the numbers in check and preserves a balance. If there's more food than people, then the people grow in numbers until there's more people than food. When that happens some die off until the food is equal to maintain the others. Is it for us to interfere? Ah, I see I've shocked you."

"Only by assuming that you yourself are different from the rest and not to be included in this stocktaking."

She smiled sweetly. "Well, of course I'm different from the rest! It's no virtue but a happy chance. I was born a Penvenen, and so am rich and educated. If I had been born poor and weakly I should no doubt die of one of your nasty diseases, but don't expect me to weep about it now!"

"It's a comfortable reasoning," Dwight said, "but dangerous. Isn't it the sort of philosophy which has caused all this trouble in France?"

Before she could reply the door opened and Ray Penvenen came in. He greeted the young doctor cordially enough, though not with the freedom his niece permitted herself. After a few minutes Dwight left, glad to escape and to sort out his impressions. The unfamiliar scent of her clung about him all the day, perhaps in his memory more than in his nostrils. Even the taste of the wine was foreign, quickening to the pulse. That philosophy, he thought; the perfect one for the middle-aged bachelor with money dulling his heart. But not for the girl of nineteen or twenty. Monstrous. And so was she; but against judgment he was deeper in than ever. There was no escape—except to hope that she would quickly become an M.P.'s wife and move up to London to keep house there. Out of sight would not be out of mind, but it would at least be out of danger.

Ray Penvenen hitched his coat to set it more firmly on his shoulders. "I hear Unwin is coming down to-morrow."

"Yes," said Caroline. "For about a fortnight."

"You did not tell me."

"I thought Sir John would this morning."

"Unwin will expect some definite word from you while he is down."

"Did Sir John say as much?"

"Not as much. But he let it be understood."

Caroline moodily picked up her skirts and perched on the window seat. " The petition has not even been heard yet. He can hardly expect me to marry a member of Parliament who doesn't know whether he really is one. That's demanding a good deal."

Ray said dryly: " My dear, you're not overtly marrying Unwin for the prestige and the position. One is supposed to marry because one loves a man."

" Oh, love, yes, I've heard of it. But is Unwin marrying me because he loves me or because he covets the twenty thousand pounds you and Uncle William have settled on me? Ask him that."

" My dear, it is for you to ask him—if you choose." Penvenen glanced at his niece and then, remembering her capabilities, added hastily: " Or perhaps you'd better not. I was only warning you that the question of a date for your marriage may be broached during his stay, and it's as well to ponder what your response will be."

" Dear, dear, it all sounds very pompous. . . . Uncle, I'm an heiress but have little money to handle. Now I rather like the feel of money, the jangle it gives, the weight in one's purse, the tawny yellow colour of the gold. Suppose you gave me some. Um? What do you say?"

Penvenen's face always looked different when this subject was mentioned. " I have no objection to advancing you something—though there's little you could find to spend it on. You're admirably clothed, well fed and housed, have three hunters and a personal maid. I should not have thought . . . How much do you want?"

" Oh . . . fifty pounds, perhaps."

A glass clattered as Penvenen locked the canary away.

" You can't be serious."

" Oh yes, indeed. Why not? It's a round comfortable sum and will last me some time. After all, what is the use of being rich if one can't have a little flutter now and then?"

" I can't possibly give you so much. For gambling of some sort it would be a sheer waste. You know I disapprove of the gaming tables—and two or three tickets is all one needs in a lottery. One is just as likely to draw a prize with few as with many."

Caroline smiled at her hands. "Oh, this is a new kind of gaming, Uncle. It appeals to me, and I have a fancy to indulge the whim."

Chapter Six

The following week, one of the quarterly meetings of the Wheal Leisure venturers was due, and it was Mr. Treneglos's turn to entertain the others at Mingoose. A distribution which was equal to a fifteen per cent return on their investment meant sixty per cent for the year and was something to be well satisfied with. Three years ago the mine had employed fifty-six men. Now it took just over the hundred and was a spot of prosperity in a depressed countryside.

Ross was not, however, altogether surprised when Mr. Renfrew again proposed that the exploratory tunnel being driven towards the ancient Trevorgie workings should be stopped and the labour turned to more productive purposes. There had been such propositions before, put mainly by Mr. Pearce, but they had been defeated. Ross had been aware for some time that some of his colleagues had been coming round to Mr. Pearce's view, so now he waited and did not speak as it was his impulse to. Mr. Pearce also was silent, and it was as if both were waiting for the neutral voters to declare themselves.

Presently Henshawe said: "I think we should persevere a month or two more. We've gone so far that it's a pity to abandon it now."

"I b'lieve we've come right past the workings," said Renfrew. "Missed them. We might go on for years more and never connect."

"Not according to that old map," shouted Mr. Treneglos, trying to make himself heard above the noises in his head.

"Remember that old map showed the Trevorgie workings as turning and branching towards Marasanvose, and we're not at the branch yet. All the same, I'm disappointed. I never thought twould be such a long job. It's a drain on our profits all the time."

Ross said: "It was the means of our finding the second lode. That's not wholly unprofitable."

"No," said Mr. Pearce, entering the lists also. "But the best mass was found in the other direction. We should do better, I declare, to strike out farther to the northeast where the going is easier and the quality promises better." He scratched himself.

Mr. Treneglos undid the top button of his trousers. "Well, tis as the majority says. There's no doubt we can afford it, what? We've a handsome profit to show, and a better in prospect. But damme, I'm coming round to the contrary view from what I've held all along. Twas not as if we was driving an adit which would help unwater the mine. We've tunnelled under the valley and now we're tunnelling under the hill. What did you say, Pearce? What?"

Pearce shook his wigged head, disclaiming speech.

Ross said: "I have talked the company into continuing twice; but I don't want to again if the feeling's against it. I still think we should do well to persevere; but the proposition was mine in the first place, and when you add up the men's wages over the months it totals to a sum in the end. So I'll say no more and leave it to the vote."

The vote was taken. Ninety parts (Ross's and Henshawe's) were for continuing, one hundred and fifty against.

Ross said: "One thing I should have brought up. I take it the men on the work will not be set off—that they'll be put to other employment."

Mr. Renfrew screwed up his eyes. "I should like to see a widening of the main shaft. The air is still bad, and we could profitably use 'em that way."

The venturers discussed this for some minutes, the matter was settled and the meeting seemed about to break up.

Then Mr. Pearce coughed and said, smiling apologetically:

"There's one other matter I should have brought up earlier. Awaiting the right opportunity, as it were. That is to say, that one of the adventurers—that is one I act for, if you understand—Mr. Benjamin Aukett, has disposed of his holding in the mine to a Mr. Henry Coke. I am not sure yet whether Mr. Coke will wish to attend the meetings, but I rather—hm—gather he will wish me to represent his interest as I did Mr. Aukett's. In any case the sale has only just taken place, and I shall be able to report more fully in April."

He went on talking, hitching up his stomach from time to time and carefully avoiding Ross's eyes.

"Who?" shouted Mr. Treneglos. "Who? Never heard of him. A Whig, I suppose. Where's he live? What's his profession? Oh. Gentleman. Well, that's a good sign. Hope he's as docile as Aukett. Bring him along sometime if he cares to come. We've nothing to conceal. That's the feeling of the meeting, I take it?"

The others agreed.

Captain Henshawe said: "I wonder if you know what his share changed hands at?"

"No, my dear sir," said the lawyer. "Not an idea in the world."

Renfrew said: "I was offered four hundred and fifty pound for my share last month. That is fifteen pounds for a five-pound part. It shows a tempting profit. An' it shows just how hard people is looking for an investment these days."

"What was the name of the man who approached you?" said Ross.

"Name of Garth. Never heard of him. A civil-spoken fellow, but not what you'd call a gentleman."

"I take it you're not intending to sell?"

"No," said Renfrew, observing Ross's expression with some surprise. "It pays me better to stay in, apart from all the tackle an' gear I supply."

The meeting ended soon after, and, as was their custom, Captain Henshawe and Ross walked home together, in the gathering misty afternoon.

"Well," said Henshawe, trying to be hearty, "it's near on

three years since you paid four-fifty for Surgeon Choake's share. At the time you'll mind me telling you I thought it a deal more than it was worth. But your belief's been justified. It's my way of thinking old Aukett got upwards of five hundred for his share to make him willing for the sale."

"That's my belief too."

Henshawe never liked it as much when the scarred side of Ross's face was towards him. The scar was more than half hidden by the long side hair, but all the same the tail of it down his cheek was a token of wildness and intractability, qualities which Henshawe deplored since he was a peace-loving and an easygoing man.

"I do not suppose," he said, "that twill make any difference to the running of the mine; in fact it cannot, for Mr. What's-it will have to tag along with the majority. Anyway, there's little anyone could cavil at while the profits are so good."

"No," said Ross.

"It's a pity the work towards Trevorgie has come to naught, but maybe we shall be able to start again in a few months."

They walked along in silence. Ross said:

"I wonder if Mrs. Trenwith will stand firm?"

"Mrs. Trenwith? You mean hold on to her share? I haven't a doubt. She's got too strong a nose for a profit, I reckon, to part with it easy."

"There are two kinds of profit."

"Yes, well, if she did, it would not be serious, would it? Interests in other mines change hands every day—when there's anyone these days to buy 'em. I agree we're very comfortable as we are, but I don't suppose a new adventurer or two will upset our applecart."

"No," said Ross.

They came to the parting of the ways.

"You'll drink with me before you go on?"

"No, thank you, sur. I'm full to the brim as it is. I'll be getting home along while the light holds."

Ross turned down through the apple trees towards his

house. As he came in sight of the front door he saw that there was a strange horse waiting.

Jane Gimlett met him in the hall. " If you please, sur, there's a gent to see you. Bin here a half-hour he has. Name of Trencrom. You asked me always to tell you so as you'd know whether to go in or no."

". . . Where is Mrs. Poldark?"

" In with Mr. Trencrom, sur."

Ross took off his hat and smoothed back his hair. Mr. Trencrom's presence explained the large horse outside; but what explained Mr. Trencrom? He was in no mood for company. Demelza alone, perhaps. No one else. He went in.

His wife, in one of her white muslin frocks, had her back to him and was pouring tea. The visitor faced him from the largest armchair.

Mr. Trencrom was one of those peculiar people who have an iron in every fire. Like the Warleggans, he had the talent for turning his interests into money, but unlike them he had no ambition to social advancement. He had been born the son of a wool stapler and that was what he would always remain. He had part shares in seines, part shares in tucking mills, part shares in tin stamps, part shares in little shops in little towns. And everywhere the money added up and brought in more. His investment in the Carnmore Copper Company had been almost the only substantial loss of his career, and Ross had not seen him since the venture failed. Of course everyone, certainly all the magistrates, knew what his chief business was.

In appearance he was very stout. He had only two enemies in the world: the gaugers and his own bronchial tubes.

" Well, Captain Poldark," he said breathlessly. " Excuse me rising. Been very ill this winter. Damp air does me no good. Your charming wife. I said I took no liquor. She made tea. Delicious. How are you? My dear sir."

" I find the climate trying," Ross said.

Demelza glanced at him and saw at once that there was trouble.

"You'll take something too, Ross?"

"Something stronger," he said. "You've ridden far on a dull afternoon, Mr. Trencrom."

"Yes, as you say. It's some years since I was in this part. What distressing news from France, Captain Poldark. They say Mirabeau is gravely ill again and nearly blind. If he should die."

"I haven't followed their politics very closely of late."

"Nor I from choice. But when one is—in constant contact. If Mirabeau goes there'll be a landslide—I'm told. The King's position. Very dangerous. England can't stand by and watch."

"I don't think it can be our affair what happens to Louis."

"Well, up to a point—that's true. But there are limits."

"Limits on both sides. For we are without an army or a navy."

"Yes, yes, of course you're right. All the same—I have grave fears for the future."

Ross sat in a chair and put his elbows on the arms.

There was silence.

"However," said Mr. Trencrom, "I have not called merely to discuss the foreign situation. As you will have guessed. No doubt." He coughed. It was an extraordinary sound for so large a man; his mountainous body quivered, and a small thin wheezy noise was eventually produced as if deep inside him a very small dog was dying of asphyxiation. Then he wiped his mouth and continued. "Purpose one. To renew our acquaintance. That is done. Purpose two. To inquire after your affairs. If they prosper. Purpose three. To speak of mine. Now if——"

"Suppose," Ross said, "that we spoke of yours first. By doing so we might come at a quicker understanding and be able to treat of mine in an incidental way."

Mr. Trencrom smiled at Demelza. "He was always one for coming to the point. I like directness. Of course. But it somewhat depends—whether his affairs prosper—as to whether he is interested in mine. However . . ."

"Half the countryside is interested in yours, Mr. Trencrom," said Ross.

The fat man's smile became a chuckle, which ended in his tiny wrung-out cough.

"It might well be—that they have reason to be anxious for my welfare, Captain Poldark. Things are none too satisfactory in the trade. I do not know—how long I shall be able to carry on to the present extent."

"I should have thought business was never more prosperous."

"Ah. Business is far from prosperous. Let me explain."

Mr. Trencrom went on to explain in his breathless voice as if he were all the time climbing a steep hill. With some horrid premonition of his direction, Demelza poured Ross a cup of tea and, forgetting his own demand, Ross drank it. Business, said Mr. Trencrom, was brisk enough so far as consumption went. People were drinking as much as ever and, although money was scarce, there was always a market for cheap good-quality liquor. Mind you, he was being frank with them as he would not be with everyone. He spoke in confidence and knew they would respect it.

Light faded in the room, but no one seemed to notice its going. At the back of the house somewhere Gimlett was chopping sticks; each series of sounds began with a tentative tap-tap growing firmer and heavier and slower until the screech of splitting wood. Through the window the cloudy fading sky was grey as iron.

The one great difficulty of the trade, Mr. Trencrom explained, was the tiresome business of the landing of the goods. Vercoe, the customhouse officer at St. Ann's, and his assistant Coppard were hard men, ever on the alert and ever ready to pounce. Attempts had been made to soften them, to bring them to a more reasonable frame of mind, but their only answer was to apply for extra help. And there was a rumour they might be getting it. How much easier, Mr. Trencrom said, if they had only been sensible like the gaugers at Newquay and Falmouth, where the officers were given a percentage of the profit on the smuggled goods and no more said.

Mr. Trencrom finished his tea and smiled an acquiescence when Demelza rose for his cup. This much, he said, was bad enough; but this had been the case ever since Vercoe came to the district four years ago. What was making it worse now was the presence of an informer or informers among the village people themselves. It had begun at St. Ann's last year, so they had brought in their cargoes at Sawle, where landing was so much more difficult. In the last six months, however, the same thing had happened at Sawle; and business was almost at a standstill. Now this, said Mr. Trencrom, would be bad enough in the south, where there were numbers of navigable harbours and creeks. But on this north coast it meant ruin and perhaps more. Only last month, in that sudden bad weather which had blown up, his cutter the *One and All* had had to be warned off from landing because the gaugers were there on the spot, and she'd been driven back towards Land's End with not a creek or a cove or a harbour under her lee but meant destruction. They had made the Scillies and come in the following night; but she might have been lost with all hands and a valuable cargo. One couldn't *risk* that sort of thing.

"You have my sympathy," said Ross. "But what's the moral to the story?"

"The moral, Captain Poldark. Is that we must find another navigable inlet. And you possess the only one for miles."

Demelza paused with the cup in her hands, her eyes going from face to face.

"I think," Ross said quietly, "that you overestimate the advantages of Nampara Cove. There is no great depth of water and several dangerous rocks at the entrance."

Don't I know it, thought Demelza, since I nearly went aground on one yesterday.

Mr. Trencrom strangled his small dog again. "I don't overestimate nothing, Captain Poldark. It's not ideal. But we could land very comfortable there on quiet nights. It's not too far from where we distribute. And tis not overlooked, like. It could all be quite private."

"Until the informer got wind of the change."

"Well, we should introduce—a closer system of secrecy. And only come in here twice or thrice a year. As for yourself you'd need to know nothing of it."

Ross got up and walked to the window. Demelza had not moved with her cup.

"As for myself," Ross said, "it would be plain that I knew everything of it. But leave that for the moment. What inducement do you suggest would make me responsive to this scheme?"

"Ross," Demelza said, but he didn't look at her.

"Oh," said Mr. Trencrom, "that would be arranged amicable, I'm sure. A percentage on the profit. Or a lump sum for each landing. We've been in business together before. We'd not quarrel over that."

There was a light in Ross's eyes as he looked out over the garden, but he was careful not to let it be seen by his visitor. "I'm afraid," he said, "I should like some proposal. One could only consider the suggestion by weighing the risks against the benefits. At present we know only the risks. . . ."

"Hm—ah. Well . . ." Mr. Trencrom stretched out a fat hand for the tea Demelza was still holding. "Thank you, ma'am. Delightful. It's very difficult betwixt friends. One wishes to be fair. But things are not what they was. Everything is more trying than it used to be. What had you in mind yourself? Would five per cent of the profits seem fair?"

"Can you suggest a lump sum per cargo?"

"Well . . . fifty pounds, say?"

"I thought," said Ross, "that you had come here to talk business, Mr. Trencrom."

The fat man wheezed over his tea, and his breath made bubbles on the surface.

"Is that a very poor offer? I don't think so. Fifty pounds is a big sum of money. What do you suggest—yourself?"

"Two hundred and fifty pounds per cargo."

"My dear sir! Impossible! You don't understand." Mr. Trencrom's feelings were hurt. "It would make the voyage virtually without——"

Ross said: "I'm not without experience of the trade myself. Fifteen years ago when I was a boy, my father and I would make the trip to Guernsey twice or so a year. We could fill our tiny cutter with brandy, gin and tea for a hundred pounds. If we had chosen to—as we did sometimes—we could have sold the cargo as soon as we landed it for double the money. Your cutter, the *One and All*, will carry a cargo of ten times that size—and of greater value, for prices have risen. It's not hard to work out the profit."

Mr. Trencrom slightly pouted. "Oh, these small private runs! They always show—the big profits. Give quite a false impression. No overheads. No organisation to maintain. Quite different as a commercial undertaking. I have the cutter to maintain. Wages to pay—usually a portion of the cargo. Palms to grease. Deliveries to arrange. Travellers who go round for orders. Storage. Mules. Ropes. Nets. Tackle. A very different thing, my dear sir. Do you know how much I pay my riders merely—for carrying away the goods from the shore? Half a guinea per night, plus all their expenses of food and drink! Plus half a bag of tea weighing forty pounds—or the equivalent, which they can resell if they wish for twenty-five shillings. Or more! All off the profits. I couldn't possibly afford to pay you more than a hundred pounds a run. After all, you would do nothing. You would sit quiet in your home here. Behind drawn curtains. Others would do it all. Merely for the privilege of using your cove."

Ross shook his head. "I'm sorry. I shouldn't be willing to do it for that."

"Don't do it at all, Ross," said Demelza.

"But why?" said Mr. Trencrom, turning to her. "I'm sure you agree it's not a wicked trade to be concerned in. Man-made laws. Not by God. Quite unreasonable that taxes should be paid on these necessaries of life. You'd make two or three hundred pounds a year. Very welcome, surely."

"Nampara Cove is my land," Ross said. "If you run a cargo at St. Ann's or Sawle or on Hendrawna Beach no one is accountable but the people who run it. If you run one here and are surprised it will go hard with me to put on a look of innocence, with mules tramping almost under my windows. I have already been at the assizes once. I don't wish to appear there again. The inducement would have to be big to make me take that risk. I've suggested to you what that inducement would be."

" No, Ross," said Demelza. " No!"

Ross turned his eyes on her. " I'll not hide from Mr. Trencrom that the money would be specially useful just now. Otherwise I should not consider it. It's really up to him to choose."

About half an hour later a big brown horse carrying a big fat man in a big brown cloak rode up the valley away from the house. Darkness had fallen, but a moon behind the clouds made it possible to see the track. It would be a lonely ride to St. Ann's and there were nervous people who would not have fancied it; but Mr. Trencrom was not as delicate as he made himself out. Also he carried a brace of pistols. There was a dejected, defeated set to his shoulders as he made his way through the trees.

When he had disappeared from view Ross shut the door and stood a moment in indecision in the hall, then returned to the parlour.

Demelza's back as she lit the candles had a taut look. Ross went to the cupboard and poured himself a drink.

" The Warleggans," he said, " have at last got a foot in Wheal Leisure. Pearce came to-day with the news that Benjamin Aukett had sold out. Their nominee is a man called Coke."

Demelza did not reply.

" I suspected it would be only a matter of time," he said. " When there are seven shareholders, one or another will sooner or later give way to the temptation of a large profit. I shouldn't be surprised if Pearce sells his share any time. So now we shall have George at our board."

She said : " What does it matter?"

" Um?" He stared at her back broodingly.

" What does it matter? Oh, I dislike the Warleggans just

so much as you; but if they come to have a share in your mine we can do naught about it. An' they can't steal *your* share. That's all that matters. It is none of it any excuse for having the tub carriers on our land!"

He said sharply: "Two hundred pounds is excuse enough for that. I want no other."

"It'll not buy you out of prison."

"I shall not be in there, thank you."

"You'll have small choice if the landing is surprised."

"Nonsense. It's a risk, I know—but not as big as I made out to Trencrom. It would be possible in fact to claim ignorance. We might not be believed, but there would be no proof to the contrary."

She put her hand on the mantelshelf. "I can't *stand* it all again! All the worrying anxious time of the trial—and before; not sleeping, like a cloud all day. Picturing this an' that. Transported, hanged, rotting in gaol. The days in Bodmin—all I did—or tried to do! It isn't fair! Not again, so soon. It isn't fair to yourself . . . or to anyone!"

He looked at her again and perceived that she was very upset. He said more gently: "Now you're seeing bogles in the dark. There's nothing to be scared of in a little free-trading. I was only afraid lest I had set my price too high. That's why I came down fifty. To-day, on top of this news of the Warleggans, if he but knew it, Mr. Trencrom was an angel in disguise."

"The devil!" she said vehemently. "No less."

"Perhaps I should lie meek under this latest of George's encroachments, but it's not in me to do so. Besides . . . you may have forgotten it, but we have recently sold *all* our stock, your brooch and horse, the clock and the newer furnishings of the house. Not, mark you, to cancel our debts but to postpone them for a mere twelve months. We're not out of the wood if we sit together in bucolic bliss and weave daisy chains. I'm more likely to go to prison that way than any other."

She said: "I can't help it! I want your child to be free from fear."

213

Ross put down his glass. "*What?*"

There was a tap at the door and Jane Gimlett came in.

"Please, will you be wanting supper at the usual time? I put the pie on to hot up just in case, like."

"The usual time," said Demelza.

"And the ham? There's a fair cutting on it yet, though 'tis largely fat."

"Put it on," said Demelza.

"The scones has come out nice, 'm. I thought I'd leave you know." She went out.

One missed the ticking of the clock in here. A new piece of wood, not quite dry, was hissing on the fire. Little bubbles of moisture were forming at one end of it, trying to escape the flames.

Ross said: "When did you know?"

"September."

He made a gesture. "Good *God* ... ! Not to tell me ... !"

"You didn't want it."

"What?"

"You said you didn't want another child—after Julia."

"Nor did I—nor do I——" He picked up his glass, set it down again without drinking. After a minute he added: "To grow into our hearts, and then to die. But if one is coming —that's different."

"How different?"

"Well ... it's different."

"I wish I could believe that."

"Why should you not? It's the truth." He turned. "I don't know what to say—how to say it ... I just don't understand you. You've been closer about it even than last time. When do you expect—the birth?"

"May."

He frowned, trying to shut out his memories.

"I know 'tis the same month," she said desperately. "I could've wished for any other. But that's the way things are. I shouldn't be amazed if it's born the same day, three years after. It's been the same so far—the visit to Trenwith and

214

all. But all history don't repeat itself. I don't believe it can. Anyway, I'm sorry."

" Sorry? What for?"

" That it's happened. That it has got to come. That you'll have this extra burden which you don't want."

He came and stood beside her at the fireplace. " Now stop crying and be sensible."

" I'm *not* crying."

" Well, wanting to, then. Is this what's been on your back all winter?"

" Not on my *back*," she said.

" As you like. Ever since September you've been withdrawn from me—poking up your head now and then like a sheep from behind a fence. I couldn't reach you. Is this child the cause of all of it?"

" If I have, then it may be."

" Because you thought I didn't want it?"

" 'Tis only what you said."

He said in exasperation: " God damn it, you should know I'm not used to dealing with women! You search the earth to find some special secret feminine grievance to *gnaw* over for months on end, and then produce it coolly on the mat to explain all the irrational hedging and dodging of an entire winter——"

" I didn't search the earth for it!"

" Well, I thought you could distinguish between a theoretical case and a practical one—evidently that isn't so."

" I wasn't well educated——"

" No more was I. Look." He thumped the flat of his hand on the mantelshelf. " Look. If you ask me, do I want more children, I'll say, no. We're nearly paupers, the world's awry, and we've lost Julia. Correct? That's a theoretical case. But if you say you're having another child, do I dislike the prospect, I'd say, yes, for all these reasons I still dislike the prospect; but a prospect is not a child, and a child can be *welcomed* for all that. D'you understand what I mean?"

" No," she said.

He stared at his tobacco jar on the shelf, his first protest exhausted, his mind leaping forward to what this news entailed. And all the memories of Julia it revived. The storm at her birth, the two christening parties, the drunken Paynters that day Demelza was out, the high hopes, the love—and the storm at her death. It had come in a cycle, had conformed to a pattern, like a Greek tragedy prepared by a cynic. It was to happen again. History had to repeat itself in the early stages whatever the later might bring.

He glanced down at her. What did it mean for her? Weeks of discomfort, agony at the end, then months of unremitting care. All that had gone to Julia and much more; yet it had all been lost. What right had he to claim a monopoly of grief? . . . He'd never done that, and yet . . .

He said more gently: " I've noticed no stoutness so far."

She said: " By April I shall look like Mr. Trencrom."

It was the first time they had laughed together for a long time; but her laughter was still dangerously near tears, his a not quite voluntary surrender of his irritation.

He put his hand on her shoulder, trying to express something that he couldn't yet say. Strange, the meaning of contacts! His firm clasp of this arm was entirely permissible, familiar, pleasurable, the touch of a known and loved person, however exasperating. His clasp of another arm at Christmas had had electricity in the touch. Was it because he loved Elizabeth more—or because he knew her less?

Demelza said: " If you—still care what is going to happen to us . . . then you must have more care in what you undertake."

" I shall have care in everything I undertake—believe me. I've every possible intention of keeping on the right side of the law." He released her shoulder. " Or at any rate the blind side. . . . Thank God at least that we have a capable physician in the neighbourhood."

" I'd still rather have Mrs. Zacky," said Demelza.

Chapter Seven

The next day Ross was up before dawn and spent the morning at the mine, arranging with Zacky Martin about the redeployment of the men who had been tunnelling towards Wheal Trevorgie. He spent longer than he need have done at the workings and went down to see how things were below grass. He felt as if the acquisitive hand of the Warleggans was already over Wheal Leisure. He had not slept well during the night, his brain being active with all the developments of yesterday.

As to Demelza's news, he could not yet evaluate his own feelings, but reflection didn't dissipate the sense of insult that he had been kept in the dark so long. To him it looked like a wilful misunderstanding of his views—or at least a painful lack of trust in his good sense. Soon after noon he walked back with Zacky, who was slipping home for a snack before returning for the change of cores. At last there was some sign of a lift in the weather; the vast burden of cloud which had hung about so long was thinning, splitting up, and drifting away before a northeasterly breeze. The contours of the land were unequivocal, demarcating the colder lighter sky.

" 'Tis a pity we've stopped that working," said Zacky. " I feel we was driving towards rich stuff. But maybe it is no more'n an old wives' dream."

" Where d'you estimate we had got to?"

Zacky stopped and rasped his chin. " Twouldn't be hard to take proper measurings, but it is hard to be sure without, sur. Just to be guessing, I'd say near on that clump of trees."

Ross scanned the distance from where the buildings of Wheal Leisure littered one skyline to where the broken wall and chimney of Wheal Grace stood on the rising ground near Mellin.

" About halfway?"

"I reckon. There's no map, I b'lieve, of the old Trevorgie workings."

"No accurate one. But I went down with my cousin seven years ago and they were pretty extensive in this direction. That air adit is the only sign, but I believe several were filled up. My father worked the newer, Wheal Grace, part towards the southwest. You were never in Wheal Grace?"

"I wasn't in these here parts till I was twenty, and then I went straight on Grambler. Of course, I've often thought twould injure no one to have a closer look at Trevorgie from that end. That's if you could get by with the foul air."

"It was none too bad when we went down. But we didn't go far. What we saw was all exhausted tin ground, and poor at that. Of course, Mark Daniel . . ."

"Mark Daniel?" said Zacky cautiously.

They went on. They were only a few hundred yards from the house Mark had built. In one part the roof had already fallen in. It seemed tactless to mention his name just here—so close to where he had killed his little faithless moonflower wife.

"I don't know if Paul ever told you," Ross said, "but the day before Mark escaped to France he hid down Grace. Before he left I—happened to see him and he told me there was a lot of rich stuff in the mine."

". . . Paul never told me. But I can add two an' two, like. Did he say where the ore was to?"

"No. . . . At least, I fancy he mentioned the east face."

"That's Trevorgie. That's sense—for your father'd never have abandoned a rich lode. Anything might've happened when Trevorgie was worked."

"Yes," said Ross, staring at the chimney of Wheal Grace. They separated just beyond Reath Cottage and Ross went up to the old mine building. There was very little left. Abandoned for twenty years, the bits of machinery had long since been carried away, and nature had licked over the scars. Ross sat down and put his chin in his hand.

It was pleasant enough sitting here among the whispering

grass, and he scarcely moved for half an hour. There was some community of spirit between the man and the scene. Strange ideas were milling in his head, at least two of them having taken shape from his conversation with Mr. Trencrom. All of them derived from the events of yesterday and all of them were moving him to one end. At length he got up and walked slowly, half aimlessly, back to Reath Cottage, pushed open the door and went in. It was dark, as it always would be except in the mornings; Mark had built it facing the wrong way. People wouldn't pass the place after dusk; they said Keren still hung there sometimes with her broken little face out of the window. The earth floor was covered with brambles and gorse, and rank white grass, predatory and unhealthy, sprouted among the stones. An old stool stood in the corner, some faggots lay by the fireplace. He went out into the open again, deriding himself for being glad to go.

From here you looked straight across the declivity to the Gatehouse. Every time Dwight Enys rode out on his doctoring this derelict cottage would stare and watch him leave. No wonder Enys still showed the scars of that time; he could not very well forget it. Ross began to walk over towards the Gatehouse. As he got near he saw Dwight at the door, and his horse was standing ready saddled. Dwight saw him and smiled and came to meet him.

"Hope this is not a professional visit? No? You come so seldom that I was a little anxious."

Ross said: "The courtesies can only be squeezed out of me like drops from a reluctant lemon. But now and then it's convenient to be agreeable for a change."

Dwight laughed. "Be careful you don't overpraise yourself. I suppose you're not responsible for my astonishing windfall, are you? Mention of the lemon came very easy to your lips."

"Just at the moment I'm praying for windfalls, not bestowing 'em. What has come your way?"

"Those sacks. They're full of oranges. They came this morning, twelve in all, delivered on three mules by a surly fellow who would scarcely open his mouth—all the way from Falmouth. I'm astonished."

" So should I be."

" Oh, they're not for me. They're for sick people in Sawle; I guess that much. I've been trying to remember how many I have mentioned this need to. You were one of them."

" Sorry. You must look among your *rich* friends, Dwight."

" I didn't know I had any," Dwight replied, knowing all the time he had one. " There must be close on a hundred dozen oranges here. Enough at least to check the scurvy if intelligently used. I have sent Bone off to borrow two old mine mules from the Nanfans. I'm waiting for him to return before I set off on my round. We must distribute some of the fruit this afternoon."

Ross glanced at his animated face. It was easy to see how Enys felt about this: to be fighting an enemy unarmed and then suddenly to find the weapons put into one's hand . . .

He said: " I came to ask you if by chance you receive any periodicals from London? The *Sherborne Mercury* is a little restricted in its news."

" Nothing—except *Medical Facts and Observations* edited by Dr. Simmons. That's sent to me monthly. I have seen a London paper sometimes at the Pascoes'."

" With the trial over my head for six months and then the business of settling back into normal life, I've had little attention for general events. What do you think of developments in Europe?"

Dwight found the query a little surprising, for he usually regarded Ross as much better informed than himself. " In France, do you mean? Have you read *Reflections on the French Revolution?*"

" No."

" Nor I. But it has had an immense sale—as of course you know. I understand Burke argues that the revolutionaries are really the enemies of liberty while doing everything in its name."

" It's not unlikely. There's strong feeling over here about the whole business; but for myself, while going into no extravagant praise of the revolutionaries, I can't help but nurse some sympathy for their original aims."

Dwight looked at Ross. " I know. There were many such to begin, but they have been steadily forfeiting such sympathy."

Bone came in sight. They waited till he reached them. Will Nanfan could lend them the mules and would send them over early in the afternoon. Ross turned to walk back. He had not told Dwight one of the things he had come to speak of, but the impulse had died when he got to the Gatehouse. Dwight would guess soon enough and he wouldn't be wanted until May.

The sun was shining brilliantly by the time Dwight turned in at the gates of Killewarren, and the wind was rattling the withered leaves on the young oak trees. The gravel in front of the house was strewn with fir twigs which had been nibbled off by the squirrels in the upper branches. He knocked at the door and asked if Miss Penvenen were at home, and was admitted to a small room off the hall. Presently the maid came back and said Miss Penvenen would see him.

She was in the usual living room, but was in a black riding habit over the shoulders of which her tawny hair fell to its full length like an escaping flame. She was standing by the fireplace when he came in, eating from a plate of sandwiches, and there was a wineglass on the mantelshelf. She laughed when she saw him.

" Good day, Mr. Apothecary. Whom have you come to blood? My uncle's in Redruth and is not expected home till four."

Dwight said: " My call's on you, Miss Penvenen. I'm sorry if it's inconvenient, but I'll not keep you long."

She glanced at the clock. " I can give you five minutes, or as long as it takes to eat these sandwiches. This good east wind won't last forever, and I've had a merry morning. Up at dawn and we picked up a fox on his drag. He was a beauty and ran straight as a die to beyond Ponsanooth. I was second at the kill, and it was lively country. Around twelve we drew

Killevreth Wood and found another, but my horse went lame just as he went away; so I'm back here for a brief refreshment while they saddle Thresher. D'you ever hunt, Mr. Sober Face?"

Dwight said: "Did you arrange for a consignment of oranges to be delivered to my house to-day?"

She looked at him widely.

"Oranges? You did say oranges? If I made you a present at all it would be a better instrument for removing fishbones. You hurt my lips with your fingers, d'you remember?"

"Yes," he said, "I remember."

They stared at each other then. He was just near enough to detect that faint unfamiliar scent she used; the mannish clothes made her look more womanly.

"So it was you," he said. "I thought it could be no one else."

"Indeed?"

"I'm—very grateful. They'll be—life-giving."

"You don't suppose I am interested in the fate of a few fishwives, do you? Heavens, what nonsense!"

"Then why did you do it?"

She looked him over, seemed about to deny it, then suddenly changed her mind. "Just to make a *mock* of you."

He flushed. "An expensive form of mockery, isn't it?"

She finished her wine. "I don't like to be under an obligation—especially to a man—especially to you. You wouldn't take my money—threw it back in my face."

"I don't want your money——"

"So I reasoned your conscience wouldn't let you be too proud to accept a present for your poor starving fisherfolk. Nor has it. It's you who are under the obligation now."

"I'm very obliged—for the condescension."

"You amuse me very much," she said.

"I like you very much too."

For the first time he saw a faint flush on her cheeks.

"Don't be impertinent."

"Wasn't it impertinence you said you admired? I forget."

"You forget a great deal."

" I shall not forget this generous gift, however hard you try to disguise it——"

She turned away from him as the door opened and Unwin Trevaunance came in.

"Oh, *there* you are! Lord, I looked everywhere. You could at least . . ." He stopped short when he saw Dwight.

" Did you get him?" she asked.

" No. . . . He ran short and the scent was confused. What was the matter?"

" Firefly went lame. It's his pastern again, so I came home. I shall be ready for off in half a minute."

" I've had nothing to eat since breakfast. I'm ravenous."

" Put something in your pocket. If we dally about we may lose the hunt. Oh. . . . Do you know Dr. Enys?"

Unwin inclined his lion's head. He didn't look too pleased to have been deserted in the field, and to come all the way home to find Caroline in earnest conversation with a flushed but good-looking young man, who might be only a country physician of some sort but had an air of his own.

" I don't think I've had that pleasure."

" Pleasure is quite the word," said Caroline, buttoning her coat. " He's most skilful in curing dogs of distressing convulsions. Horace has not been troubled near so bad since he took that mixture you prescribed, Dr. Enys. He has a little spot on his ear now, which you might look to after we've gone."

Dwight refused to be provoked. " For twelve bags of oranges he shall have the best attention I can give him, ma'am."

Unwin looked irritated. He began to take some things from the table and Caroline wrapped them in a napkin for him.

" You'd better attend to him this morning then," said Caroline, indicating Horace, who was snuffling round and round in his basket to find the most comfortable spot. " Next week we shall be gone."

" Gone?" said Unwin, looking at her. " Gone where?"

" Oh, didn't I tell you? Dear Unwin; I'm so sorry. Uncle

William said I should go back there in February. After all, I've been in these parts since September, and the hunting's so much better in Oxfordshire."

"You certainly did not. I——" Unwin stared at Dwight, plainly wishing him in Hades.

"Do you intend to be away long, Miss Penvenen?" Dwight asked.

"It will depend what entertainment there is. Usually there's plenty. But don't worry: I've ordered more oranges for you next week also."

"Oranges, oranges?" Trevaunance said impatiently. "Come, Caroline, I hope I can persuade you to a delayed departure—but in the meantime we should make the most of this lovely day while it's here." He went to the door and opened it for her.

"No, no, you cannot come, my sweet," said Caroline in a honeyed voice to Horace, who had slipped out of his basket like lightning. "You would be frightened by all the bigger doggies. You shall stay at home with the nice doctor who'll cure your ear and your fits and maybe take away any bones you swallow. There, there." She put the dog into Dwight's arms and smiled at him. Their eyes were on a level, and, out of perversity and knowing herself doubly safe in Unwin's presence, she allowed the full challenge of her interest in him to show. There were tiny specks of amber on the pupils; the long lashes, so often narrowed, were for one second wide to show the grey-green depths.

Then she laughed. "Good-bye, Dwight. May I call you Dwight? It's a quaint name. One thinks of someone shy and a little unprogressive. Your mother must have thought of something different, mustn't she? Who was right? I don't at all know. Perhaps we shall meet again someday."

"I shall look forward to it," said Dwight.

She went out, leaving him with the struggling dog. Unwin glanced at him with an unfriendly assessing eye as he followed. Dwight heard them going down the passage, heard him speaking and her laughter before their footsteps died away.

Chapter Eight

Ross's idea would not let him alone. For a long time he did not speak of it to anyone, not even Demelza, whose eager brain might have been useful in helping him to a decision. But the consequence would be such that he felt he could not decently expect anyone else to take a share of the responsibility. Besides, Demelza, for all her acuteness, was a woman and would probably be swayed by considerations that hadn't any business to be brought in.

He spent a great deal more time than hitherto reading the *Sherborne Mercury* and other news sheets which he borrowed and bought where he could. He also read Pryce's book, *Mineralogia Cornubiensis*, and several other treatises on the history and practice of mining, before making any overt move.

Henshawe was the first man to approach—straight, canny, the best judge in the district, and as close as a clam.

One day in early March, after an hour's talk in the library of Nampara, during which old samples were thumbed and old maps pored over, Henshawe and Ross, with candles in their hats and some tackle over their shoulders, walked casually up the hill to the weather-beaten stone chimney of Wheal Grace; and no more was seen of them for three hours. When they returned to the house, muddy and tired, Demelza, who had been anxious for the last ninety minutes, restrained an impulse to scold them and gave them tea laced with brandy, scanning their faces for unspoken comment. It was queer, she thought, that people should find Ross hard to read. She couldn't tell what he was thinking—any more than you could tell what a lot of those smiling-faced people were really thinking behind their smile—but she could usually tell what he was *feeling*; and she knew now that he was not displeased with the outcome of the afternoon's business.

When Henshawe had gone he was more cheerful than he

had been for a long time, much more like his old self. She realised more clearly than she had ever done before the need that Ross had for some continuing activity of mind and body. He was essentially a person who wanted to be planning and moving ahead, and however agreeable he might find the life of a country gentleman under its most favourable conditions, in poverty and frustration the life was intolerable. Further, the unseen but oppressive influence of the Warleggans was something which sooner or later must produce an explosion. If this business that was now afoot provided some sort of a safety valve, she was thankful for it.

There were more hours spent in the draughty old library the next day and the next. One evening Zacky Martin was called in, and after that he seemed to be there most of the time. Later Ross and Henshawe rode to Camborne, and another time to Redruth, to discuss certain problems with certain people. But no strangers called at Nampara. On the twenty-third of March, which was a Wednesday, Ross rode into Truro and called on Harris Pascoe to tell him he had decided to sell half his holding in Wheal Leisure.

The banker took off his spectacles and looked at him cautiously before commenting.

" I think it a wise move. There is a stage at which one has to f-face facts and cut one's losses. Of course, in a sense, it is not a loss but a sizeable profit; and that's satisfactory. All the same, you have my sincerest sympathy; I know how much this venture has meant to you. I suppose you want to repay half the debt you contracted with Pearce. Very sensible indeed."

Ross frowned at the brand-new clock above the counter. " That's the only new face I see about. Is that Mr. Tresize or Mr. Spry?"

Pascoe smiled. " The change isn't yet quite complete. But I'm sure you'll like my new partners when you meet them. Now t-tell me: what do you want for your shares in Wheal Leisure?"

" Twenty pounds a share."

The banker whistled. " Will anyone *pay* that? It's a very

high price. And you know how cautious people are about investing these days."

"Not in a profitable concern."

"No. . . . Perhaps you're right. Well, I can let it be known they're in the market." Harris Pascoe looked up at his client again, remembering an incident not so long ago. "I s-suppose you have no objections whom the shares go to?"

Ross picked up a pen and ran his fingers slowly along the feather. "Beggars can't be choosers, can they?"

"No-o."

"Except as to price. Naturally I don't want it known that I'm eager to sell or someone may start making lower offers."

"It's a change of front for you, Captain Poldark. But I think you're wise."

Soon afterwards the first "run" was made into Nampara Cove.

In the late afternoon of a quiet damp day Jud Paynter, of all people, came rolling down the combe on his bowlegs with a letter from Mr. Trencrom, touching his fringe to Ross in the old way, whistling almost noiselessly between his front teeth and glancing in an inquisitive hangdog fashion about the house where he had spent many years of his life.

Ross read the note and said: "That's convenient. Does Mr. Trencrom expect a reply?"

"Not bi word o' pen. I'll tell 'im tes all fitty. 'E depend pon me, do Mr. Trencrom these days. His right-arm man, I reckon. Couldn' do without me. Proper job I got now."

"You've the knack with a cutter," Ross agreed. "But then, you were always one for sailing near the wind, weren't you, Jud?"

"Wind or no, it d'make no difference," said Jud, blinking. He was never quite comfortable in Ross's presence, faintly defiant, faintly resentful, wanting to be cocky and familiar but never gathering the courage. As long as he lived he would never forgive Ross for turning him out of the house; but his resentment was always nearer indignation than spite.

Some such thought as this crossed Ross's mind, and he

227

said: " I haven't thanked you for your peculiar testimony at the assize court. I don't know what you intended to say when you first went into the box, but in the end no one knew whether you were for me or against me, and even the judge was arguing. It's no mean feat to confuse the law."

Nature had not designed Jud's face for the expression of pleasure, but the way he wiped his nose on the back of his hand suggested he was gratified.

" Aw . . . I always d'say to Prudie, when a man's in trouble, then he d'know his neighbours. I won't disknowledge twas a tryin' time to be stood up afore this judge just like as if I'd been the 'ardened lawbreaker. But I've mind of you since you was a little tacker no biggerer than pot high, so what was there to do else?"

" What puzzles me is how you came in that position. There's rumour about that you were paid money to swear against me. That isn't true, of course?"

" Never no word of it! Tedn true, tedn right, tedn proper! There's nasty lying tongues about tryin' to make grief betwixt us. Don't ee believe a word of un. If the truth be told . . ."

Jud paused, sucking his teeth. " If the truth be told," Ross prompted.

" If the truth be told, tes all on account o' my good nature. Don't like to say no, see. People d'come an' asks me one thing an' I say ais and naw just to be easy, like. They get very friendly along of you, an' a drop o' gin; an' afore you can spit they've congled up some notions you never thought 'pon, not in your wildest dreams. That's how tis, as sure as me mother was married. Then when tes time for the court o' law, what's to do? Only to act like you was put in wi' the bread an' took out with the cakes, like. That's the truth if I go around land to-morrer."

Ross looked down at the shifty bulldog face. He didn't believe a word of it, but he laughed.

" Go tell your new master that I'm ready to draw my curtains."

In fact on this first run, because of Demelza's anxiety and

228

because of her condition, Ross observed all the prohibitions, though it went against the grain to do so. As dusk was falling he had the candles lighted and the curtains drawn, and they sat reading together until they heard the first clink of horses' hooves by the stream. Then Demelza got up and played on the spinet, and hummed and sang a little. Later they had supper, and presently the horses began to pass again, though this time it seemed their hooves were heavier on the ground. Occasionally a gruff voice could be heard and a footstep or the chink of metal.

In spite of all the precautions Demelza's heart thumped alarmingly; and as soon as supper was over she went back to the spinet and drowned the noises outside. The Gimletts had been given sufficient information to guess the rest, so they sat quietly in the kitchen and did not stir from the house. Once or twice Ross lifted his head from his book and glanced at Demelza. Once or twice his thoughts wandered to the informers, and he asked himself if the whole operation would go through without mishap. Mr. Trencrom had assured him that every effort would be made to keep the landing secret and that only twenty riders would be used as against a larger number usually. Watchers would be posted all along the cliffs and valley so that decent warning might be given of any gaugers about. But many must know of the run. If there was an informer, he must know that the cutter had been gone some days and was due back. Did he know where?

At ten the sounds began to taper off, and by eleven all was peace again. At midnight they went to bed, but both slept restlessly, imagining from time to time they heard noises around the house. No caller, however, came to disturb them, and just before dawn Ross got up and went down to the cove.

A restless white fog moved over the land, and he thought it lucky it had not come down to impede progress last night. Great care had been taken to remove any signs of the operations. Above high-water mark the sand had been rolled or scraped with flat boards so that no one could tell the amount of disturbance there had been. Horse tracks all the way down to the cove in the soft ground could not be so easily hid, but a day's rain would wash them away. It smelt like rain. The undergrowth had been crushed down in places. A curlew was crying in the colourless dawn light.

He walked across to the cave where the dinghy was kept. It was a buoyant little craft he had bought in St. Ann's just before last year's collapse to replace the one in which Mark Daniel had made his escape. As he bent over it a footstep sounded on the dry seaweed behind him, and he turned swiftly to find that Demelza had followed him. Her face looked small, detached, like a sculpture, framed in its dark hair on the pedestal of her dark cloak.

He said: "You shouldn't have come out so soon. The air is chill."

"I like it. I feel I've been behind those drawn curtains for a week."

"Our visitors have been very careful. Nothing scarcely to show. I think they have moved this boat—they or someone else. When I left it on Thursday it was farther up the cave."

"Was it, Ross?" Why do I not tell him that I was out in it myself yesterday, that for the first time I managed without Gimlett and caught eight mackerel and a dab? Because I know he would stop me and I don't want to be stopped. Ross could not have been more thoughtful for her, but sometimes all the restrictions and prohibitions oppressed her and made her feel caged and constricted. The Gimletts were faithful watchdogs; too faithful. Oh, she was comforted and warmed by Ross's consideration—yet he had not altogether convinced her. It seemed to her that on the night of their return home after the trial he had spoken from his heart. Since knowing there was actually a child on the way he had spoken out of a confusion of feeling and a kindness of disposition. It might be she was wrong, but that was how it seemed to her.

"It's good to feel last night is over," she said.

"It's good to feel we're that much better off."

"I'm still afraid. Promise you'll not go on with it a minute longer than we really need."

"Well, I've no real fancy for commercialising our little

cove. Are you well or ill this morning that you're up so early?"

"Well if other things are well. The brume is lifting, look."

The shallow fog was smoking in the widening light, as if someone had lit a bonfire for a mile or so upon the sea. Out of the darker mist the sun already threw premonitory beams; and across the swept-clean upper sky a single smear of cloud was lit a brilliant cadmium yellow. They watched the fog grow luminous along its higher reaches; then familiar landmarks began to jut out with startling clearness, like stage scenery unveiled. The sea licked quietly at the sand, uncommunicative, saying nothing of the night.

Ross stirred. "Did you know Ruth Treneglos was safely delivered of a baby daughter early yesterday?"

"No! At last. Are they well?"

"Well except in temper. I hear they're monstrously disappointed it's a girl after all this delay. They say old Horace is so furious at not having a grandson that he's refused to speak to John since."

"Poor Ruth!"

"I should save your pity for the baby, who may deserve it."

"Who told you, Ross?"

"Dwight. He was not there, of course, but is almost on their doorstep."

Full dawn had crept round them hardly noticed so that suddenly, instead of being unobserved figures discussing the night, they had become the observed, focused by the absence of darkness, conspicuous under the rose-flushed sky. With a common instinct they drew back into the mouth of the cave.

Ross said: "I've been talking to Dwight about Francis."

"Oh?"

"Dwight tells me that Francis's quarrel with George Warleggan was over me."

"How does he know?"

"They shared a bedroom in Bodmin. Francis wanted to do away with himself. It all bears out what Verity wrote in her letter—and much more besides."

She said: "I'm glad we made it up at Christmas."

"So am I—now."

As they turned to plough across the sand she said: "I'd like to put my feet in the water."

"It would freeze your vitals at this hour."

"My vitals feel peculiar enough," said Demelza. "Perhaps I'd better leave them be."

That day Ross went to Truro and heard that the shares had sold. They had been bought by Mr. Coke, and had fetched their price. The newcomer, the unknown Mr. Coke, was now the largest shareholder in the mine. It was a wrench at the last, hearing they had irrevocably gone. On his way home he made a detour to call at Trenwith.

He found Francis beside the lake, sawing up a tree. The occupation came strangely to him. Fate would never make Francis anything but what he had been born.

"I always dislike the burning of ash," Ross said as he dismounted. "One feels it has grown for better things."

"Perhaps that's why it resents the saw," said Francis, whose face had coloured more at sight of Ross than from the exertion. There was no ease between them yet. "Elizabeth's indoors, I think, and will be glad of a visitor. I'll follow in two or three minutes."

"No, it's you I want to see. We can talk here."

"Any excuse to stop." Francis wiped his hands. "How is Demelza?"

"Well enough, thank you. Better than last time."

"What can I do for you, Ross?"

Ross tethered Darkie to a sapling and sat on a piece of the fallen tree. He picked up a thin branch and began to trace thoughtful squares and circles in the sandy gravel of the path. "Have Ellery and Pendarves found you buried treasure yet?"

". . . Hardly so much as that. There's a likely place where my land abuts on the head of Sawle Combe. But it would be right on Choake's front door, and he would squeak at that. Also the signs are for tin and I've still a special attachment for copper."

"I'm opening Wheal Grace," Ross said.

232

"What? You don't mean it? That's cheerful news! What made you change your mind?"

"Circumstances. We hope to start in three months. It's a gamble, of course."

Francis put on his coat. "You're going to follow the Trevorgie workings?"

"Henshawe and I have been down several times. God knows who did all that work but the place is honeycombed. It's mostly shallow but even so the lower level is flooded and we haven't been able to explore it. So we expect to put up an engine. We reckon there's enough ore in the shallow levels to make the venture worth while."

"Who is investing the money?"

"I am. I've sold half my shares in Wheal Leisure and can realise six hundred pounds."

Ross began to pull off his gloves. They had both been carefully mended by Demelza, and for a moment he looked at them with distaste at the thought of the necessity for darning.

"D'you see anything of George these days?" he asked.

"I haven't seen him since September. Our quarrel was not the sort that is likely to be made up."

"Not ever?"

Francis looked at him. "I can't answer for what may happen in heaven."

"This feud," Ross said carefully, "between George and *me* is one which it can be to nobody's advantage to join. It would be particularly to your detriment to take up more than —say—a neutral attitude. Although he's made no move against you up to now, he could do so any time."

"My dear Ross, my attitude has gone far beyond the neutral. You may not welcome me as a fellow standard-bearer, but I'm afraid there's no choice."

Darkie stamped her foot and whinnied.

"You've told me more than once," Ross said, "about this money you're saving to invest in a mine. How much was it: six hundred pounds or thereabouts?"

There was a sharp silence.

"Thereabouts."

"With twelve hundred pounds we could do a great deal."

"Yes?"

"It could be."

"You're suggesting—we should go into partnership?"

"Yes."

"There's nothing at all I'd like better. But—it's rather taken my breath away. Are you sure you want that?"

"If I'd not wanted it I shouldn't have suggested it."

"No. . . . God, it's a strange world." Francis wiped his forehead again, put the handkerchief away, wriggled the saw out of the half-sawn log.

"It may be a fight," said Ross. "You would do better to keep out. George has a long arm."

"To the devil with George."

"If this prospers, then I want no outsiders who can dispose of their shares just as and when they please. But you may well lose your money."

"I like a gamble. . . . But if anyone had told me six months ago . . ."

"One can gamble on a man as well as on a mine."

Francis stirred the shavings with his foot. "I can't guarantee the *mine*. . . ."

"If you feel like that, that's all that matters."

"I feel like that. . . ."

"Forget the past," Ross said. "Take this proposition or leave it on its merits."

"I take it, of course. Come up to the house and we'll seal the contract in a glass of good brandy."

As they walked along they did not speak at all. Ross's proposal had astonished Francis and excited him; but he was not easy in his mind. Two or three times he glanced at his cousin, and almost at the door of the house he stopped.

"Look, Ross, I . . ."

"What?"

"Don't think I don't want this. It—could mean a lot to me. But before we—go any further there's something it's necessary to tell you. If it were not for your offering this—

this thing it wouldn't be in me to blurt it out. But now. . . .
The proposition shouldn't go forward until you know . . ."

Ross stared at his embarrassed face.

" Is it something that is past?"

" Oh, God, yes. But all the same——"

" If it's past, then forget it. I don't think I want to hear
what you may be going to tell me."

Francis flushed. " If that's the case, I don't think I want to
hear it myself."

They stared at each other.

Francis said: " The Poldarks, then."

Ross nodded slowly.

" The Poldarks."

Chapter Nine

Widow Tregothnan's kiddley in Sawle was crammed to the
doors.

Two unmistakable signs that a cargo had been successfully
run in the neighbourhood were a relaxation in the tension
of day-to-day living and an increase of drunkenness. Money
was temporarily easier, and gin and rum were cheap. The
little subwave of prosperity ran right through the villages,
beginning among the men concerned in the run and losing its
height and momentum the further it spread from them.

Sally Tregothnan—a loud, laughing woman of forty-odd—
was herself behind the counter that served as a bar, and
giving as good as she got. The four public houses in the
village were enjoying their fair share of trade, but Widow
Tregothnan's was the meeting place of the choicer spirits.
The widow was often known as Sally Chill-Off. She was not
supposed to sell anything stronger than beer, but there had
never been a moment in the village's history when she had
not been prepared to add a little something to her ale " to take
the chill off," even when her customers were on their beam

ends. So prosperity brought her a roaring trade. Among those present to-night were Ned Bottrell, Jud Paynter, Charlie Kempthorne, Paul Daniel, Jacka Hoblyn and Ted Carkeek. Men like Pally Rogers and Will Nanfan, though they were ringleaders in the trade, frowned on drink for themselves as contrary to their Methodist principles.

Jud Paynter was at his happiest. He had gin at his elbow, gin in his stomach and an audience.

"Now then," he said, "now then, if you d'want to know what tis like to stand up in a court o' law an' speak the words o' truth an' have the judge an' jury an' all the lawyers listening openmouthed, I'll tell ee. There they was, jury row on row like sparrows on a branch, lawyers in their black nightshirts like they was ready to leap into bed, fancy doxies wi' parasols, the whole darned, danged, blathering boiling of 'em, mured together cheek to cheek. Twas some handsome sight, I tell ee."

"Go on," said Sally Tregothnan. "Go on."

"Tes true. Without a word of a lie. When first I stood up there and looked around, I was sweatin' like dung. But when I got goin' I give 'em a fair proper talking to, as if I was the shepherd and they was the sheep. Damme, twould've done ye all a power o' good to have 'eard'n."

"Reckon you did oughter have been a preacher," said Charlie Kempthorne, winking at Ned Bottrell.

Jacka Hoblyn drained his glass and looked at Jud from under his heavy brows. "I'm sick and tired of hearing all this spudder. Tis over and done with these pretty many months and there's no more to it. Who knows what you was like in the court when there's nobody but you to tell us?"

"I'm *tellin'* ee," Jud said, showing his two teeth indignantly. "If ye've got ears to hear, I'm telling ee. Here was I, say this pot, and there was Judge, say Paul Daniel, but not grinning like a ram's cat; and there was Ross Poldark in the dock, say Jacka Hoblyn, but not squattin' down like a hen wi' the cluck; and Judge says to me, 'Mester Paynter,' he says, says he, 'did this man do wrong or no?' an' I says to him I says, 'Judge,' I says, 'this man once done wrong by me but I aren't one to carry a grudge where it don't belong to be carried, for who d'know betterer'n Jud Paynter what the Good Book d'say, which is if the Lord do strike thee upon one eye turn thou the other and let'n 'ave a good clunk at that too. So tis fair to say that I'm speakin' the honest truth an' no word of a lie when I d'tell ee this man Jacka Hoblyn, Ross Poldark I d'mean, is as innocent as a new-dropped babe in its first wettels. Grudge,' I says, 'I've no judge against ee or any man living or dead. I b'lieve in all as tes written for all to read. Thou shalt not move thy neighbour's landmark. Nor shalt thou covet thy neighbour's wife, nor his mate, nor his hoss, nor his axe, nor anythink that is his.' "

"Here, mind where you're sweeping wi' your great hands!" said Sally Tregothnan.

"So I goes on till nigh every soul to be seen has melted into hot tears, hardened sinners and doxies alike. Then the grudge turns to the court an' opens up his arms like a huer that's seen the pilchards an' 'e says, 'My friends, my friends, my friends, my friends, my friends, my friends . . .' " Jud paused and groped for his glass, found it, and carried it along a winding lane to his lips.

"Stuff an' nonsense," said Jacka Hoblyn in a disagreeable voice. "No judge never said nothing of the sort."

" 'Old hard, me dear," whispered Paul Daniel. "Give 'im a bit more rope an' who knows but what he'll 'ang hisself."

But Jud had lost track of his remarks. He tried hard to put his glass down until at length Sally took it from him. He mopped his forehead with his coat sleeve and looked round with a glassy eye. He began to sing in a broken quavering tenor.

"There was an old couple an' they was poor. Tweedle, tweedle, go-twee. They lived in a sheep shed without any door. By the side of an elmin tree."

"Dear Jakes, it is more than I can stomach," said Hoblyn. "Sitting up there like an Aunt Sally at a Christmas fair."

Charlie Kempthorne coughed as he moved surreptitiously

nearer to Jacka. Smoke and drink still touched up his chest at times. "I seen Rosina out this morning," he said confidentially. "She's growing away into a 'andsome girl."

"Eh?" said Jacka, staring at him suspiciously.

"She'll be wedding soon, I suppose? Though maybe there'll be some as is put off like wi' that leg, on account of 'er walking lipsy."

Jacka grunted and finished his drink. Charlie blinked and glanced at the other man's heavy brow.

"Twouldn't do for 'er to live an' die a maid just on account of being clecky in one leg."

"She's but seventeen," said Jacka, filling his pipe. "There's many a young rip'll be coming after she afore long."

"Maybe an olderer sort of person would be more fitty like," said Kempthorne, licking his lips.

"An' this old couple," sang Jud, "'ad got no gold. Tweedle, tweedle, go-twee. So they was feelin' fair bedoled. In the lewth of the elmin tree."

"Now me," said Kempthorne, "just for instance, as you might say. I aren't doin' so dusty out o' my sailmaking an' suchlike. Gettin' a little nest egg together. Mind, I got two childer, one of——"

"Aye," said Jacka, "poor little brats."

"There's naught amiss with them that growin' up won't cure. What they need more'n aught else is a woman's care. I've had a thought for Mary Ann Tregaskis; but——"

"If she'd 'ave you." When he was in his first drink was not the time for Jacka Hoblyn's nature to show at its most agreeable.

"Well, that's as may be. I 'aven't asked her. But there's many as would jump at the chance. I got a bit o' ground back of Andrewartha's for swedes, an' I shall be havin' a litter of veers next month. An' sailmaking's maybe not all I shall do with the needle afore I'm through. I got me ten yards o' black velveteen in to Redruth last week, cheap, at two shillings the yard, and I've a mind to cut it out and make it up as breeches in a genteel way; twould sell to folk aiming to be gentry if not to the gentry themselves. And there's other things I got, picked up here an' there, that'd maybe surprise you."

"Yes?" said Jacka, pouring another drink.

"Yes. An' I 'ad the thought twould fit in very well for a girl as is 'andy with a needle to fix up with a man who's 'andy the same way, like. I 'ad that thought."

"You 'ad, eh?" said Jacka, and stared appraisingly at Kempthorne. He brooded for a minute. "How old are you, Charlie? Nearly so old as me, I reckon."

"I'm only thirty-nine," said Charlie.

"And d'you spit blood still?"

"Nay, I've not done that for near on two year. Look, Jacka, I tell ee, I'm getting on in the world, and, there's many a maid could do worse . . ."

"Maybe the maid would have somethin' to say 'bout that herself."

"Nay, Rosina's an easy-natured sort o' girl—takes after her mother. An' you, Jacka, o' course. An' you. She'd do what her dad thought right, I'm sure of it."

"Aye," growled Jacka, "maybe she would. Maybe that's the way she's been brought up. But I aren't one for doing things in haste—except when there's need for haste. And there'd better not be now."

"No haste at all! Just think around it in your leisure, like. And maybe I'll drop in an' see Rosina now and then, if tis all the same to you, just to see how the land lays . . ."

"Now, this old couple," sang Jud, "was poddlin' around. Tweedle, tweedle, go-twee; when they seen a long-cripple come out o' the ground. From under the elmin tr-tree. . . ."

Later that night Jud made his stumbling way home towards Grambler under the hasty light of a half-moon rushing through high white clouds. The air had turned keen, and if April had not been well advanced one might have expected frost. Jud was still in a jovial mood, though not untinged with forebodings about the eternal damnation of the world. Now and then he forgot it and went on with his interminable song, for which there always seemed to be a new verse; now and then he stumbled over a rut or a stone and consigned the world to the hell-fire and brimstone from which he'd long been trying to save it.

But it was after one of his rarer quiet periods that he heard the footsteps behind.

Time had partly lulled the fears of autumn and Christmas, and to-night the drink had warmed him and given him courage; all the same he turned quickly, his hackles up and reaching for his knife. It was the lonely stretch just before you reached the first cottage of Grambler; gorse bushes and heather and a few wind-contorted trees.

There were two men, and in the half-darkness he realised with a sinking feeling that they were strangers; one was tall, wore an old hat pulled low over his eyes.

" Mister Paynter," said the short man, and Jud thought he had heard that voice somewhere before.

" What d'ye want?"

" Nothing partic'lar. Just a little talk."

" I don't want no talk. Keep yer distance or I'll slit you wi' this knife."

" Oh, indeed. Quite a warrior now, eh? More of a warrior than you were last September."

" I don't know what yer mean," Jud said anxiously, backing away. " Tes all foreign to me."

" What, don't remember getting some money on the cheap, like, eh? Just thought you could tell as many lies as you liked and get away with it, eh? Clever, aren't you? Smart. All right, Joe, let 'im 'ave it."

The little man sprang forward and Jud's knife flashed in the moonlight, but before he could turn, the tall man lifted a heavy bar he carried and crashed it down with great violence upon Jud's head. There was a rush of moonlight and then his knees gave way and he fell forward into the enduring dark.

When Prudie heard that her husband had been murdered she

gave a piercing scream and rushed out in the early morning light to greet the cortège that wormed through the village towards her. Two old scavengers, Ezekiel Scawen and Sid Bunt, had found the body in the ditch beside the road, and some miners had brought a board and were carrying him on his last journey home. Whether the attackers had intended to make it a killing job or whether the savage blow and the night's exposure had together proved too much for a constitution weakened by years of drinking no one would ever know. Robbery was generally believed to be the motive, and two crippled sailors working their way along the coast to St. Ives were set on and might have been roughly handled if they had not been able to prove they had spent the whole night in the lowly house of the Rev. Clarence Odgers.

Ross wouldn't let Demelza go over, but he went himself and conveyed his sympathy to Prudie. In a queer way Jud had become an institution, not merely in the neighbourhood but in his life. Though they saw little of each other these days, Ross had always been aware of Jud's existence, grumbling, drunken, and self-righteous in his blundering hang-dog way. The district wouldn't ever be quite the same without him. He said something of this to Prudie, who sniffed into a red duster that had been Jud's and confessed to Ross her suspicion that Jud's death was a result of something that had happened at Bodmin, because he'd never been easy in his mind since then—always he'd seemed to be expecting something. Now it had come with a vengeance. Ross didn't speak, but stood staring thoughtfully out of the window, considering the possibility. After waiting hopefully for some response, Prudie gave it up and said, Well, dear life, whatever was at the root of it, she didn't know how she'd ever make out now he was gone. And her cousin from Marasanvose, who'd come over for company, sniffed in a corner and wiped her nose on her sleeve.

They had put the body in the lean-to shed that communicated with the single-story two-roomed shack by way of the back door, and after staring at his old servant for a moment or two, Ross returned to the two sniffing women and said they must tell him if there was any way in which he could help.

"We'm going to teel 'im Thursday," said Prudie, her hair over her face like a horse's tail, "an' I want for to give him a rare good berryin'. 'E was always one to like the best, and the best we shall give un, shan't us, Tina."

"A-a-is," said Tina.

"'E was a proper man, was Jud," said Prudie. "Reckon we had our ups and downs together, an? Reckon he could be a rare ole ornery monkey upon times, but that didn't count nothin' wi' me. He was my old man, see, and now 'e's dead an' gone, strick down from be'ind in the night. Tis 'orrible, 'orrible to think on!"

"If you'll let me know the time of the funeral, I'll be at the church," said Ross.

"Ned Bottrell's making a box for'n. I d'want it all done proper, like he was a gent, see. We'm goin' t'ave hymns an' all. Mester Ross . . ."

"Yes?"

"I want for ee to tell me if I'm doin' right. This forenoon when we'd laid 'im out decent I went for to empty out his 'baccy pouch—one 'e carried along with 'im most times everywhere he went, and twas a mercy he didn't take it Tuesday—for when I come to empty of it, damme if golden sov'reigns didn't scatter 'bout all over the floor like mice that's seen a cat. Fifteen of 'em there was, and me never knowed nothin' about'n! Where he come by 'em gracious knows—in the trade, I reckon—but what's plaguing me is whether tis right and fitty to spend the gold on 'is berrying, an?"

Ross stared out through the open door. "The money is yours now, Prudie, to do with as you will. Everything that was his passes to you; but there's better uses you could put it to than to squander it on a big funeral. Fifteen pounds is a tidy nest egg and would keep you fed and clothed for a long while."

Prudie scratched herself. " Jud would've wanted berryin' respectable. Tes a matter o' being *respectable*, Mest' Ross. Load me if it ain't. We must give the ole man a send-off fitty ways. Mustn't us, Tina?"

" A-a-is," said Tina.

Chapter Ten

Jud's send-off fitty ways began at two o'clock the day before the funeral. Prudie had submerged her grief in the preparations, and a long table made of old boxes had been fastened together in the larger of the two rooms. More old boxes outside served as chairs and tables for those who couldn't squeeze in. And there were many such until the heavy rain of nightfall drove them away.

Prudie as chief mourner had managed to gather together enough black clothes to make an impressive display. Her cousin had lent her black stockings, and she'd made a skirt out of a piece of serge bought at Aunt Mary Rogers's shop. An old black blouse of her own was decorated with mourning beads and a bit of ragged lace, and Char Nanfan had actually produced a black veil. Barely recognisable in this array, she sat in a place of honour at the head of the table unmoving throughout the meal and waited on by Cousin Tina, Char Nanfan, Mrs. Zacky Martin and a few of the younger end.

The Rev. Mr. Odgers had been invited to the feast but had discreetly declined; so pride of place next to the bereaved widow was given to Paul Daniel, who was Jud Paynter's oldest friend. On the other side was Constable Vage, who was conducting the inquiry into the murder, and others present were Zacky Martin, Charlie Kempthorne, Whitehead and Jinny Scoble, Ned Bottrell, Uncle Ben and Aunt Sarah Tregeagle, Jack Cobbledick, the Curnow brothers, Aunt Betsy Triggs, and some fifteen or twenty assorted hangers-on.

Soon after two the feast began with a long draught of raw

brandy all round, and then everyone set to eating and drinking at a great rate as if there wasn't a minute to be lost. At the outset the splendid widow ate more genteelly than the rest, taking in nourishment under the heavy veil as under a visor. But as the brandy warmed her vitals she threw back the emblem of bereavement and tucked in with the rest.

About five the first part of the feast was over, and by sunset many of the women began to drift off, having families or homes to see to, and the number in the room came down to about a score. This was twice as many as could decently breathe in a cramped space already full of smoke and steam and tobacco fumes. Jugs of brandy, rum and gin were going round freely, with hot water and sugar to be added to taste. At this point the hymns began. Uncle Ben Tregeagle, as doyen of the church choir, was allowed to lead them, and Joe Permewan scraped an accompaniment like rusty metal on his bass viol. They sang all the hymns and anthems they knew and some they didn't know, and then got on to patriotic songs. They sang " God Save the King " four times and " And Shall Trelawney Die " twice, and a few ditties that weren't too savoury if looked at in the most formal light.

But now no one was feeling formal, least of all Prudie, who, her nose shining like a hurricane lamp, allowed herself to be persuaded to get up and sing a song which had the chorus:

" An' when he died, he shut his eyes,
      An' never saw money no more."

Then Aunt Betsy Triggs got up and did her famous dance, ending up sitting in Constable Vage's lap. The roar that greeted this dwindled to a shamefaced silence as everyone came to realise they were overstepping the traces.

Prudie worked her feet into her tattered carpet slippers and slowly got up again.

" My dear, *dear* friends," she said, " don't take on on account o' me, I beg you. Take no heed of my grief. An' take no heed of the ole man out there that's going to be teeled to-morror. Tis just a per-personal matter twixt 'im and me.

244

No reason why ye have got to stay quiet as meaders just on account o' that. Eat, drink an' do what you will, for tis no affair of his what I do with his money now 'e's going to his long lie." She hunched her great shoulders and glowered. " I-facks, tis more'n I can b'lieve 'ow he did conceal the gold away from me all these many year. Hid it from his own wife, 'e did. Or as near his wife as makes no concern."

Charlie Kempthorne tittered, but Constable Vage poked him solemnly in the ribs and shook his head; it was not the place to show vulgar amusement.

" My blessed life," said Prudie, and hiccupped. " He was a whited sepulchre, was my old man, if the truth be known! An' old cloamin tomcat hollow to the toes. As cuzzle as they come. I'd as lief trust a beaver. But there twas, that's how tis, an' no one can deny it. 'E was my old man, see."

Paul Daniel grunted. After the merriment everyone was feeling sentimental and full of liquor.

" An' he was a talker when the drink was in him. Talk! 'E'd outtalk preacher any day of the week, Sundays including. But I seen him goin' down'ill for months. Twasn't all murdering lyin' thiefs what done for him. Twas semi-decay. Tha's what twas. He'd lived a hard life an' it told in the end."

She sat down abruptly before she had finished because her knees gave way. Constable Vage got up. At ordinary times he was a wheelwright.

" Brothers and sisters," he said. " I aren't one for slack-jaw as ye all well know; but it wouldn't do if we ended this feastin' without a thought or two for our dear brother Jud, newly departed to the flowery fields and green meads o' paradise. Wicked men 'as struck him down, but the law will track them out, never doubt." He folded his hands over his stomach.

" 'Ear, 'ear," said Prudie.

" So we must not forget the vacant chair at this table." Vage looked round but could not see even an empty packing case. " The vacant chair," he repeated. " And it is only right an' proper that we drink a toast to our dear departed brother."

" A-a-is," said Tina.

" To our dear brother," said Prudie, raising her glass. The toast was drunk.

" May he rest easy," said Joe Permewan.

" Amen," said Uncle Ben Tregeagle, shaking his ringlets.

" Tis a poor life," said Aunt Sarah. " From the cradle to the grave in two snaps of the fingers. I see it all. Layin' out and lyin' in. That's me job, but it makes you think."

" Amen," said Uncle Ben.

" I'd sooner be a fish jouster any day," said Betsy.

" There's many I've found worser to lay out than Jud," said Sarah. " 'E stretched out a good deal of a long man, but there warn't so much round the middle as I suspected."

" Amen," said Uncle Ben.

" 'Old hard with your 'amens,' old man," said Prudie. " We aren't in church yet. You can say yer prayers to-morrow."

Charlie Kempthorne began to giggle. He giggled and giggled until everyone hushed him for fear he'd wake the guests already asleep on the floor.

" I aren't partic'lar what I do for the living," said Betsy. " But when they ain't living they give me the shrims. Even poor Joe I didn' dare touch—an' him me own brother these fifty year or more." She began to weep gently.

" 'Ere, Ned," said Prudie, " do ee go'n draw the spigot of that next keg of brandy. I'm as thirsty as a cat wi' nine chets. Tis early yet."

Bottrell winked at her and went into the other room, which had served as a kitchen to-day. Prudie sat back, her massive arms folded, surveying the scene with a satisfied expression. Everything had gone off handsome so far. Most of the remaining guests would sleep here the night, and to-morrow, pleasurable thought, it would all begin again. The burying was at noon, so they'd have the coffin out early if it was fine, and placed outside the door on a bench of chairs and packing cases. All the other mourners would be back straight after breakfast, and they'd begin singing hymns. One hymn and then a glass, another hymn and then another glass until about eleven o'clock. Then the bearers would take up the coffin and carry it a hundred yards or so, and Ned Bottrell would follow behind with an anker of brandy and they'd have a hymn and refreshments, another hundred yards and more refreshments, until they got to the church. They should manage that by twelve o'clock, if they managed it at all. Prudie remembered that real bumper funeral of Tommy Job's when the bearers had been stretched out flat with half a mile still to go.

Aunt Sarah Tregeagle said: " When I first started layin' out, mind, it used to shrim me up too, so I did used to say a little charm over to meself that I'd learned from Grannie Nanpusker, that was a white witch. Afore ever I laid me 'ands on one that'd gone dead I used to say: ' God save us from mystifications, conjurations, toxifications, incantations, fumigations, tarnations, devilations and damnations. Amen. Rosemary, tansy, sweet briar, herb o' grave.' An' I never come to no 'arm at all."

" My blessed Parliament," said Prudie.

" Amen," echoed Uncle Ben sleepily.

But there was nothing sleepy in the way Ned Bottrell burst back into the room. He wasn't carrying any brandy, and his face was white.

" It's gone!" he shouted.

" The brandy!" said Prudie, lurching to her feet. " 'Ere, who's stolen it? Twas there an hour gone——"

" Not all *three* kegs!" said Constable Vage, instantly alert. " Why we did oughter have heard them. They couldn't move three kegs without——"

" Nay," said Ned Bottrell, shouting above the clamour. " Not the drink, the corpse!"

They got it out of him bit by bit, in a rising clamour of voices. Lured by morbid curiosity and professional pride, he had carried the lantern from the kitchen and taken a peep in the shed, just, as he put it, to see if the ole man was comfortable in his nice new box. And there was the coffin, but the body was gone.

Some of them were as shaken as Ned, but Prudie took the situation firmly in hand. First she said Ned was as full as a

247

can and couldn't see straight and the ole man was still there, she'd lay a guinea. But when Ned invited her to come and see, she said her feet was hurting her and sent Constable Vage instead. When Vage, clearing his throat a good deal and patting his stomach, returned to confirm the story, she drained another glass and stood up.

"'Tis they body stealers," she said in a booming voice. "You d'know what tis like! I reckon tis those same thievin' lyin' murderers that corpsed him on Monday night. Come us on, my sons."

With a great show of resolution a dozen of them, led now by the widow, pushed through into the lean-to shed and stared down at Ned Bottrell's box. It looked a good bit of carpentry, and even in this moment of crisis Ned couldn't refrain from giving it an admiring glance. But it was quite empty.

Prudie nearly tipped it up by sitting suddenly on the edge and bursting into tears.

"There, there, now," said Paul Daniel, who had been wakened from a sound sleep and dragged in here without a full explanation. "It edn as if he'd been took sudden. We was all prepared for the worst."

"He's been took sudden, sure 'nough," said Joe Permewan. "'Tis *where* 'e's been took that's mystifying me."

"We can't 'ave a funeral without someone to teel," said Betsy Triggs. "Twouldn't be decent."

"There, there, now," said Paul Daniel, stroking Prudie's lank hair. "You must be brave, my dear. We've all got to come to it sooner or later. Rich an' poor, gentle an' simple, saint an' sinner. We all must be brave."

"Brave be *danged*!" shouted Prudie, reacting ungratefully. "Go hold yer 'ead! I want to know what they done wi' my ole man!"

There was a brief silence.

"We must look," said Constable Vage. "Maybe he hasn't been took far."

This suggestion seemed better than doing nothing, so two

more lanterns were lit. When they opened the door it was raining heavily and was pitch-dark, but after some shufflings and hesitation three small search parties were organised, while the women went back to the feast to console Prudie.

Prudie was inconsolable. It was the disgrace, she said. To have a husband an' then not to have a husband, that was how she saw it, and she said she'd never live it down. Betsy Triggs was quite right, you couldn't have a burying without someone to bury. The lying murdering thieves had not only robbed her of her old man, they'd even taken away the pleasure of seeing him planted decent. Everyone was coming back to-morrow for a proper slap-up funeral, and there was three ankers of brandy not touched yet, and all those pies and cakes and the preacher engaged, and the hole dug, and nothing to put in it. It was more than flesh and blood could stand.

Aunt Sarah Tregeagle thought she'd help the time away with a story of one of her layings out, when a man had died with his knees up; but no one seemed to want to listen, so in in the end she tailed off and silence fell. This was nearly as bad, they found, so Uncle Ben, who had been excused the search on account of age, turned to Joe Permewan, who had been excused the search on account of rheumatics, and asked him to play a tune. Joe said, all right, it was just what he'd thought of suggesting himself, and got out his bass viol; but he was so fuddled with drink that when he came to play, the noise he made was even worse than the silence. As Prudie said, it was just as if he was drawing the bow over his own guts.

Ben then suggested a singsong, but nobody had the breath for this, and Prudie began to take offence at Jack Cobbledick's snores from the corner under the window. It was insult on insult, she said. However, no amount of thumping would wake him, so they just went on and on.

Then Betsy Triggs heard footsteps at the door and they all waited eagerly to see what news the returning searchers brought.

Jud Paynter limped in. He was in his best underclothes

and was very wet and very cross. The tablecloth he'd borrowed from the kiddley down the lane wasn't much protection
from the rain.

" 'Ere," he said truculently, " what's all this? An' where's
my pipe?"

Chapter Eleven

Jud's recovery was a nine days' wonder and scandal in the
district. The doctors and apothecaries who had not bothered
with him when he was supposedly dead now rode long dis-
tances to see the freak who had recovered. They peered at
him and sounded him and took samples and talked in long
Latin names about it. They prescribed febrifuges and anti-
monies and inserted setons and administered glysters, and one
of them even wanted to fire off a pistol near his ear to help
to disperse any lingering fever. Only Jud's language made it
impossible. After the first impetus of his recovery he was very
ill again, and he lay in bed with a dirty bandage round his
head glowering up at his tormentors.

Ordinary people in the district also flocked to see him, but
when he began to get better their presence annoyed him so
much that Prudie couldn't let them in any more. Even then
they clustered round his window and peeped in through the
broken boards, and when he saw them he would shout and
swear and aim anything he could lay his hands on, so that
Prudie had to hide even her best boots.

Gratitude for his escape didn't stir him deeply; his chief
feeling was anger with Prudie.

" Darned old fool," he said to Ross when Ross called.
" Darned old fool. She spends all me money on me funeral,
and I aren't dead. All me money! Drunk away, like it was
poured down a drain. She could as lief've throwed it to the
crows!"

" How did you first—come round?"

Jud said with dignity that he had been lying quiet in his

coffin when the rain coming through the leaky roof had begun to fall on his face, and this had wakened him. He explained that he had been dreaming of gin but the taste was wrong, and when he first sat up he thought he was at sea in the *One and All*. It seemed to be a rough night so he climbed out of his bunk and went on deck, but when he got there it was raining faster than ever and he saw trees and knew he was home after all.

" Then I feels thirsty so I goes down Jake's lane to Jake's kiddley and goes in wanting for a drop o' custom to ease me, like, and damme, what d'you think, they all ups and screams like they was stuck veers and goes scrabbling over each other to get out o' the other door—and leaves me all alone. So I finished up the drinks they'd left, an' puts the table sheet round me 'ead and goes home to find Prudie."

" She thought the money was hers," Ross said. " Everyone thought you were dead. It was her wish to give you a fine funeral."

" It was her wish to have a rare old caprouse, that's what twas! Drunk they all was! Drunk as emmets round a jam pot! And on *my* gold! When I was strick down there was fifteen gold sov'reigns. What is there now, eh? Three sovreigns and two kegs of brandy an' a wooden coffin standing on its end like a grandfather's clock wi' no face! Tedn right, I tell ee!"

In the weeks that followed Jud made a slow recovery. He limped about with a stick, one leg dragging a little, and would speak to no one. Nor did he take kindly to the inquiries of his friends. It was almost impossible to go out for a drink without being asked what Heaven looked like or whether Gabriel hadn't answered his knock, and if there was gin or brandy up-along.

All his life he'd been a disgruntled man, but what made his present grievance almost impossible to bear was that he could tell no one the worst of it. He had risked the reprisal to gain the guineas, and now had suffered the reprisal and lost the guineas as well. If he ever did see Gabriel there would be a fine tale to tell.

On the first Friday in May Ross and Francis rode in to make final arrangements about the opening of the mine. They explained something of their plans to Harris Pascoe in the back room of the bank, and Pascoe eyed the cousins and wondered how long the partnership would last. He had only the outsider's view of their misunderstandings, knowing nothing of the long friendship of their youth, and he was grateful for being spared the necessity of refusing them a loan on their venture.

Francis said: "There is one point on which I already have Ross's agreement. I want my interest in this mine to be vested in my son's name."

"Your little boy? He's only a child, isn't he?"

"I'm heavily in debt to Warleggan interests and have recently quarrelled with the family. So far, I'll give 'em credit, no pressure has been put on me; but you know how Ross and the Warleggans get on, and if they learn we are in partnership they may try to get at him through me. If this interest belongs to Geoffrey Charles, no one can touch it."

"We c-can arrange that. There are, of course, a few extra difficulties which may crop up in the possession of this sort of property by a minor. I suppose you would not prefer it in your wife's name?"

Francis looked at his fingers. "No. I would not."

"Just so. Very well, then. When do you intend to begin work?"

"The first of June," Ross said. "The engine pieces are already well ahead, but of course we shall not need pumping gear right at the outset."

"I suppose you're having a Boulton and Watt?"

"Well, no. There are two young engineers from Redruth Henshawe speaks highly of, and we think they will build a more efficient one at a smaller cost."

"Only t-take care not to get involved in litigation over that. Watt has the important patent, and I believe there are some years for it yet to run."

Soon after, they called on Nat Pearce, who was to draw up

the deeds of association; then they had a meal at the Red Lion Inn. Francis had some business of his own to do, so he left Ross talking to Richard Tonkin, who had joined them at the meal. Tonkin had news of many of their former associates, but Ross would have welcomed this at any other time more sincerely than now when he was trying his best to forget all the circumstances of twelve months ago.

Tonkin went on to say he had heard that Margaret Vosper, née Cartland, née nobody knew what, had left her husband and was making up to Sir Hugh Bodrugan. Ross said, Indeed, indeed, thinking, Well and good if it keeps him from sniffing round my home like a mangy old tomcat. They rose from the table and moved to go downstairs. At the top of the stairs they saw George Warleggan coming up.

Tonkin half hesitated, glanced at Ross, saw no change in his expression, and continued down a step behind him. George had seen them now, but he made no effort to avoid them. Indeed avoidance was impossible; they would meet at the bend in the stairs.

Ross would have gone down as if the other man did not exist, but George put his long malacca cane against the banisters waist-high, barring his path. It was a dangerous thing to do.

" Well, Ross!" he said. " This is favourably met. We've not seen each other for some time."

Ross looked at him.

" As you remark."

A ruby as big as a pea made oriental gleams in George's extremely expensive neckcloth. Ross, by comparison, was shabby.

George said: " You're not looking so well as when I last saw you. Can it be the anxieties of the trial?"

" Nor you," said Ross. " Can you have had some disappointment?"

George poked the rail with his stick. " I know of nothing to cause me disappointment. I am well satisfied with my many enterprises. I hear, by the way, that you're embarking on a new one."

"As usual you have your ear well to the ground," said Ross. "Or should it be to the keyhole?"

The sense of inferiority in the depths of George's consciousness was one that Ross more than any other man could call up. It was altogether the strongest element in his lust for power and far more important as a cause of his hatred for Ross than any of the more obvious reasons.

He withdrew his stick. "I like a gambler. Especially one who plunges when the luck is running against him."

"A good gambler," said Ross, "always knows before other people when his luck is beginning to turn."

"And a bad gambler believes it when it isn't true." George laughed. "I must confess I found some amusement in your choice of partner. Francis of all people! Have you forgotten what he did for the Carnmore Copper Company?"

Ross was well aware that Richard Tonkin was listening intently.

He said: "By the way, one of the witnesses at my trial was only three weeks ago set on and nearly died from an attack made by hired bullies of some sort. I shouldn't like to feel that this kind of retaliation was to become a common practice."

The flicker of surprise in George's eyes looked genuine. He leaned against the wall to let two people pass up the stairs.

"He must be an idle creature who has time to carry on personal vendettas with village riffraff. But why should you suppose it to be anything of the kind?"

"Whoever is behind it would be mistaken if he thought intimidation could remain one-sided. The miners, you know, have their own way of showing their displeasure."

"We all have," said George politely. "Oh, I hear you've been disposing of part of your holding in Wheal Leisure—one of the few really profitable ventures in the county. A grave mistake, I'm sure."

"Time will show."

George said: "Of forty-four engines built in Camborne and Illuggan during the last ten years only four are still working. In Leisure you had a rare combination of good ore and easy drainage. At Grace you have certainly not the drainage. What are you looking for—gold?"

"No," said Ross, "freedom to call our souls our own."

George, flushing, said quickly, spitefully: "I suppose you know where Francis got the money he's investing in your mine, do you?"

"I've an idea. It was very obliging of you."

"Yes, we paid it him—the Warleggans—for services rendered. Six hundred pounds . . . or thirty pieces of silver."

Down in the taproom two men were quarrelling over a mug of beer: their rough growling voices seemed to Tonkin like the reverberation of some worn-out clockwork mechanism which failed to move the arrested figures on the stairs. Then before he could do anything they slipped into motion.

Ross reached out a hand and grasped George by the neck-cloth. It had annoyed him from the first moment he saw it. With it he pulled George towards him and shook him. For a second of surprise George did nothing, but choked with the sudden tightened clasp about his throat—then he lifted his cane to hit Ross across the head. Ross grasped the hand at the wrist and twisted it down. George bunched his other fist and hit Ross a swinging blow on the side of the head. They overbalanced and crumped against the banisters which, being immensely strong, did not give way.

Tonkin stepped forward with an appeal to their common sense, but he was ignored; for a moment they were beyond common sense; a man below had seen them and was calling for the innkeeper.

George, empurpling, swung his great fist again, but he was off balance and the force was half astray. The cane clattered to the floor, and Ross, loosing his grip, hit George in the mouth. Then at last he released the neckcloth and grasped George about the waist. Like two bulls they swung across the stairs, knocking Tonkin out of the way. There was little in it for strength, but Ross had led the harder life. George felt his feet going. Raging angry at this exhibition, he sought Ross's eyes with his thumbs; but it was too late. He was lifted off his feet, was going over the banisters. At the last moment he sought to cling to something, but only tore the front out of Ross's shirt. With a great crash he fell to the floor below, landing on a chair and a small table and smashing them as if they were matchwood.

Ross swayed and gasped and spat, began to come down the stairs. His forehead was bleeding and the blood was trickling along his eyebrow and down one cheek. George was twisting and groaning on the floor. The landlord came rushing out and halted appalled at the sight; then ran to the foot of the stairs.

"Captain Poldark, sir . . . disgraceful! What is the meaning of it, please? . . . Mr. Warleggan, what has happened? . . . Are you hurt, sir? Captain Poldark, I want an explanation. . . . Mr. Tonkin, pray give me an explanation. One does not expect the gentlemen . . . a table and two good chairs . . . damage perhaps to the banisters. Captain Poldark . . ."

As Ross came down the last step the little innkeeper got in his way; Ross saw the red waistcoat and, in the last flicker of an anger such as he had not felt for years, he shoved it out of his path. He meant it as no more than a gesture but the little man staggered back and sat down abruptly against the wainscot, and a plate came down from the wall and smashed beside him. As Ross walked out of the inn George Warleggan was just getting to his knees.

At Nampara they were cutting hay. The crop was good this year, and John and Jane Gimlett and Jack Cobbledick were at work together with two of the younger Martin children, superintended a little discontentedly by Demelza, who had been forbidden to take a hand in it. She was proscribed so many things these days and didn't like it. She felt fine, and it was a waste loafing about when there was much to do.

It was a bright day with a strong southeast breeze, and after dinner she didn't follow the haymakers up to the field again but fed her small stock of poultry and did a few odd jobs about the house—all this with a restless air, as if mere activity brought no satisfaction in itself. Verity had written last week, saying with some obvious apprehension that her two stepchildren were coming to visit her *at last*—but most of her space was filled with loving concern and advice. Demelza thought: Don't overtire myself indeed; I never get a chance; Ross has set the Gimletts on me like terriers. I should not be astonished if they do not drop their scythes soon and come scurrying back to see if all is well.

She went to the front door and looked over her garden. The soft winter had suited it and the flowers were forward. Strange, she thought, if women were like that—brought on by the warm weather, retarded by the cold. The wind was fluffing the tulips about; she picked off the heads of one or two dishevelled ones, then went back through the house to the little dairy where the cheeses were standing to ripen, lifted the cloths to see that no mould was forming, moved through the outbuildings. From there it was a natural progression to the Long Field and the headland beyond.

A considerable swell on the sea to-day; the waves ran into Hendrawna Beach like brides to their wedding, a veil of spray blowing round their heads. Near the rocks the swell moved more sleekly, the veils sank as they were left behind, white lace first in the shallower green, then misting to a mottled luminous cloud in the darker depths. Beyond the breakers were two fishing boats from St. Ann's. She turned and clambered down, treading on the curled fronds of the new bracken, to Nampara Cove.

In the shelter it was quite warm and quiet and the sea rippled invitingly. She took off her shoes and stockings and let the water lick her feet. Very pleasant and soothing. After a while she went over to the dinghy and found that the last time she had used it—with Gimlett a week ago—they had forgotten to carry the rowlocks up to the house. Ross would have been cross, since anyone could use or even steal the boat if they could row it away. In the bottom of the boat was a tin with some bait in it; it would be smelly by now.

Within the cove the air was still, and, looking out, the bright day glimmered like a cameo. The waves seemed small enough, and she realised that, so long as she kept within the protection of the cove, they would be innocuous. Of course if anyone knew she had taken the boat out there would be a great to-do; but Ross was miles away, and the others could whistle if they chose.

She had learned from experience how to drag the light craft over the sand without straining herself; it was a knack; and, taking special care now that it was May, she got the boat to the edge without difficulty. Then she tucked up her skirts and pushed the boat into the water. In a minute she had climbed over the side and a pull or two at the oars straightened her up so that there was no danger of being pushed back broadside on.

She rowed out until near the mouth of the cove and dropped her anchor overboard. It caught almost at once. There was more swell here than she had expected, but it was a pleasant sensation. In triumph, though with some distasteful wrinkling of her nose, she began to bait her line.

Chapter Twelve

The sudden brawl with George Warleggan had left Ross in a ferment of angry thoughts. He didn't remember in his life having lost his temper in quite that way before. George's face, George's sneers, the oppressive influence of the Warleggans over all his life, had suddenly boiled up into a moment of uncontrollable fury. There had been at least one instant in the past when it might have done so with greater reasonableness; but that was the way things happened. Now the murder was out with a vengeance.

(It was lucky, he realised, that George *hadn't* killed himself, that *he* hadn't killed him. From the way he was getting up from among the ruins of the table it looked as if he was not even seriously hurt.) But news of the fight would spread like a fire in dead gorse. In an hour it would be on everyone's lips in Truro; in a day . . . Not that that mattered—except for the subject of the quarrel. There lay the poison.

It was a poison not only on people's lips but in Ross's mind, and a mere brawl wouldn't exorcise it. While he washed himself and bought a new shirt he tried to see the thing reasonably.

That Francis had in some degree let down the copper-smelting venture was a circumstance which Ross had come in an unspecified way to accept. Something had happened which must be overlooked and forgotten. That Francis had suffered in his own conscience because of it was plain to anyone who had met him in the last twelve months. Well, it was over and past. It was likely that the company would have crashed just as completely without his help; and if there *had* been a betrayal it had taken place in sudden anger during the quarrel over Verity's elopement. It had never once occurred to Ross that Francis could deliberately have " sold " them for money. Even now, out of some knowledge of Francis's character, he rejected it; it was the impulse to reject it which had led to the fight; it was because the insinuation couldn't be denied in words that violence had been necessary.

So the fight had been in defence of Francis's character, and yet the defendant was unsure of what he defended. An uneasy stand. The grim little confirmatory details gathered themselves and stuck. The Warleggans had certainly paid Francis the money. Was Elizabeth's explanation—presumably obtained from Francis—a reasonable one? Would the Warleggans part with six hundred pounds on a point of principle? What other reason, except a revulsion of feeling at his own treachery, could Francis have for being reluctant to spend the money on his own comfort and convenience? Why did the great window at Trenwith lack an elementary repair?

What then if it were true? If it were true, better go across and tell Pearce not to waste his time drawing up a document which never could be implemented. But how be sure? Only by challenging Francis outright. And the very challenge, showing that he considered such a betrayal for money possible, would end their association either way. He understood Francis well enough for that.

There was trivial shopping to be done in spite of all this upset. Ross went about it in an angry daze which made him a tribulation to the shopkeepers. They stared curiously at his bruised forehead and preoccupied face as they laid out their wares. One moment he would think, George is a liar and got his deserts; the next the poisonous doubts would creep back. Was this enormity what Francis had been about to confess at Trenwith last month?

If the cause of the fight got about and people believed what George said, Francis's position would become impossible anyway. Ross had glimpsed Tonkin's expression. If people believed George, Francis would not be able to show his face in Truro.

Thank God at least that Trencrom had paid up and that money at this important time was not quite so tight. Four yards of pink ribbon, four yards of blue ribbon, at sixpence a yard. Seven yards of lace edging cost five shillings. It would most likely be the wrong sort when he got home, but Demelza would make the best of it, as she made the best of everything. More huckaback towelling. These were things Demelza herself would have bought while she was still able to ride, but they had simply not had the money. A pair of blankets. There was a pair at sixteen shillings and one at twelve. In a sudden economy he bought the cheaper, and then squandered the difference on some yards of crimson velvet for a sash for Demelza for use when she was again the shape to wear it.

Her time was likely to be any day now. The sooner the better. A new comb. That was the usual cry. She always broke them pulling them through her hair.

What would she say about this new development? She had always been for reconciliation—but would she urge him to forgive and forget if *this* were true? She might say, why let everything be ruined at this late stage by a wild accusation from George? A quarrel between the cousins was exactly what he desired.

That at least was common sense. And if they quarrelled,

who *was* to finance the mine? His own money wouldn't go far enough. Was the planning of the last two months to end in futility without even a gambler's throw? Exactly what George would wish.

As he finished what he had to buy Ross realised he had arranged to meet Francis at the coaching inn. That could not be now. He was sorry he had pushed the little innkeeper over —somehow the damage and the insult should be made up to him—but he couldn't go back there to-day. (There might be formal repercussions from his fight with George but he rather doubted it: George might wish he had met him with bare fists in a place with more room for manoeuvre than a flight of stairs, but it was unlikely that he would risk his skin with weapons against a soldier. All the same, it would be open war in every other way.)

He went to the Seven Stars Tavern and sent a potboy who knew Francis by sight to keep watch for him at the entrance to the Red Lion. Then he sat in a dark corner and ordered brandy and tried to force a decision before they came back. On it, on what he decided now, from his reasoning mind's absolute freedom of choice, would spring the whole pattern of the future. Everything was done or undone, promised or forbidden, fecund or sterile according to the judgment of to-day. To-morrow it would have happened. There were two choices open to him, not three. He could not accept George's word before Francis's. Either he challenged Francis with the story—with the inevitable result—or he trusted his cousin's integrity. Even compromise would be fatal. To ignore everything George had said and yet let it fester in his mind would be worse than a clean break.

The grandfather's clock ticked in the corner. Outside in the narrow street the warm gusty wind stirred the dust in sandy whorls; it lifted the coattails and ruffled the wig of a fat old gentleman with a stick and unsteady legs who made his way laboriously past the inn; it pushed a ball of paper delectably nearer the nose of a watching cat; nine miles away the dinghy dragged its anchor an inch or two and Demelza's hair blew across her face as she pulled in an empty line. In

261

the inn, from the dark corner opposite Ross, a man stood up and came across to him. It was Andrew Blamey, Verity's husband.

Ross stared at him, trying to collect his thoughts, then, more from instinct than conscious will, got up and took the extended hand.

Blamey said gruffly: "Well, sir, it must be more than two years."

"I should have said a good deal more." There was a perceptible hesitation. "Will you join me?"

"I come seldom to Truro these days, but I brought a schooner up for a friend who is unfamiliar with the river and am waiting now for the five o'clock coach home."

They talked for some minutes, though not easefully. Andrew Blamey asked with real concern after Demelza's health. It was always a surprise to Ross how Demelza seemed to have the respect of so many of these difficult men. Francis would do anything for her. Sir John Trevaunance had sent over some hothouse peaches last week. These men were not in the Bodrugan-Treneglos class who paid her attentions because she was physically exciting and had a sharp wit.

In return he politely asked about Verity and noticed a little flicker across Andrew's face.

"Does that mean she's not well?"

"No, she was in excellent health when I left this morning." He cleared his throat. "There is one small matter—though no doubt to an outsider . . . My two children will be visiting us for the first time to-morrow, and I shall be at sea."

Ross glanced towards the door. As the other dilemma was shifted from the dead centre of his attention he tried to concentrate on what the sailor said.

"H.M.S. *Thunderer* is due in Falmouth to-night or early to-morrow. James has been away two years—I fully expected to be ashore all this week, so ordered my daughter, who hitherto has refused to come—purely out of shyness, I imagine— to pay us a visit at the same time. But last night *Arwenack* fouled an old wreck as she came into the roads and will need repairs to her bows. So *Caroline* must sail in her place to-morrow."

Time was getting ever shorter—and he no nearer the crucial choice. Belatedly, with a quickening of eye and thought, a sharp apprehension of the other issues, he realised that another explosive situation was threatening here. Francis and Blamey had never once met except to quarrel violently in seven years. Blamey must be warned now, got away. And yet . . . if *he* was expected to make a gesture of trust and forgiveness and understanding, who else might not be expected to do the same?

He said abruptly, harshly: " You see something of Europe in your travels. What do you think are the prospects for peace?"

Blamey stopped at this new tack. " What? Well, I see little of Europe beyond Lisbon. But I hear a good deal. It's a sounding board. There is nervousness about."

" On account of France?"

" On account of the revolutionary parties. They spring up everywhere, encouraged by the French. I mean the minorities in Germany and Austria and Portugal who really owe allegiance only to Paris, as you might say. That's the danger, for if war breaks out one feels they will side with the French against their own countryfolk."

" There are such parties in England, but I think they make a noise beyond their size."

" In England, yes. Elsewhere I'm not so sure."

" And the temper of the French?"

Blamey shrugged. " One hears the side of the émigrés, of course. But if conditions inside the country become intolerable, I should be inclined to think——"

He stopped. Francis had come in.

It was dark in the low-roomed inn after the brightness outside, and he only saw Ross. So he came up to the table smiling.

" Well, so I hear you've been in parlour games with George! He has marked you. But they tell me he has a

sprained shoulder and can hardly stand. What was the spark
that——?"

Francis saw Blamey and came to a stop. Blamey got up
bristling like a dog ready for a fight.

And quite suddenly the situation crystallised itself for
Ross. The disorderly segments of his own problem became
formalised by this new situation in which he was hardly
more than a spectator. With time for thought it might have
seemed an oversimplification, but the time for thought was
past. Here was the acid test for Francis. Forgive us our
trespasses . . .

Francis said: "*You . . .*"

Ross did not get up. "Sit down, Francis. I'll order you
drink."

All the old arrogance was back in Francis's face. "Thank
you, I'll not trouble you in this company. . . ."

Ross said: "This is the last moment to wipe out the past."

Something in his voice caught Francis's attention. He
looked at Ross and Ross was looking at him. He flushed and
hesitated.

Uneasily, from under frowning brows, Blamey glanced at
Ross too. The special significance of the moment had somehow communicated itself to them both. Neither spoke for a
perceptible space while the potboy who had brought Francis
hovered near waiting for his tip. Ross gave it him and ordered
brandies. The boy went away and the three men were alone
again.

Blamey said: "The quarrel has never been of my seeking."

Francis dusted his cuff and swallowed something.

"My sister seems to find her new life agreeable," he said
bitterly.

"So she should," said Ross. "It's natural for a woman to
be married, and we can't forever be scratching over it like
cocks on a dunghill."

"In any case she takes no account of my approval or disapproval. . . ."

"She would be very much happier with a reconciliation,"
Blamey said. "That's why I desire it."

It was quite handsomely said. Francis stared across the room at the returning boy, thrust his hands in his pockets as if seeking something.

"If that is the case . . ."

The boy put down the drinks and left. Ross glowered up at the other men, the new bruise on his forehead showing red and angry above the white of the scar. He wasn't saying any more. It was up to them now. If they could not find the formula he was done with them both.

Appropriately it was Francis who made the decisive move. He sat on the arm of the settle and picked up his glass.

"The Warleggans'll be raging mad after this brush, Ross. I've come near to laying hands on George myself but never quite found the opportunity." He glanced at Blamey and seemed to force himself to speak. "You haven't heard the news perhaps. That Ross and George Warleggan met on the stairs of the Red Lion this afternoon and that Ross took George in as pretty a hug as has been seen in the county for a twelvemonth and threw him from top to bottom. It's all over the town." He looked at Ross. "It's true, I suppose?"

"A thought exaggerated, but the substance is correct."

Blamey had quietly seated himself again. He twisted his glass but did not drink.

"Verity told me of a developing feud. But what was the cause of the quarrel to-day?"

Ross looked past them at the old grandfather clock. It was nearly five.

"I took a dislike to his neckcloth."

Demelza had caught two infant dabs who obviously didn't know any better, but in the main the fish were not biting. She didn't blame them. The bait was too smelly even for mackerel. After a time she decided to call the attempt off; and she threw the fish she had caught back into the water, since their food value wouldn't be worth all the inquiries and concern and the near scolding.

Looking back for the first time for some minutes, she saw that the anchor must have been dragging a bit, for she was almost out of the mouth of the cove and the land looked farther off than usual. It was a pleasant sight, the low-lying black cliffs, the curve of the sand, the pebbles and scraggy vegetation where the Mellingey ran into the sea. You could feel and see the swell of the waves as they moved past the cliffs on their way to Hendrawna Beach.

She went to the end of the boat and pulled in the anchor. Then she scrambled back and took up the oars and set her face to the sea. A few pulls and she would be home.

She wondered how Ross's business in Truro was going. This gamble on Wheal Grace had been taken without her knowledge, and although she would never criticise after the event, it had never quite won her approval. Grace was the shot in the dark, the guess that might go wrong. It was the sort of venture to indulge in when you had a thousand pounds to spare, not when you were living on the precipice of debt.

Out here you could feel the breeze quite strongly, and the dinghy was so light, almost keelless, that it was inclined to be blown off its course. Several times she corrected it after glancing behind her, and the third time she was a little perturbed to see the cliffs no nearer at all. Up to now she had pulled only with her arms and not at all with her body, knowing that she must be careful of that; but now she began to put more weight behind the oars and was comforted to feel the boat respond on the heaving sea.

Sometimes she suspected, while considering it rather disloyal to do so, that Ross in opening a new mine had allowed his judgment to be warped by his detestation of the Warleggans—so that his desire to be free of their interference had led him to overoptimism about Wheal Grace. As for Francis, he, she knew, was a gambler too, but a much less astute gambler than Ross, so that his participation in the scheme was no reassurance at all. It was well enough for the rest of them. Henshawe risked a hundred pounds which he could comfortably spare. The two young engineers from Redruth were to be paid for their engine as they built it. The tutworkers and spallers got their monthly wages; the tributers spent only their time and trouble; it was the Poldarks who risked all the rest.

She had been rowing for two or three minutes, confident she was gaining ground, but when she looked round she saw that her progress had been diagonal and towards the sharp rocks of Damsel Point. They were only fifteen or eighteen feet away and the sea slithered and slapped around them, not making a lot of fuss but rising and falling enough to knock the bottom out of a boat. She veered quickly away and in doing so lost most of the ground she had won. It was while righting her course again that she began to feel queer. At first she thought it was a touch of the seasickness. Then she knew it was not.

On the clifftop, half in the shadow, half in the sun, some jackdaws and some choughs were quarrelling. The sweep of black wing against black wing glinted like jet. The sky was an indefinite pallid blue with faint streaks of sunlit cloud trailing across it from the south. She began to row in earnest, putting all her strength into it, knowing now it was touch and go. In the roots of her hair where it grew at the sides of her brow tiny beads of sweat formed. Her bottom lip was caught up and her eyes went cloudy.

She thought, Well, this is my own fault, nobody's but my own. So I get through it myself or go under. This will be a nice homecoming for Ross. Then it seemed for a minute that she must give up rowing, that her life must be sacrificed for two minutes with her head between her knees; but with the horizon blurring and the noise of sea rushing into her head she kept on. A beast, a devil, had seized her and she must give up or die.

Then when it seemed impossible to breathe any more the grip was suddenly relaxed. The beach was perceptibly nearer now. No distance. Like a mirage it danced over her shoulder, luring her with its safe dry sand and its promise of home.

The choughs flew off, quite low over her head, glints of red about their legs; they were defeated; the jackdaws were triumphantly settling into the hollows on the cliff edge. They were farther away. Progress. But the Beast was nearer again, waiting to pounce. She thought, Ross will be home at seven; I shall not be home by then, never home again. But somehow I must get home. He will have no one to tell about the mine. Wheal Grace. Named after his mother. Perhaps it will be lucky. It was lucky once. The house had been built from the proceeds. There'd been money enough in mining in the past. Trenwith built out of Grambler. Tehidy from Dolcoath; half the big houses of Cornwall had come that way. But money enough had been lost too.

The wind contrarily, wickedly, had grown stronger, the ebbing tide pulled at the light boat, out towards the open sea. Perhaps there would be someone about who would see her, someone walking along the cliff. Or if she allowed her dinghy to drift out one of the St. Ann's fishing boats would surely catch sight of her. While there was life . . .

Unexpectedly a wave broke under her and she missed her stroke; the boat moved as if an arm six times as strong had used the oar. She turned and saw she was nearly ashore. It was the wrong end of the little cove, by the stream, not so sheltered and the waves were breaking; but it would do. She tried to guide the craft, but a second wave turned her broadside on and almost upset her. Then it burst upon the beach, dropping the dinghy on the stones before sucking it out again with a rattle and a roar. She climbed over the side and as another wave burst jumped into the sea and clutched the boat, trying instinctively to pull it ashore. The effort wrenched her and she gasped and let go. She had hurt herself. Then she fought her way through the returning surf and found herself on hands and knees on dry land. The Beast had come back, and she crouched there unable to move, in its direst grip.

Three minutes passed. The waves continued to beat out their rhythm; but the sun had gone behind a tiny cloud. Robbed of its colour, the cove looked suddenly shabby and cold and the sea dangerous. Halfway across the cove it deposited the dinghy upside down, its oars lost and a plank staved in.

Demelza stirred and got to her feet. She was soaking wet and could hardly stand. She squeezed out the front of her skirt and blouse and began painfully to limp up the valley to the house.

Chapter Thirteen

On the following afternoon Verity stood at the window of her house overlooking Falmouth Harbour, listening for the arrival of the Plymouth coach. She would have dreaded this coming meeting even with Andrew at her side. In his absence the situation, in occasional moments of panic, seemed unfaceable. Then she would rally and ask herself what but a little constraint had she to fear from two young people still only in their middle teens?

Although James must have been in the town some hours he had not shown up yet. She glanced at the clock behind her, and as she did so the horn sounded clearly. She could not see the coach from here, but she could picture it turning into the yard of the inn, the lathered horses, the passengers climbing down, the bells ringing, the sailors yawning at the door, the man she had sent to meet Esther scanning the faces; Esther herself, the girl, half woman, the face in that miniature but older by five years.

Verity swung round on the small circular mirror, peered at herself. To the girl she would seem old, dowdy, a usurper. Youth was so mercilessly hard in its decisions; it had its own unyielding standards and had not yet learned enough to know that time would prove them arbitrary. She stood there until the doorbell rang; then she took a deep breath and went down. Masters was at the door with a slight, rather tall girl.

" You're Esther? Come in, my dear. I've been looking forward to meeting you. You must be tired. Can you take the box right up, Masters; you know the room? Do come in, my dear."

Cheek was cold. Face a little broad over the cheekbones,

noticeable grey eyes, honest but self-centred, slightly hostile. "Mrs. Stevens is in bed with stomach trouble," Verity explained. " She has been ailing on and off for weeks. I have a meal ready for you."

" Thank you, ma'am. May I first go to my room?"

" Of course. Come down just at your leisure."

In the upstairs parlour again Verity walked to the window. No warmth. Did her own welcome ring false?

A three-masted packet boat was shaking out her sails as she moved slowly among the other shipping towards the open sea, taking advantage of the first ebb. Captain Buckingham in *Percuil*, bound for the West Indies. Verity forced herself to sit down, pick up her embroidery. Calm and unstrained friendship. *She* was the adult, must set the temper of the stay.

Esther was a long time, but when she came in she looked older without her bonnet. Verity got up.

" I've set our meal in here, Esther. I always dine here when I'm by myself, for I love to watch the shipping."

" Yes, ma'am." Those eyes. So small and *so* direct. Could it be fright, not hostility?

" Your father was greatly disappointed to have to sail. He had looked forward to this moment for a long time."

" They did not tell me he wouldn't be here, not until I had taken my seat in the coach."

At supper the girl toyed with her food. A slight smear of pockmarks on her cheeks.

" You know your brother's in port, Esther?"

" I knew he was coming. I did not know he was here."

" The *Thunderer* dropped anchor this morning. Your father had a note from him last month when a frigate put in with mails."

" Yes, I heard too."

So he wrote to his sister. " I believe he has been with the East Indies Fleet. . . . Are you happy at your school?"

" Yes, ma'am. I leave at the end of the year."

They talked awhile but made no progress. She parried questions like a swordsman parrying dangerous thrusts. It

270

was impossible to get near her. With a sinking heart Verity rose and went to the side table to carve the beef. She could see a nightmare week end terminating in complete failure. Esther would go away, and when Andrew came back he would know that she had failed.

"I don't think you're at all like your father, are you, my dear?"

Esther's lack of response had forced it out of her. She could feel the girl's eyes boring into her back.

"No, ma'am. I take after my mother."

"Oh, I didn't know that. . . . Well, I think you are going to be very attractive."

"Mother was *very beautiful*," said Esther. "I wish I was like her in that."

Verity looked up and suddenly found that the oval mirror with the convex surface reflected the dining table. The girl was sitting straightly in her chair, white frilled dress cascading from narrow shoulders. Her face wore an extraordinary expression of pride and resentment. Verity's knife wavered, slid across the beef. She looked down.

"Of course," she said, "I can never begin to replace your own mother, but I hope you'll always look on me as a loving and well-wishing friend."

"You know Father killed her, don't you?" Esther said.

There was silence.

Verity turned. "I know all I want to know." She put the plate before her stepdaughter. "That there was a terrible accident, and——"

"He killed her. Ever since then people have been trying to teach me different, but I know! He went to prison for it, didn't he? She hadn't any near relatives. They sent me to his. They've tried to poison her memory, but they'll never do that. I know she was good and a saint. I know!"

Verity brought her own plate and sat down. Unhappiness and resentment put an edge on her voice. "I know it's not a fit subject for discussion between us. Please finish your meal."

"So I'm to be forbid to speak of Mother before you too, ma'am."

"Certainly not. Unless speaking of your mother means speaking against your father."

"He has plenty to speak for him. She hasn't one but me."

Verity's heart was thumping. "It's right and good," she said, "that you should think and speak of your mother. But it is neither right nor good to dwell on her death. Remember the happiness she had, not the——"

"She never had any happiness!"

Their glances met.

"How do you *know*?" Verity said angrily. "I think it's necessary that we should come to an understanding, Esther ——"

She broke off and listened to a loud rantan at the street door. I *can't* face the other one to-night, she thought. Between them they'll . . . I can't. I can't.

Esther's eyes were lowered at last. "That's James," she said.

In dead silence they sat there together, listened to the front door being opened and feet on the stairs. The feet hesitated for a moment, then there was a rap at the door and it opened and a square-built boy came in. Darker than his sister, smart uniform of a naval midshipman, curly hair, brown eyes.

"Well, I wondered if there was anyone aboard," he said in an unnecessarily big voice. "I thought as the door was unhitched there'd most likely be a skeleton crew. Good day to you, Essie. You've grown." His eyes wandered to the other person. "I suspicion you'll be . . ."

With a great effort Verity rose. "Come in, James. I've been looking for you all day."

He banged the door behind him. "Are you Miss Verity?"

"Well, I was. Now I am——"

"Ha! I know. May I call you Aunt? Twould split the difference, so to speak. Sorry I missed Father. If I'd known I should ha' spoke to the captain sharp and told him to make haste. He and I are on good speaking terms, though for the most part the speaking is on his side!"

He came across, flung his cap on the window seat, patted

272

Esther on the head, came round the table to Verity, looked her up and down. He was taller than she. "I've heard a lot about you, Aunt."

He put his hands on her shoulders and kissed her just below the ear. Then he gave her a hug that squeezed all the breath out of her.

"You'll pardon the liberty," he said, speaking as if he was in a high wind, "but one don't get a new mother every day o' the week! When I had the letter we were in Penang, so I says, 'Come, lads, we've a toast to drink, for I've a new mother, an' that's better than a wife any week, being more comfort and less responsibility.' I never wrote, not being over-handy with a pen, but drink your health we did with a will."

"Thank you," said Verity, feeling suddenly warm. "That was kind of you."

"Well"—he glanced round—"nice to be home again. Though the walls are uncomfortably steady! D'you know, I truly believe that is why sailors get foxed so soon as they come ashore, it is so that the deck shall rock again like they've been used to. Esther dear, do not look so sour at me."

"You've not changed a bit," said Esther.

The boy turned and laughed aloud at Verity. "That, ma'am, is not intended as a compliment. D'you save any supper?"

"Yes, I did!" said Verity. "Mrs. Stevens is in bed, so I'll fetch it."

"I'll go below myself! That's if you'll trust me in the galley. Mrs. Stevens will not."

"Go down and bring up anything you want," said Verity.

They ate in stony silence until he came back.

"You've not been aboard a man-o'-war, ma'am?" said James, stretching his legs in satisfaction. "I wonder if I could arrange it. I wonder if you'd pass as my real mother. No, you're too young. Still, stepmothers have rights. Ha! I think it could be arranged."

"Perhaps Esther would like to come."

"No, thank you, ma'am."

"Essie doesn't like the sea. More's her misfortune. But I fancy a good sailor has been lost in you."

"It remains to be seen, for I've never sailed. Do you take sugar, James?"

"Thick wi' sugar. So as the spoon will stand. As for sailing in bad weather, I never knew what rough weather was till we ran into a hurricane off the Nicobar Islands. . . ."

"Sugar, Esther?"

"Thank you."

"We were out for a cruise after the Malay pirates when the weather blew up. . . ." Firmly launched on his story, James talked and sipped and sipped and talked. Esther had shown no friendliness for her brother, had unbent in no way. Her eyes still had that hurt, hostile look, as if she had just witnessed something shameful, as if the world was against her and she knew it was only waiting its chance to pull her down.

". . . We squared the boom, saw the boats made fast, lashed the guns afresh, double-breeching the lower deckers, then we got the t'gallant mast down on deck, in fact everything to set up a ship safe and snug. D'you follow my meaning, or do the words confuse you, eh?"

"Very much," said Verity, "but go on."

"Ha! Well, at four bells the hurricane broke, with the sea fairly raging; it was a terrible thing to be in! After an hour or so I thought to turn in but my bunk was full to the brim with water so I decided twould be drier on deck." James laughed and made the ornaments rattle. It caught at Verity and made her laugh too. "Comic to look back on, but at the time wi' the waves riding beside us fit to swamp an island and the gale screeching like a thousand hungry parrots there was another face to the picture!"

"I think I will go to bed," said Esther, "if I may be excused."

Verity said: "You'll be tired after your journey. Would you care to lie on in the morning?"

274

"Thank you, I always wake early. Good night, James. Good night to you, ma'am."

Again Verity touched her cold cheek, and then she was gone.

James said: "Mind if I smoke, ma'am? It is a dirty habit one gets into."

"No, of course not."

"Well, just then the captain called me up on the poop, and as I got there I heard him say to the lieutenant: 'The ship makes a very good weather of it upon this tack,' he says, says he; 'but we must wear her. Do you go forward and have the hands stand by.' 'There's no canvas can stand against this,' says the lieutenant. The captain says: 'We must take the risk,' he says, 'for the wind have backed, and we are drawing close upon Sumatra.' I should not worry over Essie, ma'am. She is not so hard as she makes out."

The change of topic was so abrupt that Verity half smiled. But she did not speak.

"Lord bless you, everyone thinks she's unfriendly; but half of it is just her trim. Different people take the same thing different ways, as you might say. You know about Mother, of course. Ha! Well, you'd say it was as bad for one of us as for the other; but you'd be wrong. I was eight when it happened and Essie nine. The year after, when I was nine, I weighed anchor and went to sea; I shook it all off as the littlest frigate will shake off the head of a comber that's flopped aboard when she wasn't looking. But Esther—Esther's been like a craft wi' no canvas. She got waterlogged with the shock and she's been wallowing in the trough ever since. Instead of trying to forget it, she's brooded and brooded and made her mother a saint. Which she wasn't, nor anything near; God forgive me for saying so. And when she meets someone fresh, especially someone new to the family like you, all that side of her comes up and she seems a bad case. I've told Father before now she needs careening; no one can sail sweet with a foul bottom—beg pardon, Aunt, if it sounds indelicate, but it's true. Howsoever, she will improve as the days go by. Mark my words!"

275

Verity moved her cup, set it down again, stared at her hands.

"Oh, James, I'm so happy that you came. I'm happy to have made one friend so soon. I am so happy that . . ." She stopped and choked.

He laughed, a sudden boyish laugh. "It looks as if I shall be spending most of my leave looking after you, Aunt."

There was another knock on the street door.

She said: "You've no more brothers or sisters, have you?"

"Not to my knowledge. Though it would be a lively enough lark, wouldn't it? Stay on deck, ma'am. I'll see who it is."

When he had gone down she walked to the window. The day was nearing its close, and clouds had gathered over the harbour. Three fishing boats, one with copper-coloured sails and two with white, were moving sedately in like swans coming home to rest. She didn't know the man at the door. He had come by horse.

James came up the stairs four at a time.

"It is a man with a letter for you he will hand to no one but you personal. He says his name is Gimlett."

Gimlett. Ross's servant. Demelza . . . "Oh," she said and flew down the stairs.

"Mrs. Blamey, ma'am?"

"Yes. You have a message?"

"A letter, ma'am. Captain Poldark asked for me to give it into your hands."

With excited and apprehensive fingers Verity fumbled with the seal and at last got it open. The letter inside was very short.

Dear Verity,

We have a son. It was yesterday evening, after an anxious time, but both so far are well. His name will be Jeremy. We wanted you to be the first to know.

Ross

Chapter Fourteen

It was just a small party at Nampara House: Francis and Elizabeth and Andrew Blamey and Verity—and Dwight Enys, who was now almost one of the family. Not a christening party for Jeremy, because it was natural to shrink from repeating anything which had happened in Julia's life; this marked the opening of Wheal Grace—the first men engaged, the first sods broken. Demelza, handicapped by weakness and a delicate baby, had left all the catering to the Gimletts, and they'd done well enough. Boiled cod with oyster sauce, a piece of boiled beef, roast neck of pork, two small turkeys with ham, fried rabbits, a plum pudding, tartlets and pies—with apples and olives and almonds and raisins for dessert. Demelza looked round and thought: This is much more than we can afford, but of course it's quite right not to skimp for such an occasion.

It was nearly a month since she'd reached the house that day, soaked and exhausted—to find no one about, the surveillance she'd disliked gone when it was most needed, the house terrifying in its emptiness, the garden and the trees rustling and the nearest help half a mile away. It seemed a year since she had fought her way from kitchen to parlour, her hands full of paper and shavings to start a fire. Minutes later, Jane Gimlett had found her crouched in a chair, unable to move in a room full of smoke; Cobbledick was sent flying on his long legs for Dr. Enys and had the luck to find him home. Ross returned at seven to find Jeremy just born and Dwight despairing of them both.

Well, all that time was over and they had both survived; though Jeremy still did not seem oversecure. Very different from Julia, who from her earliest moments had put forward all the claims she could to be considered a permanency. Perhaps it was an omen, Demelza thought, that this frail one would survive where the lusty one died.

Over the meal the men had been talking of a book called

The Rights of Man in which an atheist, Tom Paine, advocated a parliament of nations to prevent war, and many other sweeping reforms; but Demelza had only been indifferently attending. She thought: So Francis and Andrew Blamey are sitting at the same table at last; it isn't *complete* reconciliation, but that will follow as they have time in each other's company—in the way Ross's and Francis's has followed. And Verity will no longer be shut off from Trenwith and there will no longer be the strain of ill feeling.

And Elizabeth . . . Elizabeth blooms like a painting; she has had a better year. By contrast, I'm dowdy and untidy, pale as a sheet from being indoors, no good as a hostess and unattractive to any man. No wonder Ross looks at her with interest. She doesn't love Francis, but she's more content.

And Dwight? He looks happy to be here. A good thing Caroline Penvenen has gone, because there was something between them. He ought to marry Joan Pascoe, who will have lots of money and yet wouldn't consider herself too good for him.

And me . . .?

They drank a toast to the new mine, and when they sat down again silence fell. On the fortunes of Wheal Grace the financial survival of all the Poldarks would now depend. It was a sobering thought. Well, at least, thought Demelza, we are all together this time. And Jeremy is in the next room waiting for me, already knowing me. And Ross is at least temporarily content in knowing the venture started. Was it time now, she wondered, to lead the way out, leaving the men to their usual talking and drinking? And if so, should she get up and then speak, or speak before she got up?

Forestalling her, Francis rose instead.

"Toasts," he said, "are a plaguey nuisance at the best of times. But I've a fancy to propose one more now, and I was never one not to indulge a fancy. I want to drink to our hostess, Demelza."

Taken completely by surprise, Demelza for once in her life blushed up to the roots of her hair. "Oh no!" she said. "Twould be most uncalled for."

In a confusion of voices she heard Andrew Blamey, siding with his old enemy, say, "It's the very thing," and the others concur, Elizabeth a second later than the rest. Then they seemed all to be looking at Ross, and Ross looked up and smiled.

"Demelza is wrong; it has been long called for. Thank you, Francis."

Francis, thus encouraged, fiddled with his glass, and looked across the table at her, embarrassed, but determined. "I was never one for speechmaking, but there it is. She came to live among us almost while we were unaware of it. But we've all come aware of it in time. There's not one among us—unless it's young Enys here—who has not had some special benefit from her coming. That's no more than the truth, and there's little more I can say! But if it wasn't for her there'd be none of us gathering here together to-day—and if there's any merit in being a united family, then the merit's not the family's but *hers*. It isn't where you're born in this world, it's what you do. She is proper that proper doth. So I say we should drink to Demelza—a lady of the first quality. . . ."

It was a lot for Francis to say. Horribly affected, Demelza sat there while they drank the toast. When it was done a silence fell more difficult than the last, because they were all waiting for her to say something.

She blinked the mist out of her eyes and stared at the magenta-coloured wine in her glass. She said in a low voice: "If I've done anything good for the family—look what you've done for me."

Outside Garrick was barking, chasing a sea gull off the lawn. It might wake Jeremy. They seemed to be waiting for her to say something more. In desperation a few words of the church service she'd attended in Bodmin came to her mind. She added: "I've only followed the devices and desires of my own heart."

Verity patted her hand. "That's what we love you for."

When the party broke up Ross went a little way up the valley to see his guests off. Demelza, being convalescent, stayed behind; and when they had crossed the river in the slanting sun she walked back into the house and peered down at the sleeping Jeremy.

A small baby, unlike Julia and dark, active, thin-featured and delicate. Strange the difference. Perhaps in some way he reflected the changed circumstances in which he had been conceived and born. Demelza thought: I am content. Perhaps not the rich happiness of two years ago, because Ross is still an uncertain quality, but content. Could one expect more? They had all come through many hazards. Of course the future was uncertain, full of dangers of its own. The mine might fail, Jeremy might die in a teething convulsion like the last of the Martin children, Ross might go off with Elizabeth, or the next " run " into Nampara Cove might be surprised by the gaugers. But was any future, anyone's future, unfraught by hazards of some sort? The only security was death. So long as one wanted to go on living one had to accept the risks. Well, she accepted them. . . .

Outside Ross saw the visitors on their way and then walked slowly back alone. The stream bubbled and whispered down the valley beside him, adding its satirical commentary to his evening thoughts.

The gamble was on. The fight was on. They were setting out on this venture in the teeth of unfavourable circumstances and all the opposition the Warleggans could muster. George had been indoors for a week after his fall, and there had been talk of a summons for assault. But nothing had come of it. George had not cut a sufficiently dignified figure to want it all thrashed out in public. Nor was the cause of the quarrel so much common property as Ross had imagined it might become. What he hadn't at first realised was that the Warleggans would show up in a very bad moral light if they accused Francis of any such transaction; and for the sake of their business reputation they wouldn't want that. George, too, had evidently lost his temper that day, had tried to poison the new friendship between the cousins with the most venomous accusation he could call up. (And nearly had succeeded!)

Francis certainly knew nothing as yet of the cause of the brawl—though last week he had complained of a peculiar coldness on the part of several people he had had dealings with in Truro. The evil rumour, once let loose, wouldn't easily die. It would be liable to smoulder underground and flicker up again where least expected. If it ever came to Francis's ears it might yet prove a menace to their new partnership.

Ross glanced across at the first signs of activity around the ruins of Wheal Grace: a few ugly sheds, a heap of stones, a mountain of cut gorse, a cart, a new track across the hillside. Nothing of beauty; in twelve months the whole hill would be disfigured. But the disfigurement would have its own appeal to a man with mining in his blood. The question was, what would a further twelve months show? Another smokeless chimney stack, silent sheds, grass growing in the mule tracks, an engine rusty and derelict? Everything seemed to point to it.

Two things could save them, could save the Poldarks and their houses. The first was rich copper at an easily workable level. The second was that the market price of the ore should not merely show its present upward tendency but should leap thirty or forty pounds a ton. Ross had gambled on both. For the first he relied largely on Mark Daniel's comments on that August night two years ago. Mark could not have been so impressed—and in such circumstances—without good cause.

For the second, Ross had gambled much more dangerously. Across the Channel a neighbouring country was in the grip of a revolutionary fervour. How long would it keep its energy within the confines of its own territory? If war came in Europe England might well stay out. The Channel was the surest wall. But it could not stay out unarmed. A defenceless country was an impotent country. A rearming country needed copper for its arms.

That was the other chance.

The air was hazy, heavy in the evening light. All the smells of the earth were strong; a blackbird twittered endlessly on a fallen stump; and the smoke from a chimney of the house grew like a slow worm, for once unhurried by the wind. In the distance a grey multitude of sea gulls were wheeling and crying over Hendrawna Beach.

That was the other chance.

He came more slowly to the garden in front of the house. At the door he stopped to sniff the lilac which in a day or two would be in full bloom. Human beings were blind, crazy creatures, he thought, forever walking the tightrope of the present, condemned to ever changing shifts and expedients to maintain the balance of existence, not knowing even as far ahead as to-morrow what the actions of to-day would bring. How could one plan a year ahead, how influence the imponderables?

A butterfly settled on the lilac and stayed a moment with poised trembling wings. Not by a hairbreadth would a single external circumstance move to accommodate him and his schemes—he knew that. As well ask, on the butterfly's behalf, for the postponement of sunset or to-morrow's gale. That was as it might be. Within the scope of his own endeavour he accepted the challenge. He might at some later date look back on this day as marking the beginning of his prosperity or the last move towards his ultimate ruin. The tightrope was there. No one could see beyond the next step.

Within the house there were movements, and from where he stood he saw Demelza come into the parlour carrying some things of Jeremy's which she spread before the fire. Her face was preoccupied, thoughtful, intent, but not on what she was doing. He realised that all the struggle and anxiety of the next few months would not be his alone. She would bear her share of the burden. She was bearing it already.

He went in to join her.

IT'S THE PEOPLE WHO CHANGE... THE TIME THAT PASSES... BUT THE TAVERN STAYS THE SAME

Alice Chetwynd Ley...
The First Lady of Romance

WHAT
TO GIVE YOUR
MOTHER, FATHER, SISTER,
BROTHER, WIFE, HUSBAND, AUNT, UNCLE,
SON, DAUGHTER, GRANDPA, GRANDMA, GIRLFRIEND,
BOYFRIEND, BEST FRIEND, TEACHER, BABYSITTER, BOSS, SECRETARY....